THE ANATOMIST'S APPRENTICE

In the first of a stunning new mystery series set in eighteenth-century England, Tessa Harris introduces Dr. Thomas Silkstone, anatomist and pioneering forensic detective... The death of Lord Edward Crick has unleashed a torrent of gossip through the seedy taverns and elegant ballrooms of Oxfordshire. Few mourn the dissolute young man – except his sister, the beautiful Lady Lydia Farrell. When her husband comes under suspicion of murder, she seeks expert help from Dr. Thomas Silkstone, a young anatomist and pioneering forensic detective from Philadelphia. Dr. Silkstone came to England to study under the ageing Dr. Carruthers, but his unconventional methods only add to Thomas's outsider status.

THE ANATOMIST'S APPRENTICE

THE ANATOMIST'S APPRENTICE

by

Tessa Harris

Magna Large Print Books
Long Preston, North Yorkshire,
BD23 4ND, England.

British Library Cataloguing in Publication Data.

A catalogue record of this book is
available from the British Library

ISBN   978-0-7505-4307-1

First published in Great Britain in 2015 by Constable

Published in Large Print 2017 by arrangement with
Little, Brown

Magna Large Print is an imprint of Library Magna Books Ltd.

Printed and bound in Great Britain by
T.J. (International) Ltd., Cornwall, PL28 8RW

To my parents, Patsy and Geoffrey,
my husband, Simon,
and children, Charlie and Sophie –
with love and thanks

Acknowledgments

The character of Dr. Thomas Silkstone was inspired by the many 'American' students who came to England and Scotland to study anatomy during the late eighteenth century, several under Dr. John Hunter, a close friend of Benjamin Franklin. These included William Shippen (Junior) and John Morgan, founders of what is now the Medical Faculty of the University of Pennsylvania.

This story was inspired by a murder trial at Warwick Assizes, in England, in 1781. It was the first ever known occasion where an expert witness – in this case, an anatomist – was called.

Although this is a work of fiction and I have taken liberties with many of the facts, changing names, places, etc., I have tried to be as accurate as possible in most historical details.

In my researches I would like to thank Dr. Kate Dyerson for the benefit of her medical knowledge and Katy Eachus and Patsy Pennell for their invaluable opinions.

My thanks must also go to my agent, Melissa Jeglinski, and to my editor, John Scognamiglio, for their belief in me.

–England, 2011

It matters not how a man dies, but how he lives.
The act of dying is not of importance. It takes so
short a time.

–Dr. Samuel Johnson, 1769

Prologue

Time, they say, is a great physician. It is not, however, a good anatomist. Time may help heal the wounds to the soul left by the physical departure of a friend or the death of a loved one, but to an anatomist a corpse, devoid of any signs of life save that of maggots and blowflies, is an altogether different matter. When the very bacteria that once fed on the contents of the intestines begin to digest the intestines themselves then time becomes an enemy.

What you are about to read is the story of a man whose name has been lost in the mists of history, but to whom modern crime fighting owes so much. Just over two hundred years ago anatomists were not afforded the luxury of cold storage to retard the putrefaction process. When a man died, dissection, if it were deemed necessary or desirable, had to be performed quickly before the body attracted flies and the flesh began to rot. The dissecting rooms of Georgian London were no place for those of a delicate constitution at the best of times, let alone in the summer, when the stench of hydrogen sulfide, mingled with methane and ammonia, was enough to make even those with cast-iron stomachs retch.

Dr. Thomas Silkstone did not pretend to be less susceptible to the grotesque characteristics of a rotting corpse than the next man. But he had forced himself, over the last seven years of his practice, since his arrival in London from his native Philadelphia, to overcome the sense of revulsion, the nausea, and the faintness so often suffered by those less experienced. He was still young – at only twenty-five at least twenty years younger than most of his fellow anatomists – yet he had a singularity of purpose and a dedication to his craft that set him apart from the rest of his fraternity. Students would flock to his rooms to watch him work deftly on a corpse, explaining each incision as he did so in a voice whose accent was not quite the King's English, but a gentleman's nonetheless.

It is to this young American doctor that today's pathologists owe their origins. He was the first to record the varying stages of decomposition of the human corpse, the first to study in-depth the effects of poisons on the lymphatic system, and the first to be able to gauge the length of time a person had been dead by the entomology on their cadaver. Suddenly he found himself embracing not only anatomy, but the disciplines of chemistry, physics, botany, zoology, and medicine, too. For many, such study and exploration would have been an end in itself and had events not taken the turn they did Dr. Silkstone may well have been satisfied with pursuing pure dissection. Had he chosen to do so, he would undoubtedly have become known as one of the most eminent anatomists of his century. But the events that began to unfurl in the autumn of 1780 turned him from being a straightforward practitioner of dissection, albeit an outstanding one, into something quite

16

new and unheard of among his peers.

On a chilly evening in October that year, in the days when King George III's government believed it would always rule the world and several independent-minded gentlemen from across the Atlantic were contradicting that notion, Dr. Silkstone received a visit from a young woman that was to change his life and give birth to a new branch of medicine. This lady of good breeding had a sorry story to tell and her circumstances conspired to lure Thomas into a situation that he felt compelled to tackle head-on. A crime may or may not have been committed, but it seemed to Dr. Thomas Silkstone that only science could provide the answers. Using his many and varied scientific skills, he set about endeavoring to solve mysteries using sound logic and pioneering techniques. In short, he became the world's first forensic scientist and this is the story of his first case.

Chapter 1

*The County of Oxfordshire, England,
in the Year of Our Lord, 1780*

A stifled scream came first, shattering the oppressive silence. It was followed by the sound of a heavy footfall. Lady Lydia Farrell rushed out into the corridor. A trail of muddy footprints led to her brother's bedchamber.

'Edward,' she called.

A heartbeat later she was knocking at his door, a rising sense of panic taking hold. No reply. Without waiting she rushed in to find Hannah Lovelock, the maidservant, paralyzed by terror.

Over in the corner of the large room, darkened by shadows, the young master was shaking violently, his head tossing from side to side. Moving closer Lydia could see her brother's hair was disheveled and his shirt half open, but it was the color of his skin as his face turned toward the light from the window that shocked her most. Creamy yellow, like onyx, it was as if he wore a mask. She gasped at the sight.

'What is it, Edward? Are you unwell?' she cried, hurrying toward him. He did not answer but fixed her with a stare, as if she were a stranger; then he began to retch, his shoulders heaving with violent convulsions.

In a panic she ran over to the jug on his table and poured him water, but his hand flew out at her, knocking the glass away and it smashed into pieces on the floor. It was then she noticed his eyes. They were straining from their sockets, bulging wildly as if trying to escape, while the skin around his mouth was turning blue as he clutched his throat and clenched his teeth, like some rabid dog. Suddenly, and most terrifying of all, blood started to spew from his mouth and flecked his lips.

Hannah screamed again, this time almost hysterically, as her master lunged forward, his spindly arms trying to grab the window drapes before he fell to the ground, convulsing as if shaken by the very devil himself.

As he lay writhing on the floor, gurgling through crimson-tinged bile, Lydia ran to him, bending over his scrawny body as it juddered uncontrollably, but his left leg lashed out and kicked her, hard. She yelped in pain and steadied herself against the bed, but she knew that she alone could be of no comfort, so she fled from the room, shrieking frantically for the servants.

'Fetch the physician. For God's sake, call Dr. Fairweather!' she screamed, her voice barely audible over the howls that rose ever louder from the bedchamber.

Downstairs there was pandemonium. The unearthly cries, punctuated by the mistress's staccato pleas, could now be heard in the hallway of Boughton Hall. The footman and the butler emerged and began to climb the stairs, while Captain Michael Farrell put his head around the doorway of his study to see his wife, ashen-faced, on the half landing.

'What is it, in God's name?' he cried.

There were screams now from another housemaid as more servants gathered in the hallway, listening with mounting horror to the banshee wails coming from the young master's bedchamber. The house dogs began to bark, too, and their sounds joined together with Lydia's cries for help in a cacophony of terror that soon seemed to reach a crescendo. All was chaos and fear for a few seconds more and then, just as suddenly as it had left, silence descended on Boughton Hall once more.

Dr. Fairweather arrived too late. He found the young man lying sprawled across the bed, his clothes stained with slashes of blood. His face was contorted into a grotesque grimace, with eyes wide open, as if witnessing some scene of indescribable torment, and his swollen tongue was half protruding from purple lips.

The next few minutes were spent prodding and probing, but at the end of the examination the physician's conclusion was decidedly inconclusive.

'He has a yellowish tinge,' he noted.

'But what could have done this?' pleaded Lydia, her face tear-stained and drawn.

Dr. Fairweather shook his head. 'Lord Crick suffered many ailments. Any one, or several, could have resulted in his demise,' he volunteered rather unhelpfully.

Mr. Peabody, the apothecary, came next. He swore that he had added no more and no less to his lordship's purgative than was usual. 'His death is as much of a mystery to me as it is to Dr. Fairweather,' he concluded.

News of the untimely demise of the Right Honorable The Earl Crick was quick to seep out from Boughton Hall and spread across to nearby villages and into the Oxfordshire countryside beyond within hours. Without a surgeon to apply a tourniquet to stem the flow, it gushed like blood from a severed artery. And of course the tale became even more shocking in the telling in the inns and alehouses.

''Twas his eyes.'

'I 'eard they turned red.'

'I 'eard his flesh went green.'

20

''E were shrieking like a thing possessed.'
'Maybe 'e were.'
'Mayhap 'e saw the devil 'imself.'
'Claiming his own, no doubt.'

There was a brief pause as the drinkers pondered the salience of this last remark, until suddenly as one they chorused: 'Aye. Aye.'

The six men were huddled around the dying embers of the fire at an inn on the edge of the Chiltern Hills. It was autumn and an early chill was setting in.

'And what of 'er, poor creature?'
''Tis said 'e lashed out at 'er.'
'Tried to kill 'er, 'is own flesh and blood.'
'And she so delicate an' all, like spun gossamer.'
''E was a bad 'un, all right,' said the miller.

Without exception his five drinking companions nodded as their thoughts turned to the various injustices most of them had suffered at their dead lord's hands.

''E'll be burning in hell now,' ventured the blacksmith. Another chorus of approval was rendered.

'Good riddance, that's what I say,' said the carpenter, and everyone raised their tankards. It seemed to be a sentiment that was shared by all those contemplating the young man's fate.

For a moment or two all was quiet as they supped their tepid ale. It was the blacksmith who broke the silence. ''Course you know who'll be celebrating the most, don't ye?' He leaned forward in a conspiratorial gesture.

The men looked at one another, then nodded quickly in unison at the realization of this new supposition that had been tossed, like some

21

bone, into their circle.

''E'll be rubbing his 'ands with glee,' smirked the miller, sucking at his pipe.

'That 'e will, my friends,' agreed the blacksmith. 'That 'e will,' and he emptied his tankard and set it down with a loud thud on the table in front of him, with all the emphatic righteousness of a man who thinks he knows everything, but in reality knows very little at all.

Outside in the fading light of the marketplace, the women were talking, too. 'Like some mad dog, he was, tearing at his own clothes,' said the lady's maid, who heard it from her cousin, who knew the stable lad to the brother of the vicar who had attended at the hall on the night of the death.

She was imparting her blood-curdling tale to anyone who would listen to her as she bought ribbon for her mistress at Brandwick market, and there were plenty who did.

So it was that inside the low-beamed taverns and in bustling market squares, in restrained drawing rooms and raucous gaming halls around the county of Oxfordshire, the death was the talk of milkmaids and merchants and gossips and governesses alike. Some spoke of the young nobleman's eyes, how they had wept blood, and of his mouth, how it had slavered and foamed and how foul utterances and curses had been spewed forth.

The more circumspect would simply say the young earl had died in extreme agony and their thoughts were with his grieving family. Nevertheless, from the gummy old widow to the sober squire, they all listened intently and passed the story on in shades as varied as the turning leaves on the autumn beeches; on each occasion embellishing it with thin threads of conjecture that were strengthened every time they were entwined.

Boughton Hall was a fine, solid country house that was built in the late 1600s by the Right Honorable The Earl Crick's great-great-grandfather, the first earl. It nestled in a large hollow in the midst of the Chiltern Hills, surrounded by hundreds of acres of parkland and beech woods. Its imposing chimneystacks and pediments had seen better days and the facade was looking less than pristine, but the neglect that it had endured over the past four years under young Lord Crick's stewardship could be easily remedied with some cosmetic care.

Lady Lydia Farrell loved her ancestral home, but now it was fast taking on the mantle of a fortress whose walls stood between her and the volleys of lies and insinuation that were being fired at her and her husband since her brother's death. The vicar, the Reverend Lightfoot, tried to comfort her as they sat in the drawing room one evening three days later. His face was mottled, like some ancient, stained map, and he rolled out well-practiced words of comfort as if they were barrels of sack.

'Time,' he told her, 'is the great physician.'

She looked up at him from her chair and smiled weakly. His words, although well meant, did not impress her. She forbore his trite platitudes politely but remained silent, fully aware that while time may have been a great physician, it was not a good anatomist. The longer her brother lay in his shroud that held within it the secrets of his death, the sooner time would turn from a physician into an enemy.

Chapter 2

A good corpse is like a fine fillet of beef, the master would say – tender to the touch and easy to slice. He neglected to make any comparisons with the odor, however. Once it began to stink any cook worth her salt would throw the offending meat to the dogs. Not so with a cadaver. Unlike the side of an ox whose texture and general flavor benefited from a few days' hanging, the human body needed to be butchered, in the technical sense, ideally within the first few hours of its slaughter, or in this case, demise.

Despite the fact that this particular corpse was relatively fresh, however, it was still proving difficult. Rigor mortis was setting in and Dr. Thomas Silkstone knew he would have to work quickly if he wanted to dissect the intestinal lymphatics before they atrophied. The translucent flexible tubes that resembled a large tangle of string were already beginning to lose their elasticity, even though their unfortunate owner, a Mr. Joshua Smollett, had died only that morning. A former patient, he was one of the few visionaries to comprehend that if any strides were to be made in the field of medicine and the curation of diseases they could only be taken via the knowledge gleaned from the practice of anatomy. 'Dissection,' as the master, properly known as Dr. Silkstone's mentor, Dr. William Carruthers, would frequently say in his lectures, 'is the key to understanding all illness.'

Thomas often found himself inadvertently reciting Dr. Carruthers's mantras. He hated himself for doing it, after all he was now a qualified surgeon in his own right, but the influence of the old man's teaching had seeped into every fiber of his being and dictated every turn of his professional thoughts, every incision of his razor-sharp knife. 'You are an artist,' Thomas recalled him saying more than once. 'You are a da Vinci, a Michelangelo. The scalpel is your brush and the corpse your canvas.' It was hard to think of himself as an artist, however, when he had to breathe in short, sharp movements to stop himself retching.

It was autumn now, and the air was cool and relatively fresh, but when the temperature rose so, too, would the reek of decaying flesh. That was the time when only those with the strongest of constitutions could stomach the vile and noxious miasma, which rose throughout every dissecting room in London, fed by sunlight and heat.

It was rare for Thomas to handle a corpse such as Mr Smollett's. Indeed, these days he was finding it increasingly rare to handle a corpse at all. When he had first come to London, a fresh-faced foreigner all the way from Philadelphia, the Corporation of Surgeons had invited him to participate in the dissection of a cadaver fresh from the gallows. He shuddered as he remembered them in their black robes and gray wigs, as they peered and prodded like so many vultures until they went in for the first incision. Even now Thomas found the whole affair utterly distasteful, despite the fact that the man they were mutilating was always a convicted felon and had, in all probability, mutilated several people himself while they were still alive.

It was only natural therefore that a man in his position and with such weighty responsibilities should seek out just a few of the many distractions that London offered. In his native Philadelphia he had enjoyed masques and balls, whereas here he found the company a little dull and markedly less refined. The ladies, too, he had noted, possessed by and large thicker ankles than their sisters in Pennsylvania. Nevertheless in London he had found salvation in the theater and, in particular, Mr Garrick's in Drury Lane. He had read all the great philosophers but nowhere was the human condition so well expounded as in the great actor's production of *King Lear.*

As he worked on the flaccid body that had once housed Mr. Smollett, Thomas was in a reflective mood. Unlike most of his patients, who would make their loved ones swear as they sat by their deathbeds that their corpses would never be handed over for dissection, Mr. Smollett had no fear of forgoing the pleasures of paradise if he allowed his body to be opened. 'St. Peter will welcome me whether I be in a shroud or in pieces,' he had quipped on Thomas's penultimate visit, before his laughter had caused him to cough up blood.

Phthisis, also known as tuberculosis, also known as the white death, was the obvious agent of his demise. Thomas had found his lungs to be badly scarred as he had expected, but it was the lymphatic system that currently occupied him and so he had taken the opportunity of slicing into the lower abdomen. Mr. Smollett had been a portly gentleman to say the least, and by the time Thomas had peeled away through layers of cream-colored subcutaneous fat, the tissues and organs were becoming increasingly resistant to his scalpel. Not only that, but the light was now fading and he would soon have to resort to candles.

Mistress Finesilver, the wily housekeeper, had already warned him that too much household money was being expended on candles but a good, bright light was essential for his work. He would rather spend money on tallow than on port wine and had told her so, much to her annoyance. He put down his scalpel, wiped his hands on his large, stained apron, and fetched a candelabrum from the windowsill. Placing it on the table just by Mr. Smollett's left buttock, he struck a flint and lit a long taper. He could not afford himself the luxury of a fire that would turn the corpse even more quickly. Cradling the flame in his bloody hands, he lit the five candles so that Mr. Smollett's abdomen was gradually illuminated in a halo of soft light.

Now that Dr. Carruthers's failing sight had forced him to relinquish his work, Thomas had taken on his mantle. Gone were the days when Carruthers would pack a lecture theater to the rafters with students eager to see the precision with which he could remove a man's spleen or amputate a limb. Unlike his teacher, Thomas was no great showman. He preferred to work quietly and efficiently alone, making detailed notes of his observations as Dr. Carruthers had taught. He now labored in his erstwhile master's laboratory, graduating from the cramped, airless room at the rear of the Dover Street premises that once served him as a study. He had inherited Dr. Carruthers's spacious rooms in Hollen Street and all that came with them and that included the grotesque and disturbing creatures that now stared out at him reproachfully from their glass prisons in the half light, like forlorn captives frozen in time.

There was, however, one other living creature in the laboratory – a creature that served as both companion and confessor. He had named him after his father's friend, the noted scientist, politician, and now war activist Benjamin Franklin, and he was a white rat. Thomas would swiftly point out to anyone who objected to his presence that he was an albino rat as opposed to a black rat. Franklin was, he insisted, not a carrier of disease, but a 'pet' – a concept that many surgeons found hard to grasp, it seemed. Dr. Carruthers was about to dissect the poor creature, but Thomas had taken pity on him and persuaded him that he would be much better off kept in the laboratory for experiments. Dr. Carruthers was persuaded of the logic of this and shortly afterward lost his sight. So Franklin – although Dr. Carruthers was unaware that the laboratory rat had been given a name, of course – came out of his cage and accompanied Thomas to his room at night, where he slept in a wooden crate on the floor.

There was something very comforting about having Franklin with him while he worked, Thomas thought, as he wiped the blood from his lancet. He liked to hear him nibbling away at the scraps he left out for him and scurrying around in his cage, which was kept unlocked so that he could, if he chose, roam freely around the laboratory. Thomas frequently talked to him, trying out new theories on him. If he understood a tenth of what he was talking about he would be the most learned rat in Christendom, Thomas thought, smiling to himself.

The smile, however, soon left his lips when he realized that Mr. Smollett's guts were still exposed like untidy skeins of wool and that, according to the large timepiece on the wall, it was nearly six o'clock. It would soon be dark and time was not on his side. Painstakingly he traced a length that ran alongside a vein and which drained into a channel connected to a vein in the upper chest. Through this branch, Dr. Carruthers had discovered that the nutritious properties of food products enter the veins, conveying them to the heart, the blood acting as a sluice. Unlike most of his contemporaries, Thomas's mentor had long held that the lymphatic flow was afferent, draining tissue fluid and chyle from the organs and gut back to the heart.

Three years before, the old man had completely lost his sight, but with the help of Thomas, he had proved conclusively that his theory was right. Prior to this most of his colleagues had believed the converse to be true and that the arterial flow was in fact the opposite, toward the heart. This, Dr. Carruthers and Thomas had been able to demonstrate, was like laboring under the delusion that water ran up a spout rather than down it.

Thomas now believed it was his duty to continue expanding on this hypothesis. He reported any new observations regularly to Dr. Carruthers, who listened eagerly to the protégé who had now become his eyes. Now and again he would inter-ject with a challenge or an adjunct, always enliven-ing any report Thomas made with a peppering of colorful expletives and jocular asides. 'The mon-key's arse, it did!' was one of his favorites. Fate had been cruel to the old man, depriving him of the very tools that were so vital to his craft, and Thomas felt privileged to be able to continue work so vital to the understanding of the human anatomy.

The young man squinted and pushed away the lock of dark blond hair that had flopped forward with the back of his bloodstained hand. For a moment he stood upright to straighten his aching back. He was fine-featured, tall and slender, and cut a dashing figure about London. The ladies especially noted his pale, flawless complexion and his smile, which revealed a mouth of perfect white teeth.

The light was poor and he knew he would soon have to admit defeat. He had no wish to put a strain on his eyes and suffer the same fate as his master. Out of respect for Mr. Smollett, he stitched up the large flap of skin over his belly, so that he now looked quite respectable, and replaced his sutures in alcohol.

Thomas rinsed his bloody hands in water and as he dried them on a towel, he heard the hoarse cry of a newspaper boy shouting out headlines through the high window facing out onto the street. Continuing to tidy away his instruments he suddenly found himself looking forward to Mistress Finesilver's venison pie, a tankard of stout, and some good conversation with Dr. Carruthers. Afterward they would sit by the fire in the master's study and Thomas would read that day's edition of *The Daily Advertiser* out loud. They would discuss the major news of the day, and then Thomas would turn to the obituaries so that Dr. Carruthers could keep abreast of old associates or adversaries who had been recently deceased.

Rarely a week went by without someone with whom he had worked, or worked on, passing away. If the person had been a patient, Dr. Carruthers would relate his symptoms at the time of his treatment, be they gout or goiter, but if they were his colleagues, he might pause for a while as if picturing them at work, and mutter some melancholy tribute into the brandy that he cradled in his lap.

Thomas had all but finished clearing away when he heard footsteps outside his door. It was Mistress Finesilver. Despite having worked for Dr. Carruthers for more than thirty years, she still had little respect for the practice of anatomy and believed in a strict mealtime regimen. It mattered not that Thomas was on the verge of some great discovery that could benefit all mankind. Dinner was at half past six sharp and woe betide any man who challenged that. Mistress Finesilver also disapproved of Franklin, but had promised not to tell Dr. Carruthers about him in return for a regular supply of laudanum, which was her evening pleasure.

'Dinner is served, sir,' she shouted through the

31

door. She knew better than to enter the laboratory for fear of seeing something she would
rather not.

The venison pie was palatable, even if the meat
was a little on the tough side. Another half hour in
the pot would not have gone amiss, Thomas
thought to himself as he champed his way through
the chewy haunch.

Mistress Finesilver had cut the old doctor's
food up for him. He insisted on feeding himself,
but did not always succeed. After the meal, he
almost invariably had spits and spots of gravy
liberally splashed over his waistcoat and Mistress
Finesilver would dab it off with a damp cloth
afterward, fussing like a mother hen.

That evening they sat as usual by the fire and, as
usual, Thomas read out loud, starting with the top
left-hand column, then working his way through
the whole newspaper. On that particular day in
October 1780 it was reported that a great hurri-
cane had killed thousands in the Caribbean and
that the ships on Captain Cook's third voyage had
returned to port in London, only without their
master, who had been slaughtered in Kealakekua
Bay. But it was the news that his fellow country-
man Henry Laurens had been seized by the
British and thrown into the Tower of London that
caught Thomas's eye and he inadvertently tutted
his disapproval aloud.

'What upsets you so, young fellow?' questioned
Dr. Carruthers. He often called Thomas 'young
fellow'.

Thomas framed his words carefully, not wishing to offend his mentor. 'We Americans are not

faring so well in our bid for independence,' he informed him.

'Independence! Balderdash and piffle!' came the swift response. 'If you colonists have your independence, then every Tom, Dick, and Harry here in England will be wanting a vote soon. Mark my words. Then what would become of us all?' exclaimed Dr. Carruthers, taking a large gulp of brandy. There was a short pause, then the old gentleman said, as he always did, 'So tell me who's died this week, young fellow.'

Thomas smiled to himself and turned the page. There was a list of five notables, starting with the most eminent. He began: 'Lord Hector Braeburn, Scottish peer and expert swordsman, aged sixty-seven.' He always paused to await a response from Dr. Carruthers.

'Expert! Tosh! I patched him up after a duel once.'

Thomas continued. 'Admiral Sir John Feltham, RN retired, fought during the Seven Years' War and sustained an abdominal wound from which he never fully recovered.'

'The old sea dog had the pox!' interjected the doctor.

Next came a lady who had done many charitable works, followed by a lesser member of the Royal Academy. A well-known musician took precedence over a mathematician and an exclusive clothier. They were all known to Dr. Carruthers and they all solicited various anecdotes and yarns, seasoned with the old physician's favorite expletives. 'All those bodies safely tucked up in their mortsafes and vaults. Such a bloody waste!' was how he would usually wind up the evening. This lament was often intoned just after the mantel clock had struck eleven.

'Bedtime for me, young fellow, and I suggest for you, too,' Dr. Carruthers would say. Thomas was usually more than ready to follow his advice. On this particular evening, however, he returned to the front page of the broadsheet, folded it neatly, and put it on the desk. It was too late to finish reading the back page, he thought, although he told himself he might return to it the following evening. Had Thomas read the final page of *The Advertiser* of that particular edition, however, he would have seen a small item, tucked deep down on the right-hand column of the newspaper under the announcements section. It read: 'Death of Young Earl.'

According to the broadsheet, the Sixth Earl Crick, of Boughton Hall in Oxfordshire, died at his home on October 12, 1780, aged just twenty-one. But the unremarkable insertion went unnoticed and instead Thomas climbed wearily upstairs, undressed, and as soon as his head hit the pillow, he fell sound asleep.

Chapter 3

The face of Lady Lydia Farrell's dead brother peered in at the window. It appeared on her dinner plate by candlelight and in flames in the fireplace. It came to her when she was walking in the gardens, or sewing in the drawing room. It was with her wherever she went and whatever she did and every time it wore the hideously terrifying expression of a young man dying in unspeakable agony.

Five days had passed since that fateful morning of Edward's death and the memory of it was seared on her brain as indelibly as if by a branding iron.

Edward had just taken his physick from a phial that had been brought earlier that morning. What was in it? Lydia's first thought was that the apothecary was to blame; that he had been mistaken in the quantities he had used, or indeed in the ingredients. It did not take long, however, for her thoughts to take a darker turn. What if someone had poisoned her brother? What if he had been murdered? Whatever the cause, he had fallen into a coma and died soon after.

Since that day doubt had hovered in the air. It had floated on the ether like some poisonous miasma, infecting everything it touched. It tinged the looks of servants toward their superiors and, worst of all, it clouded the vision of Lydia toward her husband, Captain Michael Farrell, like a malevolent mist that shrouds the truth.

'You must try and eat, my dear,' urged Farrell, sitting at the other end of the long oak table. He tucked into his ham and eggs as if nothing was untoward. 'Your brother was ill,' he said. 'That is why he needed medication. The pity of it is, none of us knew just how ill he was.'

Lydia watched her husband pierce the pink meat with his fork and envied his appetite. To say that he and Edward did not like each other would

35

have been an understatement. They loathed and detested one another. Yet despite the ever-present acrimony between them, they did at least tolerate each other, for her sake as much as anything else. For her sake, too, Edward, in the will he had written on inheriting the Boughton estate and another in Ireland, had named Farrell as the chief beneficiary, should he die without issue. It was a fact that was lost on no one.

Aware that she was gazing at him, Farrell looked up at her, as if he could read her innermost thoughts. He smiled, yet there was no warmth in his eyes. It was so different from that captivating look he had bestowed on her at their first meeting three years ago.

Lydia and her mother, the Dowager Countess Crick, were on a visit to Bath when, at the height of the season, an unfortunate lack of communication left Lydia, her mother, and their maid Eliza without a room for the night. As Lady Crick waxed and wailed about their unenviable circumstances, Captain Michael Farrell, lately of the Irish Guards and Director of Entertainments at the famous London Pantheon, happened to be walking by on his way to the gaming tables. While Lady Crick's protestations assailed his ears, it was her daughter's elfin looks, together with her fine jewelry, that attracted his eyes. He swiftly introduced himself and offered his own room to the forlorn ladies. In the process he won Lydia's heart.

As a show of gratitude the charming captain was invited to accompany them to the Pump Room the next day and thus he began inveigling his way

36

into Lydia's heart. At the various balls she attended he would always be given the first dance, and many more besides, and it soon became clear that this dalliance was more than a passing fancy. There were other suitors, of course, but the captain's Gaelic charm seemed to give him the upper hand.

After Lydia returned home to Boughton Hall the captain would send her letters almost daily and trifles of affection – books of poetry and ribbons. The young noblewoman was completely entranced by the handsome lothario and it was soon evident that she only had eyes for him.

Michael Farrell was debonair, handsome, and utterly charming. He was also a gambler, a flirt, and a fashionable profligate. Ever since Lydia found the maidservant Hannah sobbing in the scullery because of the 'bad things' they were saying about the master in the village after that fateful day, she had looked at her husband in a new light. She had watched his long, tapered fingers pour wine from flagons. She had breathed in his musky scent laced with cheroot smoke and oilcloth and listened to him give orders to servants in a cultured Irish brogue that was as soft as brushed velvet. She had seen his green eyes play on the white necks of the pretty servant girls and knock back a bottle of brandy before midday. Admittedly, he was no saint, but could he be a murderer, she asked herself?

'Why do you not go into Brandwick this morning, my dear? 'Twill take your mind off things.'

Farrell obviously had no comprehension of just how wretched his wife was feeling. Lydia's brother would be laid to rest, aged just twenty-one, in the family vault the very next day. She marveled at his insensitivity. Were she to set foot in the village she would be forced to run the gauntlet of rumor and innuendo. She dared not tell him that the draper had even refused Cook credit for a new apron. Yet she had no stomach for a confrontation. She said simply, 'I think not,' and was about to excuse herself from the breakfast table when Howard, the butler, entered with a letter held aloft on a silver salver. He presented it with great ceremony to Farrell, who opened the seal with a knife.

Lydia watched as a frown settled on her husband's brow.

'What is it, Michael?' she asked with trepidation. It took a great deal to make her husband frown. He unfolded the parchment and scanned it for what seemed like an age to her. He then looked up and paused for a moment, as if wondering how to frame his reply.

''Tis from your brother's godfather.'

'Sir Montagu?'

Farrell was studied, yet forthright. 'He has heard gossip.'

'Gossip?' Lydia found herself echoing her husband and the very word chilled her to the bone.

'Rumors about Edward's death.'

Lydia breathed deeply. It was almost a relief that someone other than herself had brought the situation to her husband's attention.

'You know something?' His voice was almost accusatory.

Lydia nodded slowly. 'In the village they say...'

She broke off, unable to bring herself to reiterate what scandalous rumors were being spread like shovelsful of dirt around Brandwick and beyond to Banbury, where Sir Montagu Malthus lived.

'What do they say, Lydia?' His voice remained calm, but she could see there was anger in his eyes.

'They say that perhaps ... perhaps Edward's death was murder.' She waited anxiously for her husband's reaction, wringing her linen napkin under the table. Although the word had been on her lips for several days, it was the first time it had been spoken.

Farrell paused for a moment. 'Then Sir Montagu is right,' he said finally, standing up. 'We must stop these vile rumors spreading.'

'Yes, but how?' pleaded Lydia.

'It was well known that Edward was sickly. We must order a postmortem to prove he died of natural causes.'

The young woman looked at her husband. There was a defiant air about him. His head was tilted back slightly, highlighting his jawline. Just then a ray of morning sun caught the blade of a knife on the table, making it glint menacingly. The thought of her young brother being opened by a surgeon's scalpel appalled her, but at the same time, she knew her husband was absolutely correct.

And so it was that a surgeon, Mr. Walton of Oxford, and a physician, Dr. Siddall of Warwick, called at Boughton Hall on the morning of October 18, 1780, six days after Lord Crick's untimely demise. Captain Farrell greeted them courteously enough and showed them to the upstairs room. Lydia watched from a half-opened door in the drawing room.

'Who is it, Lydia?' Her mother, seated in a large, high-backed chair, heard the men talking in the hall and became agitated. In fact these days agitation was her natural state. The death of her husband had had a profound effect on the woman, who was now in her early fifties. She had lost what little ability she ever had to concentrate and her addlepated mind flitted butterflylike from one often unrelated subject to another. Lydia was sure she did not realize her only son was dead, or indeed how he had died. She had heard her daughter screaming for help on that terrible morning and had screamed with her, but Lydia did not believe she had any idea why.

'Funeral? Who's dead?' murmured the dowager, her lace cap tilted at a rakish angle over her gray, wiry hair, which she wore in the old-fashioned way. Lydia envied her sublime ignorance.

As soon as Farrell opened the door for the medical gentlemen, the young earl's corpse made its presence felt. The room was filled with the unmistakable stench of decomposing flesh. The cadaver lay covered under a white sheet on the bed, and with handkerchiefs over their faces, the surgeon and the physician approached it with caution. Captain Farrell watched their fearful expressions with muted amusement. Dr. Siddall stepped forward first and gingerly pulled the sheet back. Mr. Walton had approached the corpse, too, out of a sense of professional duty. Neither of them, however, was prepared for the grotesqueness of the vision that awaited them.

Crick's hideously contorted face had already fallen prey to livor mortis and proved too great a challenge for the mortician. Although his lids were closed, his mouth was open and a foul-smelling liquid oozed from the orifice. The pallid cheeks had been almost comically dusted with rouge, but they were bloated and maggots were already feasting inside the nasal cavities. Both doctors let out a simultaneous groan.

'My brother-in-law is not a pretty sight, gentlemen,' remarked Farrell wryly.

The two men looked at each other gravely and retreated to confer. After no more than a minute Mr. Walton spoke for them both. He cleared his throat, turning away from the cadaver. 'Have you any notion as to how...?' He did not finish his sentence, as if not wishing to appear indelicate.

Farrell nodded his head slowly. 'Indeed, gentlemen,' he began in a sombre tone, 'you have heard directly from his physician, have you not, that my brother-in-law was a sickly youth?' The doctors, who were aware of the young lord's general malaise, nodded sympathetically in unison. Leaning forward, rather conspiratorially, as if about to let the men in on some terrible secret, Farrell continued: 'It is an indelicate matter, gentlemen, and not one that is common knowledge, but poor Lord Crick lay with a doxy in his first term at Eton and was never the same again.'

This news, however shocking, seemed to satisfy the medical men that Lord Crick's death was perfectly natural. If the French pox had not killed him, then some complication of the vile disease had. There was no more to be said.

41

It was therefore with great relief that Mr. Walton concluded to Captain Farrell: 'We fear that his lordship's corpse is in far too advanced a state of decomposition for us to draw any conclusions as to the cause of his death other than the fact that he was' – Dr. Siddall cleared his throat and obligingly finished his colleague's sentence – 'infected.'

The captain nodded and looked at them earnestly. 'There is, too, a risk of contamination, is there not, gentlemen?'

Suddenly finding a sympathetic ear, the two doctors nodded their heads vigorously with one accord.

'Indeed so,' retorted Mr. Walton eagerly.

Farrell looked solemn. 'Would I be correct in assuming that you agree with Dr. Fairweather that my brother-in-law passed away through natural causes, then, gentlemen?'

The two doctors looked at each other somberly and, once again, nodded their heads eagerly in agreement.

'Then I am free to bury him?'

'By all means and with the greatest of haste for all our sakes,' urged Dr. Siddall obligingly.

From the drawing room, Lydia could hear footsteps descending the stairs. She rose and walked softly toward the door. She could hear her husband bidding the gentlemen farewell and waited till the front door was shut before confronting him.

'They were here not ten minutes,' she said, frowning.

Farrell turned and held her hand. 'Your poor brother is too far gone, my dear. We must bury him at once.'

Lydia's heart sank. She feared Edward would take the secrets of his death with him to his grave and no one in Brandwick, nor in the whole of Oxfordshire, would ever know the truth. More importantly, nor would she.

Chapter 4

Very few people mourned Lord Edward Crick. He was interred in the family vault in the estate chapel the following day, watched only by his mother, sister, and his brother-in-law; his cousin Francis Crick, an anatomy student in London; and James Lavington, a neighbor and friend of the captain's. His legal guardian, Sir Montagu Malthus, was suffering a severe attack of the gout and was unable to attend.

How different it had been when they were children. She remembered playing with her brother in the woods, skimming stones on Plover's Lake and, on warm summer evenings, taking bottles of lemonade up to the ridge that looked down on the house. Sometimes they would be joined by Francis and all three of them would roll down the slope, falling down from dizziness as soon as they tried to stand up at the bottom. She remembered, too, the heartache when her father sent Edward to Eton. He was thirteen. On his return home after the first term she no longer knew him. He was so changed that he would not even stroll with her in the gardens, caring more for his card games with his newfound friends than for either her or the estate he would one day inherit.

The insipid October sun offered little comfort as the small procession entered the musty chapel. Lady Crick thought it was an ordinary Sunday and wore a bright bonnet trimmed with roses. Lydia placed her mother's ice-cold arm around her own and choked back acrid tears as the vicar read from the gospel.

Captain Farrell thought it right that he should deliver the eulogy. If she had felt stronger, Lydia might have insisted that Francis, who had been closer to Edward, address the congregation, but instead her husband, the man who loathed her brother perhaps more than any other in life, now sang his praises in death. He found himself having to dig deep to find good things to say about his brother-in-law and even Lydia was forced to admit to herself that Edward Crick had not been a likeable young man.

'Those who knew Edward, as I did, will remember him as a private person.' Lydia knew what her husband would say next: that her brother may not have been very forthcoming, but that he was quietly dedicated to the estate, even though its burden had been placed on him at such a young age. He worked, he told his meagre audience, quietly behind the scenes to ensure that all ran smoothly. She could not force herself to listen to the clichés that were as empty as most of the pews in the chapel. Instead she let her eyes roam around the porticoes and columns, lifting her gaze to the ceiling. She settled on a face carved in stone and framed by large oak leaves at the top of a pillar to the left of the altar. Its mouth was drawn tight and its eyes were bulging and immediately she saw Edward's anguished face once more. Was he listening to her husband's lies? She prayed to God that this final ordeal would soon be over.

Afterward they gathered in the drawing room in an uneasy atmosphere that was thick with nagging suspicions and thinly veiled recriminations. Farrell smiled calmly through it all, making small talk and frowning sympathetically now and again when someone invoked Edward's name, until, that is, a grotesquely disfigured gentleman limped over to him from the other side of the room.

'You play the part of the bereaved brother-in-law well,' remarked James Lavington when he finally had Farrell to himself in a corner. He had known the Irishman since their days in India. It was there that the accident had happened, leaving him partly paralyzed down one side of his body and his face horribly disfigured. A prosthetic nose of ivory had replaced his own, which had been blown away. The captain allowed himself a fleeting smile.

'What I do, I do for her,' he told him in his soft Irish brogue. He looked over toward Lydia, who was talking to Francis. 'It has hit her hard.'

Lavington nodded and gulped back a sherry. He and Farrell were of the same ilk. The only difference between them was now the captain had the means to sustain his lifestyle and Lavington, disabled as he was, did not.

'You're a fortunate man, Farrell,' he said, looking at Lydia in profile as she talked earnestly with

Francis. The Irishman nodded.

Francis was roughly the same age as his beautiful cousin and as a boy even nurtured dreams of marrying her when he was old enough, but she had chosen otherwise. His features were smooth, almost feminine. People said they looked alike and although they both always denied it, Lydia liked to think it drew them closer.

'Your husband delivered a good eulogy,' said Francis, being unusually formal. Lydia knew that what he really meant to say was that the captain concealed his relief at Edward's death well.

'Yes,' she replied, but it suddenly struck her that if he could lie that well in church before a congregation, maybe he could lie to her, too. She hesitated, wondering whether or not to reveal her fear. She decided she must.

'You have heard the rumors?'

Francis feigned ignorance. 'Rumors?' he repeated.

Lydia sometimes wished he were not so polite and proper. 'Francis, I must be truthful with you. 'Twas bad enough losing Edward, but now all this scandal—'

Francis nodded, making Lydia break off. 'I must admit I have heard talk.'

'What are they saying?'

He took a deep breath, but in the end there was no tactful way of putting it. 'They say that Edward was poisoned.'

Lydia knew that was only the half of it. 'And do they say by whom?'

Francis bit his lip, as if apologizing for the accusations of others. He did not have to speak

46

Farrell's name. It was written in his eyes.

Lydia felt the anger that had been so unfamiliar to her before surge through her veins once more. Seeing her distress, Francis put his hand on her shoulder.

'Please, dear Lydia. They are just cruel rumors.'

'You call them rumors, but what if...' Lydia stopped short of saying what she truly felt, but went on: 'The fact is Edward is dead and we know not how nor why.' Hannah the maid, who was handing around a tray of savories that nobody wanted, looked startled and Lydia tried to regain her composure. Her back stiffened. Francis sought to ease her obvious pain. 'The results of the post-mortem will reveal all,' he ventured.

Lydia frowned. 'But there lies the problem,' she confided. 'There was no postmortem.'

Francis looked bemused. 'But Farrell told me a surgeon and a physician were here yesterday to perform one.'

Lydia felt panic suddenly take hold. 'Michael did not tell you? They said Edward's body was too badly decomposed. They said they could not perform one.'

Francis swallowed hard and looked at Lydia. 'A misunderstanding,' he replied quickly, not daring to look her in the eye. But it was too late and both of them understood the gravity of the situation.

Later that night, when Farrell came to her in bed, he put his arm around her waist and drew her close to him. His body was cool and she felt his breath against her warm neck. He stroked her long chestnut hair tenderly, breathing in its lemon scent, before sliding his hand up her smooth

47

thigh, taking her nightgown with it. She felt him hard and hot between her thighs, but she did not respond. Instead she feigned sleep.

Chapter 5

The old man was sitting in a chair near the open window, listening to the din below. 'Must be a hanging,' he said knowingly. Thomas always marveled at how, despite being only relatively recently deprived of his sight, Dr. Carruthers's perceptions had been sharpened to compensate for the loss of his most precious sense. 'Who is it?'

Thomas had turned his face toward his master, so that he could be heard better above the passing furor outside. 'There are three of them, I understand, sir. One is a sheep stealer and the other two are said to have killed a lawyer.'

Dr. Carruthers chuckled. 'A lawyer, eh? Then surely they did the world a service.' His rounded shoulders, hunched from years of poring over dissecting tables, lifted slightly then sank down again into the winged chair. 'You're not watching it, then, boy?'

Thomas did not have the stomach for such a show. He could drain a man's carotid artery once he was dead without a second thought, but watching the life drain away from someone still alive was a different matter. 'I think not. I have too much work to be getting on with,' he said, taking his leave and heading off for the laboratory.

He did indeed have work. He had just taken delivery of a stillborn child from St. Bartholomew's Hospital. The specimen remained wrapped in swaddling cloths and had arrived in a wooden box. Thomas took the tiny bundle out and laid it, still covered, on the marble slab. He paused before his fingers gently began unwrapping the frayed kersey bands. He had lost count of the number of fetuses he had preserved in alcohol, but he never found it any easier. He tried not to think of each specimen as a life lost, as a mother's child gone forever, as a soul trapped in eternal limbo. He brushed such morbid thoughts aside, but they always came back to him each time he unclenched tiny fingers or touched tiny toes.

Anxious to get to work quickly, he had just reached for a bottle of preserving fluid from high up on the shelf when there was a knock at the door.

'Dr. Silkstone.'

Thomas was surprised to hear Mistress Finesilver. He had assumed that she had gone along to witness the hangings. He let out a spontaneous groan, then immediately regretted it, hoping it had not penetrated through the door.

'Yes, Mistress Finesilver,' he said, not bothering to get down from the stepladder. He watched the door open and saw the housekeeper standing at the threshold, but instead of her usual pinched, self-righteous expression, she wore a wry smile.

'There is a Lady Lydia Farrell to see you, Dr. Silkstone,' she informed the young doctor. As he could see no one, he assumed that this 'lady' must be one of Dr. Carruthers's old trouts – the sort

49

who felt they required a compress if they had so much as a twinge in their little finger. He was minded to tell Mistress Finesilver to ask Lady Lydia to make an appointment at a more appropriate time, when the housekeeper elucidated, 'Her ladyship says she is here on the recommendation of her cousin, who has attended your lectures.'

Thomas paused for a moment. Either Lady Lydia had a cousin who was about forty years her junior, as none of his students was over twenty-five, or, more logically her ladyship was actually quite young herself.

'Show her in, if you please,' he instructed.

Lady Lydia was indeed young. He put her at no more than in her mid-twenties, although it was difficult to see her face properly as her head was swamped by a large bonnet, and her slight frame was concealed by a velvet cape. For some reason Thomas found himself feeling slightly awkward.

'I am honored that one of my students should think so highly of me,' he said, hating himself immediately for sounding so crass. 'Please come in.' He gestured to the young woman.

The housekeeper was about to follow, but was put very firmly in her place by a stern look. 'I am sure Lady Lydia would prefer her consultation in private,' he told her. Mistress Finesilver bit her thin lips and conceded defeat, flouncing out of the laboratory on the pretense of having to attend to one of her pies.

There was a difficult silence as Lady Lydia stepped inside and looked around the laboratory, letting her gaze settle on anything but Thomas.

He, on the other hand, was fascinated by the young woman. He watched her expression change from one of curiosity to wide-eyed repulsion as she surveyed the flint glass jars that lined the walls. Chestnut curls peeped below her bonnet and long lashes fringed large eyes.

'May I take your cape?' asked Thomas. She looked at him as if he had just asked if he could remove her tonsils.

'I find it a little chilly in here,' she replied. It was the first time he had heard her speak and he thought her body might break with the effort.

Suddenly he remembered the stillborn. Of course she found it cold in the laboratory – any normal person would. He was accustomed to working with the windows open to keep down the temperature and to let out the stench of rotting flesh, but she was not. Like one of those exotic orchids Dr. Carruthers used to keep, she belonged in a glasshouse, in need of cosseting and cherishing. And what of the stillborn? What if she saw it? He backed up toward the dissecting table.

'I shall close the windows,' he assured her, surreptitiously pulling the sheet over the tiny child as he did so. But it was too late. Lady Lydia let out a gasp. Thomas was horrified. How could he have been so careless? Feeling embarrassed that he could so abuse a lady's sensibilities he was rushing forward to apologize when he realized her horrified gaze was not directed at the babe, but at Franklin as he scurried about in the corner. Her gloved hand rose in fright as she pointed at the hapless rodent.

'A rat,' she shrieked.

Thomas was half relieved to hear that Franklin was responsible for her outburst. He quickly went over to him, picked him up by the scruff of the neck, and put him back in his cage, fastening the lock. 'He always escapes,' he smiled, adding: 'We keep him for experiments.'

She nodded, seemingly satisfied by this explanation, and Thomas had to remind himself of what he was doing before she had interrupted him.

'The windows. Yes,' he said purposefully, but Lady Lydia shook her head.

'No, please,' she interjected as he walked toward the casement. 'The smell.'

From out of a small drawstring bag, she pulled a white linen handkerchief and held it to her nose. Thomas felt mortified. Not only was the air heavy with the smell of putrefied flesh, but he smelled, too, of formaldehyde. He looked down and immediately removed his large, stained apron. 'Perhaps we should walk in the garden,' he suggested. Lady Lydia nodded her head. 'I should like that,' she replied and she rose slowly, still clutching her handkerchief to her pale face.

Outside there was a small but pleasant courtyard. Underfoot Mistress Finesilver had planted sweet thyme that fragranced the air whenever it was stepped upon. Clumps of faded lavender, too, lined the wall, giving off the last of its pungent perfume. Thomas brushed against it deliberately so that its fragrance might permeate his own tainted clothes. He motioned toward a stone bench nearby, but the young woman declined.

'So, your cousin attends my lectures? Might I know him?'

52

'His name is Francis Crick. He is only a first-year student at the Company of Surgeons, but he commended you to me because of your work in a certain field.'

Thomas raised a curious eyebrow. 'And what might that be?' He covered many aspects in his lectures, although these usually focused on a different part of the anatomy or a different pathological system each week.

The young woman looked at him earnestly. 'It is the study of poisons,' she said.

It was a strange enquiry, he thought, to come from the lips of such a beautiful woman. 'I know something of the subject, yes,' he acknowledged. He had lectured on the topic only a few weeks ago, but that was before he had begun his in-depth studies into the lymphatic system and its reaction to poisons.

'May I ask why it concerns you?' He did not mean to sound patronizing. Lady Lydia became agitated, shifting her weight, such as it was, from one foot to the other.

'You may have heard of my husband, Captain Michael Farrell.'

Thomas turned the name over in his head. He was not familiar with it. He looked at the young woman once more as she waited patiently for some glimmer of recognition. It did not come.

'Forgive me, I...' Thomas began apologetically.

'The talk has not reached London, then,' she interrupted approvingly. 'If it had you would know the name.'

Thomas was beginning to feel rather foolish and at a loss. Aware that she was traveling down

53

a dead end, the young woman changed course.

'What if I were to tell you that I am the sister of the Earl Crick?'

It was a name that was vaguely known to Thomas. He recalled that one of his students had asked to be excused a lecture to attend the funeral of his cousin called Crick.

'Indeed, I know the name,' he acknowledged, although in reality he was still floundering in ignorance. Without lifting her head, the young woman said softly, as if she wanted no one to hear, 'He is dead.' Thomas felt awkward.

'I am sorry,' he said politely, bowing his head slightly in a gesture of sympathy. But it was clearly not sympathy the young woman wanted. She looked directly at him and her voice was no longer soft.

'People are talking, Dr. Silkstone.' Thomas was taken by surprise. 'They say my brother was murdered and that it was my husband who murdered him.' She was indignant. 'I must know if he did, Dr. Silkstone.' Thomas could see that her hands were clenched below the folds of her cape.

'Why should they suspect your husband, my lady?' he found himself asking.

She looked up, fighting back the anger. 'They say he poisoned Edward for his inheritance.'

'And you are asking me to prove that your husband is innocent,' said Thomas. He did not wish to prolong her agony.

She looked at him with large, frightened eyes that were glassy with tears and said, 'I believe you are the only man in England who can discover the truth.'

Chapter 6

Oxford lay beneath them like a gleaming necklace of cream-colored knuckle bones threaded on a tendon of river that ran through a narrow valley below. The coach was now descending a steep, tree-lined hill and the young doctor peered out of the window like an eager child who had been promised a treat. He had heard so much about the university, even when he was a sophomore in Philadelphia, the so-called Athens of America. It was, according to his medical students, a hotbed of rebellion, of debauchery, of fine minds and loose morals. Instead of Plato and Aristotle, college talk was of port and allowances. The professors of the university rarely gave lectures and, as for examinations, most undergraduates had never even entered a library, let alone opened a book.

Thomas suspected a little bitterness and rivalry on their part, however, and he could not wait to find out if there was any foundation to these scurrilous accusations. When he had asked Dr. Carruthers about his students' harsh opinion of the place, the old gentleman had tried to dampen his interest. 'Full of markets and cutpurses and muckworms who try to pass for scholars,' he had chuntered over a glass of brandy. He had paused for a moment, then chuckled. 'But if they're agin' the Hanoverians, they can't be all bad,' he mused. This enigmatic dismissal had left Thomas even

55

more determined to one day visit the fabled city of academia, of John Milton and Jonathan Swift, and that day had now come about in a rather unexpected way.

As the coach bounced and lurched its way down the hill, Thomas turned toward the young woman who sat opposite him; the young woman who had come to him at his rooms in London in such desperation, pleading for his help, only the night before. He would never forget her large, pleading eyes as she begged him to help her solve the mystery of her brother's death. Yet now, there she sat, not deigning to look at him for fear that one of the other passengers might suspect they were traveling together.

Joining Lady Lydia was her maid, Eliza, a full-bosomed wench, whose eyes strayed coquettishly now and again toward him. The doctor's gaze, however, was firmly fixed on her ladyship and he watched her as she stared vacantly out of the window. In the cold light of day, those eyes looked smaller than the night before. It was Cicero who had called the eye the interpreter of the mind, mused Thomas. They may be silent today, he told himself, but her beauty was in no way diminished. He studied the carved helix of her ear and the delicate ovals of her nostrils. Her china white skin was completely flawless, except for a tiny exquisite mole to the left of her lips and yet he still found himself wondering what lay beneath this super-ficial epidermis. She must have been aware that he was looking at her, yet she deliberately ignored him.

'We must remain strangers on the coach,' she

told him after he had agreed to travel to Oxfordshire with her. 'It is imperative that people do not
realize we are together.' There was an urgency in
her voice that made him accept her instruction
unquestioningly.

Now and again when she had lifted her gaze
during the arduous journey from London, it had
been to acknowledge some ribald comment made
by the fat cleric who sat to her right. Thomas had
made the mistake of revealing his profession
before they were clear of Holborn and the well-
built clergyman had insisted on divulging the
grisly details of the lithotomy he had undergone,
which had produced a stone as big as a plover's
egg. He enthused at great length about how the
sizable stone had been excised by the surgeon in
less than two minutes flat. Indeed, the description
had been so graphic that the elderly woman who
was on her way to visit her undergraduate son had
almost passed out, and probably would have done
so had Thomas not wafted some smelling salts
under her nose.

The one saving grace of the journey had been
the fact that the woman had been so grateful to
Thomas for his care that she had shared the entire contents of a hamper originally destined for
her son with her fellow passengers. Thomas had
tucked into a pheasant leg, three oatcakes, and a
flagon of cider on her insistence. It had helped
pass the time and taken his mind off the unenviable task he might be asked to perform. He
did not relish a postmortem on a corpse already
in the advanced stages of decomposition. His
desire for dissection was not as rapacious as some

of his fellow anatomists. He did not seek out corpses with the appetite of a gourmet, keen to sample corporal delicacies. The examination of a cadaver in this advanced stage of decay would be an unpleasant means to a sought-after end, not an anatomical celebration.

The coach turned into Broad Street and came to a halt outside the White Horse. Lady Lydia had already gathered her belongings together. She had been reading what appeared to be letters for part of the journey and had folded them neatly, returning them to a small wallet she carried. As she rose from her seat, smoothing her skirts, Thomas looked at her deliberately, wondering if she might dart him a surreptitious glance. She did not and he watched, irritated, as the coachman helped her alight first.

'You are to wait at the White Horse. I will send a messenger presently,' she had instructed him the night before. He did not take kindly to being treated like a servant, but he told himself that Lady Lydia was in mourning and could therefore be excused.

On the newly laid pavement by the side of the road stood a liveried servant, and behind him a man with a pockmarked face. The servant bowed and took Lady Lydia's gloved hand, escorting her to a waiting carriage. It stood a few yards away outside the Sheldonian Theatre, whose walls were adorned with the busts of famous philosophers. Socrates and Aristotle looked down upon the bustling street below, like Greek gods watching over mere mortals. A carrot-haired boy of no more than ten years of age followed behind, struggling with his mistress's luggage.

Thomas had kept his precious instrument bag with him at his feet throughout the journey. The driver handed him the only other bag he possessed, containing an apron and a change of clothes, and he began to make his way toward the White Horse, just as Lady Lydia's carriage moved off. He could see the brim of her hat and the curve of her nose through the window and, just as he had given up all hope, she turned, as if she knew he had been watching her, and fixed him in her eye. There was no smile, no nod, no gesture of recognition; just a silent, motionless look. It was enough and Thomas was made to feel he was the most important man in the whole of Oxford.

He did not know how long he would have to wait at the inn. Lady Lydia had been very vague about her intentions. It may, she said, be only two or three hours. On the other hand he might have to wait overnight before he was sent word of her plans. She had gone on ahead to Boughton Hall, about six miles north of the city, and would consult with her husband before deciding whether or not she required Thomas's services.

The young doctor made his way inside the inn, carefully ducking under the low lintel at the entrance. After such a tedious journey, Thomas thought himself entitled to a little relaxation. The inn was cramped, with several small rooms leading off each other, like a rabbit warren. The air was thick with pipe smoke and the sickly sour smell of beer.

'A tankard of your best ale,' Thomas asked the ruddy-faced landlord. There was a moment's pause as the man processed Thomas's demeanor and his accent in particular. Detecting this new patron was from the Colonies, the innkeeper raised a disapproving eyebrow and the frothing tankard was duly dispatched, without any pleasantries, on the bar together with a few farthings in change.

Three other men who sat at a nearby table also turned to look at this traitor in their midst. Thomas was aware of an undercurrent of hostility, as their eyes bored into him with a steady pressure, but he had become used to it, as if such regular contempt had anesthetized his senses. It no longer bothered him and he simply took his ale and sat down at a small table by the window.

A sickly fire flickered in the inglenook and despite the fact that the inn was by no means empty, Thomas felt oddly alone. He took out his purse and was about to drop in his change when he saw a scrap of paper. He suddenly remembered Dr. Carruthers had slipped it in there the night before when he had told him he would be visiting Oxford for a day or two. 'Might be worth your while looking this chap up,' the old gentleman said. Despite not being able to see, he had scrawled a name on the paper in a spidery hand and pressed it into Thomas's pocket. ''Course he could be dead by now. Always ill, but he was a good anatomist in his day,' the old doctor had chuckled.

Thomas squinted as he tried to read the almost illegible hand. After a few moments of holding the parchment up to the light from the window he was able to decipher it: 'Professor Hans Hascher, Christ Church Anatomy School.' He took a large gulp of his ale. It was weak and tasted of watered-down vinegar. He did not like this place and he had no reason to stay here, at least not for the next few hours anyway, he told himself. He memorized the name and address, pushed the half-empty tankard to one side, and stood up. The three heads turned once more and watched him walk toward the door. As Thomas reached the threshold he heard someone utter, 'Bloody New Worlder.' He paused to register the insult, but chose to ignore it, then walked out into the watery light of an October day.

Chapter 7

Jacob Lovelock carried the coal scuttle across to the kitchen fire as his wife, Hannah, struggled with sticks and tapers at the grate. Wiping his forehead with a sooty hand, he left coal dust in the pockmarks that pitted his face, turning some of them into small black volcanic craters.

'I don't know as how you could,' scolded Mistress Claddingbowl, the cook. Hannah had allowed the fire to go out and now there was no hot water for Captain Farrell's morning tea, let alone his toilet. The flustered maid was trying desperately to rekindle the flames, blowing frantically when a spark caught hold of a stick, but her task was made all the more difficult because the wood had been allowed to get damp.

'So, you've let the fire go out.' The voice of Raf-

61

ferty, the captain's manservant, sent a shudder down Hannah's spine. Mr. Rafferty – no one knew his first name – had served with Captain Farrell in India for ten years. When a back injury forced him to leave the army, the captain eagerly employed him as his valet. He had an air of quiet authority about him. He never raised his voice to the other servants, although his sharp tongue could sting as much as any birch. Hannah stared at the floor as Rafferty approached. ''Tis a good job the master does not have need of it yet,' he told her, softening his tone a little. 'He still sleeps.'

Jacob shrugged his broad shoulders. ''Tis a wonder he can sleep at all,' he muttered, shoveling coals onto the fire.

Rafferty's back suddenly stiffened. 'What was that?' The smirk suddenly disappeared from Jacob's face and he stood upright.

'I said the master needs his sleep and all, Mr. Rafferty, sir.'

The valet narrowed his eyes. 'The master's going through a bad time. We should all support him,' he growled in his low Irish brogue. Tugging indignantly at his waistcoat, he turned and walked toward the pantry.

Jacob waited until the manservant was out of earshot. 'Bad time? He seemed right enough to me yesterday,' he said as he poked the coals fiercely.

Hannah laid more kindling. 'What do you mean?' she asked in a half whisper. Jacob smiled smugly, cocking his head to one side. He did not bother to lower his voice.

'He told me now that his lordship was out of the way, my life would be easier.' He paused for effect. 'That all our lives would be easier.'

Mistress Claddingbowl, who had gone back to mixing batter, stopped stirring. 'I'm sure he meant nothing by it,' she huffed, returning to her pancakes.

It gave Jacob great pleasure to see the cook writhe. 'But 'tis not the half of it, Mistress Claddingbowl,' he told her. Hannah frowned at him, silently reprimanding him, but he took no notice. 'He says to me: "Now that I'm master, there'll be some changes 'round here."'

'There've been changes enough already,' snapped Hannah, suddenly bursting into tears once more.

Jacob put his grimy arm around her. 'There, dearest. I know 'tis hard,' he comforted. Everyone understood, but his words did not soothe his wife.

'She's gone, Jacob. Rebecca's gone,' she sobbed.

Twelve-year-old Rebecca Lovelock, the eldest daughter of Hannah and Jacob, had fallen in the lake on the estate earlier in the year and drowned. Since then a malaise hung in the air, sucking out any lightheartedness there may have been at the hall. In fact the only person who appeared to have taken these calamitous events in his stride was Captain Farrell, who still slept upstairs.

Yet his sleep was not a righteous one, but fitful and broken. Beads of sweat dotted his forehead and his hair was matted. He tossed and turned and mumbled and now and again the name 'Edward' was discernable among his rantings. His sleep, it appeared, brought with it nightmares.

Suddenly he sat bolt upright, jolting himself

out of his slumber to find his bed empty. Lydia was absent. It was then he remembered she had gone to London to see her cousin. He slumped down again.

The first blackbirds were already chirping out their throaty chorus before sleep finally got the better of him once more and it was shortly after midday before Rafferty entered the chamber to check on his master. His footsteps on the polished oak floor woke the captain and he turned over, opening a cautious eye. A shaft of light beamed down through a chink in the heavy velvet drapes.

'What time is it?'

'Past noon, sir,' Rafferty replied. 'Shall I draw the curtains?'

Farrell sat up quickly. His loose nightshirt was open at the neck, revealing a large expanse of his chest. He ran his fingers through his dark, shoulder-length hair and tossed his head as if he were trying to shake off the uneasy sleep that had enveloped him so entirely for the last three hours.

His thoughts turned to Lydia once more. 'I must dress. Her ladyship will be back soon.' He flung back the covers and leapt up out of bed. Walking over to the washstand in the corner of his room by the casement, he splashed his face with the water that Rafferty had just poured.

''Tis cold,' he remarked.

Rafferty shifted awkwardly. 'I'm afraid the fire went out earlier this morning, sir,' he replied apologetically.

Farrell took the towel his manservant handed him and, patting his face dry, walked over to the window and looked out over the tree-lined drive.

It was a beautiful autumn day, with clear blue skies. The avenue of horse chestnuts was turning orange and gold, their large green leaves edged in rust-colored lace. The lawns, too, had lost their summer verdure. Nevertheless Michael Farrell felt a sense of pride as he surveyed the scene.

He had loved the estate before when it had belonged to Edward, but now that it was his, for all intents and purposes, he loved it even more. As far as the eye could see – beyond the thick copse, across the river, and over toward the rolling hills beyond – was now in his possession. Even the bridge in the distance, over which a lone horseman now rode, was his.

'This is a fine place, Rafferty,' he said, easing his arms into the waistcoat his manservant held for him.

'Indeed it is, sir,' came the sought-after reply. As Rafferty helped his master dress, Farrell continued to gaze out at the vista, drinking it in like a good glass of claret. He saw the cattle grazing in the water meadow and he saw the buzzards circling on the noonday thermals above the Chiltern Hills. He saw, too, that the horseman, who had appeared as an insignificant dot on the horizon only a few moments ago, was drawing near at speed and was now approaching the drive that led directly to the front of Boughton Hall.

Chapter 8

The ghastly moaning grew louder – an aria of pain that plucked at raw nerves and pressed on tissue. It was a sound so familiar to Thomas, yet as he stood at the top of the narrow stone stairway and listened to the excruciating cacophony with increasing concern, it occurred to him that, rather than enter the room, he should turn tail and flee. Staccato cries punctuated the low groaning now and again, but just when a musician might have expected a crescendo, the low droning resumed, offering no hope of any eventual relief.

Thomas had been standing outside the brass-studded door of Professor Hans Hascher at Christ Church College for what seemed like an age. In his imagination Thomas pictured a hapless patient having his leg sawn off without any form of anesthesia, or worse still, a criminal being dissected whilst he was still alive. This last vile scenario was too much for even Thomas to contemplate and he had just made up his mind to leave there and then when he caught a brass nameplate that was loosely fixed on the door and sent it crashing to the ground. The horrific moaning suddenly ceased and Thomas stopped dead in his tracks.

'Who's ... who's zhere?' asked a feeble voice.

Thomas hesitated. He cleared his throat. 'I am looking for Professor Hascher,' he called through the door.

'Co ... in,' came the barely intelligible reply.

Thomas straightened his waistcoat and shuddered slightly as he obeyed the command. The door creaked open to reveal a large, book-lined study, with a long desk at the far end. In front of the desk was a winged chair and Thomas could just make out a stockinged leg slung over its side, with its foot braced against the desk. A quick survey of the room told him there was no one else in it, so he could only presume that the gentleman was gravely ill. He walked forward.

'Sir, can I help you?' he asked, striding toward the chair, uncertain as to what he might find.

The reply was difficult to make out. The words were so poorly formed, as if the speaker had a mouth full of nails. 'Are ooo a su ... en...?'

Thomas drew nearer. 'I am a surgeon, sir. May I help you?' As he approached the desk he could see an array of surgical instruments laid out on green cloth; forceps, sutures, scissors, and gauze. A nearby white napkin was drenched in blood. It appeared to Thomas that the man might be performing some sort of surgery on himself.

All the young doctor could see at first was a mop of wild gray hair that reminded him of the tumbleweed in his homeland, then the head turned to reveal a swollen, pain-racked face.

'Zank God,' said the man, holding up a large pair of pliers.

He handed the instrument to Thomas, who took it without question. In a way it was a relief to know that the object of such exquisite agony was merely a decayed molar and not a diseased limb or organ that required removal.

'I have just the thing,' he told the man, who he surmised to be in his seventies, but whose features were so obviously distorted by the swelling of his jawline.

Opening his instrument bag, Thomas took out a blue glass bottle and, taking a pad of gauze from the desk, he soaked it with purple liquid.

'Open wide,' he ordered his new patient, who had become totally compliant. Thomas was allowed to dab his throbbing jaw with tincture of iodine before taking up the pliers once more. 'Brace yourself.'

The man's gnarled knuckles took hold of the two chair arms as Thomas steadied himself, wedging his feet on either side of the legs. The patient let out a long, low cry as the young doctor wrestled for a few seconds with the offending tooth before it finally came free at its roots with such a force that Thomas almost fell backward.

Holding up the pliers, with the blackened tooth still in the pincers, Thomas displayed it to its erstwhile owner as a hunter would a prize catch.

'A fine trophy, sir,' he smiled, inspecting the specimen that was as jagged as a granite outcrop. It took a moment for them both to regain their composure. Finally it was the old man who spoke first.

'After ze pox, caries is one of ze greatest scourges of humanity,' he mumbled, dabbing the blood from his mouth.

Thomas handed him a glass of water and smiled. 'Is it Professor Hascher?' he asked as he watched his patient swilling the water around his gums and spitting the bloodied liquid out into a bowl on the desk beside him.

He looked up at Thomas. 'You are ri..., young man,' he replied, still unable to enunciate properly. 'And you are?'

'Thomas Silkstone. I have taken over Dr. Carruthers's practice in London.'

Professor Hascher smiled. 'Zhat old devil. I zought ze pox would have killed him years ago!' His face suddenly split into a smile, which he instantly regretted, and his sinewy hand flew up to his swollen jaw once more. Still in pain, he pointed to a large glass bottle on a shelf behind Thomas's head. The young doctor took it down and watched bemused as the professor uncorked it and began to gulp down the clear contents, which Thomas had assumed to be formaldehyde. After four or five mouthfuls, the professor stopped drinking and wiped his tender chin with the back of his hand. 'Schnapps,' he explained. 'From Prussia. If I'd known you vere coming, I'd have had some before I tried to take ze tooz out,' he quipped.

Thomas smiled. He could see how this Saxon professor and Dr. Carruthers had been such good friends. The old man motioned to a set of what appeared to be decorated glass stirrup cups on another shelf behind him and Thomas took two down and watched as the professor filled them both to the brim. 'Prost,' he toasted, and Thomas watched a little shocked as he downed the liquid in one. Thomas followed, jerking his head back so he could swallow the alcohol in one gulp. He felt it burn the back of his throat immediately, as if he had poured flames down his gullet, then his neck began to stiffen.

The old man watched his stunned reaction. "'Tis an excellent anesthetic. Two glasses of zhat and one wouldn't feel a zing,' he laughed. This time he did not wince in pain. The schnapps was obviously working its anesthetic magic on him, thought Thomas.

The professor motioned to him to pull up a chair from the other side of the room. 'Tell me what brings you to this den of iniquity,' he said, settling back into his winged chair, relishing his newfound freedom from pain.

'When I was a young sophomore in Philadelphia' – Thomas broke off – 'in America,' he said for the sake of clarification, 'my father, who was a physician, introduced me to the work of Dr. Carruthers. I read all his seminal treatises and we began corresponding. Eventually I came to London and was fortunate enough to enjoy his tutelage.'

'But my old friend is blind now, is he not?' intervened the professor.

'Sadly yes,' replied Thomas. 'But he has given me his mantle.'

'Zen you are both fortunate to have found each other,' nodded the Saxon, adding: 'But you are a long way from your dissecting rooms here...'

The young doctor shifted uneasily in his chair and reflected. 'The other day,' he began, 'a lady of some breeding came to my rooms. It was clear she was in a state of anxiety.'

The professor listened sagely, like a priest hearing a confession. Thomas went on: 'She told me that her young brother had died in ... in, well, mysterious circumstances and asked me – no, implored me – to help her uncover the cause of his death.'

Professor Hascher, whose expression had been reasonably passive up until this point, now nodded knowingly.

'And zis lady,' he began, 'might her name happen to be Lady Lydia Farrell?'

Thomas suddenly felt awkward. How could he have been so indiscreet? Professor Hascher saw his pained reaction and was quick to try and ease it. 'It is ze talk of the county, my dear fellow,' he told him. 'Zere are rumors and more rumors. Was he murdered? And if so, by whom? Zere are plenty who would gladly claim to have done it – behind ze judge's back.'

The young doctor looked deep into his empty glass, as if regretting the fact that its contents had so loosened his tongue. 'I must go,' he told the professor, setting it down on the desk and starting to pack his bag. But the old man reached out and stayed Thomas's hand as he tried to fasten the clasp.

'If you are called upon, you will need instruments, preserving fluid, much more zan you have in zhat bag of yours.' His watery eyes were earnest. 'I want you to know zat my laboratory is at your disposal.'

Chapter 9

Lydia knew something was wrong the instant her carriage turned into the drive of Boughton Hall. The dogs did not come bounding to greet her and, worse still, Michael was not standing there by the front doorway. Had he not received word of her arrival? Suddenly she saw Howard, the butler, and Rafferty emerge down the front steps. They both looked grave. Mistress Claddingbowl and Mistress Firebrace, the housekeeper, followed, both of them with downcast eyes, as if trying to avoid her questioning gaze. Hannah, Jacob, and Will, their son, completed the entourage.

As the footman helped her alight from the carriage, Lydia's sense of unease deepened. 'Where is your master?' she asked Howard. The butler threw a worried glance at Rafferty, as if not knowing how to reply.

'He is up at the pavilion, your ladyship,' said the manservant sheepishly.

The pavilion was a summerhouse, perched on a ridge overlooking a valley, about half a mile from the house, that had been built by Lydia's father as a retreat from the troubles of daily estate life. Michael had also found solace there when her brother was being troublesome, failing to address pressing business, as he so often did, preferring instead to gamble or ride or lie with women.

'I shall go to him,' she said.

Rafferty frowned. 'Please, my lady. You must be tired after your journey.'

'I shall go to him,' she repeated, doing little to hide her anger. 'Jacob, harness the dogcart.'

The track that led up to the pavilion was rough and pitted and once or twice the pony lurched and stumbled. The spring rains carved deep gullies in the sandy soil, leaving the surface quite treacherous in places. The wooden wheels of the dogcart gouged into the waterlogged ruts and flung a muddy spray on either side. Lydia, however, was used to taking the reins. She often made the trip, especially in the summer when they were first wed. She would bring a flask of lemonade and drink it with the captain, watching the sun go down over the gentle valley.

As she urged the little bay on, up the track where it grew steep and even more difficult to negotiate, her sense of foreboding increased. Her husband would not have ignored her homecoming lightly. There must be something that was troubling him deeply and she was worried she knew what it might be. The whitewashed pavilion, with its ornate roof and narrow windows, looked so out of place set against the Oxfordshire landscape, she thought as she approached it. Her spouse was sitting on the steps, his head in his hands. He looked up when he heard the sound of the cart and struggled to his feet. Lydia tugged at the reins and the horse halted just a few feet away. He looked years older, as if the last forty-eight hours had aged him by a decade. His complexion was sallow and the skin beneath his eyes was puffy.

'What is it, Michael?' she asked. 'What has

73

happened?' Her husband held her gaze but did not speak. 'Is it about Edward?'

Her husband nodded. 'The coroner's man came this morning. There's to be an inquest.'

This did not come as a surprise to Lydia. She had been anticipating it, ever since Sir Montagu's letter. Now, however, she made little attempt to mask her relief.

'But this way, we can know for certain that Edward was not...' She broke off, unable to bring herself to say the word.

Farrell darted her a fiery glance.

'Do you not see? This way we can put paid to all the rumors,' she continued.

Farrell shrugged. 'How? His corpse has rotted so much he may as well have been burned at the stake.'

Although Lydia did not reply immediately, the captain could tell from her expression that she had something to say. She lifted her head. 'I have a confession to make.' Farrell turned, frowning. 'I did not go to London to see cousin Francis.'

'No?' He seemed more curious than shocked.

'I went to see the surgeon who teaches him.'

Farrell rolled his eyes in frustration. 'A surgeon? Not another accursed surgeon!' he groaned through clenched teeth, but Lydia pleaded.

'He is the only person who can help us, Michael, and he is waiting for you to give the word.'

The captain looked at her contemptuously, wishing that she would not meddle in affairs that he felt were beyond her grasp. 'What can this surgeon do that others cannot? Raise the dead?' he sneered.

Lydia turned and walked a few feet away, putting a short distance between them. 'This surgeon is different. He can tell things from a corpse that no others can. If we exhume Edward's body, he will be able to silence the rumors once and for all.'

'Exhume Edward?' He looked at her incredulously.

''Tis the only way,' she pleaded, walking toward him once more.

Farrell stared at her in disbelief and shook his head in a way that made her feel like a child. 'And what if he finds Edward's death was not an accident?' He glared at her with piercing green eyes. She turned away from him once more, feeling discomfort at his reproachful gaze.

For the first weeks of their marriage he had been attentive enough and his marital appetites were certainly voracious. She willingly consented at first, but as his physical demands on her grew and her energies and sensibilities did not always match his, she began to see flashes of temper. These would be compounded by his regular bouts of drinking and he increasingly forced himself on her in drunken frenzies. Beyond the confines of the bedchamber, his ill humor began to manifest itself regularly, too. He had never disguised his dislike of Edward to her, but now he allowed his sheer resentment and loathing to show itself quite openly in her presence. She had little doubt her husband could kill, as indeed he had in the army. But she was convinced it would be in hot Gaelic passion, over a card game or a woman, not cold calculation.

'I know you think I had something to do with

your brother's death,' he said softly. His words pricked at her skin like so many hot needles and she suddenly felt a pang of disloyalty. Her husband's accusations, delivered as they were with all the vulnerability of a wounded child, jolted her back to reality and she darted 'round to face him.

'You are my husband,' she began, 'and my first duty is to you, but we need to rid ourselves of this suspicion once and for all.' She went to him and tried to take his hands in hers, but he pushed her away.

'Rather you feel *I* need to rid myself of suspicion,' he corrected her.

She sighed deeply and looked into his eyes. It was almost as if they belonged to a stranger. There had been a time when she could gaze far into his soul, as if it were a deep pool, and know exactly what lay at the bottom. Now suspicion muddied those clear waters until they had become unfathomable. 'I beg you, for all our sakes,' she pleaded, 'let the surgeon do his work.'

Chapter 10

The call came at dusk. Thomas was seated on a chair by the window reading, endeavoring to catch the feeble rays from a streetlamp outside in Broad Street. Now and again he became distracted by calls from drunken scholars, pouring out of the tippling houses, or by the rattle of a carriage. In the distance Great Tom, the Christ Church bell,

76

was striking a seemingly endless toll. He thought it quaint to give a bell an intimate name, like an old friend. He thought, too, of Professor Hascher, ensconced in his study there, surrounded by books and body parts. The effects of the schnapps would be wearing off now and the cavity where once his tooth had been rooted would be throbbing. He had been generous enough to offer the services of his laboratory and Thomas wondered if he would be called upon to need them.

He returned to his papers once more. The author's hand was difficult to decipher and he found himself squinting to try and make sense of the treatise. He had been given only one candle to last him the night, but he knew the light would soon defeat him. His eyes were strained and he was just about to submit to the darkness when there came a knock at the door. His heart missed a beat. He had been half expecting it, but not quite so soon.

Jacob Lovelock stood nervously at the doorway. Thomas recognized him from earlier on in the day by his pockmarked face.

'Dr. Silkstone?' The servant spoke in a coarse whisper, as if it was something that was quite alien to him to speak in a hushed tone.

Thomas nodded and bade him enter immediately, checking that no one was loitering on the darkened landing. The servant wasted no time in delivering his message. 'Her ladyship says you must present yourself to the Oxford coroner first off tomorrow morning. There is to be an in ... an in...' He stumbled over an unfamiliar word, which he had been obliged to learn specially for the mission.

'Inquest?' coaxed Thomas.

'Yes, sir,' nodded a grateful Jacob.

The young doctor delved into his purse and pressed a few coins into the man's grimy hand. 'Go back to your mistress and tell her I will do as she bids.'

The servant touched his cratered forehead with his forefinger and was turning to go when Thomas called him back.

'Be careful,' he warned. 'No one must see you leave.' Jacob nodded once more and slipped out into the shadows. A moment later he emerged at the front of the inn and Thomas watched him mount his horse that had been tethered outside and then ride off. He only hoped no one else had noticed him, too.

He turned and looked around the unfamiliar room that was now in almost total darkness. The bed, the solitary chair, the washstand in the corner, and the wardrobe by the door made him crave the comforts of his own room in London and he suddenly found himself wondering what on earth he had become involved in. All this secrecy and intrigue – he was a surgeon, not a spy. The next morning he would present himself to the coroner and offer his expertise in the service of an inquest at the behest of a total stranger. What the coroner must never know, of course, was that Thomas had come to Oxford at the request of Lady Farrell, sister of the deceased in question. If any link were discovered, his integrity and independence would be immediately called into question and any of his findings thrown into doubt. His career would be over, his reputation in tatters. Yet he was prepared to risk it all. Why, he asked himself, as he sat watching the flame of his candle flail around as if gasping for oxygen. It was certainly not for monetary gain. He had already made up his mind not to accept any payment for his services. He gazed into the dying flame and saw Lydia's hauntingly beautiful face appear, and just before it breathed its last and expired, his question was answered.

Michael Farrell sat alone in his study, cradling a glass of brandy in his hand. He had allowed the fire to die down so that it was now only a mass of glowing embers. Lydia had retired shortly after dinner, excusing herself with a headache after the journey from London. She had sensed his anger toward her, although he had tried to hide it. He felt she was clinging to some naive belief that once this surgeon had wrought his magic they would know, for sure what had killed her brother and that he, Michael, would be able to clear his tarnished name.

Sometimes he wondered at his wife's gullibility. He was angry, too, that she had gone behind his back, deliberately deceived him and called in this anatomist from London, whose presence would surely only complicate matters. He had no faith in these quacks. After all they had shown themselves to be a lily-livered lot, allowing themselves to desert their professional duties because they did not have the stomach for a turning corpse. What could this charlatan, a colonist according to Lydia, be capable of that English doctors were not?

The captain shrugged, as if reiterating to himself the futility of it all. The brandy was calming him down, but making him feel moribund. He prodded the fire with the poker and it momentarily sprang into life, spewing out red-hot embers and letting out an odd hissing sound. Once more he was reminded of Edward's last moments; the cries, the blood around the mouth, those bulging eyes. Again, he cast his mind back to that fateful morning. Nothing had seemed out of order. The bout of vomiting and diarrhea from which he had suffered the previous week only troubled him for a day or two and he was shortly restored to his normal spirits.

Edward had risen earlier than usual, perhaps, that morning, recalled Farrell, but he assumed he went for a ride along the gallops. He saw him go out of the back door and cross the courtyard toward the stables. It was not uncustomary for him to rise at dawn on light mornings and saddle up his mare. His medication sometimes caused him severe headaches and he would often say that fresh air and exercise were the only palliatives that eased his discomfort.

He had taken his breakfast in the company of his mama and then announced he would be going fishing down at Plover's Lake on the southeastern corner of the estate. Farrell recalled he had been reading the newspaper at the time. He never liked to engage in conversation with his brother-in-law. It almost invariably ended in a row. He endured his endless prattling for Lydia's sake, but now and again he succumbed to the urge to throw the odd barbed comment toward Edward.

Farrell had taken an instant aversion to the spindly youth when he first clapped eyes on him while visiting him at Eton. He saw him boxing his fag around the ears for no good reason other than he looked him in the eye, and from that day he realized that his young brother-in-law was not only puny and physically unappealing, but a coward and a bully, too. Of course he had hidden his contempt for the young lord until he had placed a wedding band on his sister's finger, but after that day he had made no attempt to conceal his disdain.

As Eliza poured tea to take to her mistress on that particular morning, he remembered reminding Edward that the apothecary was bringing a new batch of physick later. ''Twould be a pity to miss a dose,' he had remarked sarcastically. The young earl had turned and snarled, baring his uneven teeth. He sometimes reminded Farrell of a rat, not only in nature but also in his rodentlike looks. He loved to bait his irksome brother-in-law, especially in front of the servants, but the irony of his words now haunted him.

The embers had settled down to a warming glow once more and the captain was contemplating pouring himself another brandy when he heard footsteps outside. Hannah suddenly appeared in the room, looking strained. The woman was still in mourning for her lost daughter and Farrell noted that her suffering had etched itself in her face. Streaks of white now flecked the auburn hair that peeped under her cap.

'Is there anything you need, sir?' she asked, but Farrell sensed there was more to her question than a mere eagerness to serve. He smiled at her.

'Yes.' He held out his empty glass and she took it over to the sideboard, set it down, and lifted the stopper off the decanter. He watched her and saw that she was shaking.

'Steady now,' he called across the room as the stopper fell out of her grasp and clattered, thankfully unbroken, onto the rug below. Once more the tears flowed freely as the servant suddenly broke down, lifting her apron up to her face. Farrell rose and went over to her, putting a comforting arm around her. He had long abandoned any sense of propriety when it came to female members of staff.

'There, there,' he comforted her. She looked at him with reddened eyes. 'What is it?'

'Will they tell me to say things in court, sir, about his lordship?' she asked with all the vulnerability of a helpless child.

Farrell paused, slightly nonplussed by the maidservant's question. 'You saw what happened to your master, did you not, Hannah?'

'I'll never forget it, sir. His eyes, the blood...'

The Irishman nodded impatiently, not wishing to relive the scene. 'Then I am afraid you must tell the coroner what you saw.'

She nodded slowly, regaining her composure. Farrell took the decanter and poured out a glass of brandy. He was just about to down it himself, when he thought better of it and offered it to Hannah. 'Here, drink this,' he told her. She looked at him and took the glass, gulping from it quickly, as if it were some vile-tasting medicine. With an outstretched hand he stroked her arm in a gesture of comfort. His hand brushed her bare lower arm and she lifted her head toward his.

'Sir, Mr. Lavington is here to see you.' Howard's unbidden voice broke the moment. He stood agitated at the doorway, then, suddenly realizing what he had just witnessed, he became even more harassed. 'Begging your pardon, sir,' he said disapprovingly, 'but he said it was important...'

James Lavington also appeared, wearing a worried expression on the side of his face that was not paralyzed. Farrell smiled. 'That will be all, Howard. Leave us now.' He turned to Hannah. 'You, too,' he instructed and he guided his friend inside the study.

'I came as soon as I heard,' said Lavington, accepting the glass of brandy Farrell handed him. ''Tis the talk of the village.' Both men sat down in front of the fire. Lavington was tense, hunching over his glass.

'The godfather is behind it,' Farrell said.

'Sir Montagu? I see,' nodded Lavington.

'He would do anything to exact his revenge on me.' The Irishman's voice was strangely measured and calm. Lavington was silent for a moment and sipped at his brandy as if taking in the gravity of the situation.

'These inquests are usually thorough affairs, Farrell,' he said earnestly. As a lawyer, he had been present at two while in India and knew that any coroner worth his salt would explore every avenue, especially in a case such as the young earl's.

The captain let out a forced laugh. 'I imagine they will try and find out how Crick died,' he countered sarcastically.

Lavington looked annoyed. 'They will call witnesses. They will probe. Awkward questions will be asked.' Farrell had rarely seen his friend look so apprehensive. He had played with him for high stakes at some of the most unforgiving tables in Bath and Cheltenham and he had always kept his composure, but tonight his nerves were clearly on edge. Farrell gazed deep into his half-empty glass. 'I do not doubt that you are right and that is why it is important that when I am called, and if you are called, we have our story straight.'

Chapter 11

Shortly after nine o'clock in the morning Thomas presented himself at Oxford Coroner's Court. The clerk, a man with a weasel face, looked at him suspiciously. 'What is the purpose of your visit?' he quizzed.

'I am a surgeon and anatomist, come from London, and wish to see Sir Theodisius Pettigrew,' said Thomas, trying to appear confident. Lady Lydia had told him the coroner's name before, but all the same a sickly feeling rose in the pit of his stomach and traveled up as far as his gullet.

'I will see if he is available,' said the clerk, rising from his desk and walking to the double doors behind him. He knocked, poked his head into the gloomy study beyond, and then nodded to Thomas.

Sir Theodisius Pettigrew sat behind a large desk,

84

eating. A white napkin was tucked into his collar and held in place by the lowest of his three chins. By the looks of it, he had been eating for some time, thought Thomas; such were the dollops of egg yolk and spots of grease on the linen. In front of him were several plates, some empty, and some still piled high with food. There was a side of ham, some quails' eggs, a truckle of cheddar, and a dish of pickles, together with a loaf of bread.

The coroner looked up and wiped his fingers on his napkin. 'Dr. Silkstone, is it?' He extended his hand, but did not rise. Thomas surmised the effort of lifting his corpulent frame from the chair would be too much for him.

'Have you breakfasted?' he asked.

'Thank you, yes,' Thomas replied, even though he had not.

The coroner dabbed the corners of his mouth with the napkin and smiled broadly to reveal two blackened stumps in his mouth. 'So, what brings you here from London?'

Thomas had anticipated the question and told Sir Theodisius that he was a student of the famous Dr. Carruthers, and was visiting a fellow anatomist, Professor Hascher, at Christ Church.

It just so happened, Thomas explained, that the professor had told him about the strange case of young Lord Crick and, intrigued, he wondered if he might be of any assistance.

'Poor devil's beyond help,' exclaimed the coroner, suddenly grabbing a chicken leg and taking a large bite out of it. 'I ordered an inquest into the death only yesterday. Funny business.' He tore away at the leg voraciously, as if the excitement made him hungry. 'Gossip, rumor, tittle-tattle. Murder. Money. Revenge! Such a to-do! Had to do something!'

Thomas, accustomed as he was to dissecting organs and dismembering dead bodies, had to force himself to look at the coroner while he ate.

'I believe the corpse is in an advanced state of decomposition,' he ventured.

Sir Theodisius shook his head so that the rolls of fat that covered his face quivered with the effort. He leaned forward, as if to impart to Thomas something that must stay within the four walls of his office.

'Two surgeons were tasked to conduct one but failed.' He paused and then lowered his voice, as if trying to be discreet. 'Too far gone,' he mouthed before returning to his chicken leg.

'That was last week?' asked Thomas.

Sir Theodisius nodded. 'Last Thursday. Surely there is nothing you can do on that score?' He tossed the fleshless chicken bone onto an empty plate and tore away a crust from the loaf.

'I would very much like leave to conduct a postmortem examination, sir,' said Thomas.

Sir Theodisius choked on his bread and reached for his ale. 'But the fellow'll be half eaten by now,' he protested.

The turn of phrase was unfortunate, given the circumstances, but Thomas ignored it. 'I know it will not be easy, but I may be able to discern certain vital information,' insisted the young doctor.

Sir Theodisius chewed his bread thoughtfully. 'You mean you might be able to ascertain the cause of death?' he asked.

'Precisely.'

'That would be most useful,' acknowledged the coroner, wiping his fingers on his napkin. He leaned back in his chair and let out a belch, which he did not try to disguise. 'I shall prepare the necessary papers.'

Thomas looked earnest. 'You understand that time is of the essence?'

Sir Theodisius tried to click his fingers, but the amount of grease on them prevented him from doing so. Instead he called out aloud and in marched the clerk.

'Personally I believe that time has run out as far as a postmortem is concerned, but I will bow to the opinion of an expert,' he said graciously. 'Fetch me the exhumation order papers,' he instructed, then, dipping the nib of his quill into his inkpot, he said to Thomas: 'The sooner we get to the bottom of this whole ghastly business, the better.'

Chapter 12

Lydia breathed in the scent of aromatic thymes and pungent sages. The delights of the potager were relatively new to her. She loved spending time in the kitchen garden, surrounded by the sweet-smelling herbs and the colors of the fruits and vegetables. The head gardener, Amos Kidd, had given her a great enthusiasm for gardening and she now found herself taking delight in the exquisite symmetry of his planting, in the manner in which he positioned arrangements of shrubs and trees to enhance their neighbors' hues and shapes and in the way that patterns could be created with plants just as tapestries with stitches. Kidd kept the garden well stocked with all manner of herbs from bergamot to bay, each having a specific purpose. For its antiseptic qualities there was woad, and to flavor beer there was costmary. The roots of elecampane were good for treating bronchial complaints and rhubarb was an excellent purgative.

The vegetable garden was no less exciting, with orange and cream squashes and cardoons planted by asparagus peas and white carrots. Against the ancient wall grew espaliered fruit trees; apples, plums, and pears. There were raspberry canes and gooseberry bushes; rows of strawberries that had yielded two crops that summer and sturdy rhubarb stems.

The kitchen garden had become her pleasure and now, since Edward's death, it was also a place of refuge. She could breathe in the heady scents of autumn roses and watch the bees gathering pollen from the dahlias and forget about what dreadful things had passed and what dreadful things might still yet happen.

It was strange, however, that she found herself, at such a time as this, thinking about food. Sir Theodisius and Dr. Silkstone would soon be arriving to carry out the most gruesome of tasks and yet she felt it her duty to be hospitable toward them. Afterward she would offer them dinner. She knew how Sir Theodisius loved his food.

In her hand she held a pannier she had taken from the storeroom, which was already heavy with the sweetest carrots and the plumpest apples she could find for her guests. She had just filled her basket to the brim and was heading back toward the house when she came across Hannah, cutting stems of white lilies and crying the tears of a woman in mourning for her child. The sight touched Lydia deeply and she was almost moved to put her arms around her maid to comfort her. Death had united them in their grief. It was no respecter of rank or privilege and now that Edward was dead, Lydia felt a special bond existed between them.

'They say the pain will lessen,' she said softly, standing behind her maid. The scent from the lilies was almost overpowering. Hannah turned around, her eyes red and watery.

'I fear not, mistress,' she sobbed. 'I fear not,' and she buried her head spontaneously in Lydia's shoulder.

The track that wound its way from the main road up to Boughton Hall meandered around copses and over a reed-fringed river. Thomas, who had never visited an English country house before, delighted in the scenery that he had viewed so many times in the paintings of Gainsborough and Kneller. He had held the delicate poplars and the romantic bridges to be fanciful inventions of the artists, but now he saw them to be true depictions. After the claustrophobic buildings and the stench of London, this was surely paradise, he told himself.

Sir Theodisius said very little on the hour-long journey from Oxford. He had opened a hamper shortly after they had left St. Clements and proceeded to consume a venison pie, half a dozen quails' eggs, and a dish of jellied eels.

Shortly after midday the carriage rounded the bend and up ahead, the spire of a chapel pierced the cloudless sky like a sharp needle through blue silk. As they approached it Thomas could see the honey-colored building, partly clad in ivy, was surrounded by a well-tended graveyard. The sight of it jolted him back to reality as he remembered the reason for his visit to Boughton Hall. He saw, too, that one of the graves in the corner of the churchyard was freshly dug. Tufts of grass were just beginning to appear on the unsightly brown mound that signified another recent death. White lilies were laid upon it and a simple wooden cross stood at its head.

'One of the servant's children,' said Sir Theodisius, but volunteered nothing further. Thomas simply nodded as the carriage now progressed up the gravel drive, past chestnut trees and laurel bushes.

The captain and Lady Lydia stood on the steps of Boughton Hall, waiting to greet their guests. It was apparent to Thomas, just by looking at his demeanor, that Michael Farrell was a military man. It was also clear to Thomas that he had served in some hot climate. His skin was of a darker hue than normal, probably due to overexposure of the epidermis to sunlight, noted the young doctor. His stance was upright and slightly arrogant, too, he thought. He towered over Lydia at his side. She looked even more fragile than he remembered. She allowed a smile to flicker across her lips as Thomas greeted her, supposedly for the first time as far as the coroner was concerned.

'I am sorry we meet again under such circumstances, Farrell,' said Sir Theodisius as he was escorted into the captain's study. The two met regularly at society functions and, as a stranger, Thomas felt a little uneasy.

The Irishman led them into the sunless room. The drapes were drawn, Thomas assumed, as a sign of mourning, and there was the all too familiar smell of damp in the air. Decay was visible on every surface as clearly as if it were a threadbare tapestry hanging on the wall.

Farrell sat down at his desk and motioned to two chairs. 'I cannot pretend the last few days have been easy, gentlemen. It was bad enough losing my brother-in-law, but these rumors–' He broke off, then suddenly rallied. 'But that is why you are here, Dr. Silkstone, I believe – to find out once and for all what killed Lord Crick.' The captain smiled graciously, but Thomas could tell that it was an empty gesture.

'That is why I have empaneled a jury,' interjected Sir Theodisius, suddenly exercising his authority.

'Quite so,' acknowledged Farrell. He clasped his hands together and put his elbows down firmly on the desk.

There was a slightly awkward pause and Thomas decided to step in. 'I believe I am not the first to attempt a postmortem,' he ventured. The captain was clearly riled and he shifted on his chair.

'There have been two before you, Dr. Silkstone, and both were afeared that the corpse was too far gone for examination and that there was a risk of disease should it not be disposed of quickly.' There was contempt in his voice that did not endear him to Thomas. 'Nevertheless, I am confident that both will testify that nothing more suspicious than natural causes ended Lord Crick's life.'

At that moment there was a knock at the door and Howard entered. 'Mr. Peabody is here to see you, sir,' he told his master.

The captain nodded.

'Show him in.'

'Mr. Peabody was my late brother-in-law's apothecary. I thought he might be able to throw light on what was in his medicine that was so disagreeable to him,' explained Farrell.

Thomas was relieved. Perhaps Captain Farrell was not going to be as obstructive as he had previously thought. Mr. Peabody was a stocky little man whose thick black eyebrows joined together in the middle of his forehead. He shuffled nervously into the room with the air of a condemned felon.

'Perhaps you could tell Dr. Silkstone what was in the phial that you gave to Lord Crick,' Farrell asked after initial pleasantries were over. The framing of his question did nothing to alleviate Mr. Peabody's apprehension.

The nervous apothecary delved into his topcoat pocket and produced a crumpled piece of parchment. 'I took the liberty of noting down the ingredients, sir,' he said, handing the list to the young doctor. The script was spiky but Thomas was able to decipher it quite easily. He read out loud: 'Rhubarb, jalap, spirits of lavender, nutmeg water, and syrup of saffron.' Thomas looked shocked. 'This is indeed an explosive mixture,' he said.

'Explosive?' echoed Farrell, perplexed.

Thomas looked up and frowned. 'This is a purgative,' he said. 'And a strong one at that.'

Mr. Peabody shot a nervous glance at the captain. 'You may speak plainly,' Farrell told the apothecary, whose hirsute brow had knitted itself into a frown.

The little man lowered his gaze and his voice. 'His lordship had the pox, sir,' he said quickly, spitting the words out as if they were poisonous.

Thomas and Sir Theodisius nodded simultaneously, as if they had half expected as much.

'My brother-in-law lay with a bunter when he was fourteen at Eton and paid the price in more ways than one,' added the captain.

Mr. Peabody blushed. 'That will be all now,' said Farrell, dismissing the apothecary, who wasted no time in bobbing a bow and taking his leave.

Thomas noted a self-righteous expression had settled on the captain's face. Here was proof, if proof were needed, that the late earl was a dissolute who was in poor health.

'In what ways did Lord Crick's illness manifest itself?' asked Sir Theodisius.

Farrell paused, looking out of the window while framing his thoughts. 'Sweats, leg cramps, palpitations. He was not in good health,' he said after a few moments.

'So, you think there is a possibility he died of

93

natural causes?' asked Sir Theodisius.

Farrell looked at the coroner, surprised. 'There is every possibility,' he replied abruptly.

'It is certainly an avenue I shall explore,' said Thomas.

The captain was becoming increasingly tetchy. 'You can explore all you like, but you still will not find anything. His corpse is too far gone,' he growled.

Sir Theodisius interjected. 'Dr. Silkstone is an anatomist with new procedures and techniques that could prove helpful,' he explained patiently.

Farrell nodded, but Thomas detected a scornful look in his eyes. 'Let us hope that they will,' he said.

Dipping his plump fingers with difficulty into a slim leather pouch, Sir Theodisius produced the exhumation orders. 'I will need a signature from you, Captain,' he said, pushing the parchment across the desk. Farrell scanned the papers, then, taking a quill from the inkstand, he signed them with a flourish.

'There, gentlemen,' he said, blotting the ink. 'Now you can proceed,' adding contemptuously, 'for what it's worth.'

Chapter 13

The grim procession wound its way toward the chapel with Captain Farrell at its head. Next followed Sir Theodisius, then Thomas carrying his large black bag. Lovelock and Kidd brought up the rear, one with a crowbar slung over his shoulder, the other with a pickax.

Lydia could not bring herself to accompany them. She chose to simply watch their progress toward the place where her brother lay and where he was about to be so rudely disturbed from his immortal slumber. She could only pray that this young doctor from the Colonies, who seemed so courteous and so confident, would return with some answers.

The door of the chapel groaned as Farrell opened it. Inside it was dark and for a moment Thomas could see very little until his eyes adjusted. The smell of damp hung heavy in the air. The captain fumbled for a candle from a box near the porch, lit it from a flame that burned in the vestibule, then led the way down the aisle.

Thomas marveled at the chapel. It was like one of the many grand churches he had attended in London – usually on the occasion of funerals – but in miniature. There was a wooden rood screen, a pulpit, a sombre effigy of a knight, and on the walls were displayed fine hatchments, topped by the Crick family crest, the likes of which he had never seen before he set foot in England. An Englishman's God was much grander than a New Englander's, he thought to himself.

After a few paces the captain stopped by a flight of shallow steps that led down to a door. 'Be careful down here, gentlemen,' he warned as he lit a torch. Handing it to Thomas, he unlocked the door. Eight more steps led down into a room.

The first thing that struck Thomas was the sudden change in temperature from cool to almost cold. This was encouraging, he told himself. At least decomposition should have been slowed down after burial. He held the torch aloft in the darkness. As the beam of light penetrated farther, he could see they were in a vault no more than one hundred feet square. The walls appeared to be lime washed and the ceiling was rounded. He bumped his head. Even at its highest point, he could not stand upright.

'I should have warned you,' said the captain, ducking ahead. Thomas had never been in a vault before and he did not much care for the claustrophobic sensation it gave him. Nor did he like the smell of damp, but he knew it was infinitely preferable to the stench of rotting flesh, which he would shortly encounter.

There was another torch at the foot of the stairs and Farrell lit it, casting more welcome light into the eerie space. Thomas could now see seven coffins lined against the facing wall. Five were placed on the floor and had obviously been there many years. The woodwork was badly decayed and the lead linings were exposed. Above was a large stone shelf upon which rested two much newer coffins.

One was adorned with silver furnishings.

'The fifth earl, Edward's father,' explained Farrell. 'He died four years ago.' He then held the torch aloft over what was obviously the newest coffin of them all. 'But this is the one that interests you, gentlemen,' he said.

Thomas motioned to Lovelock and Kidd. 'The candles, if you please,' he said. From out of bags tied to their belts, the men produced several tapers and began arranging them on the shelves. Thomas had thought the young lord's body would be in such an advanced state of decomposition that it could not withstand removal to the chapel itself where the light would have been better. Instead he had ordered as many candles as possible. As the men lit them one by one the light grew stronger until Thomas could see into the farthest corners of the vault.

'How picturesque,' commented the captain glibly as Lovelock lit the last of the tapers.

'They serve their purpose,' whispered Sir Theodisius disapprovingly.

For a moment they stood in a reverent silence, aware that they were in the presence of death, before Sir Theodisius spontaneously put his hands together.

'Let us pray,' he said softly. Thomas lowered his head, as did Kidd and Lovelock. Farrell looked slightly bemused, but nonetheless followed suit.

'Lord, forgive us for disturbing the body of thy servant Edward Crick, and grant us that we might find the truth as to how he came to you so suddenly and in his prime. Through Christ our Lord, amen.'

'Amen,' answered everyone in unison.

There was another respectful pause before Farrell motioned to the men. Each threaded a rope around the casket handles on either side and pulled gently until they could get a good purchase on the coffin. They then proceeded to slide their shoulders under it, taking the strain. Groaning under its considerable weight, they were able to lower it, albeit fairly rapidly, to the brick floor.

Thomas knew what he was about to witness would not be pleasant, but he had learned to control his reactions. Sir Theodisius took out his pocket handkerchief and nervously wiped his forehead. The coroner braced himself as Thomas looked at Farrell to give the order. The captain said simply: 'Proceed,' and Lovelock and Kidd began prizing off the coffin lid. After a few jabbings with the crowbars it was loosened, and with one final push the men managed to lever it off entirely so that it fell clattering to the floor.

No one was prepared for what happened next. In the very same instant a cloud of black flies rose like a plume of smoke into the air, resembling a scene out of a biblical plague. They filled the vault with their buzzing and scattered, crashing into their unsuspecting victims in their droves. Sir Theodisius let out a cry as he tried to fend off the insects. There was worse to come. Behind the flies rose unseen vapors of choking gas. The men groaned and Lovelock retched. Farrell dashed up the steps and opened the door, taking deep gulps of fresh air. Most of the flies flew out immediately. Sir Theodisius, Lovelock, and Kidd followed swiftly.

Thomas grimaced and wafted the last of the flies away with a kerchief he had pulled out of his pocket. He was willing his senses to overcome this vile assault, but it was hard. He held the square of cloth to his mouth and made his way back up the steps, shutting the door behind him.

'Now do you believe that he's too far gone?' asked the captain, still struggling for breath.

Thomas, too, was finding it hard to breathe. ''Twould be better for all if I worked alone,' he ventured.

Farrell looked at him in disbelief. 'You mean to tell me that you plan to go back to that ... that hellhole?' he cried.

Sir Theodisius had collapsed onto a pew but was regaining his composure. 'Surely you jest, Dr. Silkstone.'

'I am here to do a job, gentlemen,' Thomas replied. He would have loved to have turned tail and run a mile from that stinking vault, but it would be a complete dereliction of his duty. 'I must go back,' he told them, 'but I will go alone.'

By now the foul stench had begun to creep up the stairs and into the main body of the chapel. Farrell shrugged his shoulders, as if abdicating any responsibility for Thomas's actions. Sir Theodisius merely looked relieved. The coroner nodded, waving his own white handkerchief as if in a gesture of surrender, before holding it over his mouth. Farrell, who had moved even closer to the door by this time, beckoned Sir Theodisius toward him. 'He is all yours,' he said ruefully to Thomas, as he and the coroner made their way out of the chapel.

Lovelock and Kidd, meanwhile, were also endeavoring to keep their distance. They had shuffled over to the vestry, as far as they could go from the opened door. Thomas looked at their pitiful faces that were so full of disgust. They silently begged dismissal and the young doctor was pleased to oblige. 'Wait outside until I call you,' he instructed.

Relieved, they simply rushed with irreverent haste to the portal and out into the chill air of late autumn. They slammed the door shut behind them, leaving Thomas alone in the eerie twilight of the chapel with only the low drone of flies and a reeking corpse for company. He knew he would have to work quickly. There was no time for prevarication, even though he felt physically sick. He simply had to go back down into the vault.

Holding the kerchief over his mouth he descended the steps once more. The candles still burned brightly and he decided it was high time to bring out his secret weapon – one that had been revealed to him by Dr. Carruthers. He fumbled in his pocket and retrieved his clay pipe. He had packed it with tobacco earlier that morning and, moving over to the candle, simply lit it with a taper. Holding the bowl, he sucked on the stem to produce large puffs of smoke that helped to dissipate the cloying stench that hung in the air.

After a few moments of trying to envelope himself in a veil of tobacco smoke, he took off his topcoat and laid it on the nearby stone shelf. Opening his black bag, he found a large cloth and laid it, too, on the shelf before proceeding to select the instruments he felt he would need for the postmortem. He now approached the coffin. Even he had to steel himself to look inside. It was a gruesome sight. What only ten days ago had been a living, breathing human being was now reduced to a decaying mass of tissue and bone. Where there had once been a soul, a spirit, call it what you will, there were maggots consuming the man's very essence.

Although his features were now barely discernable, there was no mistaking the hideously contorted mouth and the swollen tongue that protruded from it, denoting he had died in great agony. Reddish purge fluid had leaked from his nose and there were signs that creamy grave wax was beginning to form around his mouth. As one might expect, the skin was badly bruised in many areas but Thomas was not sure if its yellowish tint was attributable to natural decomposition or, alternatively, the result of massive liver or kidney failure.

The young anatomist had never worked on such a badly decomposed cadaver before and did not relish the prospect. Water. He remembered he would need water, but where might the nearest source be? It suddenly came to him there had been a font in the chapel. Ascending the stairs once more he walked over to the large stone receptacle near the altar. In the unusual circumstances, he decided he would be forgiven if he scooped a few jugfuls out in order to clean his instruments and his hands. He had just dipped his hands into the font when there was an almighty flapping of wings. Terrified, he looked up, only to see a bewildered pigeon teetering on the rafters. His heartbeats matched the rapid flapping, then slowed when he realized the bird had entered through a broken pane of glass. He was now ready to proceed.

Once more in the bowels of the chapel, he knelt down beside the coffin and stared at its grisly contents. As he started to examine the corpse, Dr. Carruthers's words began to ring in his ears. 'Keep an open mind,' he would say. Any number of factors could have combined to end this young man's life and Thomas could not rule out any possibility or discount any suspicion without having thoroughly checked it out. So, despite the fact that he did not want the procedure to last a moment longer than it had to, he knew his examination would have to be thorough.

Thomas puffed on his pipe once more before reaching for his knife. With a steady hand he cut away the white linen shroud from the corpse's torso to reveal graying, bloated flesh. His blade sliced through the epidermis swiftly and cleanly, letting the foul smelling gas that had built up inside the body cavity escape, as if he had just deflated a ball. For a moment he retched, then recovered his composure, puffing voraciously on the pipe. He did not have high hopes. He knew that bacteria would have fed on the contents of the intestines and would have started to digest the intestines themselves.

When he reached the stomach, however, he discovered that although it was much distended, not all of the tissue was in an advanced state of decomposition, thus enabling him to cut through the pyloric sphincter and remove a large portion of the lining. While his knife did its work, Thomas noticed the intestinal lymphatics, or lacteals, that resembled cream-colored skeins of wool were still intact. He was reminded of poor Mr. Smollett, lying on his dissecting table in London, and taking a scalpel, he carefully began to untangle the threadlike channels so that he could cut off a good length. It suddenly occurred to him that these might harbor vital evidence. Satisfied with a foot-long section, he put the lacteals in a jar of preservative and the stomach tissue in another. He puffed once more on his pipe.

Next Thomas turned his attention to the chest cavity and examined the heart and lungs. He could not rule out the possibility that young Lord Crick had suffered a heart attack, or some form of lung disease, but neither showed any signs of anything untoward.

Undaunted, Thomas continued on his journey, focusing on the liver. There it crouched in the shadow of the belly, divided into two great lobes. Like a large brown-stained snail its smooth back nestled into the dome of the diaphragm, unwilling to yield up any of its secrets.

'I will have you,' muttered Thomas, slicing through the large internal ropes that once tethered the slain beast to its cavity. A man's liver could be read like a private journal, divulging many of his secrets, and Thomas intended to peruse it in his own time.

It only remained to conduct the most unsavory part of the examination. The words of the apothecary returned to him as his eyes worked their way down to inspect the genital area. 'Lord Crick had the pox,' he had said.

'Indeed he had,' muttered Thomas to himself as he looked at the chancre. He suddenly wondered if the young earl's dalliances might have any bearing on his death.

Usually, out of deference to his patients, he would sew them up after a dissection, but this corpse was too far gone for the needle. Instead he merely folded the cut shroud back into place and stepped away from the coffin as soon as he could. He quickly cleared his instruments away and, without bothering to rinse them, returned them to their bag. The sample jars he placed carefully into lined cases and strapped them into his bag for safekeeping.

Still with his pipe in his mouth, he rinsed his hands in the holy water and dried them on a small napkin he had brought with him. Putting on his topcoat once more, he walked up the narrow flight of steps and through the open door at the top, back into the deserted chapel. Here the air was fresher. The outside door had been left open and Thomas began to breathe deeply once more. He poked his head outside and saw Kidd and Lovelock standing outside. 'If you please, gentlemen,' he called. They simply looked at each other before venturing forward with as much enthusiasm as schoolboys for a caning.

Captain Farrell, who had also been waiting outside, followed them back into the chapel. 'Find anything, Dr. Silkstone?' he asked in what to Thomas seemed a casual manner. He may as well have been enquiring after a country walk or a foray into Oxford.

'I will have found something, all right,' replied Thomas. 'But everything will need to be analyzed first.' He did not like Farrell. He found him to be arrogant and flippant. Nevertheless he doffed his hat to him. He would make his way up the path and back to the hall, where he would take his leave of Lady Lydia and collect Sir Theodisius, who had taken refuge at the dinner table.

Meanwhile Kidd and Lovelock had reluctantly returned to the vault, still gagging with the noxious fumes that filled the entire chapel. They deliberately tried to avert their gaze from the grotesque being that lay inside, but picked up the coffin lid and struggled, as quickly as they could, to position it on top of the casket. Farrell had followed them, but this time he was seemingly oblivious to the stench. Instead of merely supervising the closure of the lid, he positioned himself so that he looked inside it once more. Just before the men were about to place the cover on the coffin for eternity, Captain Farrell simply stared at his brother-in-law's distorted, bloated face and with a sneer said softly, but quite deliberately: 'I always said he was rotten to the core.'

Thomas breathed in deeply the scents of a fine autumn day: damp, fallen leaves melding back into the earth, smoke on the air from a nearby bonfire. His senses were heightened after having to keep them so tightly in check in the stinking vault. He could smell the heavy sweetness of the late honeysuckle in the hedgerow and the acidity in the brambles. Colors, too, took on a new in-

105

tensity, as if sunlight had penetrated every blade of grass and every leaf on the trees, making them somehow radiant and magical.

For a few seconds he forgot the reason for being in this place. His sense of reality was momentarily suspended as daylight lifted him out of the gloom. It was only when his eyes began to focus and he saw the gravestones peering out at him through the long grass like uneven teeth that he remembered his purpose. The dead man's hideous face flashed into his consciousness once more and it took all of his strength to banish the grotesque image. He walked on toward Boughton Hall. He was so preoccupied that he did not notice a woman and her two children in the far corner of the churchyard. The girl was placing a posy of flowers on a fresh grave: poker red dahlias from the kitchen garden. The young boy was messing around in the soil, picking up pieces of flint and pocketing them.

'Stop that. You'll go through your pockets,' scolded his mother. The boy duly ceased his activities and, looking around, wiped his hands on his shirt.

'Who's he?' he asked, pointing a muddy finger at Thomas in the distance.

'I know not, Will,' replied Hannah. She knew full well, but did not want her children to find out that this was the man responsible for disturbing their erstwhile master's rotting body. They would only worry that the same awful treatment might be meted out to their own dear sister.

Chapter 14

James Lavington watched Michael Farrell's elegant fingers as they held a fan of playing cards. He could still see the thin white line left by the band he used to wear on the third finger of his right hand. Out in India they had called him 'Diamond' Farrell because of the magnificent gemstone he used to wear mounted on a gold ring. The story was that he had stolen it from a dead merchant, but Lavington had never pressed him on the subject.

Lydia had apparently protested about the band shortly after they met, calling it 'vulgar.' Farrell had obliged her by removing it, but his time in India had left his skin permanently colored by the sun, hence the white line that served as a reminder of his cavalier days in the Irish Dragoon Guards.

Howard poured them both a glass of sack, as was customary, and set a loaf of bread and a small truckle of cheddar on the sideboard. For the last two years this had been the Thursday night ritual. Last Thursday – just three days after Edward's death – had been the only game of cards they had missed in all that time. It had been their pleasure, their distraction, and now, Lavington feared, their undoing.

'Relax, will you, man,' ordered Farrell shortly after Howard shut the study door behind him. 'The servant will suspect.'

Lavington gulped back the sack. 'Did the anatomist find anything?'

Farrell let out a staccato laugh. 'Plenty of flies, but I'm not sure what else,' he said, laying out his cards on the green baize in front of him.

'When will the inquest open?' Lavington was in no mood for cards. He placed his hand faceup on the table.

'The old duffer said in a couple of weeks,' replied Farrell. He found Sir Theodisius irksome in the extreme.

The captain possessed the ability to brush even the most serious of matters aside with a quip or a derogatory remark. It galled Lavington to see him behave thus, as if without a care in the world, but he needed him, so he let his arrogance pass. He took another gulp of sack.

'Farrell, what if this colonist finds out that Edward was murdered?'

The Irishman's gaze darted up. His friend was looking tense and pale. There was a grayish hue to his complexion and his brown eyes looked dull and listless. His demeanor reminded him of the time when General Lavington had got wind that his first son and heir planned to marry an Indian woman and disinherited him. Despite the fact that James quickly fell out of love with the exotic beauty, the damage was done and his father pledged the two-thousand-acre estate in Dorset to his younger son.

Shortly afterward came the accident, so, when Farrell landed on his feet and married Lydia, he had persuaded Edward to let his friend become a tenant on the Boughton estate. Two years ago,

Lavington had moved into a humble cottage about a mile away from the hall.

Farrell smiled and nodded slowly, as if the possibility of such a conclusion to the postmortem had also occurred to him. He fixed a penetrating stare on Lavington. 'Then, my friend, we better start covering our tracks.'

Great Tom was tolling when Thomas arrived at Christ Church. The carriage had dropped Sir Theodisius off at his house on the outskirts of the city and Thomas had carried on, clutching his precious cargo in his black bag. Under the college's great pepper pot dome he went around the eastern flank of the large quadrangle. There he alighted and made his way through the arch to the Anatomy School. It was almost dusk, and he feared Professor Hascher might have retired, but when he saw a chink of light piercing the bottom of the door, he knew he was in luck and knocked.

'Well, well, Dr. Silkstone. And to what do I owe zis unexpected pleasure?' The elderly professor was seated at his desk, but rose as soon as he saw Thomas. As the young doctor approached with an outstretched hand, however, he could see the doctor flex his nostrils. It was then he remembered he must still stink from the postmortem. He had not had a chance to wash properly since his visit to Boughton Hall. Sir Theodisius had been unusually quiet in the carriage, holding his handkerchief to his nose and complaining of a 'slight cold.' Now Thomas realized why.

'You have been busy zis afternoon, yes?' asked the professor with a knowing smile.

'I am so sorry, sir, perhaps I should go and change my clothes.'

Hascher shook his head. 'A rotting corpse vaits for no man. We should get to work.'

Thomas smiled. He knew he could count on the old anatomist's help. He walked over to the dissecting table as Professor Hascher brought more candles and placed them nearby. Delving into his black bag, Thomas pulled out three jars: one containing tissue he had taken from the earl's stomach lining, another a cross section of the liver, and another holding the lacteals. He held the first up to the light and both men looked at it in silent reverence. The velvety mucosa lay folded like a bolt of rich, red fabric.

'What do you propose?' asked the professor.

Thomas sighed. If the truth were told, the young doctor had hoped to have found some simple reason for Lord Crick's death by merely examining the corpse: a blood clot or a tumor would have been all that was required. But there was nothing. The earl was as unyielding in death as he had been in life.

'I only wish I knew, Professor,' he answered.

Thomas hired a horse from the inn and rode to Boughton Hall early the next morning. It was a dull, autumn day and the air was full of the foreboding of winter. Reaching his destination shortly before ten o'clock, he rode 'round the side of the great house and into the courtyard at the back. He found the place deserted, except for young Will, who was polishing some tack in the corner. The boy immediately stopped what he was doing and rushed to take the doctor's horse.

'Good morning,' greeted Thomas.

''Morning, sir.'

Thomas dismounted as the boy held the reins. The youth seemed cheerful enough, he thought, and he put his hand in his pocket and pulled out a farthing. Will beamed his thanks as he tethered the horse in front of the water trough.

'Now tell me, young man, where might I find your mistress?' He bent down close toward Will so as not to appear too intimidating. The lad had a thin face with large, sad eyes.

'She be in the kitchen garden, sir,' he said, pointing toward the walled potager.

'Thank you,' said Thomas, feeling in his pocket once more. 'And here's another farthing for your pains.' But just as he reached out toward the boy, the still air was pierced by a scream, coming from behind the wall.

'Her ladyship,' cried Will.

Thomas rushed toward the gate in the wall and ran through it to see Lady Lydia, her hands clasped against her breasts, looking intently on the ground. Just what she was looking at with such fear and apprehension, Thomas could not see. His view was obscured by one of the low box hedges that sectioned off the various plots.

'Your ladyship!' he shouted, running toward the stricken young woman. She looked even more vulnerable than usual. Her face was ashen. An upturned pannier had deposited its cargo of onions all over the path.

'There!' she screamed. 'There.' She was pointing at a corner of the hedge. Thomas drew level with it, but could see nothing.

'What? What is it?' Thomas was puzzled.

'There. Under the hedge,' she cried. She was trembling with fear.

Thomas looked down and peered into the dense, mottled green foliage. There, in the blackness, he suddenly saw two beady eyes staring out at him. A rat. The cause of Lady Farrell's great consternation was a humble rodent. He remembered how she had reacted when she encountered Franklin at his laboratory in London. He smiled to himself, but emerged from the hedge looking grave.

'Boy,' he called to Will, who had been watching somewhat bemused a few feet away. 'Go to the kitchen and fetch some scraps.'

Will nodded his carrot-colored head and scampered off toward the scullery.

'I thought they were all gone,' she said softly, as if thinking out loud. She looked so vulnerable, thought Thomas.

He approached her, walking sideways so he could still keep an eye on the rat's hiding place.

'Do not fret, my lady,' came a deep voice from behind. It was Amos Kidd, net in hand. Just then Will came running back with a bowl full of victuals from Mistress Claddingbowl. On Thomas's instructions, he sprinkled them on the path, near where the rat was hiding, then moved behind the hedge. Kidd joined him and lowered the net by the bait.

'Shall we go now?' asked Thomas. 'I am sure you do not wish to see any more, my lady.'

She took a deep breath and nodded. Together

they walked toward the house. Ahead of them lay opened French doors and Lydia led the way into the garden room. Inside it was warm and restful. A vine wove its way through rafters above them, heavy with purple grapes. The young woman sat on a white bench and motioned to Thomas to sit opposite.

'We shall take refreshments,' she said, looking everywhere but at the doctor. She appeared nervous and agitated, fiddling with the ribbon on the cuff of her dress. She rang a small bell on the table beside her and Hannah appeared almost immediately.

'Tea for Dr. Silkstone and me,' she instructed. Hannah cast a quick glance at the doctor. He noticed more than a passing resemblance to young Will.

'Am I to assume you have come here with news of the postmortem?' Lydia's voice was quiet and her nervous fingers now moved to her wedding band

Thomas nodded. 'Indeed, your ladyship.' There was no easy way to tell her, so he had promised himself he would get it over with quickly. 'I am afraid I have not been able to come to a definite conclusion,' he said softly, ashamed that he had not been decisive. He saw her narrow shoulders drop in disappointment.

'Was the body too...' It was difficult for her to bring herself to say the words.

'No,' Thomas interrupted. 'I am still hopeful of finding the cause, but I need to do more tests.' Lydia nodded, but her sense of frustration was palpable.

'All is not lost,' assured Thomas. 'But I need to return to London before I can be sure.'

He saw her body heave in an inaudible sigh before reaching for a small velvet bag at her side. She handed it to him and he took it, hesitantly.

'Your fee,' she said coldly.

Thomas bridled, but before he could protest, Hannah returned with a tray of tea and poured the hot black liquid into porcelain cups. Thomas could tell she was oddly nervous and the servant sensed he was looking at her. The spout strayed from the cup and, to her dismay, she spilled tea on the table.

'Begging your pardon, my lady,' she blurted, almost distraught at her mistake.

''Tis of no consequence, Hannah,' Lydia said kindly. Nevertheless, the maid rushed off distraught.

Lydia shook her head. 'Poor woman.'

Thomas looked at her questioningly, awaiting an explanation.

Lydia knew she would have to give him one. 'Hannah lost her daughter a few weeks ago.'

Thomas frowned. Lydia continued: 'She was drowned in the lake. A tragic accident.'

'A terrible loss,' sympathized Thomas.

Lydia fingered the handle of the delicate porcelain cup that remained empty before her. 'Yes, and now I know how she feels,' she said softly.

Thomas saw the emotion rise in her face. He wanted to reach out and clasp her soft hand that played so forlornly with the teacup, but all he allowed himself were a few words of comfort across the great abyss that divided them.

'I will find out how your brother died, your ladyship. That I promise you, but I will not do it for money.'

She lifted her gaze to meet his and for the first time she looked at him as an equal.

'I will not accept payment for my work,' he reiterated.

She was about to protest, but saw the resolve in his face and detected a note of hurt in his voice. Instead, she tilted her head slightly in a gesture of thanks.

'You colonists are very proud,' she observed.

Thomas was not sure whether she was reprehending him or admiring him, but he dared to suspect the latter. The uncertainty was short-lived, however, as Hannah returned with another teacup and poured once more, this time without incident. Any mutual understanding there had been between them in that split-second smile was now lost.

Decorum and cool politeness reestablished themselves for the next few minutes. In between sips of tea, her ladyship spoke of the weather and the garden and Thomas, who had become accustomed to English reserve, could do little but nod and agree and punctuate the awkward silences with inane pleasantries until he felt it politic to take his leave.

Lydia escorted him through the garden to the courtyard where Will was waiting with the horse. He smiled at Thomas, who gave him another farthing.

'I meant what I said, my lady,' he told her just before mounting his mare.

'Thank you, Dr. Silkstone,' said Lydia, allowing a smile to flit across her lips.

She felt a strange compulsion to watch him ride off through the main gates, then turned to walk back through the garden. Passing the low box hedge, she was reminded of the unpleasant incident with the rat not an hour before. She could see Kidd through a half-open door planting seedlings in the glasshouse nearby and went over to speak to him.

When the gardener saw his mistress approach he put down his trowel, wiped his muddy hands on his breeches, and stood to attention.

'Your ladyship.' He nodded.

Lydia did not return the greeting, but looked at him sternly. 'You know I cannot abide rats, Kidd. Can you see to it that more poison is put down?'

The gardener's expression suddenly changed. He looked awkward.

'What is it?' she quizzed.

'I fear 'twould be hard, my lady,' he told her.

Lydia raised an eyebrow. She was not used to being crossed by the servants. 'And why might that be?'

Kidd fixed his gaze on the earth floor. 'There's no more poison left, my lady.'

Lydia looked at him quizzically. She had seen several jars of the laurel water herself only three or four days before.

'Where has it all gone?' she demanded.

Knowing there was no easy way out of his predicament, the gardener raised his bearded face toward his mistress and looked at her sheepishly. 'His lordship ordered me destroy the retort and

116

all the jars yesterday,' he mumbled.

Lydia paused for a moment, surprised at the revelation. Not wishing to register her shock, however, she simply shrugged her small shoulders. 'Of course he did. I was forgetting,' she said and, lifting the hem of her muslin gown slightly so as not to trail it in the dirt, she walked off back toward the hall.

Chapter 15

'If God had intended men to lie in water, he'd have given them fins,' chided Mistress Finesilver, pouring the last of countless jugs of hot water into the tin tub.

Ever since Thomas had announced his intention to take a bath shortly after his return from Oxfordshire that morning, the housekeeper had been complaining about having to heat so much water. Moreover, when Thomas told her that he wished to bathe in the privacy of his room, he thought the old harridan would explode. A compromise was reached, however, when it was agreed the young doctor would soak in his laboratory, where there was a water pump just outside the door. He would give the irascible matron an extra phial of laudanum for her pains, he told himself.

The click of the laboratory door came as an enormous relief to Thomas. At last he was alone and he walked naked across the room. The past two days had been rather disturbing and slightly traumatic. He was used to dealing with dead people, but dead people who had died without any real mystery. True, sometimes the cause of death was not straightforward. Was it an aneurysm or a heart attack, a burst appendix or a duodenal ulcer? Yet there was so much more to the case of young Lord Crick.

For now, however, he would let all thoughts of the hapless aristocrat, his beautiful sister, and her arrogant husband float away in his bathwater as he attempted to slough off the gruesome events of the past forty-eight hours.

Dipping his hand into the tub, Thomas smiled at the comforting warmth of the water. It was then he remembered the essence that one of his wealthy Jewish patients, Mrs. Margolis, had given him. He had lanced a particularly aggressive boil for her and, to show her gratitude, she had given him a bottle of scented water.

'A token of my appreciation,' she had told him, handing Thomas the clear glass bottle. He had taken it graciously and put it away in the top drawer of his desk, never giving it another thought, until now. With only a towel to protect his modesty he tiptoed across the slate floor to his desk drawer and retrieved the bottle. Uncorking it he sniffed it and found the scent to be very pleasing. He then returned to the bath and poured in most of the contents of the bottle. A powerful perfume was immediately released, enticing him, as if he needed enticing, into the deep, soothing waters of a battered old tin tub.

Never had water felt so warm, so comforting, so relaxing. He immersed himself in it totally so that it enveloped him entirely from head to toe. As it did so, Thomas could almost feel the layer of death that had clung so avidly to his body for the last twenty-four hours ease itself from his skin and drift away. He did not close his eyes, so that he could see ripples and currents whirl and eddy before him, making him feel like a fish swimming through fresh water. For a split second he almost believed he could breathe, but then, as his lungs began to burn, reality returned and he reemerged from the depths, taking a deep gulp of air.

Thomas surfaced and lay back. Baths are inspirational, he told himself. After all, did not Archimedes formulate his great principle of water displacement while indulging in one? He smiled at the thought of making his own great discovery in the bath. But his breakthroughs, his advances, such as they were, never came to him in a blinding flash, but rather through a chink that allowed a narrow shaft of light to penetrate and gradually illuminate the darkness of ignorance.

Thomas put out an arm and reached for a strange, fibrous object that lay on a chair nearby. A naval friend of his had presented him with the curio after one of his voyages to Africa, telling him it was the skeleton of a fruit called a loofah, that the natives used to slough off dead skin. Thomas began to rub his arms vigorously with it and found it quite a painful, yet strangely satisfying experience. He even started to sing, something he very rarely did. The words of a sea shanty, taught to him by the first officer of the frigate that brought him to England, sprang to mind and he embarked on the first verse with great gusto. In fact, so engrossed did he become in his song and in his rubbing that he did not hear the latch lift on the laboratory door. Nor did he notice a figure approach the bath until it was too late to protect his modesty.

'A fine tenor you have there, young fellow,' came a familiar voice. Thomas sat bolt upright in the tub and instinctively placed his loofah strategically over his manhood. He need not have bothered. It was Dr. Carruthers.

'Sir. I did not hear...'

The old anatomist laughed. 'So, you are bathing, Dr. Silkstone – a very worthwhile habit. Do I detect bergamot with a hint of hop blossom?'

Dr. Carruthers never ceased to amaze Thomas. He had seen those very ingredients written on the bottle.

'You are right, sir,' he replied. 'But how did...?'

'You forget, Dr. Silkstone,' replied the old surgeon, smiling. 'I may be blind, but I stare with my ears and detect with my nose.' Thomas was slightly puzzled by this revelation and, sensing this, Dr. Carruthers laughed and changed the subject.

'So, tell me, Thomas, I want to know all about your mysterious liaison with a certain young lady up in the wilds of deepest Oxfordshire,' he chortled.

Thomas did not feel like obliging his mentor. Despite the fact that Dr. Carruthers could not see him, he still felt oddly vulnerable. Once again, as if detecting his young protégé's unease, the old doctor said: 'But it can wait until dinnertime,' and he left Thomas alone once more, but the glorious peace he had felt earlier, prior to Dr. Carruthers's interruption, had deserted him. Instead his eyes were drawn to the small, cobalt blue bottle that sat on his desk.

Just before he took the coach back to Oxford, he had paid a visit to Mr. Peabody, the apothecary, whose premises were in Brandwick. The nervous little man had not expected Thomas to call and seemed quite out of sorts when he appeared at his door. Nevertheless he led Thomas into the back room of his business where he mixed all his salves and febrifuges. Large glass jars containing powders of crimson and saffron, of sickly green and charcoal gray were ranged on dusty shelves, interspersed with boxes of bark and tubs of lard.

Soon Mr. Peabody's eyebrows were knitted once more into a frown when Thomas enquired if any of Lord Crick's purgative might remain. He suspected not, but was delighted, and somewhat shocked, to find out that the apothecary had preserved some of the batch.

'You want to test it, you say?' he said, suspiciously handing over the small blue bottle to the young doctor. 'Looking for poison, I assume?'

Thomas nodded earnestly and Mr. Peabody's brow creased once more. 'Well, you'll not find any, I can assure you,' he jibed, suddenly seeming less recalcitrant than before, like a rabbit that suddenly bares its teeth.

Thomas had promptly put the bottle in his topcoat pocket, trying not to show his relief at discovering what could be a key piece of evidence, and left as quickly as he could in case the apothecary changed his mind and asked for the phial to be returned. And now that bottle, made of glass as

121

blue as the sea off the coast of Maine, sat enticingly on his desk, ready to offer up its secrets if he could but devise a method of separating its ingredients. Rhubarb, jalap, spirits of lavender, nutmeg water, and syrup of saffron: he had memorized the list on his return journey to London, wondering which one of these natural components, if any, could have had such a fatal effect on the young lord.

Later, over a dish of roast mutton and capers, Thomas told Dr. Carruthers about the strange circumstances surrounding Lord Crick's death and the postmortem he had conducted. He saved the intricate details until after Mistress Finesilver had cleared their plates.

'So, now you have the purgative, you can test its effects,' ventured Dr. Carruthers, tucking into an apple.

'In theory,' replied Thomas. 'But I need to find a way of separating out the components that might be involved.'

'Just as I could tell the ingredients of the individual scents in your bathwater,' ventured the old man.

'That's it,' exclaimed Thomas, suddenly realizing the significance of Dr. Carruthers's skills.

'But surely you know what was in the medicine? The apothecary gave you a list,' said the old doctor.

'But what if that list was added to or tampered with?' asked Thomas.

For once Dr. Carruthers did not have an immediate answer. He simply toyed with his napkin.

'There has to be a way,' mused Thomas.

His companion grunted, then pointed out rather unhelpfully: 'And only a week until the inquest.'

The rest of the evening Thomas spent in deep and uncomfortable thought, going down dark routes that only ended in blind alleys. The clock struck eleven when he decided to retire and he was just about to climb the stairs when a troubled-looking Mistress Finesilver entered the room, carrying what appeared to be a letter.

'Begging your pardon, Dr. Silkstone,' she said warily. 'But this has just come for you.'

Thomas looked at her, puzzled, as she handed the parchment to him.

'Strange at this time of night,' he muttered, breaking the seal.

'There was a knock at the front door, but when I opened it there was no one there,' explained the agitated housekeeper.

As soon as he opened the missive, Thomas could see why the bearer had wished to remain anonymous. In strong, bold script the message read: *STAY AWAY FROM BOUGHTON HALL.*

Chapter 16

'You have eaten nothing, my dear,' remarked Michael Farrell to his wife as Hannah disappeared from the room with the last of the dirty dishes.

'I have no appetite,' came Lydia's terse reply.

'You have been through much lately,' said Farrell, standing up and walking toward her at the other end of the table. As he put his hands on her shoulders, she winced.

When her husband had first fashioned the chemical retort, which he kept in the glasshouse, he had told her it was to distill attar from the garden flowers and she had welcomed the idea, envisaging a plentiful supply of exquisite floral fragrances with which to perfume her clothes, her hair, and the soft furnishings in the house. Last year, however, rose petals had been replaced by black laurel cherries. 'We are overrun with rats,' he had told her. 'We need to rid ourselves of the wretched things.' She did not disagree, for she loathed rats more than any other living creature. And so it was that in autumn, as soon as the plump cherries that looked like black olives appeared on the laurels on the estate, Kidd would harvest them and fill the retort with them in order to distill their powerful poison.

Lydia had been brooding on the destruction of the retort all day, wondering whether or not to confront her husband with the facts. She stiffened her back and felt his hands lift quickly, as if he had touched something hot. He drew out the chair next to her and sat down. Now was the right time to ask him, she told herself.

'Why did you order the retort to be destroyed and all the poison with it?' Her words came flooding out in a rapid torrent. Farrell looked momentarily fazed. He paused and picked up a silver fork that had been left on the table.

'How did you know?' he asked, fingering the

fork nervously.

'I ordered Kidd to put more rat poison down and he said he could not,' she replied, looking at him straight, watching his reactions intently.

Farrell smiled at her. She found him infuriating at times. She was anticipating some glib, plausible excuse and he did not disappoint. Turning 'round on her chair, she faced him and waited.

'The poison was useless,' he told her dismissively. He paused for dramatic effect, knowing that she wanted more. 'It did not work. You know that yourself. I hear you had an...' his lips curled slightly, 'an encounter with a dirty vermin today.'

Lydia felt the blood rising to her cheeks. He went on: 'The rats, for some reason, were not dying, so I told Kidd to destroy the still and we would find a better way to rid the place of the vile creatures.'

He has done it again, she told herself – extricated himself from a difficult situation, like some master contortionist. He smiled and kissed her on the top of her head triumphantly. He had delivered a perfectly legitimate reason for destroying the still.

'Does that satisfy you, my love?' he asked, still stooping over her chair. She detected something slightly superior in his tone and it riled her, yet she managed to smile all the same.

'Yes,' she replied softly.

'Good,' he said, as if he had just concluded some sort of deal. 'Then I shall take my leave and catch up on some reading in my study.'

She watched him go, then looked out of the half-open window at the rose-tinted sunset that made the lawns and the hills beyond them glow. She walked over to the casement and inhaled the scents of jasmine and late-flowering honeysuckle that released their unctuous perfume into the evening air. She decided she needed a walk. There was no chance of sleep coming to her that night unless she vented some of her frustration. She could not possibly bear the thought of her husband's hot breath against her neck, or the touch of his thighs against hers, unless she left the four claustrophobic walls of Boughton Hall, albeit for a few minutes. The need to distance herself from the deception and intrigue was overwhelming.

Wrapping a shawl around herself, Lydia slipped out of the French doors and through the kitchen garden. Glancing over her shoulder to make sure she was not being watched, she opened the heavy gate in the wall and took the path that led past the game larder and onto the track up to the pavilion.

The path was dry underfoot as it had not rained for the past three days. She walked quickly, now and again stopping to catch her breath and to take in the view. Halfway up she allowed herself a moment to drink in the vista of the dark clumps of trees and the sweeping parkland below before marching on toward the top of the hill.

The wooden structure of the pavilion looked inviting in the sunset, the gentle rays reflecting off the white painted planks. She remembered her father designing it with the help of an architect, the long piece of parchment laid out on his desk in the study. She had spent many a happy hour playing in the copse nearby as her father had sat

126

and drawn or written inside his retreat and now she felt it was hers. She was glad in a way that her dear Papa had been spared the nightmare of Edward's death. He and his only son had not always seen eye-to-eye. He did not approve of his libertine ways and on more than one occasion had withdrawn his allowance, but he would have been heartbroken at his death.

Lydia opened the glass-paneled doors and walked inside. It smelled damp and uninviting, so different from how it used to be when Papa was alive and the smell of his tobacco hung sweetly on the air. Cobwebs were now festooned in the corners and rats had chewed a hole in the floorboards, leaving a pile of droppings in their wake. She made a mental note to tell Kidd to see that the place was thoroughly cleaned.

Such neglect made her feel uneasy again and the anger returned once more. 'I should not have come to this place,' she told herself and was just about to close the door behind her when she saw, tucked away in a corner, a stone jar, about the size of a pitcher, with a narrow neck plugged by a cork. She stopped for a moment, then bent down and picked it up. Liquid slopped around inside as she did so. It felt quite heavy, so she balanced it on the window ledge as she gently tugged at the stopper. It came off with little resistance. Cautiously she put her face closer to the neck so that she could sniff the contents, but she did not have to bend too far before she knew. It was that smell that was so familiar to her, which she had smelled so often in the glasshouse and outside by the compost heap in the kitchen garden and by the rubbish pile at the back of the stables. The smell that was so com-monplace and so repellent. It was the smell of bitter almonds.

Chapter 17

Thomas worked into the early hours of the morn-ing. It was as if that small blue bottle, given to him by Mr. Peabody, had wrought a spell on him. He was convinced it held secrets; strange and exotic properties that could exercise the power of life or death over living beings. By themselves they may seem harmless enough, yet mixed together, in certain ratios, they may prove lethal.

When he became too tired to stand at his work-bench, he sat down at his desk. First he would test whether the substance was acid or alkaline by dipping in a piece of litmus paper, which had been impregnated with dye obtained from lichens. If the substance was an acid, the paper would turn red, if alkaline, blue. Each result he recorded, with meticulous precision, noting the exact measure-ments, but none produced any surprises.

Next he began pouring a few droplets of the mysterious liquid from one phial to another. To one container he might add a few grains of sodium, to another a drop or two of citric acid, all the time waiting and watching for a reaction, a discoloration, a fermentation, or a separation. Quill in hand, Thomas was poised to record every observation. Yet after each experiment, the result was always the same. Nothing untoward or unexpected happened. The contents of the bottle remained steadfast in their refusal to yield up their secret properties.

The clock struck two and Thomas leaned back in his chair, stretching out arms that felt as tense as steel. A pain shot across his shoulders and he rubbed his aching neck with the palm of his hand. He thought of Lydia, with her large, vulnerable eyes. He had to keep going for her sake as much as his own. The inquest was only three days away and there were still so many tests to be conducted.

At that moment there was a sudden movement in the corner of the room. Thomas looked 'round quickly to see Franklin the rat, who had been content to sit in the corner all night, venturing out, as if sensing his master could do with some company. He scuttled across the floor, jumped up onto a stool by the desk, and then onto the desk itself.

Thomas smiled and held out a hand to the rodent. The rat drew nearer and sat himself down contemptuously on the pile of notes, as if he were telling Thomas to rest. But instead of shooing Franklin away, the young doctor began to stroke his furry companion.

'Tell me what I should be doing, boy. Where am I going wrong?' whispered Thomas, running his fingers gently against the rat's back. As he did so, the rhythmic motion of the stroking made him feel even drowsier and he let his head rest gently on a pile of books that lay on his desk. But even if Franklin had been able to voice a reply, he would not have been heard, for within a few seconds, his master had fallen fast asleep. His hand fell motionless against the rodent's back and, feeling trapped, it wriggled out of his senseless grasp. As it did so, however, it knocked over a glass jar that had contained a little water. It spilled over onto the desk and a rivulet just skirted the edge of the parchment on which Thomas had written his meticulous notes.

The clatter of hooves on cobbles woke Thomas from his deep sleep. It was the milk cart doing its early morning rounds. The recognition of the familiar sound came slowly, however, and it was not until a few seconds later that Thomas realized what had happened. He sat upright. He was still at his desk; still fully dressed and several of the phials full of ingredients that were ranged before him in a rack were still all to be tested. He felt angry with himself, but even angrier when he saw the upturned jar and the water spilled on his notes. The telltale signs of rat's footprints were traced across another blank piece of paper.

'Franklin,' he scowled, looking at the rat preening himself disrespectfully in the corner.

Thomas picked up the sheaf of ink-written notes and stared in wonderment at the top sheet. A strange rainbow pattern had formed. Starting from the edge of the parchment where the water had been spilled, the ink had been separated into various shades and tones; each a band of color with its own distinct color. He wondered what it could mean – these strange pigmentations ranged so precisely and so orderly.

Quickly he took up another sheet of paper,

dipped his quill into ink, and scribbled along the bottom. He then poured a little water into a tray that was on his desk and dipped the bottom of the paper into it. Nothing happened. Why would it? he asked himself. Wait, be patient, he told himself. Science must not be hurried. It is like a fine wine. It must be given time to mature. He would fetch Dr. Carruthers. No. He glanced at the clock. He would still be abed and besides, there was nothing to show him, apart from a strange rainbow on a page. There was nothing and there was everything. He waited, pacing the room, allowing himself only now and again to see if any more magic was being wrought by some great, unseen magician.

Five minutes past, then ten. Still nothing. How long had he been asleep? His last recollection was of the clock striking three. It was now six o'clock. This magic had been wrought in less than four hours, but if it was to occur again, it may take another four. He would have to occupy himself fruitfully in the meantime. He could not forbear like the husband of a woman in labor, waiting for the miracle of life to appear. He would carry on examining the ingredients. Next the jalap – a purgative used widely in Mexico, so he believed. Should he allow himself one more glance at the paper? He did and – what was this? As the water was sucked up into the paper, the ink began to separate, slowly but surely. Before his very eyes he saw the dyes and pigments emerge, first into red, then into light blue, then to green.

It occurred to him that if ink could be separated thus into pigments and dyes, then surely the same could be done for the purgative? He felt his hands

131

start to tremble with excitement, but he must remain calm. He would conduct a similar experiment, this time using the purgative instead of the ink. If the mixture behaved in the same way, separating out into various components, then he would be making progress.

Chapter 18

Michael Farrell watched Lord Crick's godfather and the executor of his late brother-in-law's will descend on Boughton Hall like a great raven. Sir Montagu Malthus's hair was jet black, his eyes hooded, his nose hooked like a beak, and he had come to pick over the carrion. He flew into his study three days before the inquest and, shoulders hunched, eyed up the family as they waited anxiously for the will to be read.

Farrell knew Sir Montagu had his own suspicions about his ward's untimely death; he was aware of the vile murmurings, whispered accusations, loose talk in the taverns. Above all he knew he disliked him as much as he had Edward. That was why, when Farrell had extended a hand on his arrival, he was not surprised to be regarded with disdain from under black knitted brows.

'I think not, under the circumstances,' countered Sir Montagu, his voice dry and crackly.

'The circumstances are very unfortunate, sir,' acknowledged Farrell, slightly unnerved, as Sir Montagu brushed past him. The man was followed by another smaller gentleman, whom he assumed was a notary. And now there the large man sat, grave-faced and judgmental.

Directly opposite Sir Montagu stood Lydia; stiff backed and tense, like the taut string of an exquisitely crafted violin that could break at the slightest vibration. Less than an hour ago he had told her that Lavington was a beneficiary and she was still reeling from the shock. To her knowledge her brother's only connection to James Lavington had been the fact that her husband had persuaded Edward to let his old friend lease a cottage on the estate for a peppercorn rent. As far as she knew his only association with Edward was through cards on a Thursday night. To her knowledge there was no real friendship between the two men.

And so the company waited nervously and uneasily as Sir Montagu Malthus took his seat behind a large desk.

'He suspects,' whispered Lavington to Farrell through clenched teeth.

'He is here to read the will, not pass judgment on it,' scowled the Irishman. Nevertheless he noted Lavington's palms were clammy and his eyes were fixed to the floor.

Beyond her own anxieties Lydia was having to contend with her poor demented mother, who kept raising her right hand and calling out, as if bidding at an auction.

'I like that painting. I must have it, my dear,' she said, pointing to the gilded mirror on the opposite wall. Her daughter was trying to calm her, like a troublesome child, but to little avail.

'Lydia, my dear, please accept my deepest

sympathies,' said Sir Montagu, taking the young woman's hand. She was unaware of the less than civil exchange that had just taken place between him and her husband and she smiled politely.

'And dear Felicity,' he said, moving on to Lady Crick, who was seated next to her daughter.

'Montagu. Is that really you, Montagu?' she asked, a glint of recognition in her dull eyes.

Lydia was surprised, but delighted. 'It is indeed Sir Montagu, Mama,' she said, almost breathless with pleasure at her mother's apparent lucidity.

''Tis I, Felicity. And how charming you look,' he told her, admiring the pink ribbons she sported so absurdly in her graying hair. Sir Montagu had been a loyal friend to the old earl and had spent many a pleasant sojourn there with his late wife.

'You will stay for dinner, will you not? I'll have Mistress Claddingbowl cook your favorite mutton pie,' she told him sweetly, clasping his clawlike hand.

Lydia was amazed. Her mother's thoughts and speech had not been so clear for weeks.

'That is kind, but my business is brief,' said Sir Montagu, managing to prize the old woman's hand from his.

Without bothering to sit down he addressed the room. 'As you know, as executor of his lordship's will, it is my duty, along with Mr. Rathbone's here' – he motioned to the little man beside him who had said nothing, but constantly shuffled a sheaf of papers – 'to read it to you, the beneficiaries.'

Farrell shifted and Lavington cracked his knuckles in a nervous gesture, but Lydia simply kept her gaze to the floor.

The formidable gentleman continued: 'As Lord Crick's executor, it is also my duty to see that there are no improprieties in the execution of that last will and testament.' He darted a pin-sharp glance at Farrell. 'However, it has come to my attention that there have been certain irregularities of which I was not aware before yesterday.'

Lydia frowned. She looked at her husband, who remained impassive. 'I am afraid, therefore,' continued Sir Montagu, 'that, under the questionable circumstances, I have decided to postpone this reading.'

Farrell remained calm, but Lavington leaned forward with indignant haste. 'What mean you, sir?' he asked aggressively.

'Precisely what I say, Mr. Lavington.' Sir Montagu remained unruffled by the confrontation. 'I have decided to await the outcome of the inquest before I read the will.'

'But you cannot do that,' protested Lavington. Farrell, clearly embarrassed by the whole episode, pulled on his friend's arm.

'No. Please,' the captain urged, drawing his friend close to him.

Lavington, swinging 'round, caught sight of the look of consternation on Lydia's face. It was enough to calm him. He composed himself.

'Of course, Sir Montagu. You are right,' Farrell conceded graciously, standing up and tugging at his topcoat. 'But might you tell us what these irregularities are? Technicalities, surely?'

'That I cannot say, Captain Farrell, until after the inquest,' came the terse reply. It was clear Sir Montagu would not be moved.

In the hallway, Howard helped the visitor on with his large black mantle and he and his small notary swept toward the front door.

'No doubt we shall see each other at the inquest, Captain,' he croaked, and Farrell watched him and his silent associate drive off in the carriage with a feeling of inexplicable dread. It was as if he had suddenly realized that the inquest into his brother-in-law's death would by no means be the formality for which he had hoped. Lavington joined him and together they watched the carriage turn out of the drive.

'He suspects, does he not, Farrell?' said Lavington when he was sure no one would overhear.

'Yes, my friend, I believe he does,' replied the Irishman.

Lydia joined the two men.

'May I speak with my husband, Mr. Lavington?' she asked urgently, taking Farrell by the arm and drawing him away. 'Michael, what is it? There is something you are not telling me.' Her voice was poised halfway between anger and disbelief.

The Irishman raised his hand and stroked her flushed cheek. 'Do not fret so, my dear. 'Tis nothing you should worry yourself over,' he told her. The charming smile appeared once more on her husband's face, but this time Lydia could see there was apprehension in his eyes. She prayed to God that by sending the stone jar to Thomas to analyze she had done the right thing.

Chapter 19

Thomas rubbed his eyes and grimaced. It was as if the lenses were covered in shards of glass and it pained him every time he blinked. Over the past two days he had slept hardly at all. He had become a voluntary prisoner in his own laboratory as he tested each ingredient in the purgative by this new separation method and with each experiment he had witnessed a miracle of nature. He had then compared this with the ingredients he knew to be pure. He had found nothing strange nor irregular.

Each finding of each ingredient correlated exactly to the other, like a footprint on the soil or a signature on parchment. Each ingredient had its own unique pattern, its own kaleidoscope of color. There was no foreign substance present in the purgative that Mr. Peabody had given Lord Crick, at least he could be sure of that; at least he would be able to stand up at the inquest tomorrow and be certain of that fact, he told himself.

Two possibilities had occurred to him during the course of his experiments. Either the young earl had reacted violently to one or a combination of the ingredients used, or the purgative had been tampered with after it left Mr. Peabody's hands.

Just then Franklin leapt up onto the ledge of an open drawer of Thomas's desk and sniffed the air disdainfully. His master looked down at the rodent and a memory flashed through his mind. He recalled seeing the rat in the garden at Boughton Hall and Lady Lydia's torment at seeing the rodent on the path. 'I thought they'd all been poisoned,' she had wailed.

Thomas wondered what sort of poison might have been used on the vermin. His duty was to report the facts to the inquest, but he was also allowed to interpret them. Was it also his place to conjecture? He was not sure, but now that the thought had sown itself in his brain, it was rapidly taking root. He had to obtain a sample of whatever poison was used to kill rats at Boughton Hall and conduct the appropriate experiments to establish the facts. But how?

Sleep did not come easily to him that night. Every time he closed his eyes he would see rats, whole plagues of them overrunning the kitchen garden at Boughton Hall and in among the hordes of squeaking, undulating rodents he could see Lydia, her face full of anguish, calling for help. His heart was pumping fast, its vibrations thumping against the pillow like a drumbeat. At times like this, Thomas thought, it was a curse knowing the mechanisms of the body without knowing where the soul lay.

Will Lovelock was also finding it difficult to sleep that night, as he had every night since his sister died. His young mind kept reliving the time he had been out looking for her. She had been missing for a few hours. It was not like her. She would normally help her mother with her duties, taking out the ashes or scrubbing the kitchen floor. But on that particular day, she disappeared shortly after breakfast and no one knew where she had gone. His father had been angry, called her a 'sluggard' and said he would take his belt to her when she returned. But Mother had been anxious. He could see it in her face, so that was why, after he had seen to the horses, he had made some excuse to go over to Mr. Lavington's cottage at the far edge of the estate.

Mounted on one of the ponies, he had crossed the bridge over the lake, keeping an eagle eye open for his sister. It was a fine clear day in May, but there was still a chill in the air and just as the pony's hooves had begun to rattle over the wooden bridge a gust of wind blew up. It caught the green reeds that fringed the lake and made them rustle in unison. Will looked at the black-domed heads of the reeds nodding in the breeze, then looked again, this time more intently. His attention had been called to something caught in the foliage: a piece of dark material, like a half-deflated balloon, that was trapped in the bull-rushes. Nudging his pony closer, he dismounted and walked toward the water's edge. It was then he realized the material belonged to a skirt. He stopped dead in his tracks and his horrified eyes traced the outline of the skirt to an arm, then to long, loose hair, and he knew. He began to scream, as if the noise might waken his sleeping sister. She was out of reach, just beyond the parapet of the bridge in water too deep for him. He looked for a branch, a stick, so that she could grab ahold of it and he could pull her ashore. He could not see one. He was helpless. He screamed

139

once more. This time James Lavington heard his anguished cries from the first floor of his cottage. He opened his bedroom window that overlooked the lake and saw the boy fixed to the spot, wailing hysterically.

'I'm coming, boy. Hold on,' he called out and he had hurried as fast as his disabled leg would allow him to where Will stood frozen with terror, glaring at the reeds.

'Oh sweet Jesus,' cried Lavington when he saw the folds of material and the hair that swirled in the gentle current.

They waded in, Amos Kidd and his father, and dragged her out, like a large wet rag doll, her dark hair streaked with green weeds. They heaved her onto the bank facedown as if she were a sack of potatoes, and then fell exhausted themselves onto the grass. It was then that Will had rushed forward and thrown himself onto her body, turning her over with all his might so that he could see her face. Her eyes were closed. He had to wake her. He began pushing her, pulling her, trying to rouse her, frantically calling out her name. His mother had rushed forward, too, prizing him away from his sister. She had lifted her head up and cradled her daughter's milk-white face in her hands.

'No. No,' cried Hannah, rocking her daughter gently, as if she were a babe. It was then that Will had seen the bulges in his sister's apron pockets, while his mother was too enveloped in her grief to see him put in his hand and reach inside. His father came now to comfort her, drenched to his waist and eyes full of tears.

'Beccy!' screamed Will and sat up in a cold

sweat in bed.

His mother came to him once more as he lay on a straw palliasse in the corner of the room, opposite his sister. In her hand she carried a mortar.

'Hush now. You'll wake Rachel,' she whispered, kneeling by the mattress. 'Take this,' she soothed and she spooned the bitter mixture into her son's mouth as she did most nights. ''Twill make you feel better,' she would say, and it always did. A few minutes later sleep would come to him like a welcome visitor that would not leave until the daylight appeared.

'I miss her,' said Will. His coppery hair was disheveled and stuck out at angles all over his large head.

'We all do,' replied Hannah, her voice cracking with emotion. She stroked his cheek for a moment and kissed his freckled forehead before returning to the warmth of the fire.

Will rolled over in bed to await the inevitable arrival of sleep that always came after his mother's remedy. As he did so, he felt under his mattress and touched the flat stones that were as cold as his sister's cheeks the day they pulled her from the lake. Now they lay underneath him, those smooth, small slabs that he had found in Rebecca's apron pockets, sandwiched between the mattress and the floor. His hand felt for them in the darkness and he shivered as he touched their cold, level surfaces. Somehow they made him feel closer to her, even though she had gone to another place.

Chapter 20

'So, we are to lose you to Oxford again,' said Dr. Carruthers over breakfast the following morning. Thomas detected a note of disapproval in his voice.

The young New Englander was toying with a rasher of fatty bacon on his plate, but had no appetite for it. He knew he had to return to Boughton Hall before the inquest convened. He would take the coach up to Oxford that very morning, so that he could endeavor to track down the poison used to kill vermin on the estate. He would need a sample of it to test.

Dr. Carruthers sipped the coffee Mistress Finesilver had just poured him. He was aware that Thomas had postponed a lecture he was due to give at the College of Surgeons the day before because he was working on solving the riddle of this purgative.

'Remember you have a duty to your students,' he warned his protégé.

Thomas rested his fork on the side of the plate. 'Indeed, I would never forget, sir, but I also have an obligation to the court. It is relying on me to determine how a young man died.'

The old doctor let out a deep sigh. 'You are not a lawyer, Thomas,' he countered, obviously annoyed.

'But I seem the only one who may be capable of

142

clearing up this awful mystery,' protested Thomas. He found himself pointing the fork aggressively at his mentor and was glad he could not see his uncharacteristically fiery gesture.

Abashed, he put his knife and fork together carefully on the side of the plate in an act of closure. 'I must take my leave now, sir,' he said, rising from the table. 'I shall be back by the end of the week.'

Dr. Carruthers nodded and wiped his mouth with a napkin. He hoped his student's brilliant young mind would not stray from the path of anatomy and serious study. Murders were best solved by lawyers and constables, he told himself, not by scientists.

Back in his laboratory, Thomas began to pack his bag with the necessary implements and ingredients he would need to carry out experiments on any samples of poison he might find at Boughton Hall. A sense of panic was rising within him as he rushed to strap ampules and phials securely into their correct cases. When he performed in front of students in the anatomy theater he was a priest. His chalice was a knife and the actions he executed were rituals; above reproach and incontrovertible. His unquestioning congregation held him in awe. They merely watched his skill and precision as he teased out long lengths of tubules and sliced through cumbering flesh. To them he was an apostle of the great Vesalius who, more than two hundred years before, had performed the first postmortem dissections. He was respected and revered on his own hallowed ground.

A court, however, was foreign territory, full of

143

nonbelievers and infidels. His audience would be made up not of students eager to learn, but of curious meddlers and bloodthirsty gossips. And he, with his science and his theories, would be regarded as no better than a common charlatan, who peddled false remedies and cure-alls at fairgrounds and markets.

Thomas shuddered at the very thought of taking the stand as he began collating his notes. He had just packed the last sheaves into a bag when a knock came at the door. He was annoyed. 'Yes, Mistress Finesilver,' he called out brusquely. The door swung open and, sure enough, there she stood, her face pinched and unsmiling as usual. Yet instead of telling Thomas that she had darned his stockings for the very last time, or that his hot meal was growing cold, she announced he had a visitor.

Immediately Thomas put down the last of his notes and turned toward the door. He was struck straightaway by the young man's resemblance to Lydia: the high cheekbones, the loosely curled hair, the same heart-shaped face.

'Please, come in,' said Thomas, holding out his hand. Francis Crick took it, slightly bemused. He recognized the young man from his attendances at his lectures.

'You bear a great resemblance to your cousin, Mr. Crick,' ventured Thomas.

'You speak of Lady Lydia?' The young aristocrat seemed shocked. 'Yes. Yes, I suppose I do,' he mused.

'You were the one who recommended me to her ladyship, were you not?'

144

'Yes. Yes, I was,' said Francis, not knowing whether he might be castigated.

Thomas paused. 'Thank you for your confidence in me,' he said, nodding his head.

'You are a great anatomist, Dr. Silkstone,' replied the young man genuinely.

Thomas smiled. 'No, not great, just inquisitive.' He fastened the clasp on his bag and turned to the student. 'And true to my nature, I must ask you what brings you here, Mr. Crick.'

Francis straightened himself, as if he had suddenly remembered the reason for his presence. 'I am come on a mission on behalf of my cousin,' he announced in what Thomas thought was a somewhat formal manner. The doctor's curiosity was roused. 'Go on,' he urged.

The young man plunged a hand into his coat pocket and retrieved a gray drawstring bag. Handing it carefully over to the doctor, he said: 'Lydia wanted you to have this.'

Thomas remained silent, but took the bag warily and laid it on his desk. Inside was a small, clear glass bottle with a cork stopper. Sitting down, he held the bottle up to the light. Inside the liquid was colorless. It could have been water, or pure alcohol, save a few minute impurities that floated in it.

Francis eyed Thomas nervously as he began to uncork the bottle. It only took a second before the doctor knew for sure what was contained inside. His head jerked back involuntarily, as if someone had punched him in the face. So strong was the smell that it sent his senses reeling. It was an unforgettable, unmistakable smell. It was a smell like bitter almonds. It was the smell of cyanide.

'And this was made at Boughton?' Thomas choked.

Francis, too, could smell the pungent odor. He turned away, panting. 'Yes. Captain Farrell made it in a still. He would make the poison from black laurel cherries every autumn.'

This knowledge came as a revelation to Thomas. 'So, there is a still at Boughton where cyanide is made?'

Francis nodded. 'There was,' he replied hesitantly.

Thomas placed the cork back into the bottle neck. 'There was?' he repeated. 'So, where is it now?'

Francis looked awkward. He knew the information he was about to divulge would be incriminating for his cousin's husband. 'Captain Farrell had it destroyed after Edward's death and all the poison with it.'

Thomas paused to process what he had just heard. 'I see,' he said thoughtfully. 'So, where did Lady Lydia find this bottle?'

'There is a place called the pavilion on the estate. 'Tis like a summerhouse. She found it there,' said Francis gravely.

Thomas held the bottle up for inspection once more. 'Then no one else knows that this bottle exists?'

'No one.' Crick shook his head solemnly.

Thomas banged his palms down flat on his desk. 'Then we must get to work,' he said emphatically.

Two large preserving jars sat on Thomas's desk. He had been about to pack them into his bag when his unexpected visitor arrived. One contained a section of the earl's stomach, the other part of his liver.

'I can test the deceased's organs for traces of this substance,' said Thomas, looking at the brownish objects that floated anonymously in preserving fluid. But just as he had uttered these words he saw the pained look on Francis's face when he realized that his cousin's remains had been reduced to tissues in sample jars. To be a good anatomist, or indeed a surgeon, Thomas had learned that compassion must be distanced and emotion suppressed, but he recognized that these were exceptional and traumatic circumstances. He laid a hand on the young man's shoulder. 'You do not have to assist me,' he said softly.

Francis looked at him vacantly for a moment; then, as if a sudden resolve had seized hold of him, he replied: 'We must do what we can to find out what killed Edward.'

Thomas nodded, satisfied in the knowledge that the young man who stood before him had the makings of a good surgeon. 'There are two aprons hanging up over there,' he said, pointing to the hooks on the far wall. Francis allowed a smile to flit across his face before he obeyed the surgeon's order.

Meanwhile Thomas transferred the sample jars over to his workbench and carefully opened the one containing the dead man's stomach tissue. Surely if cyanide had been added to the purgative, he would have smelled it during the post-mortem, he told himself.

Francis brought the aprons over and together

they put them on. Next Thomas laid his instruments out on the bench and using tweezers lifted the large section of stomach out of the jar and onto a porcelain dish. Now he was looking at this pulpy bag with fresh eyes and a heightened sense of smell. He lifted the dish and sniffed, then passed it over to Francis.

'One in six people is not capable of smelling cyanide,' Thomas told him, 'but I do not believe we would both suffer from anosmia, especially as we both detected the odor from the bottle.'

At that moment the latch on the laboratory door clicked open and Dr. Carruthers appeared. 'Are you still there, Thomas?' he called.

'Indeed, sir,' he replied, wiping his hands on his apron and walking over to greet the old doctor.

'I did not want us to part on difficult terms,' said Carruthers, taking Thomas's hand.

'There is no bad feeling on my part, sir, let me assure you,' replied Thomas, feeling a little embarrassed that such a conversation should be taking place in front of one of his students. He changed the subject as quickly as he could. 'You have come at an opportune time, sir,' he continued.

'How so?' replied the old doctor, making his way slowly into the center of the laboratory. His progress was suddenly halted, however. Like a rabbit that has sensed the approach of a fox, he stiffened and sniffed the air, his nose twitching violently. 'Heavens above, I smell cyanide,' he exclaimed.

Thomas and Francis shot a glance at each other. "'Tis something I've not smelled since I did a postmortem on a young fellow who drank a tankard of the stuff in the winter of '72.'

Thomas's eyes opened wide. 'Sir, you've performed a postmortem on a cyanide death?'

'Unrequited love, I believe. Messy business,' reflected the old doctor, unaware of the significance of his revelation.

'And do you still have the stomach?' Thomas realized that this postmortem took place eight years ago. It was too much to hope that the sample still remained.

'Still have the stomach?' repeated Dr. Carruthers. Thomas held his breath. 'Of course I do,' he chuckled, as if there was any question that he had not kept it.

'You'll find it on the top left-hand shelf in the cupboard in the storeroom,' he revealed.

Thomas smiled broadly with relief, knowing he should never have doubted his mentor.

The storeroom lay through another door and down a narrow passage. Thomas rarely ventured into it. Dr. Carruthers often referred to it as his 'medical encyclopedia' and Thomas had vowed one day to familiarize himself with the contents of all the mysterious jars and carboys it held, but he had simply been too busy.

The young anatomist and his student ventured into the damp, windowless room. Holding his candle aloft, glass containers came into view one by one, each labeled in Dr. Carruthers's spidery scrawl and there, sure enough, on the top left-hand shelf was a jar labeled 'stomach – cyanide poisoning.' He could scarcely believe his luck.

As Francis Crick held the candle, Thomas carefully reached up for the container and gently brought it down. Taking it to the light of the passageway, the two men inspected the macabre cargo. There it was: the perfectly preserved stomach of someone whose life had been so blighted that he had killed himself in one of the most agonizing ways imaginable.

Back in the laboratory Thomas and Francis returned to the workbench.

'You've found it, then?' asked the old doctor, smiling.

'Indeed we have,' replied Thomas, eagerly prizing off the lid of the jar.

Even after eight years in preserving fluid, the smell was still unmistakable. The acrid odor immediately wafted into the air.

Thomas lifted the sample carefully onto another dish. The most striking difference between this sample and that of Lord Crick's was the color.

'Well, look at this,' whispered Thomas to himself as much as to Francis. The mucosa of the stomach was a deep inky blue, with a heavy staining of the fundus, yet the antrum was spared.

''Tis a deep blue if I remember correctly,' ventured Dr. Carruthers, now sitting at the desk.

'Indeed it is,' replied Thomas, surprised by the comparison. 'It bears no resemblance whatsoever to Crick's stomach. So 'twas not rat poison that killed him.'

'How can you be so sure?' asked Francis.

'This is proof, Mr. Crick,' he countered. 'A negative proof, but proof all the same.'

'So, what *did* kill Edward?' asked the student.

'That,' replied the young doctor, 'is what we still have to find out.'

150

Chapter 21

If death, mused the great thinker Dr. Samuel Johnson, is merely a gateway on the path from life into eternity, a portal from mortality to immortality, then what does it matter how a man dies? The act of dying is not of importance. It is how he lives that counts.

'What say you to that, Mr. Crick?' asked Thomas at the end of a long afternoon in the laboratory.

The young student had remained to assist him in his tests on the contents of the jar of rat poison. The process of elimination was a laboriously slow one, as the liquid had to be broken down into its various components and each one tested for its toxicity. Now, however, at least one conclusion could be scientifically proven. Edward Crick did not die from cyanide poisoning. Dr. Carruthers's specimen had proved vital to Thomas in this respect. It was the one aspect about which he could be certain should he be questioned in the witness stand at the forthcoming inquest, assuming the matter of the still and the rat poison came to light.

Thomas studied Crick as he rinsed the phials in a bowl of water. Even his gestures, the angle at which he held his head, the cadence of his voice, reminded him of Lydia.

'Are those not the thoughts of Dr. Johnson?' replied the student.

151

Thomas was duly impressed. 'Indeed so.' He had been fortunate enough to be introduced to the great thinker by Dr. Carruthers when he first came to England and he found him to be a most convivial fellow, with a sharp wit and a tongue to match. His visits to Bedford Coffee House were legendary and the discussions that his forthright remarks provoked were always as lively as a fireworks display.

'He is a man of great erudition and humor, but I am not sure I agree with him on that particular point,' he said, securing the lid on a sample jar.

Crick turned to face his mentor. 'How so, sir?' he pressed.

'It matters greatly if the man's dying was by the hand of another.'

The younger man paused and looked away. 'And you are still convinced my cousin was murdered?'

Thomas wiped his iodine-stained hands on a damp cloth. 'The more I see, the more I believe he was,' he replied earnestly. 'And you?'

Crick sighed deeply. 'I do not know what to think, sir,' he replied, as if the very effort of forming an opinion or making a decision was far too much for him to bear.

Thomas chided him for his ambivalence. 'Come, come, you are a scientist, Mr. Crick. We are traveling down the path of discovery and soon we will come to a fork in the road. Which route do we take?'

The young man looked at Thomas blankly. The doctor waited for a while, but seeing that no reply was forthcoming from his student he obliged him with the answer. 'The one of which we are sure, of course,' he said. 'The one where we can tread heavily and not be afraid that we will sink. Our path must be built on fact, not on assumption, Mr. Crick.'

The problem that confronted Thomas was, of course, that there were so few facts at his fingertips that no path presented itself more than any other and he was in danger of finding himself utterly lost.

The next morning Thomas left London for Oxford once more, only this time he was accompanied by his eager assistant. He had found Francis Crick to be a personable young man, although somewhat lacking in the tenacity needed to pursue the truth. He suspected a certain sloppiness in his manner and haphazardness in his methods that were not conducive to thorough anatomical investigation. He had much to learn, thought Thomas, as their coach bounced and bumped along the main road leading northwest through the rolling Chilterns.

Once they reached Oxford, Francis Crick was to journey onward to Boughton Hall where he would spend the night and accompany Captain Farrell and Lady Lydia to the inquest in the morning. Thomas was to stay, once more, at the White Horse. First, however, he walked to Christ Church, to pay a visit to Dr. Hascher.

Thomas found the old professor hunched over a weighty tome in his study. The men greeted each other as old friends and Thomas asked if he might store his various samples and equipment in the professor's laboratory for safekeeping. They then enjoyed a schnapps together.

'You are troubled about tomorrow? Yes?' The professor sensed Thomas was as tense as a tendon at full stretch as he sat in a chair opposite him, staring into his glass.

'It troubles me that I have such little real evidence to present to the court,' acknowledged Thomas. He was used to standing up in front of dozens of students and delivering lectures whose foundations were laid on indisputable facts, but tomorrow he would face a court with little more than a handful of straws. 'And yet...' He broke off.

The professor frowned. 'What is it, Thomas?' he asked, seeing a look of fear shoot across the young doctor's face as he remembered the scribbled note of warning.

'And yet someone is worried about what I may find,' he said, delving into his waistcoat pocket and handing the professor the piece of crumpled paper.

The old man hooked a pair of spectacles onto his nose and looked at the note. 'It seems as zough you have disturbed a nest of vipers, Thomas,' he said gravely. 'Be careful.'

An hour or so later Thomas took his leave. The night was as crisp as starched sheets and the air so cold it could have been sliced with a surgeon's knife. The black dome of the Radcliffe Camera loomed large against the star-studded sky as Thomas made his way across the cobbles toward Broad Street.

Great Tom was tolling the hour as he walked

briskly past the Camera's steps. From the shadows of the great portico he could hear a girl's staccato pants of pleasure, punctuated by the rhythmic grunts of a man. They cared nothing for the great works that lay inside: the papers of John Friend's original chemistry lectures or the collections of such notable scientists as Nathan Alcock. They cocked a snook at scholarship by their actions and their complete lack of respect angered Thomas. He quickened his pace now, past Hertford College in Catte Street.

A little farther on a group of begowned drunken scholars crossed the street under the disapproving gaze of the great philosophers of the Sheldonian, squawking obscenities like a flock of crows. Their existence was so very different from his own sophomore days in Philadelphia, where the distractions from the labor of the medical book and the apprenticeship of the knife had been more genteel. Thomas shook his head absentmindedly as he thought of what Aristotle and Plato might make of these ignorant dolts.

The White Horse now lay within sight. Candles burned dimly in its frosted windows. Even his spartan room, with its damp bed linen, seemed inviting now as the chill air began to seep into his very bones.

He was looking forward to a sound night's sleep before the inquest tomorrow. He had just begun to cross the last few yards of pavement before he reached Broad Street when he suddenly became aware of a presence beside him. He turned swiftly to see who was there, but he felt only the crushing force of a fist to his jaw. It sent him

155

reeling backward, so that his left shoulder smashed into the wall behind him. Now another blow was struck to his guts, doubling him over. He let out a cry as he felt his diaphragm go into spasm, and then dropped to his knees on the icy ground. As he did so he searched for his purse. 'Here, take my money,' he pleaded hoarsely, pointing to his belt. But his pleas fell on deaf ears as yet another blow was rained on his head, striking him just above his left eye. This time he dropped like a stone onto the pavement.

''Tis not your money that's wanted, Doctor,' came the gruff voice in the darkness.

Thomas tried in vain to lift his head, but the pain was so great it felt that flames were licking every nerve ending. Putting his hand to his forehead, he felt a warm trickle of liquid gushing from a wound just above his left eye. It was a feeling so familiar to him, he did not need to see the color of it to know it was blood.

'For God's sake, have pity,' he pleaded as he felt another sharp jab under his ribs as his assailant kicked him. The sound of his own cries now filled his ears as the sharp stabs of pain penetrated him like the blade of a stiletto. Again and again the jabs came until the cries died down, the whimpers were silenced, and the night belonged once more to illicit lovers and rowdy scholars.

The night watchman found him sprawled along the pavement outside Exeter College. Thinking him to be the worse for drink at first, he had kicked him soundly in the ribs, but when he received no response, he bent down and held his oil lamp over the man. It was then that he saw the trickle of blood seeping from a wound to the head. With his foot the night watchman turned the man over, so that he now lay on his back. From his dress and his face he could tell he was a gentleman. Bending down he placed his grimy fingers around the throat, feeling for a pulse. He could find none. So, satisfied that this gentleman would no longer be needing any money, he delved into the purse that hung on his belt and brought out two guineas.

The find brought a smile to his stubbly face. Not bad for a night's work. 'A brace of shiners,' he said to himself, but that, of course, was not an end to it. He could not move the dead weight. He would have to enlist help. Disappearing down Broad Street, he turned into Turl Street and into the Turf Tavern, where he knew he could find a willing assistant.

'You've a good 'un here,' puffed the night watchman's accomplice, as he helped his friend lift the body from the pavement and into a handcart.

'At least four pounds, I'll wager,' replied the night watchman, gleefully tucking the gentleman's limp arm into the cart for fear of further damaging his precious cargo. Together they pushed their prized load back down Turl Street. Warily they crossed the High Street, then trundled down Oriel Lane, arriving at Christ Church by a narrow back gate – the one they always used for such occasions.

Usually it was an old one they brought, or a young child, often a fetus, but no matter their age, they were always poor, scrawny specimens without flesh on their bones or money in their pockets. This one was different and Professor

Hascher, they told themselves, would pay over the odds for it.

'This one'll please ye, doctor,' said the night watchman, as he let his burden land on the dissecting table with an unceremonious thud. But as soon as he pulled back the hessian from the man's face, Professor Hascher's interested expression turned to one of horror.

'*O mein Gott!*' he cried when he set eyes on the man's features as he lay limp and crumpled on the dissecting table. The elderly anatomist's hands flew up to his lined face.

'It cannot be,' he cried, leaning over the pallet.

Both the night watchmen were shocked by his reaction as they saw him bend down and put his ear to the man's mouth. He felt for a pulse in the man's wrist and his expression suddenly changed.

'Zis man is not dead, you fools,' he muttered under his breath. 'He is unconscious. Stand back,' he barked and, pushing them both aside, he reached for his instrument bag on the desk. Pulling out a pad of gauze and a bottle of iodine Professor Hascher began dabbing Thomas's head wound.

By now the blood had congealed around the abrasion. The skin is at its most delicate above the eyes, and the skin on Thomas's face was like a taut drum hide that had been hit too hard and split. Professor Hascher knew he would need to stitch the wound. He had to forget that this was his friend, his colleague who lay supine and helpless before him.

As the needle pierced the skin for the first time, he was glad that Thomas was still deep in a crevasse of oblivion, unaware of all feeling and therefore all pain. It was a merciful escape for him because the wound was a long one and the needle penetrated and reemerged several times before the professor's work was complete.

A row of black, flat stitches now adorned the young doctor's bruised brow and Professor Hascher took a small step back to inspect his work from a short distance. He was pleased with its neatness, its precision. He may have been more used to suturing corpses, but he could still turn his hand to a trim piece of handiwork when required.

The wound now cleaned and sutured, the professor's attention was diverted to the rest of Thomas's battered body. His patient made no move throughout the stitching and this troubled him. He opened the young man's bloodstained shirt and saw there was a wound on his abdomen and severe bruising all around, consistent with having been repeatedly kicked.

'Pass me more gauze, will you,' he instructed the night watchman's assistant. The man, of rough appearance, whose stench of stale sweat fought with the smell of preserving fluid in the laboratory, obliged. It occurred to Professor Hascher that if these men would have been prepared to sell a corpse to him, as they had done before, they would also rob it beforehand.

'Where is the money you stole from zis man?' he asked, taking the gauze.

The ruffian looked shocked and darted a glance at the night watchman, who now struggled to his feet. Simultaneously both men delved into their pockets and each brought out a guinea, stolen from Thomas as he lay helpless on the pavement. They placed the coins on the desk nearby under the professor's reproachful eye.

'If you want zem back, and to avoid ze wrath of ze magistrate, you will have to earn zem zis time,' he told them mysteriously.

The men looked on puzzled as the professor sat at his desk and scribbled a note. 'You will ride to Boughton Hall near Brandwick at first light,' he told them. 'And deliver this to Lady Lydia Farrell,' he said, handing the night watchman the sealed piece of parchment. 'You will wait for her reply, zen, if she so wishes, escort her back here. Do you understand?' The men nodded vigorously. 'Zen we shall talk about reimbursement,' added the professor, dismissing them with a contemptuous wave of his hand.

The old anatomist watched the men go before returning to his unconscious patient, who remained silent and deathly white on the dissecting table. For all anyone else knew he could have been the next corpse to be sliced open in front of eager anatomy students the next day, so still and pale did he look. His ribs had been cracked like dry twigs and his head delivered a fearful blow, but the life that could so easily have been taken from Thomas had been spared. Whoever had done this to the young surgeon, thought Professor Hascher could so easily have killed him. They had not. Whoever did this to him could so easily have robbed him. They did not do that, either.

Slipping his hand into Thomas's waistcoat pocket, he withdrew the anonymous note that the young doctor had shown him earlier that evening.

The villain that had so cruelly treated his friend, he concluded, did not want him to delve any further into the death of the Earl Crick.

Chapter 22

As Thomas gazed through the thick fog of returning consciousness, he became vaguely aware of strangely familiar objects around him. In the half light rows of books came into murky focus before retreating into a blur once more. Ill-defined shapes, a table, or perhaps a chair, emerged from the shadows. The smell, too, that met his nostrils was recognizable to him, yet he did not know why. Now he could hear voices at the boundary of his vision. He turned his head in their direction, but felt pain sear into his brain like a red-hot spear.

'Lie still, Dr. Silkstone,' came a soft voice. Someone was bending over him. He squinted against the daylight that burned into his eyes.

'Lady L...?' His throat felt scorched.

Lydia was indeed there. 'Professor Hascher,' she called. Thomas now recognized the outline of the wiry-haired anatomist. He held a cup of water to his lips and Thomas felt the cool liquid trickle down his throat and soothe his parched gullet.

Shapes now became better defined. Colors returned. Sounds and smells began to make sense once more. 'What happened?' he asked faintly.

Professor Hascher answered. 'You were attacked opposite the White Horse. You suffered a blow to the jaw and head. You have cracked three ribs and have a gash on your leg, but you'll survive.'

Thomas tried to acknowledge that he had heard the prognosis with a nod, but the pain returned once more. He stifled a cry.

'The night watchmen brought you here because zey took you for dead and wanted to make a shilling or two out of your corpse,' the professor told him.

'You must rest, Dr. Silkstone,' said Lydia softly. She held a damp cloth in her hand and dabbed his forehead gently.

Thomas focused on her face. She was wearing that same anxious expression as when she had first come to his laboratory, but her very presence was as soothing as any balm or unguent could be.

'What...?'

Lydia put her finger to his lips and he felt a tingling sensation run through his body. 'You must not talk, Dr. Silkstone, only listen.' She sat down on a chair next to the table and took a deep breath. He felt its moist sweetness against his face as she bent low over him.

'This is all my doing, Dr. Silkstone,' she sighed, shaking her head. Thomas opened his mouth to protest. 'Please,' she urged. 'Let me say what I have to.' She stilled the hand he had raised and he felt her cool skin against his. 'I came to you seeking your help because I knew that you were the best in your field and you willingly agreed to help me find out how Edward died.' She bit her lips, fighting back tears. 'I prayed that it would all be very straightforward; that you would confirm that my brother died from natural causes and

162

that he could rest in peace. But it was not to be. It would seem that someone is afraid you will be able to find out the cause of his death, which, God forbid, may well be far from natural. It will be murder.' She took a deep breath once more. 'I have made you risk your own life, Dr. Silkstone, and for that I can only apologize.' She gripped Thomas's hand tighter. 'You must not give evidence at the inquest.'

Thomas felt one of her tears fall on his cheek. He wished he had possessed the strength to rise up and comfort her, but all that he was capable of was to summon what little energy he could muster and lay his other hand on top of hers, reciprocating a moment of forbidden intimacy.

She studied his long surgeon's hands as if she had never seen fingers before; as if they were something new and wonderful and as she did so, Thomas allowed himself to gaze on her face. It was Professor Hascher's voice that broke the moment in two like the snap of a bone when it is amputated.

'Ze inquest will start within ze hour, your ladyship,' he reminded her, moving closer to where Thomas lay.

Lydia's hand withdrew instantly from Thomas's touch. 'Yes. Thank you. I must go,' she replied awkwardly, not sure whether or not the professor had witnessed her indiscretion. She rose quickly. 'I wish you a speedy recovery, Dr. Silkstone,' she said formally.

'Thank you,' croaked Thomas weakly. They were all the words his swollen mouth and tongue could form.

Chapter 23

The inquest into the death of The Right Honorable The Earl Crick, late of Boughton Hall in the county of Oxfordshire, opened at Oxford Coroner's Court on November 16 in the year of our Lord 1780.

At eleven o'clock precisely, Sir Theodisius Pettigrew walked into the courtroom and was more than a little surprised by the scene that greeted him. Where usually only a few grim-faced relatives sat to hear of the last moments of their departed loved one replayed in distressing detail, there now stood and jostled and elbowed scores of noisy, restless, and decidedly malodorous members of the general public. Indeed the tableau that met Sir Theodisius was more akin to the gallery from a variety theater than a court of law; more like a vicious caricature from the pencil of Mr. Hogarth than a solemn and sober occasion. Painted trollops vied for space with black-toothed ruffians. They called out to each other. Some whistled shrilly to attract attention. Others shouted obscenities and swore oaths if they felt they were being crushed in the melee.

As soon as the clerk announced the coroner's arrival, the fracas died down. Even the common throng, it seemed, knew when respect should be shown at an inquest.

'Looks more like a hanging trial,' commented

164

Sir Theodisius to his clerk as he settled his corpulent frame into its seat. Under his voluminous black gown he had smuggled in a small case. It contained neither papers nor textbooks that might help him fathom this most complicated of fiscal procedures, but two chicken legs and a venison pie to see him through the morning until the adjournment for luncheon at one o'clock.

Below on pews sat the more normal breed of attendee: nervous witnesses and pale-faced relatives. A short distance away sat the jury, twelve men of good character and, it was trusted, sound judgment. Sir Theodisius perched his spectacles on the edge of his nose and surveyed them all imperiously. Captain Michael Farrell, confident to the point of arrogance, thought Sir Theodisius, sat next to his pretty young wife, dressed in light blue with a matching hat. Next to her was her addle-brained mother, who, to the coroner's great surprise, sported a necklace made of dried daisies. To Farrell's right James Lavington, wincing now and again in pain, stretched out his right leg in front of him as he perched uneasily on the edge of his seat. Next to him sat Francis Crick, fresh-faced and earnest. Behind the family and close friends sat the servants, all dressed in their Sunday best, looking as solemn as if they were at a funeral.

'Order,' called Sir Theodisius before slamming down his gavel to produce absolute silence. He glanced down at the list of witnesses who were to give evidence. He was acutely aware that this would not be a straightforward inquest. Not only had Lord Crick been well known in the community – particularly among a certain sector of the

165

community, he noted, looking at the paphians and doxies in the gallery – but his death, at the tender age of twenty-one, remained, to date, shrouded in mystery.

After he had dispensed with the usual formalities, Sir Theodisius nodded to the clerk to call the first witness, Mr. Archibald Peabody.

The apothecary from Brandwick shuffled nervously up to the stand and swore on the Bible that his testimony would be truthful.

'Tell me, Mr. Peabody, why did Lord Crick require an apothecary? Was he not in good health?' It was the question that Mr. Peabody was dreading. He looked at Lady Lydia sitting in the front row, as fragile as a flower, and he knew what he was about to say would be deeply offensive.

'His lordship suffered from a very' – the apothecary hesitated, searching for a gentler word to describe the young man's plight – 'a very personal illness,' he blurted.

At these words several women in the gallery dissolved into raucous laughter until Sir Theodisius brought down his gavel once more. He glanced at Lady Lydia, who remained stone-faced.

'And this illness was of a sexual nature?' probed Sir Theodisius.

'Yes, sir,' came the mumbled reply.

There followed more questions as to what treatment was given for this most intimate of afflictions and what ingredients were used in any palliatives.

'In your opinion, Mr. Peabody, was Lord Crick in reasonable health?' asked Sir Theodisius.

The nervous little man took a deep breath

once more. 'He did not take care of his body, sir,' he replied.

'So, is it possible that he may well have died from natural causes?'

Again Peabody paused. 'It is possible, but unlikely,' he replied.

Next to take the witness box was Dr. Elijah Siddall, the physician whom Farrell had called upon to conduct a postmortem on his brother-in-law.

'The corpse was a health hazard,' said the doctor under scrutiny. 'No surgeon in his right mind would have examined it.' He stiffened with indignation.

'I agree with Dr. Siddall,' concurred Mr. Jeremy Walton when it was his turn to take the stand. 'Lord Crick's body was badly decomposed and required immediate burial.'

'I should now like to call upon our third medical witness,' announced Sir Theodisius. 'Dr. Thomas Silkstone.'

There was a hushed silence as the court waited for Thomas, followed by a ripple of murmurings when he failed to appear. 'Dr. Thomas Silkstone,' repeated the clerk.

Lydia looked agitated. She turned in her seat. 'Did you not tell the clerk?' she asked her husband. Farrell shrugged dismissively.

'Rafferty cannot have delivered my message about your doctor friend's unfortunate disposition,' he replied.

'Dr. Silkstone,' boomed the clerk once more. When no reply was forthcoming Sir Theodisius scowled and the drone of the rabble rose like the sound of flies around excrement. 'Then we must move on,' he said, bringing down his gavel to restore order in the court. 'Call the next witness.'

Chapter 24

'Zis is utter madness,' scolded Professor Hascher, helping his patient up from the dissecting table.

Thomas winced and clenched his teeth to try and stifle a reflexive cry. His bruised abdominal muscles were straining with the effort of sitting upright.

'You are correct,' he replied, gasping for breath. 'But you know as well as I do, Professor, that if there is mention of that rat poison in court, everyone, including Sir Theodisius, will jump to the wrong conclusion.'

For a moment Thomas held his head in his hands as lights danced before his eyes and the room oscillated around him. So many times he had treated men with head injuries and wondered at their pain. Now that he knew what it felt like he could share in their misery with an intense empathy.

After a few moments he lowered his stockinged foot to the floor. Slowly, by degrees, he increased the pressure he applied to it and felt the fire travel up from his ankle to his knee joint, as surely as if someone had put a match to the bone.

'Drink zis,' said the professor, handing him a glass of schnapps. Thomas took it with a smile and a shaking hand. He downed it in one and felt its effects almost immediately.

''Tis good physick,' he said, easing himself up on his knuckles.

'The court calls Hannah Lovelock,' announced the clerk. All eyes now turned on the slight woman in a drab brown shawl and battered bonnet who was being helped to stand by her husband. She looked drawn and unsteady on her feet as she made her way to the front of the court.

In a hushed voice she gave her name and swore her oath, all the time looking at her husband in one of the pews, as if drawing strength from his very presence.

'You have clearly been through a terrible ordeal, Mistress Lovelock,' soothed Sir Theodisius. 'But the court understands that you were present when Lord Crick took his physick and therefore your testimony could prove vital.'

Hannah nodded slowly. 'Yes, my lord,' she replied softly, wringing her hands self-consciously.

'Tell us, then, what happened on that morning. In your own time.'

Hannah took a deep breath to compose herself and began. ''Twas when his lordship had just come back from riding. He came up to his room. I were tidying. I saw the bottle of physick on the mantelpiece, but it weren't opened, so I says to his lordship: "Your medicine is here, master." And he says, "Yes, Hannah, I shall take it now."' The maid's face suddenly puckered into a grimace as she recalled the event. 'Them were the last words he said,' she blurted to Sir Theodisius.

'Calm yourself, Mistress Lovelock. We know this is very difficult for you, but you must not upset yourself,' the coroner told her as she dabbed her eyes. There was a note of irascibility in his tone and it was clear he was beginning to lose his patience. 'Can you tell the court what happened next?' he urged.

No sooner had the murmurings in the gallery died down, however, than there was more commotion at the main entrance. Sir Theodisius leaned to one side to see if he could determine its cause and slammed down his gavel once more. But the source of the disturbance soon became apparent as Thomas, propped up on a crutch and with a bandage around his head, staggered to a seat near the front of the courtroom. His face was the color of pumice stone and it was clear that every step pained him.

'Dr. Silkstone,' cried the coroner, more out of surprise than by way of reprimand. 'You are late.'

Thomas, who had managed to seat himself with the greatest of difficulty, was now forced to rise once more to address Sir Theodisius.

'I offer you and the court my sincere apologies, sir,' he said against a background of murmurings. 'But I met with an accident.'

'That we can all see,' replied Sir Theodisius sarcastically. 'I trust we can look forward to hearing your expert evidence later in the proceedings?'

'Indeed, sir,' replied Thomas, longing to return to the comfort of his seat.

'Very well,' said the coroner and he dismissed Thomas with a nod of the head before turning his attention once more to the anxious maidservant, who had been waiting patiently in the witness stand. 'Now, where were we? Pray continue, Mistress Lovelock.'

Taking another deep breath Hannah went on: 'He took the bottle and pulled the cork out.' Her voice trembled as she delved into the deep recesses of her memory, recalling how her master drank down the medicine in one, then walked over to the bed. 'He looked a bit strange,' she remembered.

'In what way?' interrupted Sir Theodisius, who had begun taking notes.

Hannah paused for a moment. 'His face changed color. It were yellowy. I said to him: "Sir, what ails you?" Then he suddenly put his hand up to his chest and began panting like a dog. Then I saw his eyes...'

'What about his eyes?' asked the coroner, setting down his quill.

'I will never forget them. Bulging, they were, as if they were going to leap out at me. They was yellow, too,' she cried.

There were stifled screams from some of the women in the gallery as Hannah continued to relive her experience. Sir Theodisius's gavel slammed down once more. 'Go on, Mistress Lovelock.'

Aware now that she had her audience completely enthralled, the servant continued: 'And his mouth ... it were covered in white, white...' She sought a word to describe the horror she had seen. 'Like froth, it was.' Another communal alarum emitted from the gallery. 'Then he just dropped to the floor, like a stone, and began rolling around like a rat on the captain's poison and

171

he held his belly–'

'Hold,' called Sir Theodisius, lifting his large hand and frowning. Hannah looked at him perlexed and stopped mid-sentence. 'What did you just say?'

Hannah paused. 'I said he held his belly and–'

Sir Theodisius shook his head. 'Before that. You mentioned poison.'

Hannah's expression immediately changed. She looked at her eager audience, as if she were acting out some dramatic role. 'Captain Farrell makes his own rat poison for the hall and the farm,' she said almost conspiratorially.

At this revelation the gallery gasped in unison once more. These men and women were neither learned in their letters, nor their numbers, mused Thomas, looking up at the pack of baying wolves. On the abacus of suspicion and calumny they found it all too easy to add two and two together and make five. He glanced over to Lydia. There had been no chance to tell her of the findings of his tests on the poison. He watched her reaction to Hannah's outpourings. She closed her eyes, hoping, perhaps, that this was all a nightmare. Thomas longed to go and comfort her; to tell her that her husband's poison had not killed her brother.

Captain Farrell, meanwhile, remained impassive, but Thomas saw the look that James Lavington darted at his friend. It was clear to him that he also doubted the wisdom of the Irishman's actions. Hannah's words could be the sparks that ignited the smoldering kindling.

'Order. Order!' cried Sir. Theodisius. He waited until the noise had died down, then turned to

172

Hannah, who seemed almost elated by her own revelation.

'Tell us what happened next,' continued Sir Theodisius.

'I screamed, of course. I ain't never seen such a terrible thing. I screamed until Lady Lydia comes running in and sees her brother lying and waving and crying like an animal caught in a trap,' said the servant. She was now flailing her arms around graphically demonstrating the agonal death throes of her young master.

'What did her ladyship do?' asked Sir Theodisius.

Hannah's eyes widened as she relived the moment. 'She rushed over to her poor brother and tried to calm him, but his body were shaking and jerking like a thing possessed. I thought the very devil was in him,' she exclaimed. Her voice was rising to a crescendo like some soprano delivering a dramatic aria.

Another collective intake of breath from the gallery echoed on the taut air.

'What happened next, Mistress Lovelock?' coaxed Sir Theodisius, every bit as fascinated as the rabble.

'Lady Crick came in to see her only son in his death throes. Thankfully she weren't quite sure what was going on, her being not quite right.' The maid pointed to her own head in a gesture that Sir Theodisius found impertinent but which caused a titter around the gallery.

'And where was Captain Farrell at this time?' urged the coroner.

Hannah nodded. 'He came in next, asked what

all the fuss was about. Then he sees his lordship, fallen on the floor now.'

'And what did he do?' pressed Sir Theodisius.

'He watched.' She paused for dramatic effect. 'Her ladyship was screaming to fetch Dr. Fairweather, but he just stood in the doorway as she rushed past him. He just watched until his lordship stopped moving in his sister's arms.'

The reply was said almost without emotion, which made it all the more shocking. Lydia could see her husband tensing at Hannah's words and she put her hand on his arm in a gesture that said the servant's account was too harsh and there was nothing he could have done.

Throughout her testimony Hannah had not once looked at anyone in the family, but had addressed all her words to the gallery. She now told them how the young earl's limp body had been lifted onto the bed and how Lady Lydia had sat by it, while Dr. Fairweather was summoned, even though it was clear it was too late.

'And what did you do next, Mistress Lovelock?' asked Sir Theodisius.

'Me, sir? I cleaned up like the captain said,' she replied in a matter-of-fact fashion, as if she had been asked to polish the silver or do the laundry.

'And in all of this obvious confusion, can I ask what happened to the bottle of physick?' quizzed Sir Theodisius.

Thomas leaned forward eagerly. Hannah looked at Sir Theodisius straight, as if he had just asked her a profoundly stupid question that was not worthy of a reply.

'Captain Farrell told me to clear everything up,

so I washed it out and put it away,' she retorted, a vague note of contempt in her uneducated voice.

Thomas tried to hide his exasperation. In her ignorance Hannah had destroyed vital evidence. He looked at the maid for a moment, then his gaze crossed to Captain Farrell.

Sir Theodisius was quick to pick up on the point. 'And you say Captain Farrell ordered you to clear everything away?'

It was the first time Thomas had seen the captain look uncomfortable.

'Why, yes, sir. I wiped the floor, took the bloodied cover off the bed, and rinsed out the physick bottle,' detailed the maid, as if she were reporting to the housekeeper.

Sir Theodisius sat back in his chair and sighed. He then shot a glance at Thomas, who seemed equally disheartened.

'This court will adjourn for lunch. We shall reconvene at three o'clock,' said the coroner, his voice perking up at the thought of a two-hour repast, and he brought down his gavel on a morning of high drama and heightened suspicion.

Thomas saw Lydia rise with Farrell. She turned and he caught her eye. He had to speak to her, but, as the hordes of people began to leave the courtroom, her husband quickly ushered her ahead of him and her blue hat disappeared into the crowd.

'Dr. Silkstone,' called a voice that rose above the general melee. The young New Englander turned to see Francis Crick standing behind him.

'My cousin told me of your misfortune. I trust your injuries are not too serious,' he enquired anxiously. He studied Thomas's distended face with a physician's eye, mentally noting the contusions and bruising.

Thomas thanked him for his concern, but was more interested in finding Lydia to tell her the results of the tests on the poison. He glanced over to the opened doorway just in time to see her blue hat once more. The crowd around the exit had dispersed and he dashed toward her as fast as his injured leg permitted.

'Lady Lydia,' he called, ducking and diving through the few stragglers who still filed out of the courtroom. She turned at the sound of her name, but so, too, did her husband, who saw the flustered look on Thomas's swollen face as he approached.

'Come, Lydia,' he instructed, taking a firm hold of his wife's arm. 'We want nothing to do with that man.' And together they walked off down Turl Street and melted into the crowd.

Francis Crick finally caught up with Thomas as he stood looking vexed at the doorway, wincing in pain caused by his exertions.

'It is vital I talk to your cousin, in private,' he told Francis. There was despair in his voice, as if the morning's events were conspiring against him. 'Can you arrange it?'

Francis nodded. 'Leave it to me, sir,' he said. 'I will find a way.'

Chapter 25

The students of Christ Church Anatomy School sat in silent respect on banked rows watching their tutor. As parishioners look to their priest during their act of worship, so did they regard Professor Hans Hascher. He now stood poised before them, no chalice but a knife in hand, like some hierophant about to perform the most invasive of rituals.

Entering almost unnoticed through the side door, Dr. Thomas Silkstone and Francis Crick took their places on the second row of the lecture theater.

The naked body of an elderly man lay on the table in the center. A sheet covered his nether regions. The grisly-haired professor paused for a moment, as if making some silent prayer, then brought his knife down, slicing a neat line into the lower abdomen.

'My purpose today, gentlemen, is to show you ze viscera contained within ze lower abdomen,' he said, still cutting through the silver-gray flesh of the corpse. He paused for a moment and looked up at his audience. 'Pray, can anyone tell me what I might find?'

Two or three reluctant hands went into the air as the professor scanned the rows of students. Thomas knew he would be spotted. He had hoped to catch the old anatomist before the resumption of the afternoon session of the inquest. There were tests he needed to carry out in his laboratory. Now that he knew the professor was engaged in teaching, such investigations would be out of the question until the evening.

Thomas could see his elderly friend was in his element. There was a sense of theater in his gestures and his words. 'What secrets lurk in zis abdomen, gentlemen?' He asked the question as much of himself as of his feeble-minded students. To him the human body was a cavern full of mysterious chemistries and inexplicable rituals, of turgid organs housed in damp, hot places.

Pointing out with boyish glee the bulwarks of the liver and spleen and the shriveled pouch of the stomach, it was a full five minutes before he finally noticed Thomas, who now braced himself for recognition.

'Dr. Silkstone!' exclaimed Hascher in surprise. 'But what brings you here?' He set down his scalpel, as all eyes now fixed on Thomas. Turning his back on his students the professor took the young doctor aside. 'You should be resting,' he scolded.

Thomas felt duly humbled and acknowledged his friend was right, but explained that he needed the use of his laboratory to conduct more tests that afternoon.

'On one condition,' replied the old professor, with a glint in his eye.

Thomas nodded. 'Of course, Professor.'

'Zat you show zese young men how ze abdomen should be dissected.'

The old Saxon had raised his voice, so that the entire auditorium had heard the request. He

178

made it impossible for Thomas to refuse.

'Please join me.' The old man motioned excitedly, beckoning Thomas to follow him onto the floor. The young doctor smiled awkwardly at Francis as all eyes turned on him and he descended the steep steps of the auditorium.

'May I introduce to you gentlemen one of the finest anatomists alive today, Dr. Thomas Silkstone,' gushed Professor Hascher.

'You flatter me, sir,' replied Thomas, feeling the color rise in his cheeks.

'Not at all,' enthused Professor Hascher and, as if to inadvertently compound Thomas's embarrassment, he handed him his surgeon's knife.

'Pray continue. Show us how a master practitioner performs such a complicated task.' The old man meant well, thought Thomas, but dissecting a cadaver for teaching purposes had not been a priority for him when he had entered the college. Nevertheless, he accepted the knife with good grace and, after a short pause to compose his thoughts, he continued making the deep incision.

Once he had finished cutting, he folded the large flap of skin back so that it lay like a square of crimson silk on the dead man's chest.

'Now, gentlemen, we can see the full viscera exposed,' Thomas announced. There was the liver, dark and majestic, while above could be seen the loops of the bowel. In a slow and precise accent that most students could not quite pinpoint, Dr. Thomas Silkstone guided his spectators through the internal workings of the lower abdomen. Inserting his hand into the body cavity, he felt the

179

lower intestines slide against his hand like indolent snakes. He explained to the students the mysteries of the spleen, the tracery of tubules and ducts worthy of a glassblower, and the eccentricities of the peritoneum.

As his explorations progressed, he was reminded of the last time he had probed the body of a dead man. He recalled Lord Crick's putrefying body, the stench, the flies. This was altogether a better specimen, he thought to himself, although he could see no obvious cause of death.

When his gruesome tour came to an end twenty minutes later, the spellbound students rose to their feet and applauded this new and exciting lecturer, who had made the cadaver on the table in front of him come alive to the sound of his voice and the touch of his hands as they explored its inner geographies.

'You are a true artist,' complimented Professor Hascher, as Thomas washed in the ewer provided.

'I prefer to think of myself as a scientist,' smiled the young doctor.

'But is zere not art in science?' chided the professor.

Thomas knew this question was more rhetorical than real and he brushed it off politely, not wishing to enter into a philosophical discussion. What interested him more were the viscera he had just dissected.

'Professor, I could see no evidence of a cause of death,' he said, glancing at the corpse.

'Indeed not. Ze fellow suffered an infected leg wound that caused blood poisoning,' replied Hascher. 'We shall amputate it zis afternoon.'

'I am sorry I will not be able to watch,' said Thomas.

The professor nodded. 'Ah, ze inquest,' he said, as if he had forgotten the very reason for Thomas's visit. 'My laboratory is at your disposal,' smiled the old man, scratching his gray head. 'You must get to the bottom of zis terrible mystery.'

Thomas took an instant dislike to the pompous prig who now took the witness stand in court. Dr. Felix Fairweather was the very epitome of everything that he hated about the medical profession. As an inadequately drained abscess discharges pus, so superciliousness seeped from every pore of this affected little man who was called to attend the young earl at Boughton Hall on that fateful morning.

'On examination I found him to have been dead for a short while,' he pronounced. His tongue, thought Thomas, was clearly too big for his mouth, and he slobbered as he delivered certain vowels.

'And can you tell us how Lord Crick appeared?' asked the coroner. Thomas knew that this was crucial.

Dr. Fairweather thought for a moment. 'His face was contorted, as if he had died in considerable discomfort.'

When pressed if he noticed any other unusual features by Sir Theodisius, the little man paused thoughtfully. 'I believe his skin was slightly yellow in color,' he reflected. 'But I put this down to his "usual" problem,' he said rather coyly.

The coroner nodded. 'Thank you. That is all for

the moment,' he said, dismissing the doctor.

Next came the turn of Jacob Lovelock to take the stand. He had greeted Lord Crick after his ride that morning.

'And was his lordship in good spirits?' asked Sir Theodisius.

'As good as ever they were,' replied Lovelock in a taciturn fashion.

'Had he been complaining of any ailments or agues to you?'

The servant paused. ''Course there'd been the sickness the week before.'

Sir Theodisius and Thomas leaned forward, almost in unison, to listen.

'Pray tell us about this sickness, Mr. Lovelock,' urged the coroner.

The servant shrugged his broad shoulders. 'The week before, it were,' he recalled. 'On the Friday. His lordship took to his bed, holding his belly.'

'And he vomited?' asked the coroner.

Lovelock frowned. 'If you mean did he spew his guts out, he did, Your Honor,' he replied, much to the amusement of the gallery.

'And how long was your master stricken with this sickness?' pressed the coroner.

The servant thought for a moment. 'For a day or two.'

'After which he seemed restored?'

'I know he stayed out the next night,' Lovelock replied, amusing the crowd yet again.

The gavel was brought down once more, but if Sir Theodisius ever imagined he could restore order to his courtroom, he was sorely mistaken, especially when he put his next question to the witness that was so necessary in light of his wife's evidence.

'Was rat poison kept on the premises?' he quizzed.

An excited murmur rippled around the gallery. Lovelock looked up nervously at the eager faces.

'That it was, sir.'

A gasp came from the crowd, even though it was perfectly normal to keep rat poison on an estate.

'Where was it kept?' asked Sir Theodisius.

'In jars in the glasshouse.'

'And from whence did this poison come?'

Lovelock paused and glanced anxiously toward Farrell. 'We made it ourselves,' he replied softly.

'And how did you make it?'

'Out of laurel cherries, sir. We made laurel water in a still.'

At this revelation the whole gallery erupted once more.

Thomas looked at the faces in the raucous crowd. For them it was now so blindingly obvious. The nobleman had died of rat poisoning. Someone had slipped it into his medicaments. There was a wonderful simplicity about the case. The reality, he knew, was not so straightforward, and there were those on the jury who would rather follow a soothsayer than a surgeon. He trusted Sir Theodisius could not be counted in that number and would steer them away from that course.

The coroner called for order once more. 'Was there a great problem with rats?'

'No more than anywhere else,' replied Lovelock with a shrug of his shoulders. 'But Captain Farrell thought 'twould be a good idea to have a retort so we could make our own poison.'

'And where is this retort, pray?' asked Sir Theodisius.

Lovelock paused for a moment and looked at the captain, who simply stared straight ahead. Any trace of the smile that often played so arrogantly on his lips had disappeared.

''Tis gone, sir,' he muttered.

'Speak up, man. Where is it?'

''Tis gone. Destroyed, sir.'

'Destroyed?' repeated the coroner. 'On whose orders?'

'On the captain's orders, sir.'

A noose was being placed around Michael Farrell's neck, thought Thomas, as many in the crowd leapt to their feet once more. With fists clenched they started shouting at the captain, who sat impassively below.

'Order. Order!' shouted Sir Theodisius several times, his face growing red with the exertion.

This inquest was beginning to show the hallmarks of summary justice. Sir Theodisius, too, perceived those in the gallery were baying for blood. He looked at the timepiece on the far wall of the courtroom. It was approaching five o'clock and the coroner felt it was high time to adjourn. Not only was there a danger of the hearing degenerating into a fracas, but he had also heard his stomach begin to rumble and decided he was in need of sustenance.

'The court will reconvene at ten o'clock on the morrow,' he pronounced before adjourning the highly charged session. Thomas breathed a sigh of relief.

The Saxon professor bent over the specimen and sniffed it eagerly as a grisly-haired wolfhound would a piece of meat.

'No distinctive smell,' he concluded, straightening his permanently arched back as best he could. 'No discoloration.'

Thomas nodded. 'We can safely rule out cyanide, can we not?'

'Zere is no question,' affirmed Hascher, his scalpel in his hand.

The two men stood in silence, staring at the curved, flaccid stomach that had once been housed inside a living, breathing being. Less than a month ago it was slung between the great bulwarks of the liver and spleen, its mouth open, receiving food like some great hairless beast within the abdomen. Now it lay motionless and unyielding, storing secrets within its voluminous antrum that it was so reluctant to reveal.

The old anatomist prodded the lumbering organ once more. It was badly decomposed, and gastric and hydrochloric acids had devoured much of its lining, but to the trained eye, there seemed nothing unusual about the inner machinations of this most workmanlike of organs. 'Zere is no evidence of poisoning,' concluded the professor, giving the specimen a final, slightly contemptuous jab.

Thomas suddenly looked at him. 'No evidence,' he repeated. Those were the precise words that he himself had used earlier on in the day when he had dissected the viscera of the corpse in front of the students. It suddenly occurred to him that whereas the dead man's abdomen was perfectly healthy, he would only have discovered the cause of death had he opened up his diseased leg.

'Perhaps,' he mused, 'we are looking at the wrong organ. Maybe our attentions should be diverted to another part of the anatomy.'

The professor nodded his gray head in slow agreement. 'So, you are saying zat different poisons may affect different organs?'

'Precisely,' said Thomas, his face suddenly animated. 'I have to return to London as soon as possible,' he told the professor and he began lifting the stomach sample back into its jar. 'Perhaps I have been looking in the wrong place.'

The Saxon scratched his head. 'But surely it is too late to look anywhere else?'

'That's where you are wrong, Professor,' smiled Thomas. 'When I was performing the post-mortem, I had to work fast. There was no time to examine the heart, so I cut it out.'

'You have ze heart?' gasped Hascher.

Thomas nodded triumphantly. 'It is preserved in my laboratory. I was so busy testing the stomach for poisons, I did not think to look at it.'

The professor clasped his hands in glee. 'Zis is indeed positive news.' He nodded.

'It is too early to say until I can start work, but yes, the heart could hold the key,' replied Thomas, fastening the lid of the specimen receptacle.

Before returning to London, however, Thomas knew he would be called as an expert witness first thing the next morning. He would have to try and convince Sir Theodisius that cyanide, the lethal ingredient in laurel water, had not killed

186

the young earl and that it may well have been some other poison. Yet there was no proof and without hard evidence it was so easy and natural to conclude that the young nobleman had been killed by cyanide.

Thomas was just about to ask Professor Hascher if he could have the use of his library to research the effects of various poisons on the heart, when there came a knock at the tutor's door.

Lady Lydia Farrell stood framed in the doorway. Behind her, dwarfing her tiny body, was Francis Crick. It was the professor who answered the door. Thomas was washing his hands at the far end of the room and turned to see his visitors.

'Your ladyship. Crick,' he called out. Drying his hands on a towel, he strode over to greet both visitors. He held the young woman's gaze for perhaps a moment longer than was seemly, then took her gloved hand and kissed it.

'I am grateful for your coming,' he told her. 'Please,' he said, ushering the visitors into the cavernous room.

As Thomas pulled up a chair, Francis approached him. 'The captain dines with a friend,' he whispered. Thomas nodded before setting down a stool next to Lydia.

The young woman was clearly ill at ease. She sat, straight backed, on the edge of a chair, her pale face without expression. Francis sat next to her. The professor had extinguished the candles at the other end of the room where he and Thomas had been working and the only light came from a candelabrum on a nearby table.

'It is good to see you restored, Dr. Silkstone,'

she said awkwardly, aware that her cousin was watching her.

Thomas nodded. 'I appreciate your coming, your ladyship, and I thought it right that I should tell you in person the results of the experiments I conducted on the poison you so judiciously sent me.'

Lydia looked nervous and corpse pale. She was aware that her actions would have met with complete disapproval from her husband. She was also painfully aware that her maid's evidence had cast doubt on the captain's integrity.

'Go on,' she urged.

Thomas took a deep breath. ''Twas not rat poison that killed your brother,' he said.

Lydia's eyes widened. She nodded slowly, then looked directly at Thomas.

'If 'twas not the rat poison, then do you know...?' Her soft voice trailed off like ether into the air.

Thomas shook his head. 'I am afraid not,' he said hesitantly.

'But you know something?' She frowned, wrinkling her flawless brow. 'You must tell me, sir,' she pleaded.

Thomas felt his stomach tense as he had so many times before when he had to break the news of the death of one of his patients to a loved one. It was never easy. But this time the words seemed to stick in his gullet like sharp blades, so afraid was he of wounding this fragile creature who sat so vulnerable before him.

'I now firmly believe,' he started, 'that your brother did not die of natural causes.' He paused to allow the enormity of this statement to sink in. He watched the young woman as her eyelids momentarily flickered, like a moth near a flame. Yet from the look on her delicate face, it seemed that such a conclusion came as little surprise to her.

'This is what I shall be telling the inquest tomorrow, but I wanted you to hear it from me first, your ladyship.'

The young woman nodded slowly. In the candle glow, Thomas could see that her large eyes glistened with moisture, yet her lips did not quiver, and he was thankful to be spared the sight of her tears. It was Francis who turned to comfort her, putting a hand on her shoulder in a gesture that was so natural and effortless that, for the first time in his life, Thomas experienced a sensation that had been hitherto utterly foreign to him – that of jealousy.

In the upper room of an inn not half a mile away, two men sat drinking in a sombre mood. Between them was a table covered with the detritus of an evening meal: a half-eaten game pie, a dish of cabbage, and the remains of a stale loaf. Taking pride of place, as the centerpiece of the table, stood a decanter half full of brandy, but the amber liquid that so often soothed Michael Farrell's tension did not seem to be working its magic that evening. The captain downed another shot, but felt no better.

James Lavington sat opposite him, the disfigured side of his face hidden in the deep shadow cast by the candle on the table. He had never seen his friend so troubled. There had been many a time at the gaming tables when he had stood to lose his whole fortune and yet he had still smiled and held his nerve until the final die had been cast or the last card revealed.

Lavington, too, was feeling agitated. The day's events had unfolded in an unexpected and dramatic fashion that not even he, the greatest of pessimists, could have envisaged. The two men had hardly spoken over dinner, so engrossed were they in their own machinations and recriminations. Hannah's words played themselves over and over in both their minds. Her outburst had thrown up more questions than answers and her testimony had been more malevolent than helpful. Her husband's evidence, too, had poured oil on the flames and the heat was growing too intense for comfort.

What Lavington feared most was that his carefully laid plans were unraveling slowly but surely in front of his very eyes. It had seemed such a simple, straightforward scheme: a comfortable living far away that would have cut the ties to Boughton Hall and to Farrell. It would have harmed no one, save for the profligate little scoundrel, who now lay dead, and he had never once visited the Irish estate anyway. He could have made a new life, independent of Farrell's charity and favors. Ensconced in his country pile, sheltered from the prying eyes of common villagers and curious ladies, he could have found the peace that he so craved. Yet now it was all in jeopardy and not only that, but because of his association with the Irishman, so was his own integrity.

Between the men on the cloth-covered table lay a wooden bowl piled high with apples, hard-skinned pears, and crimson plums. A sharp knife rested nearby and Farrell picked it up, calmly inspecting the blade in the candle glow, then suddenly he lunged at an apple, stabbing it with such ferocity that Lavington felt alarmed. He knew that the shiny pink skin that had been so viciously pierced could well have been Hannah's breast in the captain's mind's eye and it made him wonder.

'So, this is how the whore would repay my kindness,' cursed Farrell under his breath, inspecting the apple that now lay impaled on the end of the blade.

'You will have your say in the stand on the morrow,' ventured Lavington, trying to ease his companion's agitation.

Farrell remained thoughtful for a moment, then his expression suddenly changed from a scowl of anger to a broad smile. 'You're right, dear Lavington,' he replied, then, taking a large bite out of the apple he still held on his knife, he quipped: 'I'll have them eating out of my hands.'

Chapter 26

The brain, mused Dr. Thomas Silkstone, as he lay listlessly in his bed, is the most complex of all the organs. From the gray, spongy marsh of the inner cerebral cortex to the fields of tubules and cobweb threads of the cerebrum, from the undulating hills of the cerebellum to the boggy lowlands of the hypothalamus, the trails and routes of the brain were charted territories inasmuch as explorer surgeons had traversed their silent landscapes many times.

Through trial and error, by scaling rocky outcrops and probing deep canyons, they had managed to ascertain that certain regions were responsible for certain functions. Their voyage of discovery was by no means ended, although they had managed to gather much invaluable information on their eventful journey. And yet, thought Thomas, no one had come near to finding the seat of the soul.

By soul, he meant not the nebulous religious concept that could bring a man closer to God in its purest state, but the very essence of a being. To him the soul was the seat of all memories, of all ideas, of all thoughts that crystalize into the character of a man and make him who he is. Somehow these thoughts were as clay, taken and molded, or hewn and sculpted with all the skill of Michelangelo and turned miraculously into the unique character and personality of the individual.

And what of feelings? What of sensations? Of inklings and forebodings? Of nagging illogicalities and inexplicable premonitions? Were they generated from the realm of the spirit or the brain? Were the questions and musings that kept darting around in his brain emitting from his cerebrum or his soul?

As soon as a pale finger of weak autumn sunlight probed its way into his room at the White

Horse the young American rose without delay. His brain, or rather the workings of it, had done him a great disservice throughout most of the night, depriving him of sleep and causing him to experience a state of acute anxiety. He had often seen such symptoms in his patients: muscle tension, sweaty palms, and a dry mouth. It did not help that his swollen jaw was still causing him a great deal of discomfort and his head still throbbed with every heartbeat.

When his patients presented themselves to him with such problems, he could do little but advise rest and a gill of brandy, although he had recently read of the restorative powers of *Digitalis purpurea* in a monograph by a doctor from somewhere in the north. He postulated that the common purple foxglove could exercise a power over the motion of the heart, which in turn would lead to a relaxation of the patient's anxiety. Thomas had yet to try this claim out on a patient, but intended to do so shortly. In the meantime, however, he must prepare himself for the day's events.

At precisely ten o'clock he found himself once more exposed to the ignorant taunts and ill-conceived jibes of the cinder sifters and coster-mongers of Oxford. They had heard him speak the previous day in court and word had spread that he was a colonist, even though his accent was virtually undetectable.

Thomas sat behind a long table at the front of the court. From the corner of his right eye he could see Captain Farrell and Lady Lydia. The latter sat composed as ever, with a yellow, lace-trimmed cape around her diminutive shoulders, but he dared not look at her for fear of incurring her husband's displeasure. He judged that she would not have imparted to him the news that rat poison was not the cause of her brother's death. Had she done so, her clandestine meeting with him at Christ Church would have been exposed. She would, he surmised, be content to let him formally reveal the results of his experiments from the authoritative platform of the witness stand.

A respectful hush settled on the rabble in the gallery as soon as Sir Theodisius appeared, the yolky remnants of the morning's breakfast clearly visible on his black robe. As soon as the coroner had settled his corpulent frame into his chair, the clerk called Thomas to the stand.

Diligently the anatomist explained how he had been summoned to Boughton Hall to conduct a postmortem on Lord Crick, who had been dead for more than six days. Sparing the sensibilities of the ladies present in the courtroom, although admittedly they were few and far between, he described how he had found the corpse in an advanced state of decomposition and how he had worked as quickly as possible, removing any relevant organs for later examination.

Thomas delivered his findings with clarity and conviction. Aware that many of the terms he used would be unfamiliar to Sir Theodisius, let alone his audience, he carefully explained each causality, each result, each influence and product with the patience of a benign pedagogue, as Gamaliel to Saul.

When it came to explaining his experiments regarding the sample of rat poison that Lady Lydia had sent him without the captain's knowledge or approval, Thomas knew he was treading on delicate ground, however. He decided to try and brush over how he came by the phial, but Sir Theodisius was as sharp as a needle.

'Pray, how did this poison come into your possession, if as we heard, the still was destroyed very soon after Lord Crick's demise?' pressed the coroner.

Thomas felt a knot in his stomach. He dared not look at Lady Lydia. 'I am a scientist, sir,' he replied, keeping his gaze firmly on the table ahead. 'It is my duty to examine all possibilities; to probe into all eventualities,' he went on somewhat enigmatically.

Sir Theodisius raised an eyebrow. 'Indeed, and I can see you are doing an excellent job,' replied the coroner reassuringly.

During most of his testimony, the gallery had been silent, unable to comprehend even the basic tenets of Thomas's scientific proposition. After ten minutes or so, one or two even dared to shout to him to 'get on with it,' or to 'speak plain,' much to Sir Theodisius's displeasure. He had ordered them out of the gallery and allowed Thomas to proceed. He did so for another five minutes, unfazed by the rude interruptions, and then finally drew to his conclusion.

'In summary, sir, I would say that after examining the deceased's stomach, I can categorically say that the rat poison, otherwise known as laurel water, was not responsible for the death of Lord Crick.'

The coroner sat back in his chair, looking singularly unimpressed. 'That is all very well, Dr. Silkstone,' he mused, 'but can you say what did cause Lord Crick's death?'

Thomas frowned. He had not expected such a response. He found himself tensing involuntarily. Once more he felt a knot in his stomach. 'I am afraid I cannot, sir,' he replied, crestfallen.

Sir Theodisius, without any seeming regard for the young doctor's feelings, raised his eyes heavenward, in full view of the throng. It caused much amusement among the painted faces and ragged breeches and Thomas felt momentarily humiliated. He looked toward Lydia, as if trying to gain strength from her.

Instead it was Farrell who caught his eye. The captain, who had been sitting quietly throughout Thomas's evidence, gestured his contempt and mouthed his exasperation into the stale air of the courtroom. Lydia held his flailing arm, trying to quieten him. She glanced toward Thomas and held his gaze and he knew then that it was she who needed his support.

'Order! Order!' cried Sir Theodisius for the third time that morning. The fracas died down once more.

'Then, if there is no more you wish to say, Dr. Silkstone,' said Sir Theodisius, about to dismiss Thomas.

'But there is, sir,' countered the young anatomist.

The coroner acceded. 'Yes, Dr. Silkstone.'

The court was now quiet, eagerly anticipating Thomas's next statement, hoping that he would totally discredit himself and his untrustworthy profession. They were disappointed.

'When I said I had not ascertained Lord Crick's cause of death, I neglected to say *so far*, sir.' There was a certain defiance in his tone. 'I do, however, have every confidence that I will be able to present the court with conclusive evidence as to how the young man died.'

Sir Theodisius nodded. 'And when may we look forward to that evidence, Dr. Silkstone?' he asked.

'I need to return to my own laboratory in London to complete more experiments, but I would hope within two weeks,' Thomas replied, knowing full well that such tests would, in all probability, take at least a month.

The coroner paused. 'Very well, Dr. Silkstone. The court notes your offer,' he said, nodding to the clerk, his quill poised over the record book, 'and looks forward to hearing a further report.'

Relieved, Thomas allowed himself a fleeting smile as he stepped down from the witness stand and walked back to his seat. He glanced across at Lady Lydia. For an instant their eyes met. He knew he could not let her down.

Back at Boughton Hall, young Will Lovelock had been tasked to go about his daily chores as if all were normal. His parents had stayed the night in a boardinghouse in Oxford, at Captain Farrell's expense, but had ordered their son to fulfill his duties the same as ever he did, as well as doing some of his mother's.

At first light he had risen and filled a whisket with kindling for the fires. Mistress Firebrace, the housekeeper, had told him to first lay one in the kitchen, then in the drawing room, even though the house was empty. Naturally he did not question her orders, but went about his business, first laying the kindling, then setting on the larger logs before lighting the taper and watching the flames take hold in the grates.

When he was certain no one would enter the room for a while, he sat back on his haunches as the warmth from the fire grew, holding out his scabby hands. Some of the sore places were still raw and moist but his mother's fragrant unguent had soothed the itching so that he did not scratch as much now. In the heat of the summer, or at night under the coverlet, the itching would be at its worst, like so many ants gnawing away at his broken flesh. Sometimes he had cried out in pain and when the patches of scaly skin spread to the backs of his knees, he thought he would scream with the fire of them. There were times when he felt the torments of demons as they prodded him and burned his skin. And when his mother tried to hold him to comfort him, he would push her away, not because he did not want her tenderness but because he could not bear her touch.

Will's suffering continued for many weeks until one day, it was early spring as he recalled, he and his mother and Rebecca were on the road to Brandwick to buy thread. The first shoots were appearing fresh and green and the scent of lily-of-the-valley hung sweet in the air. It was then that they met her – an old didicoy, making her way out of the village. Her skin was nut brown and as lined as a hornbeam and when she spoke Will could see

198

no teeth in her head. His mother had told them about Gypsy folk; how if they were to see one on the road, they should run away as fast as they could. But instead of ignoring the old crone, Hannah returned her greeting and stopped to talk. Will was all for ignoring her, but Rebecca chastised him and said the old woman would only put a curse on him if he should bolt. He was still too afraid to listen to their conversation, however, and stayed a few paces away, so that he could run if the old witch suddenly began ranting. Neither his mother, nor Rebecca, seemed in the least bit concerned. The Gypsy showed them something in the whisket she was carrying and then, to Will's dismay, his mother summoned him to her side. Gingerly he walked over to the women and, at his mother's bidding, he held out his hands to be inspected by the Gypsy.

The didicoy nodded. 'Yes,' she spat through smooth, pink gums, 'this should ease it.' And so Will's mother parted with half a penny and came away with a small hessian bag.

On their return home Hannah and Rebecca had begun to gather herbs from the potager and pick wildflowers from the meadows. In her pestle his mother ground them with her mortar, releasing strange, pungent, unfamiliar smells. Some leaves she seeped in viscous oil, others in spirit that made his eyes sting. To these ingredients she added the contents of the little hessian bag.

Shortly afterward she came to him in his suffering and smeared his suppurating flesh with a balm so cool and soothing that it would have quenched the fires of hell. She rubbed it lovingly onto his bleeding wrists and the backs of his hands and smeared it into the crevices between his fingers, bringing him a relief so instant that it might have been a miracle from heaven.

His mother had made a large bowl of the balm and Rebecca spooned it into a jar, so that when the fire flared up again, his torments might be eased quickly. He could still see his sister, standing at the kitchen table, carefully ladling the brown mixture, then looking up and smiling at him.

Now that the wounds were healing, he could once more relish the warmth of an open fire on a chill autumn morning and he thanked his mother for her ointment and he thanked God for giving her such healing powers. But nothing would bring back Rebecca.

It was Mistress Claddingbowl who broke his reverie. 'Will ... Will,' she called. 'You good-for-nothing...' She opened the drawing room door to find him clearing up the last of the kindling from the hearth.

'You should've finished that by now,' she scolded. 'I need some apples from the store. Go fetch me a good dozen cookers for a pie,' she ordered, wiping her plump fingers on her stained apron. This was another task his mother usually fulfilled, but he did not mind. He liked the sweet liquor smell of the apple store that reminded him of his father's cider.

Will rose immediately, nodded an acknowledgment, then, taking the same whisket that had held the kindling, he made his way to the store that lay off the courtyard. Dust motes danced in the autumn sunlight as he opened the door.

Inside it was dark and it smelled sickly sweet with the fragrance of the fruit.

The cooking apples lay in a barrel at the back. Large, waxy, and bright green, many of the late picked ones had brown spots, but in the half light it was impossible to see which were good and which were not without taking each one out of the barrel and inspecting it at the door.

Delving deep, Will heard the apples tumble about, rumbling like a drum. He pulled one out, held it to the light, and judged it passable. There followed another and another until his basket was almost full. Once again he plunged his hand in, this time much deeper, so that his hips hung over the neck of the barrel and his toes were on their tips. It was then that he heard it: a foreign, clanking sound against the iron frame of the cask. He felt once more. There it was again, an alien presence among the overripe mush of fruit at the bottom. His enquiring hands explored even deeper, probing to the very floor of the barrel, then, fanning his fingers out, he felt something hard and cold and angular. It was most definitely not an apple.

Chapter 27

Jeers and catcalls rang out in the courtroom as Captain Michael Farrell took the stand to give evidence at the inquest of his late, and not much lamented, brother-in-law. The rabble had already made up their minds, casting him as the villain of the piece, branding him a murderer before a verdict on the cause of death had even been reached.

Yet as Sir Theodisius once more called for 'order,' Michael Farrell's disarming smile was having more effect in quieting the common horde than any blows of the coroner's gavel. He wore the expression of a gentleman on a Sunday picnic, such was the ease and nonchalance of his demeanor, and he was dressed to match his mood. A lavender-colored topcoat, cream silk breeches, and a pink brocade waistcoat gave him an air of fashionable sophistication that was quite out of place in a courtroom. Yet he seemed not in the least bit concerned that his appearance caused Sir Theodisius to raise an eyebrow.

The catcalls had soon turned to wolf whistles as the gallery mocked the captain en masse, but not a hair on Farrell's immaculately groomed and powdered wig turned. He simply surveyed his audience and curled his mouth in a curiously wry smile.

Under examination Sir Theodisius asked the captain to describe exactly what had happened on that fateful day and Farrell had obliged, speaking calmly and clearly. He neither refused to answer any question that was put to him nor failed to elucidate when the coroner deemed it necessary.

'In what state did you find Lord Crick?'

'He was moaning and flailing about.'

'Did you try to help in any way?'

'I feared there was nothing I could do. My brother-in-law was clearly in terrible distress, so

I immediately sent for Dr. Fairweather.'

'Did you have any idea what might have caused this terrible spasm?'

'I cannot be certain, sir, but my brother-in-law was not a well man. His blood was a mass of mercury and corruption and his intellects were very much affected,' replied the captain.

'Are you saying Lord Crick was mad, Captain Farrell?' pressed Sir Theodisius.

'I am saying, sir, that at first I thought his distemper was down to the pox. I had no inkling that it might have been the contents of his physick bottle that did for him. That is why I asked Hannah to clear up afterward. Had I known there were any suspicions surrounding the medication, I would naturally have seen to it that the bottle be salvaged.'

The coroner nodded sympathetically. The captain's evidence seemed perfectly logical. 'I see,' said Sir Theodisius and noted something down on a sheaf of paper before him. 'And pray tell me, have you any idea what happened to this bottle?'

Farrell shook his head. 'I thought nothing of it, sir. I do not know what became of it. I believe Mistress Lovelock is the one you must ask, sir.'

'I do not need you to tell me my job,' countered Sir Theodisius, clearly irritated by what he regarded as the captain's impertinence. He stroked his flaccid jowls for a moment. 'One more thing, Captain Farrell. Can you tell me why you ordered the destruction of the still in which the laurel water was made?'

Shouts went up from the gallery. 'Yes, you scoundrel. Tell us,' they called, shaking fists and biting their thumbs at him.

The Irishman paused for a moment, smiled disarmingly, and said: 'Why sir, yes. As soon as my dear wife,' he motioned to Lydia, who sat close by, 'told me of the upsetting rumors circulating among the servants that her brother may have taken poison in his medicine, she told me she wanted nothing to do with the retort.'

There was a murmuring in the gallery. Lydia looked uncomfortable.

'So, it was *she* who asked you to destroy it?' pressed Sir Theodisius.

The captain nodded. 'Indeed, yes, sir. I tried to persuade her that it would not be a good idea, but the very sight of it so vexed her that I thought it best to obey her wishes.' He looked pointedly at Lydia, as if reaffirming his devotion to her.

The coroner gave out an audible sigh. 'I see, Captain Farrell. That will be all.'

The Irishman walked back to his seat with the air of a man who was quietly confident. He sat down once more next to Lydia and gave her a smile. It was not returned.

'This court calls Hannah Lovelock,' announced the clerk. The servant had not been expecting another appearance in the witness stand. She rose, but seemed unsteady on her feet. Jacob helped her walk the few paces to the box.

Sir Theodisius noted her pained demeanor. It was clear to him that the whole hearing had been an ordeal for the poor woman and he apologized for recalling her. 'However,' he continued, 'I feel it is imperative to ask you what became of the bottle of physick after Lord Crick's body was removed from the room.'

Hannah's bowed head now lifted and her gaze met the coroner's. 'It broke, sir,' she said, her voice cracking. 'I was in such a state that, when I went to put it in the cupboard, I dropped it and it shattered on the floor.' With these words she broke down, sobbing silently, her shoulders heaving rhythmically, and Sir Theodisius felt he had no choice but to let her step down. The clerk escorted her back to her seat against a backdrop of shouts and jeers from the gallery, whose sympathies lay fairly and squarely with the poor maid who was so fearful of her master.

Sir Theodisius looked at the clock on the wall. It was nearly noon and high time, he felt, to draw proceedings to an end, not least because his empty stomach was making a tumultuous protest. As coroner it was his duty to decide how the deceased had died, not to occasion blame. He had strong suspicions that the young braggart had been poisoned, but in the absence of hard evidence, it was difficult to be categorical. As to the possible perpetrator of any crime that may or may not have been committed, it was neither his duty nor his wish to point the finger unless he had very strong grounds to do so. He would go away and consider his verdict over a jowl of salmon and a brace of stewed carp. Such sustenance, he told himself, would undoubtedly sharpen his wits.

Thus, Sir Theodisius was just about to adjourn for luncheon when the clerk approached, looking very agitated, with a note in his hand. Taking the piece of parchment, the coroner unfurled it and saw it contained a painstakingly written message,

205

executed in an ill-educated hand. Its author was one Eliza Appleton, Lady Lydia's maidservant. She was requesting to be called to give evidence. She had, she wrote, 'a burning memory of something said before his lordship's passing.'

The coroner had little choice. Intrigued, he summoned the young woman to take the stand. All eyes immediately focused on the voluptuous maid, who looked uncharacteristically demure. There was no sign of her cleavage and her pert breasts were covered by a dark shawl. She wore no rouge, and her hair was tucked under a neat lace cap.

'Your name,' instructed the clerk.

'Eliza Anna Appleton,' came the soft reply. 'I be Lady Lydia's maid.'

'And what is it that you wish to tell this inquest, pray?' Sir Theodisius was gentle with her, aware that she was frightened and intimidated.

The young girl straightened her back and cleared her throat. ''Tis something I 'eard, sir,' she replied.

'Well?' coaxed the coroner.

''Twas on the morning, sir, before 'is lordship ... before 'e...' Unable to bring herself to say the words, her voice trailed.

'On the morning of Lord Crick's death, yes, girl,' urged Sir Theodisius, whose patience was wearing thin.

'Lady Lydia told me to fetch 'er shawl, which she 'ad left at the breakfast table,' began the maid. 'So I went down to get it and I sees Lord Crick and the captain in the breakfast room.' She paused and turned toward the coroner, as if shying away from Farrell's gaze.

'Well?' urged the coroner once more.

'Then I sees the master is going out.' She paused once more.

'And...' Sir Theodisius cajoled.

'And the captain says to him: "Do not forget the apothecary is coming ... we would hate you to forget your medication."'

With these last words a wave of indignation swept across the courtroom, followed by the swell of a murmur.

Once more the coroner had to call for order. It was not his job to apportion blame, he told himself, but so many fingers of suspicion were pointing at the same person that he would be failing in his duty if he ignored them. He had reached his verdict a while back and would direct the jury accordingly. He felt no compulsion to wait for Dr. Silkstone and his high-falutin tests. The evidence was overwhelming: 'unlawful killing' would be the outcome and the perpetrator of that killing was plain for all to see.

Michael Farrell came late to the marital bed that night. Lavington had accompanied him and Lydia in the carriage from Oxford and an icy silence had pervaded. When they arrived back at Boughton Hall, the captain asked Lavington to join him for a drink in his study and it was shortly before midnight that he climbed into bed. Lydia had not been able to sleep. She lay on her side, with her back to her husband, her pillow wet with tears. She smelled Farrell's brandy breath and tensed. He reached out his hand and began to stroke her chestnut curls on the pillow. The moment he did so, she felt she could contain her anger no longer. She bolted upright.

'How could you?' she asked incredulously. 'How could you perjure yourself in court?' She looked at him with eyes full of rage. Her expression shocked even her husband for a moment.

'My dearest, I thought you might want to help me. If I had admitted that I ordered the still to be destroyed, I would have looked even guiltier than I do already,' he whispered in his soft Irish brogue.

'But you lied and you used me to protect yourself,' she told him through clenched teeth. Trying to disarm her with charm, he took hold of her hand, but she brushed him away and began to sob once more.

Farrell did not enjoy seeing his wife cry, but it was something she had been doing with relentless regularity over the past few days. He knew that what he had done was morally reprehensible, but his instinct to survive had taken over in the courtroom. Nevertheless he felt chastened by her tears.

'I did not do it, Lydia,' he said softly in the darkness. She could barely hear his words above her sobs, but she stopped crying and turned to face him.

'What did you say?'

'I did not kill Edward,' he told her. 'You do believe me, do you not?'

There was a note of pleading in his voice.

She looked at him and saw the creases in his brow had grown deeper over the past few days. His face was at last showing the strain, but still doubt clouded her mind.

'I cannot be sure, Michael,' she said. 'I really do not know.'

The next thing Lydia knew was that Farrell had risen from the bed and was donning his dressing robe.

'Where are you going?' she asked.

'I cannot share my bed with a woman who thinks I am a murderer.'

She swallowed hard and turned toward him, but she was glad she could not see his face clearly in the darkness, nor he hers. That way he could not detect her tears. She did not try and stop him as he walked out of the room. As soon as the door was shut she slumped back on her pillows. Perhaps she was being too harsh on him. He had a temper and more than once she had been on the receiving end of it, but Edward's murderer was cold and calculating. Whoever was responsible had harbored such deep hatred for her brother that they had thought long and hard about his death and the manner of it. The notion chilled her to the very bone and no matter how closely she wrapped the coverlet around her body it was no substitute for her husband's warmth.

Chapter 28

Like a strange exotic fruit waiting to be sliced, Earl Crick's heart floated in a large glass jar. Suspended in a syrup-colored liquid, it would soon be cut open and its contents revealed. There were those who might have wagered it would be black inside, because of the evil doings of its owner, but Dr. Thomas Silkstone had no such misgivings. All he could hope for would be that this once garrulous, now silent heart would reveal to him the secrets of its master's death.

Lifting the jar, he held the specimen up to the light from the window to examine it more closely. Outwardly it looked quite normal: the size of a clenched fist and with no unusual discoloration or contusions. Carefully he opened the lid and, delving into the jar, slid his hand under the bulbous organ, easing it out gently. He laid it on the cool marble slab before him and pondered for a moment. He was about to enter the red pavilion of the heart, drawing back the vermilion curtains of tissue to reveal this man's inner room; the sanctum where, some believed, his thoughts and emotions reposed. Now, more than ever before, he felt like an intruder, but he needed to find out the truth.

The scalpel sliced through the pericardium as easily as a knife through a ripe peach. The heart divided into two perfect halves. Thomas strained his eyes, inspecting the organ. Reaching for a magnifying glass, he peered at the septum that separates the two sides of the heart, before inspecting each of the four chambers in detail. He could see nothing untoward. It was only when his examination moved to the ventricles and then to the atria that he noticed anything out of the ordinary. The aorta, which carried fresh blood from the heart, seemed to be constricted. It was considerably smaller than he would expect in a healthy adult male.

Next he carefully cut across the pulmonary artery. Again it was much smaller than he anticipated. If, as appeared likely, the earl had been poisoned, then this poison seemed to have had an effect on his circulatory system. What was it that Hannah had said at the inquest? Lord Crick had put his hand up to his chest and begun panting like a dog. It made perfect sense. The young man was clutching his chest because he was experiencing cardiac arrest. No wonder his eyes bulged from their sockets and his breathing became difficult. He was suffering from a constriction of the heart, which affected his oxygen supply. If Thomas could ascertain which poisons might have such an effect on the heart, he could then test for traces of the toxin in the young lord's remains.

Thomas had felt a huge sense of relief to be back in his rooms in London. The courthouse had been an alien environment, hostile and ignorant, but here, surrounded by his beloved books and his precious specimen jars full of gleaming membranes and delicate tissues, he felt as at ease as a fetus in the womb.

Franklin was pleased to see him, too. Mistress Finesilver had locked him in his cage while Thomas was away and the rodent had sat on his haunches and stretched upward as soon as he saw his master. The young doctor had allowed the animal to roam freely around the laboratory all day, talking to him now and again, playfully asking his opinion from time to time.

'We have work to do, Franklin,' smiled Thomas as the rodent climbed onto his desk. 'Much work,' and with that he went over to his book-shelves and started studying the spines. His long surgeon's fingers stroked the leather-bound volumes thoughtfully, passing over such seminal works as Hooke's *Micrographia* and countless volumes of *Nature* until they came across a volume of *Philosophical Transactions of the Royal Society*, something he had often consulted on Dr. Carruthers's recommendation. Next to it was a thick tome entitled *The Poisonous Properties of Botanics in the British Isles*. Thomas took them both out of their shelf and staggered under their collective weight as he walked over to his desk. He was just about to open the first book when a knock came at his door.

'Thomas, will you dine with us tonight?' It was Dr. Carruthers. The men had barely spoken since the American had returned from Oxford the day before, and the young doctor felt obliged to eat with his mentor.

'I am looking forward to it, sir,' he replied.

'I'll wager you missed Mistress Finesilver's pies in Oxford,' chuckled the old doctor. Remembering the paltry fare he had been offered at the White Horse, Thomas had to agree.

Over a hearty slice of game pie, Thomas told Dr. Carruthers of the revelations at the inquest and how Captain Farrell had not fared well in the various testimonies.

'And did he do it?' asked Dr. Carruthers with his usual candor. Thomas's ensuing silence spoke volumes. 'Ah, there is great doubt in your mind,' said the old physician.

'I need to base my conclusions on facts, sir, and

at the moment these are sadly lacking,' replied Thomas.

'But only you can do that, Dr. Silkstone,' countered Carruthers. ''Tis a weighty duty on your shoulders.'

Thomas was all too aware that his experiments on the dead man's organs were the only real hope of providing the key to Lord Crick's mysterious death. An image of Lydia's beautiful face suddenly darted through his consciousness. 'Aye, sir, but it is a duty I must see through,' he replied.

Dr. Carruthers sensed that his protégé was in a black mood. 'But where is my newspaper?' he suddenly said cheerfully, trying to lift Thomas's spirits.

The young doctor glanced over at the writing desk. Mistress Finesilver had laid the copy of *The Daily Advertiser* on the salver as usual and Thomas settled himself into a chair opposite the old doctor to read aloud.

There were the regular tedious proceedings in Parliament and a report on the growing schism between the Anglican Church and Nonconformists. Aside from this, Dr. Carruthers only knew one of the worthies in the Obituaries column and did not rate him very highly. It was only when Thomas turned the final page that his attention was captured. The headline was small, but it sufficed. It read: 'Verdict of Unlawful Killing: Young Lord Was Poisoned.' The account that followed gave a summary version of proceedings in three paragraphs, but it was enough for Thomas. Sir Theodisius had judged that young Edward Crick had been deliberately poisoned, without waiting for the results of Thomas's findings. The ugly word that had hovered on the lips of every gossip in Oxfordshire for the past few weeks could now be proclaimed out loud and that word was 'murder.'

Chapter 29

James Lavington felt himself harden in anticipation of Eliza's arrival. He lay on her iron bed and thought of her creamy thighs and voluptuous breasts and grew urgent and excited. She was late, but he could guess why, and when she finally did arrive, a few minutes later, she was crying. He put his arm around her shoulders as they heaved with emotion.

'Come, sit down,' he urged her gently, leading her to the bed. Her pretty plump cheeks were puckered and red, like a shriveled plum, and he thought she looked quite ugly when she cried. Nonetheless, he forbore.

'She said I was disloyal,' sobbed the maid, looking at Lavington for some reassuring refutation.

'That is unfair,' replied Lavington, easing off Eliza's cap and watching her black hair tumble onto her shoulders. He began stroking her tresses, but the girl pulled away suddenly.

'You said she would thank me for it.' Her tone suddenly became recriminating and Lavington was taken aback by the outburst. Of course he knew that Lydia would be enraged by her maid's revelation in court.

'You were only doing your duty to your mistress,' he insisted.

'I didn't want to say it,' she countered like a petulant child.

She was beginning to irritate Lavington. 'I said I'd pay you for it,' he replied churlishly.

The maid ignored his protest and continued: 'I'm just glad that that little shit is dead and good luck to 'im that did it.' She rose in anger and stormed over to the other end of the room. "E didn't deserve to live. Not after what 'e did to Beccy.' She stopped suddenly as if she had realized she had said something she should not, as if the lock on Pandora's Box had come unfastened and a terrible secret had slipped out.

'Tell me, Eliza,' said Lavington gently. 'Tell me what your master did to Rebecca.' He patted the bed cover and she slowly walked back toward the bed and sat down beside him. Her shoulders heaved as a great sigh came out, as if she knew she would have to divulge a most hideous taboo.

"E had 'er just like 'e 'ad me and all the other servant girls that 'ave worked in this 'ouse,' she blurted, 'whether we wanted it or not.'

It came as no revelation to Lavington that Crick had bedded Eliza, but what surprised even him was that he had violated one so young.

'But Rebecca was...?'

'A child. Twelve years old. But 'twas worse. She found out she was...'

Her voice trailed off and Lavington could tell the rest. He nodded. It was all beginning to make sense now.

'So, her death was no accident.'

'She could not bear the shame,' said Eliza, staring ahead of her with unseeing eyes.

Lavington rose and walked to the window that looked out over the courtyard and to the Lovelocks' accommodation. He suddenly remembered seeing Crick, on the morning of his death, coming out of the door. It was not the first time, either. He had seen him once before, only a few days prior to Rebecca's death. He had thought nothing of it at the time. Edward had once told him it was a master's right to have his servants, whether willing or not, whether male or female. He said it 'made good sport' and Lavington had laughed and downed another brandy. Now, perhaps, that 'sport' had turned into something far more dangerous and sinister.

He turned and saw Eliza prostrate on the bed, facedown, weeping into the coarse blanket. She looked meek and vulnerable. Her disclosures would be vital in finding Lord Crick's killer and that could only be to his advantage. She would tell him more in due course, he knew, but in the meantime, he felt himself harden again and this time he would not be refused.

'Did you deal with the maid?' Michael Farrell's tone was brusque. He had just returned from a long ride, 'to clear his head' so he said, but the fresh air and exercise had obviously done nothing to lift his mood.

Lydia knelt beside him as he sat in his chair and took off his riding boots. 'I reprimanded her,' she replied in a conciliatory tone, but Farrell withdrew his foot straightaway.

'You reprimanded her?' he repeated incredulously. 'I want that whore out of this house by tomorrow.'

Lydia's heart sank. She had feared that her actions would not be sufficiently harsh to please her husband.

'But Eliza has been with me for five years, Michael. 'Tis not right that I should dismiss her without notice.'

Farrell looked exasperated. His Irish charm was ebbing away fast. His skin was gray and there were bags under his green eyes that once twinkled so brightly. 'She virtually accused me of murdering your brother,' he cried, loosening his cravat and flinging it on the floor.

'She was only repeating what she'd heard,' appealed Lydia, but her words made her husband even angrier.

'So, you would defend a servant against your husband, now, would you?' He leapt up and went over to the sideboard to pour himself a brandy.

'Of course not, but you make such...'

'Such what?' He swung 'round, a glass in his hand.

'Such thoughtless comments sometimes. People who do not know you can ... can misconstrue them,' said Lydia, choosing her words carefully.

His wife's words enraged Farrell. He raised his voice. 'You had no business to go against my wishes. Am I not the master of the house now?'

'You are indeed,' Lydia acceded reluctantly, even though it was she who actually inherited the estate, as Edward had died without issue.

'Then you are just as bad as that whore of a

servant of yours. You have been as disloyal as she has and I've a good mind to send you away, too.'

In fact his rantings were so loud that they carried down the stairs and could be heard in the kitchen below. The assembled servants listened to him cursing and railing at his distressed young wife. Such was the distraction, both upstairs and down, that no one heard the horses' hooves thunder along the driveway of Boughton Hall, or the clatter of the wheels of a carriage. Nor did anyone see the procession draw up in front of the main door or hear the riders' crunching dismount on the gravel underfoot.

As it was, the loud banging of the knocker was the first the Irishman, or anyone else in the house, knew that four constables and a reeve had arrived to arrest him for the murder of Edward Crick. Naturally he protested his innocence. Naturally he was reluctant to go with them. Naturally he resisted the chains they put about his wrists. But as Lydia watched the procession leave for Oxford, she was sure of only one thing: that she no longer knew the man she once loved.

Chapter 30

Will Lovelock held the blue bottle in his hand for a moment. With its long neck, stopped by a cork, and its smooth shoulders, it would be, he told himself, by far the best piece in his collection.

A shaft of sunlight beamed through a hole in the

barn roof and he lifted it toward the light to study it more carefully. He noticed there was a small amount of clear liquid left in the bottom. It looked like water, but he decided he would sniff it and see. A strange, pungent odor emanated from inside. It was a smell that seemed strangely familiar to him and yet he could not place it. He was tempted to taste it. He put his finger on top of the neck and was about to tip it up, when he suddenly remembered the fate of the master. Had he not drunk something that disagreed with him? The agonizing cries still rang in Will's ears and collided with his own mother's screams. She had been unable to sleep for days after. Recalling the whole ghastly episode, he was about to push the cork back when he suddenly decided that one drop would do no harm. He tipped up the bottle once more and allowed a little of the liquid to coat his forefinger. Surprised to find it thick and syrupy and obviously not water, he lifted his finger to his tongue and licked it.

It tasted quite pleasing, moderately sweet, but there was a bitter back taste to it that made him shiver. He pushed the cork back into the neck and placed the bottle carefully on the rafter to admire it, next to a brass button, a locket, and a hairpin.

It had all begun last summer, when he had come across a silver spoon on the path in the vegetable garden. He knew he should have taken it back to Mistress Claddingbowl in the kitchen, but it was bent and covered in soil and good for nothing. So, he put it in his pocket when he was sure no one was looking. This very act of secrecy, of subterfuge, gave him a feeling of independence that excited him. But what to do with this new-found booty? He had to find somewhere to conceal his treasure.

He had climbed up on top of the bales in the hay barn and put it on the rafter in the corner out of sight. He often spent time up there, among the hay, where the color of his own hair blended in so well with the straw that if he lay flat, no one could see him. Sometimes he would hear his mother or Mistress Claddingbowl calling for him, but he made it a rule never to move until his father started to shout his name gruffly. That usually brought him out of hiding, but he was careful to cover his tracks. He would climb down from the bales and then slip through a small hole in the back of the barn, so that he would always appear to have been somewhere else.

No one ever suspected that he had a hideaway. It was his secret. Had his mother known, she would have forbidden his forays into the barn for many reasons, not least because the hay made his hands itch. Nor would she have approved of his collection. The week after his first discovery, when he was in the stable yard, he spied a shoe buckle made of brass on the cobbles. A horse had trodden on it and it was misshapen, so it was of no use and it joined the spoon. Within a month the collection included a toothpick, a broken piece of porcelain, and a jam jar.

Now, one year on, Will's eclectic array of ec-centric collectables amounted to more than forty pieces occupying two rafters in the corner of the hay barn. Among the buttons and the broken clay pipes were two unlikely specimens – the flat stones he had found in his sister's apron pockets when they pulled her out of the lake. No one had seen him remove them, but he kept them as a memory of her. They were probably the last things she touched on this earth and they made him feel closer to her. He had removed them from under his bed as soon as he could and now they took pride of place on the beams. Rebecca had been the only one who knew about his secret stash. She had come upon it by mistake when she was looking for him one day, but she had promised not to tell and she remained true to her word.

This latest acquisition, this magnificent cobalt bottle, that now stood so handsomely on the rafter, surpassed them all in beauty. He allowed himself to gaze at its elegance. He did not know how or why it had ended up in the apple barrel, but he was delighted that he had found it. Had his mother set eyes on it, she would have laid claim to it herself as a receptacle for her salves and febrifuges; she must not see it and it would be his to keep forever.

He settled back on a bale and smiled. There was little fear he would be called upon to complete more duties. Ever since Captain Farrell had been taken away two days ago, the big house had been in turmoil. Hardly anyone had called for him and no one seemed to care where he was. Since Rebecca's death, his mother had seemed in another world. Now and again she would weep for no apparent reason, but otherwise she seemed to walk around in a daze, as if her mind was somewhere far removed from Boughton Hall. He knew his secret would be safe for a little while longer at least.

Chapter 31

Since his return to London, Thomas had been in emotional turmoil. Had he suffered an ache, or a minor infection of some kind, it would have been simple to treat. A dose of feverfew or a dab of iodine would have eased his discomfort – he had not time for bloodletting – but this, this stirring deep down in his very soul was untreatable.

Poets speak of the heart as the organ from which love emanates, thought Thomas, but this sensation that he now experienced was affecting his whole body. He had lost his appetite. His pulse raced at the very thought of her and he was unable to concentrate. Sleep now escaped him and he felt agitated and anxious. He longed for the sight of her, the scent of her, her touch, her voice. Just as Mistress Finesilver craved the laudanum he supplied, so, too, did he crave Lydia. She was the only balm that could soothe his ills and she was forbidden.

As he walked wearily up to his room, knowing that he would be unable to sleep once more, there came a loud rapping at the front door. Mistress Finesilver, dressed in her nightgown, emerged to answer it, but Thomas, fearful of cutpurses at this time of night, told her he would see to it.

A troubled Francis Crick stood on the threshold. 'Dr. Silkstone, something terrible has happened,' he panted.

Thomas said nothing, but quickly ushered his visitor in, not wishing to alarm Mistress Finesilver. He showed him into the drawing room and bade him sit down.

'You look like death, man,' he said, handing him a hastily poured brandy. The young man's complexion was white and his hands were shaking as he tried to steady the glass.

'Captain Farrell has been arrested,' he blurted. 'They've charged him with murder.'

At first light Thomas hired a horse and galloped as far as the George and Dragon at West Wycombe. There, without bothering to refresh himself, he changed his mount and rode on, not stopping until he reached Boughton Hall. It was late afternoon when he arrived and the sound of hooves on stone alerted young Will up in his hideaway. Seeing Dr. Silkstone, he jumped down from the bales and hurried to take his horse in the yard.

'Ah, Will. There's a good lad,' Thomas greeted, giving the young boy the reins of his mount. Will smiled. The doctor was the only one who ever showed him any kindness.

'She's ridden hard, sir,' he remarked, seeing the flecks of white foam on the mare's fetlocks and hindquarters.

'We both have,' smiled Thomas, taking off his hat and wiping his forehead with the back of his hand.

'Can I get you something, sir?'

'You look after the horse,' replied Thomas. 'I'll take care of myself,' and with that he pressed a farthing into Will's hand.

The boy's freckled face broke into a broad smile. 'Thank you, sir.'

Thomas entered the house via one of the back entrances. No one saw him as he made his way through an ill-lit corridor that led out onto the hallway. He walked toward the drawing room. The door was closed and he put his ear to it. He could hear movement inside. Light footsteps paced up and down on the wooden floor. He had just raised his hand to knock when he heard a voice – a man's voice.

'Can I help you, Dr. Silkstone?' came another voice from behind. Thomas jumped. It was Rafferty, the manservant. He was caught off-guard and felt awkward.

'I am come to see Lady Lydia, but I believe she has company.'

Rafferty looked at the young doctor imperiously. 'I shall see if her ladyship is available to receive you,' he replied. He disappeared momentarily, then reemerged to open the door wide, gesturing inside.

Thomas was not prepared for the scene that greeted him. It was not the fact that James Lavington was in the room, nor that he was standing by Lydia. It was the air of intimacy that was almost palpable, as if in Captain Farrell's absence the lawyer had quickly and easily filled the errant husband's shoes.

'Dr. Silkstone,' Lydia greeted him warmly. 'I am

so pleased you are here.' He wondered if she really was, or if his appearance had thwarted a secret tryst.

Thomas gave a half bow and kissed Lydia's outstretched hand. He acknowledged Lavington with a nod. 'I came as soon as I heard,' he said. He was unsure how she would react to his unannounced arrival, but she was unfazed.

'You know Mr. Lavington, do you not?' said Lydia.

Thomas had seen him at the inquest in Oxford, but the two men had not been formally introduced. He could not help looking at his disfigurement and what an excellent job the prosthetician had made of the ivory nose.

Lavington, who was obviously acutely sensitive to even the most discreet of glances, turned his face the other way toward Lydia.

'I must go now, your ladyship,' he told her, taking her hand in an intimate gesture. 'I shall call by tomorrow.'

Lydia smiled and nodded in a noiseless language that spoke volumes to Thomas. Lavington gave a polite bow and took his leave.

As soon as he had left the room, Lydia's countenance became graver. 'Francis must have told you,' she said, settling herself on a chair by the fireplace. 'Please,' she said, gesturing Thomas to sit opposite her.

She looked pale and her eyes were red from crying. She seemed even more fragile than when he had first seen her, he thought. He felt an overwhelming urge to put his arms around her.

'You have ridden all this way. You must be exhausted, Dr. Silkstone.' She deliberately used his title, as if to distance herself from him. 'I shall call for refreshment.'

She reached for the bell and rang it. 'Bring Dr. Silkstone a pitcher of wine,' she ordered Rafferty.

'Yes, my lady,' replied the manservant rather warily.

'And Dr. Silkstone will be dining with us tonight, too,' she added.

'You are too kind,' said Thomas.

'It is the least I can do, seeing you have come all the way from London,' said Lydia, smiling.

Rafferty bowed and was just about to leave the room when his mistress called him back. 'And Rafferty. See that the blue room is ready. Dr. Silkstone will be staying with us tonight.' The manservant raised an imperious eyebrow and Lydia noted his expression, but said nothing.

'I appreciate your generosity, my lady,' remarked Thomas, feeling a little awkward.

'As I said, it is the least I can do,' she repeated firmly.

He looked at her, seated a few feet away across the room, and it may as well have been a thousand miles that separated them. Lavington's presence had unsettled him. There was an awkward silence, which Thomas broke.

'How was your husband when you saw him?' he enquired. Francis Crick had told him of Lydia's visit to Oxford Prison, much against his own advice.

'How well can a man be when he shares a cell with cockroaches and the threat of death hangs over him?' she asked bitterly.

226

Thomas felt insensitive. 'I am sorry. I did not mean...'

Lydia looked at him and shook her head. 'No. 'Tis I who should be sorry. You travel all this way to assist us and I snap at you like that. Forgive me, Dr. Silkstone.'

Her pain was as real and as obvious as if she, too, were caged in a stinking cell awaiting trial.

Rafferty returned carrying a tray. He set it down on a table by Thomas and poured a large glass of claret. Before the manservant was out of the room, Thomas took a large gulp.

Lydia watched him in the half light. His face was intelligent and earnest, although she had seen him smile, and she knew there was humor and warmth there, too, albeit hidden from her at that moment. A frond of long hair flopped forward across his face and he brushed it back with a firm hand. He looked disheveled and his breeches were covered in dust.

'I need your help, Dr. Silkstone,' she said. She paused. 'But of course you knew that.'

Thomas looked up. 'You can be assured that I will do everything in my power to establish who killed your brother,' he said earnestly. He omitted to say that he would endeavor to prove Captain Farrell's innocence. It was an omission that did not go unremarked by Lydia, but she let it pass.

Chapter 32

Hannah Lovelock was preparing herbs in her kitchen. She had been out and about earlier on that evening with her whisket, looking for plants to dry and preserve. She had almost reached the bridge when she decided to turn back as the light was growing dim. Now the fruits of her evening forage lay before her on the wooden table: bunches of feverfew, whose white flowers soothed the most violent of headaches, and of meadow-sweet that she had found growing in the damp meadows by the lake. The latter was good for the digestion and Jacob took it when he had an attack of bile.

There was henbane, too. Her late mother had sworn by it. It was, she had told her daughter, a good eryngo, promoting ardor in a man. The Egyptians smoked it to relieve toothache, while the ancient Greeks believed that people under the influence of the herb became prophetic.

These powers were, however, as nothing compared with those of this common plant that stored its magic in its purple bell flowers and its tall, thin stems. It hid itself away in wooded areas in the shade and only a fortunate few knew of its incredible properties.

Taking a handful of spiky leaves, she chopped them till they bled green, then packed them into a crock before pouring over enough oil to steep them. She returned to the table and was just about to start on a batch of wild garlic when she heard a noise in the front room.

'Is that you, Will?' she called. 'Where've you been all day, young man?' She was clearly annoyed with her son, but there was no reply. 'Jacob?' Perhaps it was her husband, come from checking the stables. There was still no reply and yet she heard more footsteps, or rather the sound of footsteps and of wood on the flagstone floor. She wiped her green-stained hands on her apron and went to see.

'Good evening, Mistress Lovelock,' came a voice. Hannah did not reply. James Lavington stood, propped on his walking stick, as relaxed in her front room as if he had been invited.

'I hope I did not alarm you,' he remarked calmly.

Hannah felt her heart begin to race and her palms grow clammy with sweat. She opened her mouth, but no words would come. Lavington shuffled forward toward her and she backed away. In the fading light, she found his scarred face was even more disquieting.

'Nervous, aren't we?' he taunted her. Still no sound came from her mouth, so to spare her more agony, he told her: 'If there is anything you want to tell me, Hannah, anything at all, I will always listen.' He waited a few seconds for an answer, but when none was forthcoming, as he had antici-pated, he turned and headed for the door.

Thomas could not sleep. He lay awake listening to the unfamiliar sounds of a strange house. He was used to the din of London, even at night, when the blackness was always alive to the sound of

229

horses' hooves and dogs barking and loud voices. But now, at Boughton Hall, above the creak of the woodwork and the mewing of a cat he heard muffled sobs.

He leapt up and put his ear to the door. There it was again, a mournful yet rhythmic sob that rose and fell and rose again. It was a woman's cry. It was Lydia's. Slipping on his breeches and waistcoat, he lit a candle and ventured out into the hallway.

It was dark, save for a shaft of moonlight that pierced a gap in the drapes on the landing, and now he could be certain the sound was coming from Lydia's room, a few paces away. Looking around warily, he walked over to her door, took a deep breath, and tapped lightly. The sobs stopped instantly.

'Who is it?'

'Dr. Silkstone,' he whispered formally.

More sounds. This time he could hear the bed creaking and rustling silk before Lydia cautiously opened the door slightly. Her dark lashes were wet and her hair was tumbling down over her shoulders. She looked at Thomas for a moment. He felt his heart beating fast inside his chest as his pulse raced.

Now she opened the door wide to allow him in, glancing down the corridor to make sure no one saw him enter. They stood in the darkness, a few inches apart.

'I thought you were ... unwell.'

'You should not be here,' she said softly.

'I am come to see if I can offer any help,' countered Thomas.

'So, you are come as a physician?'

'If that is your wish, then I can offer you a draught to make you sleep, my lady.' His words were measured, uncertain. To act out his feelings now would be a violation of the Hippocratic Oath. She looked so vulnerable, so helpless, yet she suddenly stepped closer to him and, taking his hand, knitted her fingers through his.

'I do not think I shall ever sleep again, Thomas,' she whispered as she leaned forward in search of his lips.

In the darkness they found each other. Their kisses were slow at the beginning, like the first few drops of summer rain, then they came quicker and more urgent as the passion took hold of them both. Thomas breathed in her perfume and ran his hands up and down the arch of her back. Her skin was silky smooth underneath her nightgown and he felt his hands traveling around her body to the cups of her pert breasts. She was so beautiful, more beautiful than any other woman he had ever seen, and he wanted her so badly, but as she closed her eyes, abandoning herself to his touch, she turned and he saw, hanging on the wall, a large portrait of the captain. Seeing his arrogant face jolted him back to reality and he suddenly broke away from her.

'Lydia, Lydia, this is wrong,' he said, holding her at arm's length. 'I am a doctor. You are a married woman. This is madness.'

There was a silence. All Thomas could hear was the blood pounding in his own ears. She lifted her face toward his and nodded in agreement.

'Just hold me,' she whispered.

She laid her head on his chest and he enfolded her in his arms and gently kissed the top of her head. After a few moments he led her silently to the bed and settled her, resting her on his chest. Tenderly he stroked her hair, listening to the music of her breathing as it rose and fell.

'Stay with me, Thomas,' she said softly.

'I am here and I shall always be, if you wish it,' he replied. She nestled her head deeper into his chest and he kissed her forehead once more.

'You are so different from Michael,' she said finally, as if she had read his thoughts. 'He is a liar and a cheat and a womanizer.'

She grew agitated and he stroked her cheek, trying to calm her.

'But is he a murderer?' said Thomas, thinking out loud.

'I wish I knew.'

'I think not,' he mused, but said nothing more.

There, lying in the silence of Lydia's room, Thomas lost all track of time, but after what seemed an age, he heard the rhythm of her breathing change and he knew that sleep had finally found her. Gently lifting her head off his chest, he laid her down on plump pillows and pulled the coverlet over her.

'Sleep well, my love,' he whispered tenderly and he quietly made his way over to the door. Nervously he turned the handle and looked outside into the dark and silent corridor. Quietly he walked the few paces toward his room when suddenly he became aware of something or someone in the shadows.

From out of the darkness stepped a figure.

Thomas turned and held his breath.

'Crick,' he exclaimed, shock darting through his body like a bolt of lightning. 'What ... what...?'

'I caught the morning coach from London, Dr. Silkstone, but it was delayed.' His voice was steady and self-assured. Had he seen him leave Lydia's chamber? The young doctor could not be sure.

'I shall go to my room now, sir,' he said, excusing himself. Perhaps he had not seen anything suspicious after all, Thomas thought to himself. But just as the young student took hold of the handle of his bedroom door at the end of the landing, he turned once more. 'I trust you know where your room is, Dr. Silkstone,' he said.

Chapter 33

Fear is easily diagnosed in a man. The physical symptoms are clear. They are writ, thought Thomas, as he looked at Captain Farrell, plain as if they had been in ink on the parchment of his pallid skin. But just as there are many types of cancer, or many forms of rash to the skin, so, too, were there different strains of fear. The fear from which this accused man suffered did not dilate his pupils nor make him tremble involuntarily. It was more a gnawing fear, noted Thomas; one that had grown slowly like a tumor, but that was now beginning to surface.

The captain had been damned by the words of his servants at the inquest and with the verdict of

233

unlawful killing had come a warrant for his arrest. And now that he was confined within the dripping walls of a putrid cell, that tumorous growth could manifest itself. No longer concealed under the captain's brocade waistcoats and arrogant manner, it revealed itself in his graying flesh, pulled taut over cheekbones, and his dull, listless eyes.

'Do you have the remedy, Doctor?' asked the Irishman, seeing that Thomas was scrutinizing him.

Thomas looked at him straight. 'Aye, sir, the truth.'

The captain nodded. 'That is what we want, too,' he said, drawing Lydia toward him. Thomas noted she winced at his touch, but did not resist and allowed herself to be pulled gently to his side. In her hand she held a nosegay, which she put up to her nostrils and inhaled deeply.

Thomas also noted the captain's dirt-encrusted fingers as he ran them through his hair, which was normally so neatly coiffured. Stripped of his finery and his normal comforts, he seemed to have acquired a humility that had been noticeably absent before and he felt oddly compassionate toward him.

'I am innocent,' declared the Irishman. His composure fleetingly cracked, but he regained it in an instant and Lydia put a comforting hand on his arm. He looked at her. 'If you lost faith in me, my love, I would not want to go on living,' he told her, tears welling up in his green eyes.

Thomas saw there were tears, too, in Lydia's, but she did not answer. A pang of guilt stabbed him as he wondered if she still loved her husband.

After an awkward moment Thomas decided it was time to break the fragile mood. 'You have a lawyer?' he asked.

Farrell nodded. 'A family friend.'

'Someone we trust,' added Lydia.

'Good, then I must speak with him,' said Thomas, addressing the captain. 'We need all the help we can muster if we are to prove you innocent of this crime.'

James Lavington found Lady Crick seated on a swing in the informal garden. There had been a hard frost and the lawn was laced in white. Blue ribbons were threaded through her grisly long hair, which hung in two braids like coarse rope on either shoulder. Her cheeks were heavily rouged and she cut a tragic figure as she quietly hummed to herself as she swung backward and forward.

When she saw him approach, she smiled but kept on swinging. It was bitterly cold and Lavington wondered that she did not seem to feel the chill. 'Everything looks so magical dressed in white, does it not, Mr. Lavington?' she asked. But as she spoke, he could see sadness in her tired, watery eyes. 'I know Edward is dead, you know,' she said. This was the first time he had heard her acknowledge her son's death. The dowager saw his face register the shock. 'Please, Mr. Lavington, do not tell Lydia I know. 'Tis less painful for her this way.'

'Indeed, my lady,' he replied, standing by her, looking out onto the white spiky carpet before them. He could not have asked for a better entree into the thorny territory he was about to negotiate.

No one had dared broach the subject of Farrell's arrest with the old woman. It was feared that the news would distress her even more, so she had lived in blissful ignorance for the past week while her son-in-law languished behind bars.

'You love Lady Lydia very much,' ventured Lavington.

Her cracked, painted lips broke into a smile. 'Yes,' she said, still swinging gently, as if cradled in a far-off memory and, without lifting her gaze from a distant horizon she repeated softly, 'Dear Lydia.'

'You have done so much for her, have you not?'

'She is my only daughter. Her happiness is my happiness,' she replied wistfully.

Now was his chance, he thought, and he seized it. 'And that is why you let her return here with Captain Farrell after they strayed.'

These last words served to recall Lady Crick from her reverie. Lavington was afraid that he had overstepped the mark. Turning her head quickly, so that her gray braids flicked 'round, she looked at her inquisitor warily. 'I did not want to lose my daughter, sir. Had I not allowed her to return to Boughton Hall I would have no one now.'

Lavington was aware he would have to tread carefully from now on. He had reopened an old wound and he knew the old dowager would find it painful. When she first encountered dashing Captain Farrell three years ago in Bath, he had not only swept Lydia off her feet. He had stolen her heart and with it any vestige of respect she may have held for her elderly mother's opinion. Hence when, after a two-month courtship, the couple asked for permission to marry, Lady Crick, who had been at that time in possession of most of her faculties, declined. Her better judgment told her that this young Irishman was a wastrel and a scoundrel and only after her daughter's wealth.

The dowager had set her sights on another young man whom she considered much more suitable. Before her encounter with the dashing captain, Lydia had also seemed amenable to the match, but all that changed in Bath. Small wonder that Lady Crick was disinclined to give her consent and was first outraged, then heart-broken, when Lydia did the unthinkable. She and Captain Farrell eloped.

It was the talk of all Oxfordshire. Fans were raised and spiteful words spoken every time the dowager entered a room. Naturally she closed her doors to the newlyweds and for almost a year the couple lived in Cheltenham, surviving on Lydia's income. Far from shunning the old woman, how-ever, and seeking to turn his bride away from her mother's affections, Michael Farrell strove to placate his estranged mother-in-law with his Gaelic charm. Forswearing his godless ways, he pledged to be an exemplary husband, devoting himself to his wife's every whim. Not only that, but word reached Boughton Hall that he publicly renounced any claim he might have to his wife's fortune and, crucially, to any property she might inherit on the death of her brother. A weary and troubled Lady Crick relented – even though no document of renunciation was ever signed – and welcomed her wayward daughter and her erst-while libertine husband back to the bosom of the family and all settled down to live in peace and harmony at their ancestral home. Or so it seemed.

Lavington watched the old woman. Her swinging had slowed down. It had become less rhythmical, as if she had lost all sense of timing and tempo, like a dancer in full flow whose music stops without warning.

'Nobody knows what pain you endured, Lady Crick,' said Lavington slowly.

'Nobody knows,' she echoed, coming to a halt on the swing.

'Perhaps it is time you told them.'

'Told them?' she echoed once more.

'Yes,' urged Lavington. 'The coroner who presided over Lord Crick's inquest never heard from you. You, the most important person in his lordship's life.'

'Inquest?' she repeated. 'No, no, you are right.'

Lavington bent down low and whispered in the old woman's ear.

'Is it not time they heard your story, your ladyship? How you were slighted and ignored.'

He could see her expression change from one of compliance to anger. 'Yes, they made me look a fool,' she said through clenched teeth, suddenly starting to swing again, only this time more aggressively. 'It was Farrell. It was all his fault. If it hadn't been for him...' She broke off suddenly, as if she had just realized some consequence or some course of action that might have changed the outcome of certain events.

'Yes, my lady?' probed Lavington.

'He led my Lydia astray,' she continued, suddenly returning from the far-off place she had been in her imagination.

'Indeed so,' nodded Lavington. In his hand he carried a large leather satchel, which he now opened to reveal a document. He brought this out, together with a quill and a bottle of ink. 'That is why I took the liberty of drafting this affidavit for you, your ladyship,' he said, handing her the large piece of parchment.

Lady Crick looked at Lavington curiously. 'What's this?' she asked.

''Tis the sorry story of your love for your daughter and how she repaid you,' replied Lavington. He placed the bottle of ink on a nearby ornamental wall and dipped the nib of his quill into it. 'All that remains to be done is for you to sign it. I shall then see that it is delivered to the coroner and that he is made aware of the whole truth.'

The old lady nodded her gray head and took the quill in her gnarled, liver-spotted hand. 'The truth must be told,' she intoned as she scrawled illegibly across the parchment.

Lavington looked at the old woman intently. 'I can assure you, your ladyship, I will see to it that it is.'

Chapter 34

Thomas could not remember it being so cold. Even when his father had taken him up the Delaware in winter to hunt elk as a boy there had been a passage through the ice, but now even the

Thames was frozen over. London became a strange landscape of drifts and dunes that rose to rooftops and fell down gullies. In the streets razors of crystal ice sliced through the frozen air as they clung from eaves and overhangs, and men's breath looked like the hot steam from cups in coffee-houses.

On the river itself children lit bonfires and enterprising traders set up their stalls on the ice. It was as if the blood that flowed through the great artery of the city that normally pulsated with ships and barges and wherries had been leeched.

At first the sack-'em-up men were worried, too. The ground was so hard their picks and shovels barely marked the surface of the graveyards, but then, as the frost took hold, followed by the deep snow, they found they no longer had to dig. The young and the old were falling in the streets, frozen to the marrow. All they had to do was pick them up and deliver them to the dissecting rooms.

There the corpses would be packed in the very snow that had killed them, waiting their turn under the anatomist's knife. Stored in outhouses, the cadavers remained intact for days, protected against the ravages of rot and worms, ensuring a regular supply for eager students.

Thomas had been approached several times. In fact there seemed to be more bodies for sale than loaves of bread that winter. He gave the scoundrels short shrift. He wanted no truck with their filthy trade and besides, he had more than enough to keep him occupied on those long, dark winter days since his return to the capital.

Christmas had come and gone and two months

had elapsed since his last visit to Oxford. In between performing amputations and lecturing to packed auditoriums, he had devoted what little spare time there was to testing for the most obvious and easily detected poisons, such as mercury and arsenic in Lord Crick's sample. He had found nothing to arouse any suspicion. If the truth were told, he felt quite wretched about his efforts and the quest to find the poison that had killed the young nobleman. He had only agreed to continue his searches on behalf of Captain Farrell because he believed there was a possibility he was innocent and because Lydia had asked him to.

Thomas had spoken with the captain at length before he left Oxford, asking probing questions about any other poisons that may have been used on the estate. Farrell insisted he had no access to any other toxic substances and knew of no others. The young doctor had drawn a blank. He was working in the dark and, without a dim and distant light to follow, however weak, his journey toward the truth remained strewn with blind alleys.

Lydia had journeyed back to Boughton Hall alone. After their visit to the prison, Thomas had put her onto the coach for Brandwick and Lovelock planned to meet her there. Their parting had been strained and muted. The mutual pleasure they once shared was a guilty secret and would have to remain so.

On cold, bleak nights, when the snow lay piled high in London's eerily silent streets, it was difficult not to think of her and long for her warmth.

He had lost count of the letters he had written

her late at night in his solitary room, longing for her presence. Yet he knew if he had sent them and they had been intercepted, both of them would be undone. If Francis Crick had seen him leave Lydia's room that night, he had said nothing. Indeed, the young student had been notable by his absence of late, attending none of Thomas's lectures since their last encounter at Boughton Hall. His disappearance troubled Thomas, but he brushed it aside and tried to concentrate instead on finding out the truth.

The body holds within it many secrets. Each organ stores its own particular mysteries, ensconced deep within its membranes, hidden in tissue or stored in beefy cliffs of muscle. How easy, how straightforward it must have been, mused Thomas, as he pored over the young earl's heart, to be a priest in Babylon or in Ancient Greece or Rome. In those days of soothsayers and oracles it was the liver that was the seat of the soul and the center of all vitality. All one had to do if advice were sought on how to outflank an enemy or gain revenge was to sacrifice a sheep or a goat and slit open the belly. By simply gazing deep into the patterns of the ducts and lobes, the markings of the liver and the lay of the gallbladder, the future would be revealed.

'Such divinations aided no lesser figure than Julius Caesar,' pronounced Dr. Carruthers one evening. He had taken to sitting with his young protégé in the laboratory every evening as he labored, seemingly fruitlessly, on Lord Crick's heart.

Thomas was feeling completely bereft of any

242

inspiration, divine or otherwise. The only revelations on which he could rely would be not from the gods but of his own making.

'Surely, sir, justice, like science, should not only be based on the natural order, but on fact,' retorted Thomas. 'In the absence of hard fact that justice is flawed and the justice that is about to be dispensed next week at Oxford Assizes is based largely on supposition and circumstantial evidence.'

'A good judge will recognize that, young fellow,' reassured Dr. Carruthers. But Thomas was not so sure. Each day since his return from Oxfordshire he had entered a surgery, much as a judge did a court of law. More than once he had seen a patient awaiting an amputation, much like an accused awaiting trial. The hapless people would be nervous, tense, unsure of what fate was about to befall them, but no matter the outcome they knew it would be painful.

'But, sir,' Thomas countered, 'it is the surgeon and the surgeon alone who is responsible. He alone makes an incision. He alone is close enough to hear the little crack at the end when the arm or the leg falls from the table. There may be students watching, but we are the adventurers. We are the ones who forge pulsing rivers of blood and bound from bone to bone.'

Dr. Carruthers nodded. 'You have a point there, young fellow.'

Fired up, Thomas went on: 'A judge, on the other hand, leads an expedition. He is not alone. True, he charts unfamiliar ground on occasion; ground that is strewn with inaccuracies, deviations, and untruths, but he can only direct what he hears. He cannot control it.'

This thought frightened Thomas. He had no control. He was in the hands of others whom he did not know and therefore could not trust. Why had Captain Farrell's defense counsel not yet contacted him, even though the trial was imminent? Surely he would be asked to give evidence?

Later that evening, as Thomas and Dr. Carruthers sat by the fire taking a nightcap before bed, the old anatomist sensed that all was still not well with his protégé. He was reading *The Daily Advertiser* in a monotone and the old doctor could tell his mind was elsewhere.

'Tell me again about that fire in Great Portland Street,' he said suddenly.

'Fire? What fire?' replied Thomas before realizing his master's ruse.

'Your mouth read out the article not five minutes ago, young fellow,' jibed Carruthers. 'But your head was somewhere else.'

''Tis true I am a little preoccupied with the trial at the moment,' he replied humbly.

'Preoccupied! A monkey's arse,' chortled the old doctor. 'Your head never came back from Oxford and I'll wager you left your heart there, too.'

Thomas was glad his mentor could not see the blood rush to his cheeks.

''Tis a good job you go on the morrow!' exclaimed Dr. Carruthers. 'Around here, you're no good to man nor beast.'

Chapter 35

At first light the following day Thomas took the coach back to Oxford, but instead of taking a room once more at the White Horse, he hired a mount to ride to Boughton Hall. It was early evening when he arrived and Will was there in the courtyard to greet him.

'Dr. Silkstone,' he called as Thomas turned in through the gate.

The young doctor smiled and rode up to the boy. 'Are you expected, sir?' he asked, taking Thomas's reins.

'No, Will, I am not,' he replied, starting to dismount. Just as he had taken one foot from the stirrups, however, something, a rat perhaps, disturbed his horse and it reared up suddenly. Thomas tried to grab on to its mane, but he could not and was knocked to the cobbles.

Will tugged on the bridle and quickly controlled the gelding, settling him once more. But the damage had been quickly done. Although Thomas had no bones broken, he had fallen against the boot scrapers near the rear door and had gashed his hand quite deeply. He held it as the blood began to surface.

'Sir, you're hurt,' cried Will, noticing the crimson slash on the doctor's hand.

''Tis nothing,' replied Thomas, knowing full well that the wound needed attention.

The young boy led the horse into a nearby stable as Thomas grasped his injured hand in pain.

'My mother has ointments to stop bad things taking hold, sir,' he said, guiding Thomas by the elbow. 'Please come with me.'

The doctor's faint protests fell on deaf ears and Will led him to his own home, just across the courtyard.

'Mother. Mother!' the young boy called out. Hannah Lovelock stood at her kitchen table, mixing dough for bread. As soon as she saw Dr. Silkstone she wiped her hands on her apron and came to see what the matter was.

'The doctor's cut real deep,' said Will, guiding Thomas toward his mother.

''Tis nothing, please,' protested Thomas.

Hannah looked uneasy, but went up to the young doctor and inspected the wound. She gestured to a chair and Thomas sat down as he was bidden.

'Fetch me that jar,' Hannah instructed Will and the boy obeyed. Thomas's eyes followed him to the shelf that would have been more at home in an apothecary's shop than a servant's home. Row upon row of tinctures and salves were lined up in jars and pots. Rarely had he seen such a gallimaufry of herbs and plants, of dried fungi and strange roots. Shelves groaned under the weight of gallipots of preserved leaves and urns packed full of petals. There were ampules of oil and pots of creams and lotions ranged in rows.

'You keep many remedies,' Thomas ventured as he watched her fetch a linen cloth and a jug of water.

'That I do,' she snapped, drawing the conversation to a close before it had even begun.

She sat down beside him at the kitchen table and cleaned the blood from the wound before taking a few crushed leaves from the jar and adding them to a little oil. Next she took a pad of gauze and poured the oil onto it before placing it gently on the wound.

Thomas noted that on each of these jars were pasted leaves or petals or pieces of root. He surmised that as Hannah in all probability could neither read nor write, this was her way of identifying their contents. He saw that the leaf stuck on the jar whose contents Hannah was using was large and oval and slightly hairy in appearance, but he did not ask his nurse what it was. Aware that she felt uneasy Thomas let her work in silence. The herb had no distinctive odor, but the oil was soothing against the heat of his wound.

'Mother says it cures all ills,' chirped Will.

But Hannah snapped at him. 'You hush your mouth. 'Tis nothing but a common weed.'

There was an awkward silence as she tore a piece of linen from an old petticoat and wrapped his hand in a bandage with great expertise.

'I am indebted to you, Mistress Lovelock,' said Thomas as she tied a knot.

She did not bother to look up. The young doctor felt awkward. If he pulled out a few farthings from his pocket she would be offended, he knew, so he simply rose and thanked her for her attentions.

Will escorted him out of the quarters. 'I told you she could help you,' he gloated.

Thomas smiled. 'Your mother has a rare knowledge. Perhaps I could talk with her sometime.'

Will shrugged. 'All I know is her ointments help the burning on my hands and her potions help me sleep at night,' he replied.

'You are fortunate,' said Thomas and young Will beamed with pride.

Thomas found Lydia cutting the first daffodil stems in the walled garden. Her chestnut hair was swept back so that he saw her in profile. She was every bit as beautiful as he remembered her. He looked around him to make sure no one else would witness their reunion.

He walked up to her and, as soon as she heard his footfall crunch on the pebbled path, she turned. For a split second she simply stared at him, then her face broke into a smile. It was something he had seen her do very rarely and it surprised and delighted him, but fearful that someone might be watching them, Thomas simply took her hand and kissed it. It was then that she saw the bandage. 'But you are hurt,' she cried.

'A scratch,' he told her dismissively.

'It is so good to see you,' Lydia told him as they walked along the box-hedged path toward the house. 'I have missed you so much,' she blurted, grabbing his arm, but then remembering herself and letting go just as quickly. 'The trial is...' Her voice waned.

'I needed to be here,' said Thomas earnestly.

'You did not write,' she said reproachfully.

'I thought it too dangerous.'

She nodded, knowing it to be true.

After a few seconds' silence, she said: 'It is not easy without...' She stopped herself uttering her husband's name, as if the very mention of it hurt her.

'How is he bearing up?' asked Thomas.

'His spirits are low and his health fails.'

Detecting a note of despair in her voice he said quickly: 'I have been continuing with the tests in London.'

'Yes?' she replied eagerly.

'But I am afraid I still cannot identify the poison that killed your brother.' He felt woefully inadequate. He knew he had failed her so far.

As they walked on, the watery March sun was sinking below the garden wall and the green shoots of bluebells were emerging from their winter beds.

''Twill soon be spring,' he told her, not meaning to sound trite.

'It holds little promise this year,' she countered.

For a moment they walked on in silence until Thomas caught sight of Lady Crick at the far end of the garden. The old woman was about to open the wrought-iron gate that led toward the track to Brandwick. Lydia saw her, too, and instantly called out to Kidd, who was hoeing a bed nearby.

'Stop her!' she called out, and the gardener sprang into action, bounding up to the old woman and taking her by the arm. She seemed agitated at first, but by the time Lydia arrived she had calmed down a little.

'Now, Mama, we don't want you getting lost, do we?' chastised Lydia gently, before Kidd led her away back toward the house.

'My mother will keep wandering off,' explained Lydia as they began their journey toward the house once more.

'She enjoys her freedom,' ventured Thomas.

'Yes,' replied Lydia, frowning. 'When Francis is here he takes her for walks in the woods. He is kind to her.' She turned her face toward his, reminding him again of her fragile beauty. Her eyes met his for a fleeting moment and darted away again. He had not told her of his encounter with her cousin on the landing and nor did he intend to.

'Francis is a good man,' she added as if talking to herself as much as to Thomas. He only hoped that discretion was another of his qualities.

Chapter 36

The young doctor's unannounced arrival had sent Boughton Hall into a flurry. Lydia ordered a bed be made for him and naturally invited him to dinner, but he was not the only guest. He had intended to ask Lydia about her husband's defense counsel and how he might make contact with him. Instead, he found himself making small talk with a man to whom he had already taken an instant dislike.

'You are not hungry, Dr. Silkstone?' asked Lydia as Thomas toyed with the trout on his plate.

'I am just a little tired, your ladyship,' he replied politely.

'Mistress Claddingbowl will be most offended,' chimed in James Lavington.

Lavington had a prior invitation to dine and Thomas soon found that his appetite had deserted him. There was a difficult pause in the conversation – it had not exactly flowed between the two men all evening – and Lydia had seen fit to bridge the gap.

'So, you two gentlemen must wish to talk about the trial,' she ventured.

Thomas was not sure what she meant. 'The trial, of course.' He nodded. He was still none the wiser and frowned.

'But Dr. Silkstone, forgive me,' she said, suddenly realizing her omission. 'Mr. Lavington is the good friend we told you about. He will represent my husband at the trial.'

Thomas felt his heart race. 'Mr. Lavington is an advocate?' he asked incredulously, first looking at his rival across the table and then back at Lydia.

'Indeed I am, sir,' he replied. 'I studied law at Balliol.'

'I apologize. I thought you knew,' said Lydia, the color rising in her pale cheeks.

Thomas, of course, did not. To make matters worse, he neither liked nor trusted the man who sat opposite him at dinner. Yet Lydia was entrusting her husband's future, his very life in fact, to this shadowy figure, who clearly had designs on her, if she could but see it.

Shortly after dessert, Lydia left her guests together, clothed in an uncomfortable silence. The two men rose as she departed, then seated themselves once more. At least without her company, they could relax a little more. From a rack on the table that Rafferty had set before them, Lavington took a clay pipe. As he packed the tobacco into the bowl, Thomas noted his left hand was also badly scarred and the tip of his ring finger was missing.

'So, Balliol,' he said, breaking the uneasy peace.

'Yes, then Gray's Inn,' replied Lavington.

'So why...?' Lavington did not allow Thomas to finish his question.

'I wanted adventure, Dr. Silkstone. For the same reason that you left Philadelphia for these fair shores, I joined the army and went out to India in search of the exotic.'

'And did you find it?' asked Thomas.

Lavington shrugged and pointed to his disfigured face. 'This found me,' he smirked.

Thomas cast his gaze down toward the table.

'Please, do not feel embarrassed,' urged the lawyer. 'Most people look away. They avoid eye contact, but you, as a doctor... I saw you studying it earlier. What do you make of it?'

Thomas appreciated Lavington's attempts to break through any barriers of pretense. True, as a physician he had allowed his eyes to study the facial disfigurement.

'I can see small pieces of shrapnel still buried in the flesh,' Thomas remarked. 'I would therefore deduce that you were involved in some kind of explosion.'

Lavington sat back from the table and nodded, smiling, as if Thomas had been some child playing a guessing game. 'Very good, Dr. Silkstone. Very good. I expect Lydia has told you how it happened.'

She had not. 'You obviously haven't been invited to one of her soirées, my good man,' jibed

Lavington, making Thomas feel acutely aware of his social standing. 'That story's another time for the telling.'

He poured a large glass of port and held it up to Thomas, who declined. He raised his glass in a toast. 'To Captain Michael Farrell, the man who saved my life and left me with this reminder!' His hand stroked the gnarled scar tissue on his left cheek and his smile suddenly gave way to a scowl.

Thomas did not pursue the matter. Nor did he discuss the captain's case. His dining companion was becoming rapidly the worse for wear as he swigged down liberal gulps of vintage port. What information he had to impart to Lavington would best be delivered in the light of day with clear heads and more restrained tongues. He decided to draw the evening to a close, made his excuses, and, leaving the hall by the back entrance, ventured out into the moonlit night to breathe in the fresh air after the tobacco smoke of the dining room. He was just crossing the courtyard toward the gate when he heard someone call his name in a half whisper.

'Dr. Silkstone.'

Thomas looked up. A head was peering out of the window in the hayloft.

'Will. Is that you?'

He could see the boy put his finger to his lips, then disappear from view to reappear seconds later at the door.

'What are you doing out this late?' asked Thomas as the boy walked furtively toward him.

He shrugged and smiled. 'I comes here to my secret place,' he confided. 'Want to see it?' Taking

253

Thomas by the hand, he tugged him toward the hayloft. The young doctor felt unsure, but allowed himself to be guided into the barn.

A lantern burned on the ledge and Will picked it up and guided Thomas to a ladder that led up to the rafters.

'Where are you taking me?' asked Thomas.

'Promise you won't tell,' Will said earnestly. 'You're the only grown-up to know.'

Holding the lantern high, Will led the way up to the loft. Thomas followed, barely able to see in the dark. There was a narrow passage between the sheaves of hay and Will made his way through them until he stopped in the far corner.

'Here, Dr. Silkstone,' he whispered.

Thomas followed the dim glow of the lantern until he came to within a foot or two of the boy. It was then that he saw what Will had brought him to see: his collection. Buckles and buttons, pieces of broken plates and a rusty key: these were the treasures of a ten-year-old farm boy and Thomas felt honored that he should have been chosen to be privy to them.

'Where did you find all these?' asked Thomas, feigning an interest in the worthless trinkets.

'Around here, mostly. On the ground; in the garden,' replied the boy. His fingers settled upon one of two large, flat stones on the rafter.

'And what are those?' enquired Thomas, slightly puzzled as to what attraction such ordinary-looking stones might hold.

Will looked up. 'These?' he queried, picking up one of the stones and stroking it lovingly. 'These were in my sister's pockets when they dragged her

254

out of the lake,' he said. 'They make me feel closer to her.'

Thomas tried to hide his shock. 'You must miss her,' he said gently. The boy chose to ignore this last question and instead turned his attention once more to his collection.

'This is a locket I found in the garden. I think it must be Lady Lydia's, 'tis so fair,' he said, holding the silver pendant up to the light of his lantern.

It was then that Thomas began to feel uneasy. Taking such items, knowing to whom they belonged, could be deemed as theft. If Will's collection was discovered, the young boy could risk a flogging or, even worse, imprisonment. He was just about to broach the matter with him when the light from Will's lantern settled on a physick bottle.

'Is it not fine, sir?' asked Will, seeing the doctor's eyes gaze at the bottle.

'Indeed,' replied Thomas. 'And where did you find it?'

Will frowned. ''Twas in the bottom of the apple barrel.'

'Strange,' replied Thomas, trying to hide his amazement. 'Do you know how it came to be there?'

Will shook his head. 'There was some medicine in it,' he volunteered. 'I tasted some, but it weren't nice.'

Had there been sufficient light, Will would have seen his newfound friend turn pale at these last words. 'You tasted some?' echoed Thomas.

'Yes, sir. Would you like to try, sir?' asked the young boy, uncorking the bottle and thrusting it

255

under the doctor's nose.

Thomas detected no odor, but he could see there was still a little liquid left in the bottle. Somehow he would have to wrest it from the boy without arousing suspicion.

'It is indeed a fine bottle and I am always in need of such vessels for my patients' medicaments,' Thomas told his young companion.

'You wish to keep it, sir?' asked Will, looking crestfallen.

'It would be of great use to me,' Thomas told him, adding: 'But of course I would not expect you to give it to me without some form of recompense.'

'Sir?' queried the boy.

Thomas had suddenly remembered the small bottle of smelling salts he kept in his pocket for emergencies. It was made of porcelain and was painted in bright colors. Surely this would be a fair exchange for the plain physick bottle?

''Tis pretty, sir,' said Will, smiling. 'I thank you.'

Thomas wanted to tell the boy that it was he who should be thanking him for possibly inadvertently providing the biggest breakthrough yet in this ghastly episode. Instead he merely thanked Will for showing him his collection, told him it would be 'their secret,' and bade him find his way home to bed. Tomorrow he would set to work revealing the mysteries contained within the glass bottle he now held in his hand. Tomorrow, he told himself, he may even be one step further to uncovering Lord Crick's murderer. Such a revelation would not come a moment too soon.

Chapter 37

A foreigner visiting the fair and esteemed city of Oxford on the morning of March 13, 1781, could have been forgiven for thinking he had stumbled across a fete, a carnival, or some such frivolous pleasure so beloved of the common horde. Booths had been set up outside the courthouse, selling everything from ribbons to cheap part-music scores. Hawkers jostled for position on the pavement, filling the air with their cries. 'Ripe peascods,' and 'Hot spiced gingerbread!' they called.

Taking advantage of the crowd that had gathered, knife grinders and even tooth drawers vied for business among those who thronged the length and breadth of Broad Street on that sunny March morning.

Gowned undergraduates rubbed shoulders with nostrum mongers and tradesmen, while even ladies and gentlemen of refinement seemed drawn into the melee, caught up in a steaming stew of intrigue and accusation.

At the heart of all this excitement and fevered activity was the fate of one man. His name was not known to most of those who gathered outside the assizes. It mattered not. He was simply called 'the Irishman'.

Folklore had already given him a familiar sobriquet and hearsay had already sentenced him. It was clear that he was guilty of the crime of which

257

he stood accused. His trial was merely a formality. The talk in the taverns was of 'the Irish murderer'. The talk on the street was of a hanging.

Thomas had feared such a scene outside the courtroom. That was why he had persuaded Lydia and James Lavington to take a coach to the back entrance of the assizes, so that they would be able to enter unnoticed by the massing crowd. Francis Crick had sent his apologies. He had been struck down by a fever but would make the journey to Oxford as soon as his health permitted.

Lydia had borne her public humiliation with great dignity. Each day since her husband's arrest she had been aware that the character of the man she once loved was being torn to shreds, as hounds would kill a fox. Now that the day of the trial had arrived, however, Thomas knew that the sight of this great throng, all baying for his blood, would be too much for her to bear.

Slipping unseen into the courtroom, Thomas made sure that Lavington and Lydia were safely inside. The lawyer seemed to know what he was doing. When Thomas had enquired if he would be called as an expert witness, the lawyer had assured him that he would if deemed necessary, although he had in his possession a written transcript of his testimony at the inquest, which may, he said, suffice.

Outside at the front entrance the rabble was kept at bay by two peace constables, but their raucous shouts and rantings could easily be heard inside. Lydia looked pale and forlorn. She sat at the front of the court, just behind Lavington's table, nervously playing with her fan.

'I shall return later this afternoon, my lady,' Thomas assured her. 'But I need to do more experiments.' She nodded but looked at him blankly, not really aware of what he was saying. He had told neither her, nor Lavington for that matter, about the bottle Will had found. He did not want to raise false hopes, so he slipped away as quietly as he had come and made his way toward the Anatomy School at Christ Church.

As Great Tom tolled the tenth hour, the constables opened the court's heavy porticos and allowed those at the front of the queue to enter, albeit in a completely disorderly fashion. The same painted paphians and trollops who had been present at the young earl's inquest now came to see the trial of the man accused of his murder.

Dressed in their frills and furbelows, they looked as though they were on an evening outing to some shilling gallery. In they swarmed, settling themselves down with baskets of food and drink, bringing their salacious banter into a court of law as if it were some bawdy music hall.

Next into this rowdy scene came the jurors – twelve men of good standing in the community. Some seemed quite intimidated by the throng, but most were simply bemused.

The star of this unseemly show did not disappoint. Farrell had ordered that his best blue silk brocade waistcoat be brought to his cell, together with his satin breeches. 'They have come to see the trial of a gentleman and a gentleman they shall see,' he had told a tearful Lydia on one of her recent visits.

259

Mr. Justice de Quincy had seen it all before in his fifty long years at the bench. He had witnessed many a medical man give evidence, but few were as unimpressive as the two who came before him on that first day of the hearing. Dr. Siddall, who was sweating profusely, conceded that he had shied away from an autopsy, but be assured, he told the judge, had he received any inclination that foul play might have been afoot, he would have risked his own life to uncover the truth. Mr. Walton was no less adamant in his devotion to duty. Had he suspected poison, he would of course have performed a postmortem.

In light of the inquest into Lord Crick's death, however, both men seemed to have acquired an in-depth knowledge of toxicology, even going so far as to conduct their own experiments on live animals.

'I favor laurel water as the poison used,' surmised Dr. Siddall in the witness stand, deliberately ignoring Thomas's findings. To this end, the doctor had fed half a pint to a greyhound, a pint and a half to an aged mare, and an ounce to a cat. 'The greyhound died in convulsions in thirty seconds,' he told the court, 'but it took the mare fifteen minutes and the cat just three,' he added almost gleefully.

'There was also the question of the smell, my lord,' recalled Mr. Walton. 'The smell described by the maidservant Hannah as the smell of bitter almonds.'

'Did you smell such a smell around the deceased?' enquired the judge.

'No,' admitted the surgeon, but that was of little

consequence, he assured Mr. de Quincy. 'The corpse was so noxious it masked all other smells.'

On such evidence, both men were, they said, drawn to the conclusion that Lord Crick had been poisoned by the introduction of laurel water to his physick.

Back in Professor Hascher's laboratory, Thomas was working on the physick bottle when his mind turned to Hannah Lovelock's kitchen. Never had he seen such an array of potions and possets outside a hospital. What if one of those gallipots or guglets contained a poison – a herb or toxic weed perhaps? What was it that Will had said about the herb his mother used on his own wound? It worked miracles? He cast his memory back to the leaf that had been stuck on the front of the jar to identify it. What was it Hannah had said as she dressed his wound? ''Tis only a common weed.'

Walking over to the dusty shelves Thomas scanned the various bottles and jars of dried herbs that Professor Hascher kept mainly for preserving. After a few moments he stumbled across the very thing for which he searched: a jar containing what appeared to be the exact same leaf. Taking the vessel out, he carefully poured some of its contents into a phial. He then repeated the same test that he had performed so many times in the last month, mixing a little of the ingredient with the medicine that the apothecary had prescribed the hapless young nobleman.

One hour later he had his answer. '*Digitalis purpurea*,' he said out loud, as if wanting to share his discovery with anyone or anything that might be listening. Could it be that the common purple foxglove was responsible for Lord Crick's demise?

Now that he knew there was digitalis present in the medicine, he could test for it in the earl's stomach tissue. But there was a problem. Fearful of damaging the specimen unnecessarily in transit, he had left it at Boughton Hall. He must return, and as soon as possible. He was not due to be called to the witness stand until the following day. There was still time for him to prove once and for all what had killed Lord Crick.

Chapter 38

Hannah Lovelock eased off her husband's hobnailed boots in front of a dwindling fire. Normally he would have scolded her for not tossing another log on it, but he seemed gleefully preoccupied with other matters that evening. The couple were due to travel to Oxford in two days' time to give evidence at the trial and Jacob had seen his wife in conversation with the local butcher, who had been among the rabble at the court that day.

'So, what did 'e say?' asked Jacob as she grasped the tongue of his boot.

'Who?' she queried, knowing full well to whom her husband referred.

'Sam Bowmaker, 'course.' He was smiling mischievously. 'I saw you lapping up his words like a cat with cream.'

Hannah thought for a moment as she pulled off his right boot first.

'He said them doctors had been telling the court what they thought.'

'And?' His breath smelt stale and unpleasant and Hannah turned her face away.

'They said they thought it was the laurel water what did it.'

'Laurel water, aye?' He paused thoughtfully. 'And did they point the finger?'

'No.' She did not elaborate.

Lovelock sat back in the chair and let his wife pull the final boot off. 'Looks like the captain's in the shit, then, don't it?' He smiled wryly.

Later that night, when Hannah was sure her son was abed and her husband was dozing after his ale by the fire, she sneaked out of the house and across the courtyard to the apple store. From her apron pocket she took out a piece of tallow candle, secured it into a holder, then struck a flint and lit it. She knew that what she sought would be difficult to find, but plunging her arm into the deep barrel, she felt the cold, smooth skins that were so fragrant and enticing.

It was in there somewhere. Down, down she delved, deeper and deeper, until the tips of her toes were no longer on the ground and her body was doubled over, swinging from the barrel neck. Suddenly her palms hit the wooden bottom, but as soon as she cleared a space, the apples descended again, filling it once more, making her search almost impossible. It was in there. She knew it was, but perhaps she needed to return in the daylight, when she could see what she was doing and not

263

have to rely simply on touch, like some blind woman groping helplessly in the sweet-smelling dark.

Hannah tipped herself backward so that both feet now touched the ground and recovered her composure. Smoothing her hair and her apron, she retrieved the candle holder and snuffed out the ineffectual flame. She then made her way back toward the door. She had almost reached the threshold when she sensed that someone, or something, was lurking in the shadows.

'Is this what you seek, Hannah?' came a voice from out of the blackness.

She gasped and turned to see a figure emerge, holding up the elusive physick bottle that she had hidden in the apple barrel. She recognized the voice instantly.

'Dr. Silkstone. You frightened me,' she told him as he emerged into the pool of moonlight that fell on the threshold.

'Is it not time you told the truth, Hannah?' asked Thomas, still holding up the bottle so that it was level with her eyes, which were wide with terror.

'I ... I don't know what you mean, sir.' She was backing away from him like a frightened animal.

The young doctor moved toward her and for the first time she could see his face quite clearly. His countenance was not threatening, but he was frowning. 'A man's life is at stake, Hannah. You must tell me all you know.'

'What's this?' asked Jacob Lovelock as his wife stood at the doorway of their home, accompanied by Thomas. 'You sick or something?'

'May we come in?' asked Thomas earnestly.

Lovelock nodded and bade him sit down. Hannah seated herself opposite, by now her shoulders heaving in deep sobs. Her breath was ragged and her words rasped like a file on metal. 'Forgive me,' she pleaded. 'Please forgive me...'

'What be the meaning of this?' shouted Lovelock above his wife's strangled protestations.

'Do you have any strong liquor in the house?' asked Thomas.

Lovelock looked bemused, then pointed to a jug on the table, half filled with ale. The doctor poured some into a tankard and eased it up to Hannah's lips. 'Drink this,' he urged her, hoping it would calm her.

She sipped it slowly at first, then began to swallow great gulps until she had downed the whole tankard. A stream of ale trickled down the side of her mouth and she wiped it away with the back of her hand.

'What ails the woman, Doctor?' questioned her anxious husband.

'No ailment but guilt, I suspect,' replied Thomas. He held Hannah firmly by the shoulders. She did not look at him at first. Her gaze was fixed on some far-off point, but when she heard the young doctor's voice calling her, she shook her head as if fighting off some malaise.

'Hannah, we need to know the truth,' urged Thomas. 'Tell us about Rebecca. Tell us what happened to her.'

Jacob suddenly became agitated. 'What's it to do with Rebecca?' he scowled. But Thomas put his finger to his lips, signifying Lovelock to hold his tongue. Hannah was about to speak. Slowly she nodded, as if she accepted that the truth needed to be told, then took a deep breath. Her voice was faltering at first.

'My Rebecca was a fair girl. Just passed her twelfth birthday, she 'ad.' A faint smile flickered across her face as she recalled some distant, pleasant memory of her daughter. But her happy expression was short-lived. 'We was in the orchard last autumn, picking the fallers,' she recalled. 'The young master walked by. 'E stopped by me and I could see 'e was looking at my girl. Eyeing her up, he was, with those weasel eyes of his that were so full of lust. I see'd it in 'im and I warned my girl to stay away from 'im.'

At the recollection of the scene Hannah's voice began to crack. She wiped away a tear. 'Then a few days later she came home all quiet and there was bruising on her arms and I knew it had happened.'

'Why didn't you tell me?' raged Jacob Lovelock, rising. 'The bastard,' he cried, clenching his fists, wanting to strike out. He caught the tankard and sent it crashing to the floor.

'Please, Jacob, calm yourself,' urged Thomas. 'Your anger can serve no purpose.'

Hannah went on. 'She said she didn't want to talk about it. I knew she felt dirty and ashamed.' The tears now rolled freely down her cheeks. 'I told 'er she must not feel bad. 'Twas not her fault, but she'd changed. 'E'd taken away her flower and I knew she'd never be my little girl again.'

The tears were flowing down Jacob's face now,

266

too. Hannah went on: 'Then, after Christmas, she was even quieter. I begged her to talk to me, but she would just turn 'er back on me. She was like a stranger to 'er own mother.'

So the silence and the isolation went on, recalled Hannah, until one chilly day in May, when the ground lay covered by a late frost, Rebecca failed to report to the kitchen to help Mistress Cladding-bowl prepare the vegetables for luncheon. They sent young Will to look for his sister and he had found her, lying facedown in among the reeds of the lake. The poor child had run to get help and they had dragged his sister out of the water like a limp doll.

'She killed 'erself, Jacob,' said Hannah, turning to her husband.

'You knew it was no accident?' asked Thomas.

She nodded. 'I saw Will take the stones out of her pockets, but I wasn't going to let them bury 'er at a crossroads with a stake through her heart,' she replied calmly. Her voice had gathered strength, just as it did on the witness stand at the inquest. 'No, I knew she killed 'erself and when I prepared her body for the grave I found out why.'

Thomas and Jacob were transfixed. 'Her belly was rounding,' she said softly, in almost a reverential whisper.

At these words Jacob Lovelock leapt up and let forth a desperate cry. Lurching over to his wife, he started shaking her. 'Why didn't you tell me? Why? I could've... I...' he shouted. Thomas tried to pull him off, but he was too strong. Hannah stood her ground and looked at her husband straight in the eye. 'So that you could've killed the man who

267

raped your daughter and left her with child?' she asked. She spoke calmly and with great clarity, like a woman who had come to terms with her actions and was prepared to pay the consequences.

'Is that what you did, Hannah?' asked Thomas. 'Did you kill Lord Crick?'

An aura of tranquillity had descended upon her, as if she had become impervious to any slights or accusations. Like Saint Sebastian, her flesh could have been penetrated with countless arrows yet, thought Thomas, from her calm demeanor not a single cry of pain would have passed her lips.

'On that morning he came to us. He said he wanted to see Jacob about one of the horses. He stood in our home and he saw our Rachel.' Suddenly there was emotion in her voice once more. 'He saw her and he took her face in his filthy hands and he said to me: "She has her sister's eyes."'

Hannah turned and looked at Thomas. ''Twas then that I knew I had to do it, before he had my Rachel, too.'

At this forthright admission, Jacob Lovelock looked at his wife, then rushed forward, kneeling at her feet and smothering his tear-stained face in her skirts. She began to stroke his tousled hair gently.

'So you added something to his lordship's physick?' Thomas continued. 'What was it, Hannah? Purple foxglove?'

She glanced across at the shelf, to the jar from which she had taken leaves to treat Thomas's wound. 'Yes,' she whispered.

'And you knew it was poisonous?'

She nodded her head. 'That I did,' she groaned. 'But I never meant to kill him. I never did.' Thomas saw her breast heave as her lips trembled. He frowned.

'But what of the cyanide? The smell of bitter almonds?'

'I took one of his kerchiefs from the laundry and soaked it in laurel water,' she said calmly. 'I knew 'twould be thought that the rat poison killed the master.'

'So you would let an innocent man hang?' he asked her.

Her face hardened. 'He is of the same sort,' she sneered. 'They treat us all like dog shit on their boots.'

Thomas shook his head. 'I do not believe that you would let the captain go to the gallows, Hannah.'

She was silent for a moment.

'No. You are right, Dr. Silkstone. I never thought 'twould go this far. I thought they'd say the young master died natural-like, but when you was called in things changed. I had to point the finger somewhere.'

Thomas sighed heavily. 'But now you will do what is right?'

She nodded and grabbed hold of her husband's hands.

'Then we shall go to Oxford at first light.'

'And may God have mercy on my soul,' she murmured.

Chapter 39

Hannah Lovelock sat straight-backed next to Thomas as he steered the cart toward Oxford. They had left at dawn, just as the sun's first beams had begun to dispel the darkness of one of the longest nights Thomas had ever known. He was acutely aware that he was, in all probability, taking this woman, this mother who sat beside him, to her death. There was a sort of dignified righteousness in her poise, strangely akin to a martyr being conveyed to an undeserved death and Thomas was feeling like her executioner.

There had been tearful farewells to Jacob Lovelock and to her children that proved too painful for Thomas to witness. It was for the love of her second daughter that Hannah had done what she had done; not out of selfishness, nor greed, nor personal gain. Her only motive had been to protect her child and now she would make the ultimate sacrifice.

As the spires of Oxford came into view, Thomas turned to his stoic passenger. 'Will you forgive me for what I am about to do?'

Hannah, her face lined and pale, took a deep breath and looked into the young doctor's eyes. 'You are a just man, Dr. Silkstone,' she said in an unfaltering voice. 'You do what is right.'

With these simple words, Thomas felt absolved, even though no absolution was needed. Grasping both reins in one hand, he reached out the other and laid it gently on her arm. She reciprocated the gesture and cupped her left hand over his, but she said nothing, because nothing more could be said.

As the cart trundled on toward Oxford, in the assizes below the wheels of English justice were also turning. Sir Montagu Malthus perched himself in the witness box, his black eyes peering out from under hooded lids. He had been called to testify for the prosecution as he had uncovered some irregularities in the late Lord Crick's accounts.

'And of what do these irregularities consist?' asked the counsel for the prosecution, a portly man in his sixties by the name of Archibald Seabright.

'Large amounts of money were withdrawn on a regular basis,' replied Sir Montagu.

'Pray define the term "large",' urged the prosecution.

'Between two and five hundred pounds each week,' came the reply.

'But could these not be considered normal living expenses for a gentleman of Lord Crick's means?' suggested Mr. Seabright.

Sir Montagu's large eyebrows met in a frown over his hooded eyes. He gave a supercilious shrug. 'These monies were in addition to his normal allowance,' he replied.

'And do you have any idea what Lord Crick might have been doing with this money?' asked the portly lawyer.

James Lavington exchanged a nervous glance

with his client, while Sir Montagu looked directly at Judge de Quincy. 'I believe he was losing it at cards,' he replied in an assured manner that left no room at all for doubt in his mind.

Lavington's damaged arm suddenly began to tremble. He tried to steady it with his good hand and hoped no one had seen.

'What gives you that impression?' asked Seabright.

Malthus looked at him straight. 'Because, sir, I also discovered a number of copies of credit notes in Lord Crick's safe deposit box.'

'And to whom were these notes made out?'

The witness paused for dramatic effect. 'To Captain Farrell,' he said.

By this point, most of the players in this courtroom drama were so immersed in the action, that, on his arrival, Thomas was able to approach James Lavington almost unnoticed.

The solicitor saw him out of the corner of his eye and turned. Thomas bent down and whispered in his ear. 'I have news. New evidence.'

Lavington frowned, waving his hand as if warning off a troublesome fly, but Thomas persisted. 'We need an adjournment,' he urged.

At the word 'adjournment' Lavington turned to face the doctor. 'New evidence, you say?'

By now Thomas's presence had been noted by the judge, who swiftly brought down his gavel. 'What goes on here?' he enquired, obviously riled.

Lavington heaved himself up, his wayward hand now under control. 'My apologies, Your Honor,' he began, then, glancing at Thomas he continued: 'I would ask for an adjournment.'

'On what grounds?' barked the judge.

'I believe there is new evidence, Your Honor,' replied the lawyer.

'Very well,' declared Mr. de Quincy. 'You have until tomorrow at ten o'clock,' and with these words not only Thomas, but Lavington, too, breathed a sigh of relief, but for very different reasons.

'So, you are confessing to the murder of Lord Crick?' James Lavington needed to make sure in his own mind that what he had just heard from Hannah Lovelock's lips was correct.

The servant nodded. 'Aye, sir.' Her voice was calm, as if she had just admitted to making a bed or stoking a fire. ''Twas not my will, sir, as I said, but it happened nonetheless.'

Lavington simply nodded. Any relief that his old friend and client could now be acquitted of a crime for which he stood to lose his life remained hidden.

The lawyer's reaction surprised Thomas, who interceded. 'Hannah will make her mark on a written statement,' he said, but still there was little reaction.

'I see,' was his only reply, as he looked at Hannah rather strangely.

'Shall I...?' Thomas was about to ask if he should call the clerk into the room so that a confession could be taken, when Lavington raised his right hand to silence him.

'Thank you for your help, Dr. Silkstone,' he said coldly, 'but I need some time with Mistress Lovelock ... alone, if you please.'

Bemused by Lavington's response, Thomas nonetheless acquiesced. 'Very well,' he replied reluctantly. 'I shall leave matters in your hands,' he said as he left.

Lavington waited until the doctor had shut the door. The maidservant was seated, staring impassively at the table before her.

'So, Hannah,' Lavington finally addressed her. 'You've done a foolish thing.' His voice was measured.

'Yes, sir,' she replied softly. He was standing beside her now, close enough for her to smell his sweat. For the first time since she had revealed her secret she felt afraid. She was prepared for her punishment to be public, so that every man and woman could see her suffer for protecting her own child, but she did not want to endure a secret pain, behind closed doors, where no one would hear her cry out the name of her dead daughter; where her anguish would not penetrate the closed doors and the thick walls that now surrounded her. She wanted people to know she died for a cause. She turned toward her inquisitor and saw that he had lifted his stick and held it by the middle of the shaft, lightly hitting the palm of his hand.

Bending down so that the hideous side of his face was on a level with hers, so that she could see the shards of metal that lay still embedded beneath his skin, James Lavington whispered: 'But Hannah, I would hate you to do anything even more foolish.'

Chapter 40

The black-toothed jailer had barely had time to hang the key back up on its hook after the accused had been brought from the courtroom when Thomas emerged at the cell.

'You 'ere to see the captain?' mumbled the burly man. It was a statement more than a question. Thomas nodded. 'His wife's in there at the moment.'

'Good,' replied the young doctor. 'The news I bring concerns them both.'

But the scene that confronted him as he peered through the grille of the cell door was not one of marital harmony. Michael Farrell and his wife stood facing each other, a foot apart, in the center of the dingy, stinking room.

'How could you let him get so indebted to you and Lavington?' asked Lydia, infuriated by the latest revelations in court. Her fists were clenched in anger.

'Your brother knew what he was doing,' sneered Farrell. 'He just wasn't very good at cards.'

Meanwhile the cheerless jailer sidled toward the cell, turned the large key in the lock, and opened the door, which creaked forlornly as if reluctant to be open.

Lydia was just about to remonstrate with her husband even more when she heard the door open and turned.

'Dr. Silkstone,' she cried.

Immediately Thomas sensed a tension between the two of them. He assumed that all had not gone well in court that morning.

'Ah, the dashing young man of science,' greeted Farrell sarcastically.

Lydia shot him an angry glance.

'Please forgive my husband,' she said quickly. 'It has been a difficult morning in court.'

Thomas looked at her questioningly, but it was Farrell who replied.

'They know that Crick lost hundreds of pounds at cards to me,' he replied, showing a little uncustomary humility, 'and–'

Thomas cut him off. 'Sir, it matters not.'

Farrell looked puzzled. Lydia frowned. 'What can you mean, Dr. Silkstone?' she asked.

'I mean I bring news, good news – for you, that is.' The couple's expressions changed from anxiety to curiosity.

'Someone has confessed to poisoning Lord Crick,' declared Thomas.

At these words Lydia lurched forward, clinging tightly to her husband, melting away the distance she had put between them.

'They have? But who?' asked Farrell, ignoring his wife's embrace.

Thomas told them of Hannah's confession. He spared Lydia the details of her servant's motivation, knowing that the grim truth would be revealed at her trial.

'But why?' asked Lydia, not knowing whether to laugh or cry.

'I am not at liberty to say, your ladyship,' replied Thomas. 'Besides, it matters not. What is important is that we get you, Captain Farrell, out of here as quickly as possible.'

'Amen to that,' smiled the Irishman.

'The clerk is taking a statement from Hannah as we speak,' Thomas explained. 'By this time tomorrow your ordeal will be over, sir,' he assured the captain.

At that moment Michael Farrell should have found it in his heart to commend Thomas for his efforts on his behalf, but he left it up to his wife to step forward. 'We cannot thank you enough, Dr. Silkstone,' she told Thomas, clearly embarrassed by her husband's churlishness. 'You have done so much,' she said as the jailer's key turned once more in the lock and the door groaned open.

'You asked me to find the truth, your ladyship, and that is what I have done.'

She smiled broadly and her small hand suddenly found its way into his in a spontaneous gesture of gratitude. 'We shall see you tomorrow in court, then,' she said.

Thomas took his leave and heard the key turn in the lock for what he hoped would be the last time.

The smile was still on Lydia's lips as she turned back from the door to face her husband, but it soon vanished when she saw his knowing look.

'So, my wife and the doctor, eh?' he sneered.

Lydia froze for a moment. 'What are you saying, Michael?' she blurted out indignantly.

Her husband's shoulders sank before he let out a strange half laugh, then raising his arm he cried: 'At least he'll be able to mend your broken bones.'

Chapter 41

A mere half an hour had elapsed since Thomas had left the assizes and now the courtroom seemed eerily quiet. The gallery mob had disappeared and only the janitor could be seen sweeping up the apple cores and various unsanitary detritus left behind on the floor of the entrance hall.

Thomas wasted no time, but went straight to the antechamber where he had left Lavington and Hannah. It was empty. There was no sign of them and he thought it strange. A feeling of great unease suddenly swept over him.

'You there,' he called to the caretaker. 'Did you see a man with a stick and a maidservant leave here?'

The caretaker's hair was matted, as if the dust and dirt from the floor had gravitated toward his shoulder-length locks. He leaned on his broom. 'That I did, sir, long time ago now.'

'And did you see where they went?'

The cleaner looked blank and shook his tousled head. 'They went that way,' he said, waving a dirt-encrusted hand in a vague and wholly unhelpful manner, leaving Thomas none the wiser and doubly unsettled. He'd assumed that once Hannah had signed her confession, the court constables would be summoned to arrest her. That'd have been the correct procedure. Now he was confused, unsure, and deeply troubled as to the maidservant's whereabouts. Without her confession, the fate of Captain Farrell still lay precariously in the balance. He told himself he was being ridiculous; that Lavington had probably taken Hannah somewhere quiet to question her. He'd go to the lawyer's lodgings in Merton Street later, but right now, he had urgent business of his own.

Thomas was relieved to find Professor Hascher in his laboratory. Here there was order amid this chaos in which he suddenly found himself immersed. Here were the labeled jars and the numbered receptacles; the surgeons' instruments, the sutures, the pliers, the forceps; their capabilities, their functions all tested, all certain, all known.

'I think I have made progress,' Thomas explained, dispensing with customary pleasantries. The professor saw that the young man looked troubled and stressed as he opened his case and took out a physick bottle and a phial containing a sample from the jar of foxglove leaves from Hannah's kitchen.

'My laboratory is always at your disposal,' the Saxon reiterated.

'And what about your mice?' asked Thomas, casting his gaze toward a large cage in the corner.

The professor nodded, looking at the rodents scurrying about in their cages, eager-eyed and twitching. Thomas was reminded of Franklin in his own laboratory and how he had saved him from the fate that he was now to bestow on one of these helpless vermin. He had no liking for it, but he could see no other way.

Carefully he picked out the plumpest mouse

and, using a pipette, he dropped a solution of the digitalis, which he had made up earlier, into the creature's mouth. He had added it to Lord Crick's physick, just as Hannah had done, and used the exact same strength of the poison that she had used. Normally the effects of ingestion in a human, he had read, were felt between thirty minutes and two hours later. It troubled him somewhat that, according to Hannah's account, the poison had taken hold almost immediately, and only a few seconds after the young earl had swallowed the physick.

Placing the mouse back in the cage, all Thomas could do was watch and wait. Professor Hascher joined him in his vigil. The minutes passed. Ten, twenty. The mouse interacted quite happily with his fellows, showing no adverse effects from the digitalis whatsoever.

'I shall increase the dose,' said Thomas. 'I shall double it.'

This he did, so that the solution a second mouse now ingested was twice the strength of the one given to Lord Crick. He waited another ten minutes, the professor at his side, watching eagerly, but again, nothing happened. Again the mouse remained active and alert. Thomas was perplexed. If such a dose had killed a man outright, why was it having no effect at all on a mouse? He grappled with the conundrum, turning the quandary around and around in his head. But time and time again, no matter how many different strands of logic he applied to the problem, he was forced to come to the same startling and wholly unexpected conclusion.

Chapter 42

Thomas made his way hurriedly toward Merton Street. He knew that Lydia and Lavington had taken rooms there. Just exactly where, he was unsure. He was grasping at straws, he accepted, but he needed to find them. Through the narrow gate he went, which led out of Christ Church Meadow and past Chapel Tower. Skirting Merton Tower with its high walls topped by battlements and massive doors, he turned right into Merton Street and proceeded to walk along the cobbles heading toward Magdalene Bridge.

Farther down, the rows of houses afforded lodgings to scholars and fellows. It was here that Thomas supposed he would find Lavington, but he soon came to the end of the street and was berating himself for his pathetic attempt to find Hannah and the lawyer when he spied a familiar figure. Walking along the street, wearing the same battered bonnet that she had worn for the inquest, was Eliza, her fulsome hips swinging provocatively down the street. He quickened his pace. She was perhaps only half a furlong head of him. He saw her stop outside a house and disappear inside.

No. 22 Merton Street was a substantial dwelling with stone columns that stood abreast a large door. It was grander than most of the other houses in the street and Thomas pulled the bell cord. Sure enough, it was Eliza who answered.

'Is your mistress at home?'

Eliza recognized Thomas instantly and was clearly a little taken aback by his presence. 'Yes, Dr. Silkstone,' she said. 'Please come in.'

The maid disappeared into the hallway and returned a few moments later. 'Come this way,' she said, leading Thomas upstairs to a large, airy drawing room. Lydia was seated at the window seat, gazing down onto the street below. She seemed strangely subdued and motioned to Eliza to leave.

It was only when Thomas walked over to her and she turned to face him fully that he saw the bruising down one side of her face. Her right cheek was swollen and inflamed.

'What happened?' he asked, taking her face in his hands and inspecting the bruises.

She remained silent, but her silence spoke volumes. 'What sort of a man does this to his wife?' he asked, the anger rising in him. 'He does not deserve to live.'

Lydia stretched out her hand. 'You must not say that,' she reprimanded him, but her voice remained calm.

Thomas took a deep breath and composed himself. 'I am sorry. I should not...' He broke off, remembering the real reason for his visit. If he did not trace Hannah, the captain might still be in danger.

'Have you seen Lavington?'

Lydia frowned. 'I last saw him when the court adjourned,' she replied. 'Pray tell me – what is it, Thomas?'

'Lydia,' he said earnestly. 'I fear that Hannah

might have escaped.'

'Your fear is well-founded,' came a voice from behind.

It was James Lavington. He stood at the door-way, looking slightly disheveled. His cravat was askew and his normally immaculate topcoat was torn on the sleeve, just below the elbow.

'The witch gave me the slip,' he panted, wiping his brow with a kerchief. 'She told me she wanted one last look at freedom before she made her confession and I, like a fool, obliged.'

'You mean you let her escape?' cried Lydia in-credulously, jumping to her feet.

'The constables are out looking for her now,' said Lavington, mopping his brow.

'God grant they find her,' cried Lydia.

The woman lay on the table in front of him; a heap of tissue and skin, of bone and muscle; a conglomeration of all that is human and yet not. Only a few hours ago she would have been alive. Her heart would have pumped, her lungs would have inflated; her liver would have drawn nourishment. Now she lay lifeless with her face so badly beaten that her features melded into one grotesque, amorphous mass.

Like a rotten piece of meat, she had been dis-carded and thrown into the Cherwell. Some bargees had spotted her floating facedown among the duckweed in a shallow channel, with only a chemise covering her breasts. With their billhooks they had dragged her to the bank, adding to her already horrific injuries, and smiled among themselves. There was money to be made from a corpse, so once again the sack-'em-up men were summoned. True to their name, they put the corpse in a sack. 'Four guineas,' demanded one of the bargees.

'Not with her face smashed in like that,' said a sack-'em-up man. 'Two.'

And so a deal was struck and, for the price of a few yards of worsted, they bagged her up, this unfortunate woman, and took her to the door of Professor Hans Hascher. It was Thomas who answered their knock.

'The foreign one not in?' asked one.

'He is here,' replied a wary Thomas, looking at the hessian sack at his side.

Professor Hascher came to the door. 'We got an adult for you.'

The old man waved his hand distastefully. 'Not today,' he said dismissively, but Thomas countermanded him.

'How much?'

'Four guineas,' replied the senior man.

'Here's three,' said Thomas, putting a handful of shiny coins into his soiled palm. The man nodded, knowing that once the doctor had seen the face, he might well not be interested at all.

The scoundrels brought in their gruesome cargo and put the sack on the table, leaving Thomas to discover its grisly contents.

'A woman, aye?' he said as the men wiped their wet hands on their breeches.

'Yes. In the river, she was. Upstream from Magdalene.'

Not wishing to engage in conversation, the two hoodlums took their leave and Thomas and the

284

professor were left to discover the macabre offering for themselves.

'You sink zis could be your woman?' asked Hascher as Thomas took a scalpel to cut open the sacking.

The young doctor looked the professor in the eye. 'I pray God it is not.'

Carefully he began slicing the hessian that covered the head and within a few seconds the woman's face was revealed.

'Dear God,' Thomas let slip when he saw the pulverized mass of tissue and bone where once there had been a nose and eyes and cheekbones. In his seven years of anatomy, he had never seen an attack so vicious and brutal as to leave a woman bereft of her entire face. All that remained were fragments of long brown hair.

For a moment he needed to calm himself, to remind himself that he was a professional and that he needed to distance himself from any emotion or repulsion that he felt.

The corpse was naked, save for a coarse, white linen chemise that was caked in blood. This woman, he surmised, was of lowly birth. He cut open the front of her shift to reveal her breasts. They were small, but quite pendulous, indicative that she might have nursed at least one infant.

Thomas noted the contusions along the length of her body. Whoever she was, the woman had been beaten before her face had been pulverized. There were long marks along her back, arms, and legs, the marks of a bar or a stick, Thomas surmised.

'She tried to shield herself from the blows,' he

remarked to the professor. 'Look, her hands, inner lower arms, and fingers are badly bruised.'

Now he moved to the abdomen and began to examine her pelvis. Thomas noticed it had widened and the slackness of her pelvic ligaments suggested she had given birth more than once.

'A mother?' queried the professor.

Thomas nodded. 'Definitely.'

There was bruising, too, around her genitalia and scratch marks on her inner thighs. 'Whoever beat her raped her, too,' concluded Thomas, a note of disgust in his voice at this final act of barbarity.

'But who was she?'

'I'd say she was in her thirties. She had borne at least one child, and was probably in service,' Thomas concluded.

'The calloused hands?' remarked the professor, looking at her palms. 'But is she the woman you were looking for?'

Thomas sighed deeply. 'Of that I cannot be sure.' He paused reverentially for a moment. 'She must have a decent burial.'

The old Saxon was about to protest, thinking the torso a fine specimen for his students. When, however, he saw the look in the young doctor's eyes, he capitulated. It was clear Thomas felt this corpse had been through too much already. She did not deserve to endure the final humiliation of the dissection hall in front of dozens of undergraduates who had no care for the fact that this was a woman who had suffered unspeakable horrors before being beaten to death.

'I shall call ze constables,' said the professor.

'Yes,' nodded Thomas, aware that whoever had committed this heinous act of savagery needed to be caught and brought to justice.

'We may have found the woman they were looking for.'

Chapter 43

Thomas slept fitfully that night. The pieces of the puzzle that only twenty-four hours ago were beginning to fit so neatly into place were now falling apart. The results of his tests on the *Digitalis purpurea,* Hannah's disappearance, and now the discovery of this woman's body all felt so wrong. It was as if an experiment he had conducted and noted dozens of times before had yielded a completely different and contradictory result when he had repeated it one last time.

He thought of Captain Farrell, too, alone in his cell. Just a few hours before, freedom had seemed within his reach, but it was dangling perilously on the end of a fragile thread and that thread had now broken.

At first light when he reached the prison gates he surmised that the jailers would run such a harsh regime and wake the prisoners at dawn, if only to prolong their interminable agony of incarceration.

He found the jailer sitting at his table with his mouth wide open, dabbing a troublesome tooth with a grubby gin-soaked cloth. When he saw the young doctor, he took his fingers out of his mouth and eyed him suspiciously.

'You're an early bird,' he greeted him warily, then under his foul-smelling breath he jibed: 'Come to see the worm.'

Thomas heard him, but chose to ignore his cheap aside. 'Is the captain awake?'

'Slept like a baby all night, he 'as,' said the jailer, peering through the grille. 'More than I 'ave,' he moaned, clutching a grubby hand to his jaw. Thomas peered through the grille, as well. He could see the Irishman was lying under his coarse blanket on the wooden platform that served as a bed. He could not see his head, only a mound of coverlet and straw, which, he assumed, had escaped from his torn palliasse.

The jailer opened wide the cell door, allowing Thomas to enter, the smell of urine and filth assailing his nostrils. As soon as the door was shut behind him, Thomas went over to the bed. It surprised him that the Irishman had not stirred when the key had clanked in the lock.

'Captain Farrell,' called Thomas, standing over the crumpled heap, softly at first, then louder. 'Captain Farrell.'

Receiving no response, Thomas lightly prodded the blanket, but his fingers felt only straw below. Shocked, he pulled back the cover. Farrell was gone. A mound of hay brought from the spoil corner lay in his stead.

'Guard, guard,' he cried, rushing to the door. The jailer came swiftly. 'The captain – he's gone,' called Thomas. But the look of shock on the young doctor's face was as nothing compared with the fingerprint of horror that had suddenly stamped itself upon the jailer. Thomas followed the man's terrified eyes to where they had rested, pupils dilated, the hairs on the back of his neck erect, then he, too, was suddenly gripped by the chilling sight – the sight of a hanged man.

Gently they cut him down. Thomas sliced through the cord as the jailer took the weight of the body, then together they carried him over to the wooden pallet. Thomas felt for a pulse. There was none and the precariousness of his own mortality flashed before him, as it had never done before. As he lay on the reeking palliasse, Captain Michael Farrell looked dignified in a place that dignity had long deserted. His eyes were shut. They had been shut when he first saw him hanging. His facial muscles were not contorted in any way, but relaxed. There was a peaceful beauty in the death that made Thomas believe for a moment that perhaps he was only sleeping.

He had seen many a man hanged, sometimes several at one go. If the drop was short they would often writhe in agony for up to an hour. Sometimes relatives would rush forward to pull on their legs to end their loved one's suffering. Michael Farrell could have been accorded no such mercy and yet, thought Thomas, his face was not contorted in any way. He was tall and his body had only dropped six inches from the ceiling and yet his lips were not bitten, as most men's are when they are gasping for breath, nor was his tongue protruding, as in some grotesque gargoyle's grimace.

The captain may have wanted to die, but even

so, his body would have put up a fight against his mind. There were certain involuntary reactions, which always occurred – the emptying of the bowels, for example – but this had not happened in this case. Such thoughts, however, the thoughts of a surgeon, had to be put aside for the moment. He had a more pressing task to which it was his grim duty to attend.

Eliza answered the door. 'My mistress is dressing, sir,' she told Thomas.

'I am afraid that I have some grave news which I must impart right away,' he told the maid. She could tell from his expression that something terrible had indeed happened and she did not argue. Instead, she ran upstairs and Thomas heard her knock urgently on her ladyship's door. There were muffled calls and shouted questions. He heard Lavington's voice, too, upbraiding Eliza for disturbing her mistress.

'What's the meaning of this, Silkstone?' the lawyer called angrily, fastening the belt on his robe as he limped down the stairs.

'Is Lady Lydia coming?'

'What business is it of yours, sir?'

'What I have to say concerns her deeply.'

Lavington could tell by Thomas's tone that there was, indeed, some disturbing news to impart.

'You'd better go in,' said the lawyer, motioning to the drawing room. 'Her ladyship will be down shortly.'

Eliza scurried in front of them into the room, which was in darkness. She went to draw back the heavy drapes, but fumbled among the folds, as if looking for something.

'What's the matter with you, girl?' barked Lavington.

'Sorry, sir, I...' she began and then, as if she had found a solution to her problem, she stopped and gripped a side of one of the curtains, pulling it back so that the watery morning light flooded the room.

Thomas did not sit, but paced the floor, trying to frame his words. He had lost count of the number of times he had had to break the news to a relative, a husband or wife, a mother or a son. It was never easy, but this time would be by far the worst.

'Good God, man. You're acting like a caged animal,' accused Lavington. Thomas ignored him until, after what seemed an age, Lydia finally appeared at the doorway.

'What is it, Dr. Silkstone? What has happened? Have they found Hannah?' she asked nervously.

'Your ladyship, please.' Thomas motioned to the chaise longue. He was afraid she might swoon when he told her the news.

'There is no easy way of putting this,' he said.

Lydia looked at him with guileless eyes. She seemed more fragile than ever to Thomas, waiting for his words.

'I am afraid your husband ... Captain Farrell is dead.'

'What are you saying, man?' cried Lavington, rushing forward.

For a moment Lydia was silent, as if her brain were processing the dreaded message it had just received, then she let out a muffled cry.

'No. No!' she screamed, leaping up and whirling around. Lavington took hold of her by the arms. She tried to fend him off.

'Lydia. Lydia. Calm yourself. For God's sake,' shouted the lawyer, gripping her tightly and shaking her.

Thomas could see the onset of hysteria, but he did not like the way Lavington was handling Lydia. He feared he might hurt her.

Quickly delving into his bag, he brought out a phial of smelling salts and wafted them under her nose. They took effect almost instantly, jolting her back to reality. Lavington lessened his grip and the young woman's tears began to flow.

'How? How?' she sobbed as Lavington eased her back onto the chaise longue.

Thomas shot a glance at the lawyer. He had agonized over whether to reveal the whole truth to Lydia, but had decided that perhaps it was for the best. 'I ... I found him hanging in his cell this morning, your ladyship,' he told her.

She looked up at him incredulously. 'What? You mean ... you mean he took his own...?'

Her voice trailed off wanly, but before Thomas could answer, Lavington intervened.

'I am afraid it does not surprise me in the least,' he said, shaking his head slowly.

'What are you saying, Mr. Lavington?' asked Thomas.

The lawyer sighed deeply and sat himself down beside the distraught Lydia.

'You remember what he said? You told me yourself.'

A look of shock darted across Lydia's face as

she remembered her husband's words on one of her last visits. In a moment of indiscretion she must have divulged them to Lavington.

'If you ever lost faith in him...?'

Lydia shot a glance at Thomas. They both knew that what Lavington was saying was true. The lawyer reached out his hand to take hers, but she withdrew instantly. 'He could not face life without your trust. We all knew that.'

Thomas watched Lydia's reaction to Lavington's cruel words. The lawyer may as well have pierced her flesh with a stiletto and then twisted it inside her, but he felt powerless to intervene.

Lydia looked away. 'No. No. Tell me this is not true,' she screamed, doubling over and sobbing uncontrollably. The lawyer put a comforting arm around Lydia's back as it heaved violently up and down, then looked up at Thomas. 'Give her something to calm her, will you?' he said coldly. 'I must away to court. The judge needs to be informed.'

As soon as Lavington had limped out of the room Thomas took his place on the chaise longue next to Lydia. He put a tentative arm around her. He was not sure how she would react. She did not prize herself away, as he feared she might, but rather sat up and allowed her face to nestle into his shoulder.

'Lydia,' said Thomas softly as she continued to weep. 'Lydia. Please, do not blame yourself.' He would never forgive Lavington for showing such insensitivity. 'I have to tell you something. Please listen to me.'

At these words Lydia raised her head from his shoulder and faced him with tear-stained cheeks.

Just as there had been no easy way to break the news of Captain Farrell's death, there was no easy way of imparting his deepest fears. 'I do not think your husband took his own life.' Her glassy eyes gazed questioningly into his.

'What are you saying?'

Thomas looked at Lydia. She seemed so delicate, he did not know if she would stand the shock of what he was about to say, but say it he must. He took a deep breath and said: 'I have reason to believe the captain was murdered.'

Chapter 44

'I am afraid that is out of the question, Dr. Silk-stone.' Sir Theodisius pushed away the remnants of a veal pie. He was so irked by the young doctor's insistent request for a postmortem that he had suddenly lost his appetite.

'But, sir, I beg you, for the sake of justice,' pleaded Thomas.

The coroner brought his fist down hard on the desk so that the knife that rested on his pewter plate jumped and clattered as it landed.

'In France justice dictates that suicides are dragged, facedown, through the streets on a hurdle, then strung up by the feet and their goods confiscated, sir,' he roared. His flaccid face had reddened with anger, but then, as if realizing that his temper was getting the better of him, his tone became measured.

'I am satisfied that Captain Farrell took his own life. He had every reason to do so and unless I see proof to the contrary, that is my final say on the matter.'

Thomas had wanted to at least have the opportunity to provide the coroner with that proof and did not see the logicality of his argument, but he could also see he was getting nowhere.

'I am sorry to have troubled you, sir,' he said, fingering the brim of his tricorn forlornly. He turned to go, but then swung 'round quickly, as if he had had an afterthought.

'I would ask just one thing of you, sir,' he said excitedly.

'Yes?' retorted Sir Theodisius, obviously irritated.

'I understand that in this country it is still common practice to bury a suicide at a crossroads with a stake through its heart.'

The coroner shifted in his seat, clearly uncomfortable that an upstart colonist should look down upon centuries-old English ways. He nodded: 'Aye, that is true.'

'And that a suicide cannot be buried in consecrated ground?' Another nod from the coroner.

'Then,' continued Thomas, 'may I make a request on behalf of Captain Farrell's widow that his body be returned to Boughton Hall and buried on the estate?'

Sir Theodisius sat back in his chair, his large frame bulging over the sides. He thought for a moment of Lydia and the pain she must be suffering. It was within his remit to alleviate some of that suffering by exercising his discretionary powers. He looked Thomas in the eye.

'For the sake of Lady Lydia, I shall permit this.'

Thomas smiled. 'You are a compassionate man, sir,' he said and, with that, he turned and left to make his way to the prison to see to the appropriate arrangements.

The same black-toothed jailer sat in his chair, still nursing his throbbing jaw. He stiffened as soon as he saw Thomas.

'I am here to prepare the corpse,' explained the doctor, lifting his black bag slightly. 'Can you let me attend to Captain Farrell's body?'

He could see clearly through the grille. The Irishman remained in the cell, where he had been laid, but he was hidden under a large piece of hessian.

'I can't let you do that, sir,' said the jailer, rising slowly to his feet.

'What do you mean? I am here to prepare the body for burial,' protested Thomas indignantly.

''Tis orders, Doctor. I am not allowed to let anyone see the body,' replied the jailer.

'Whose orders?' snapped Thomas.

'Mr. Lavington's.'

The young doctor nodded. He should have expected as much. As his attorney, Lavington had a right to claim jurisdiction over access to Farrell's body. Now he would never be able to examine the captain's neck properly to see if it was as he suspected and that it remained unbroken. The silken cord that he had found around his neck seemed too delicate to have withstood a struggle or a sudden jolt. A sense of powerlessness suddenly enveloped him.

'I shall go and speak with Mr. Lavington,' he told the jailer.

'No need to go anywhere, Dr. Silkstone,' came a voice from the stairs. Thomas turned to see Lavington limp into view. 'I am here.'

'I am glad of it, sir,' said Thomas. 'I have been told by Sir Theodisius that I am not allowed to conduct a postmortem on the body.'

Lavington frowned. 'Indeed you are not, sir. Lady Lydia has expressly said she does not want her late husband filleted like a side of beef.'

'Very well,' replied Thomas. 'But you might at least allow me to prepare the captain's body for burial.'

Lavington looked contemptuously at the young doctor. 'Yes, I hear that Sir Theodisius has generously suggested that he be buried at Boughton.' Thomas knew the lawyer made a deliberate error to discredit him, refusing to acknowledge the fact that it was he who had interceded as regards the burial. 'But your help will not be necessary, Dr. Silkstone. They are well used to dealing with the dead here,' he said, glancing toward the jailer. 'It is in their hands,' he said finally, not brokering any discussion on the subject. With that he bid Thomas a good day and made his way back up the steps.

The young doctor felt humiliated. He looked at the jailer taking a swig of gin from the bottle on the table. One side of his stubble-covered face was noticeably bulging. His instinct as a surgeon was to offer to remove the offending tooth for the wretched man; his instinct as a man in search of the truth was to bargain.

'Do you want me to take it out?' he said, pointing to the man's inflamed cheek.

At the very suggestion the jailer's eyes lit up and his head nodded so vigorously that it made his tooth hurt even more.

Thomas smiled. 'I'll tell you what I'll do. I remove your rotting tooth and in return you do a little something for me.'

'Anything, sir,' whimpered the man.

Thomas opened his black bag and took out a pair of pliers. He held them in front of the man's terrified face, as if they were an instrument of torture rather than relief.

'First tell me who was the last person to see Captain Farrell alive.'

The jailer looked at Thomas shiftily. 'Me, sir. It was me.'

Thomas thrust the pliers nearer to the man's face. 'I can take this tooth out quickly, or I can make you suffer. You choose,' he warned.

'He ... he gave me money not to tell,' he squealed.

'Who? Who gave you money?' Thomas lunged for the man's head and stood behind him, holding it in a lock, the pliers poised to draw.

'Mr. Lavington, sir.'

The man's garbled words merely confirmed Thomas's suspicions.

'Good,' he said, relaxing his hold on the jailer's head. 'We shall proceed presently, just after you have agreed to one more thing.'

The helpless man grunted his assent. 'You see that bottle of gin on the table,' said Thomas. 'You

298

will douse Captain Farrell's body in it before wrapping it in sacking.'

Again a grunt from the man, followed by a loud cry as Thomas swiftly and with infinite dexterity extracted the rotting tooth by its root from the gum.

The great gargoyles of Merton College glowered down on Thomas as he made his way along the cobbled streets to Lydia's lodgings. He needed to speak with her in private, so he planned to deliver a note via Eliza, requesting a secret assignation where he could tell her his fears.

Eliza did, indeed, answer the door, but before he opened his mouth, she pressed a wad of bank notes in his hand.

'Lady Lydia has asked me to pay you your fee and bid you farewell, Dr. Silkstone,' she said, not daring to look Thomas in the eye.

The young doctor stared in disbelief at the money in his hand. He had not undertaken this tortuous journey that had ended so tragically for financial gain. Feeling tainted he returned the notes to Eliza. 'Please tell Lady Lydia I cannot accept her money for a task I have not completed,' he said and with those words he handed back the bills.

Upstairs Lydia looked out of the window. She saw Thomas below and, unaware of the alter-cation, was about to instruct Eliza to allow the doctor inside immediately when James Lavington entered the room.

'Dr. Silkstone is downstairs,' she told him, walking toward the door. 'I must see him.' But as she passed him, Lavington took hold of her arm.

'I think not,' he said firmly.

She frowned. 'What do you mean?' she asked, looking at her wrist, which remained in his grip.

Lavington smiled his twisted smile. 'I'm afraid your doctor is no longer welcome here,' he told her.

'But I must...' Lydia tried to break free of his grip, but he held on tight.

'You must agree it is not seemly for a new widow to see her lover on the day of her husband's death.'

Lydia froze. 'What are you talking about?'

Lavington shook his head. 'There's no denying it, my dear,' he smirked, then reaching into his coat pocket he brought out a button and held it up in front of Lydia's face. 'Eliza found this in your bed; from Dr. Silkstone's waistcoat, I believe.'

Lydia felt her heart beating in her chest and the blood coursing through her veins. 'No. It wasn't like that. He...'

Lavington reached out his index finger and pressed it against her lips. 'Save your excuses, dear Lydia. I need no explanation, just your obedience.'

Chapter 45

Thomas Silkstone sat alone in his laboratory, as he had done ever since his return from Oxford three days before, and pondered on the events of the past few weeks. He could not dispel his last image of Lydia in Merton Street. He had backed away from the front door and looked up at the drawing room window. There, standing gazing down, he saw her. Her face was expressionless and she did not try to speak. For a second or two he held her icy stare, hoping it might melt. He willed her to say something, to show some emotion, but she did not and he turned reluctantly to walk away.

Shunning the wit and conversations of the coffeehouse, the distractions of the theater, and the company of his students, he emerged only to take meals with Dr. Carruthers. His mentor always seemed eager to discourse and Thomas did not wish to disappoint. Perhaps he had been wrong, after all, to venture out of the confines of his own world. His fingers were more at ease exploring the moist, familiar landscapes of the human body than in the dry and combative environs of the courtroom. He was after all a surgeon, not an enforcer of the law. He was a man of science, not of letters. His mission was to wield a knife as an instrument of healing, not of torture.

Time and time again he asked how he had allowed himself to be lured away from all that he knew, all that he could be certain of, and into a world of duplicity and intrigue and mistrust, and time and time again, he came to the same conclusion. At first he had lied to himself. He had deluded himself about some higher cause: a search for truth and justice. But in the end he had to admit he had been guided by an undeniable, unquenchable, and forbidden love for Lady Lydia Farrell.

Poets talked of broken hearts, but at the

moment he felt as though someone had wrenched out his own heart and pulverized it. Lydia had reciprocated his feelings for her, had she not? She was willing to give herself to him. He could not believe that her touch was not genuine, her kisses a sham. The recollection of her icy stare as she looked down at him from the window in Oxford was burned indelibly on his memory, as if it had been etched in acid. He wanted to forget it, but her face came back to haunt him time and again and on each occasion he found himself asking the question, 'Why?'

When the captain was alive their love was forbidden. True, he had died in tragic and mysterious circumstances, and now a respectful period of mourning was in order. Thomas would have been discreet. Surely she knew that? Perhaps she was feeling guilty, he told himself, for her infidelity.

And what of James Lavington? Had not the captain nominated him as Lydia's guardian should anything happen to him? He mixed in the same social circles. Moreover, he was not a foreigner. Lavington would be the logical successor to step into the captain's shoes and he, Thomas, would be consigned to a mere memory.

After Lydia had dismissed him so summarily, Thomas had made his way back to Christ Church Anatomy School to see Professor Hascher. He had told him of events and asked him to see to it that Jacob Lovelock was summoned to try and identify the body of the battered woman. This, Hascher had duly done and earlier that morning Thomas had received word that the woman's corpse was not that of Hannah Lovelock. He was relieved, of course, but the maidservant's where-abouts still remained a mystery. Thomas was convinced that she held the key to at least some of what had happened in the past week and until she was found, he would not be able to move forward.

Since his return Thomas had tried to busy himself. There were new specimens to dissect and notate and medicaments to make up for aged ladies with nothing better to do than count their agues as they awaited death. He glanced toward his shelves and saw the neatly labeled jars that held Lord Crick's stomach and other tissue samples. If only they could speak, he thought, their eloquence and insight would put an end to this charade immediately.

Dr. Carruthers had tried to persuade Thomas to accompany him to the coffeehouse, but he had declined. He did not feel that he would add anything to the gathering in his present state of mind. The only living thing whose company he could tolerate right now was Franklin's. The rat suddenly appeared from a pile of papers on the floor and meandered over to his desk. Whiskers twitching, nose to the ground, he scurried in-tently past Thomas and headed for the young doctor's coat, which hung on a peg adjacent to the desk. There the rodent stopped and began sniffing at the pocket, which was level with his nose. Next he sat on his hind legs, and with his front paws, he began clawing at the pocket, as if attracted by something inside.

'What is it, Franklin?' asked Thomas puzzled. 'You'll not find any scraps in there, boy.'

It was then that Thomas remembered what the

rat would find. He rose and walked over to the coat. Thrusting his hand deep into his left pocket, he brought out the object of Franklin's curiosity – the bloodstained silken cord, which Thomas had cut from the neck of Captain Michael Farrell.

'Clever boy,' said Thomas, looking at the thin rope. He had put it in his pocket almost immediately at the jail. In all the subsequent drama it was something that had completely slipped his mind. He unraveled the cord and laid it out on his desk. It was around seven feet long and at one end it was stained with what appeared to be blood. Thomas assumed that this was where it had sliced through the epidermis at the neck as the body hung. A section of about three inches was stained, but one small patch was darker than the rest.

Holding the silken cord in his hand, his mind suddenly flashed back to his penultimate visit to Lydia's lodgings at Merton Street. Eliza had been fumbling with the curtains as Lavington came downstairs. Why? Could it have been that the pull cord had disappeared so that she had to draw the drapes by hand?

Thomas reached for his microscope. He then took a glass slide from one of the small drawers on his desk and positioned it. Next he secured the cord onto the slide and peered through the lens. What he saw, magnified one hundred times, confirmed his analysis. The cells that lay before him, like so many brown roof tiles, were those of blood, but their density varied. Where the stain was darkest, there were more of them, indicating the possibility of a much deeper wound. It was something that puzzled Thomas and unless he could gain access to the captain's corpse, it would forever remain a mystery. Each day that the decay spread was a day the truth rotted, too.

Lydia bent down, took a handful of loose earth, and threw it on top of the simple pine coffin that held the body of her late husband. There was a tragic finality about this act, as if she had just closed a book or drawn a curtain. James Lavington stood at her side, supporting her throughout. He nodded to Lovelock and Kidd to proceed shoveling in the dirt.

The burial was a private affair. No pastor was there to lead prayers; no friends to eulogize. Lady Crick was attending an imaginary bridge party and only the servants had shown their loyalty by paying their respects. Lydia had bid a dutiful farewell and Lavington, too, had said a few well-chosen words, designed to ease her burden of guilt.

Lydia had selected a place for the burial just a few yards away from the pavilion at the top of the hill, so that when she came to visit the grave, she could look out at the rolling vista and remember the times they had shared up there. A simple wooden cross rested at the head of the grave that gave no hint of the tragic circumstances that lay behind this shocking death. No future generations would know the true facts of this tragedy if Lydia had her way. But as she watched Kidd and Lovelock shovel the earth back over the coffin, it occurred to her that there might not even be another generation. With Michael's death, she might never bear a child to carry on the line at Boughton. The thought of it was too much for her and she broke down in tears, so that Lavington had to help her onto the dogcart and drive her down the hill and back to the hall.

'My dear Lydia, please calm yourself,' he urged her. They were sitting in the darkened drawing room later that afternoon. She had asked him to leave her alone earlier, and he had respected her wishes, but she remained inconsolable and he was becoming increasingly concerned, showing her slow gestures of care. Easing himself down on the settee beside her, he put a comforting arm around her. She pulled away at his touch, but he persisted. 'Do not fear,' he told her. 'This is what Michael wanted. You know he asked me to look after you, if anything happened to him.'

Lydia looked up at him suddenly, shocked at the impropriety of this last statement. Lavington reached out for her hand and kissed it, allowing his lips to linger on her wrist, but she withdrew it quickly.

'Come, come, Lydia. Why do you shun my concern?' he asked her.

Lydia's back stiffened. 'You speak to me in terms which are not seemly, sir,' she scolded gently.

But instead of feeling duly humbled by this chastisement, Lavington simply smiled in the half light, the hideous part of his face hidden in shadow, so that he looked strong and handsome. He pulled her gently toward him and said sweetly: 'That is where you are wrong, Lydia. I have every right.'

Unable to bear his touch, she leapt up from the sofa and hugged herself, as if she felt a chill. 'I am in mourning, sir. Please respect that,' she rebuked him, more sternly this time. 'I would ask you to leave now.'

Lavington looked at her contemptuously. 'I doubt if you would treat Dr. Silkstone the same way,' he ventured, his lip curving in a sneer. She resented the remark, but said nothing. Now she knew how her dead husband must have felt – alone and in a prison of his own making.

Chapter 46

With the twenty guineas James Lavington had paid for her silence, Hannah Lovelock caught a coach to London and took rooms in a lodging house for gentlewomen in Bedford Lane. She had bought herself a dress of printed calico and a thick woolen cape and passed herself off as a married woman come to London to visit her ailing father in hospital. The rules of her boardinghouse dictated no visitors, and lodgers were to be in by dusk, but that suited Hannah's purpose very well.

London, to her, was a frightening and strange place, far removed from Brandwick, or even Oxford. From her upstairs room, all Covent Garden lay before her in all its squalid, frantic, and colorful glory. Strolling performers beat their salt boxes, making music with rolling pins; crows fired cannons with their beaks; and she had even seen a pig arrange lettered blocks with its snout. Quacks called out their cures for the French pox and merchants with baskets on their heads hawked live mackerel, lemons, and fine Seville oranges.

This was a world where Hannah Lovelock most definitely did not feel she belonged, but she had come here on a mission. She needed to find the man who had wanted to take her to her death. Thomas Silkstone had uncovered her darkest secret. He had made her stare into the cold, unforgiving eyes of reality. He had made her confess. But despite the fact that she had faced the gallows, and still did for all she knew, she was grateful to him. She could not have lived with herself with the young lord's death staining her soul and she was glad that her misdeeds had been uncovered.

It mattered not that Dr. Silkstone thought he was driving her to her trial and ultimate execution. She would have died for a noble cause. As the hangman placed the noose around her neck, she would have cried out the name of her dead child and died for her. What really mattered now was that she had escaped from the clutches of a man whom she thought she could trust, but who had threatened to make the rest of her family suffer if she had not left the courtroom that day, vowing never to return. That man was James Lavington and now she sought to expose him to the only man she felt could help her.

She walked the one and a half miles from her lodgings in Covent Garden to the sprawling mass of St. George's Hospital, just beyond the western gates of the city. This is where she told her landlady her stricken father lay and the woman had obligingly given her directions, but now that she had arrived at the forbidding building, she had no idea which way to turn. It was her hope that someone, somewhere in this vast edifice might have heard of Dr. Thomas Silkstone, so they could tell her where she might find his rooms.

As she walked through the giant portico, the porters bustling around her helping patients with bloodied bandages walk along its vast corridors, Hannah Lovelock felt alone and very frightened. The sickly sweet smell of vinegar that washed the walls and floors assailed her nostrils and the distant groans of patients in distress droned in her ears.

'Oi, you. Nurse. Give us a 'and,' commanded a gruff voice nearby. Hannah turned to see a porter trying to lift an elderly woman who had fainted. 'Come on, then,' urged the man, struggling with the limp patient. Hannah looked nervously around, hoping he was addressing someone else. But no, his eyes were firmly fixed on her and she walked over to him and took some of the woman's weight, while the porter eased her onto a bench 'Don't just stand there. Go fetch a physician,' he barked.

Hannah felt helpless. She began walking, frantically searching for anyone with an air of authority. A few yards down the corridor, she spotted a white-haired man with a kindly face who was carrying a black bag.

'Doctor?' she said tentatively.

'What is it, Nurse?'

'I am no nurse, sir,' she replied timidly

He looked at her incredulously. 'Then who are you, pray?'

'I am but a visitor, sir,' Hannah replied.

'Then, my dear lady, I suggest you report to the reception,' he said, pointing to a large sign over a door on the opposite side of the corridor.

To a woman who could not read, such a sign was of little relevance, but at least she now knew where to seek help.

'Thank you, sir,' she said, curtsying.

The hall was lofty, with a large table on the left, behind a wooden screen, behind which lay wooden cubbyholes that bulged with packets and documents. Young men swarmed about them, like drones on a honeycomb, filling and emptying the spaces, opening packages or thrusting in documents.

As Hannah approached the desk, she could see a bewigged porter seated behind it, only the top of his head and his eyes visible from where she was standing.

'Yes,' came a voice from above, as the porter looked down on her.

'Please, sir, I am looking for a Dr. Thomas Silkstone,' she said in a thin voice.

The porter consulted some sort of ledger that lay open on the desk, tracing the names on it with his quill.

'Silkstone, you say. What department?'

Hannah looked puzzled. She had no idea what the word meant.

'I do not know,' she replied.

'Um,' said the porter unhelpfully. 'Silkstone.'

Nearby, one of the young men at the cubbyholes turned 'round as soon as he heard the name.

'No. No Dr. Silkstone here,' said the porter.

Crestfallen, Hannah thanked the gentleman for

his pains and slowly turned away, bumping into a young man as she did so.

'Hannah?'

She looked up.

'Hannah, what on earth...?'

The face of Francis Crick stared down at her and she could have almost fainted with relief.

'Please, sir. I can't talk here,' she said self-consciously. 'I need to see Dr. Silkstone.'

Francis looked puzzled but nodded. 'Very well, then I shall take you to him.'

Chapter 47

James Lavington was not a patient man. A full week had passed since Lydia had laid her Irish husband in the ground and still she spent the day in a darkened room, still she refused to take food, and still she wept at the slightest reference to the captain.

'Michael would not have wanted this,' he told her softly at first.

Lydia raised her tear-stained face and looked at Lavington disdainfully. 'You would upbraid me for grieving?'

Limping over to her, Lavington put a hand on her shoulder. 'Grief or guilt, dear Lydia? How much longer can you keep up this pretense?'

Lydia sighed deeply, then looking at him directly and with desperation in her voice she pleaded: 'What is it that you want of me, Mr. Lavington?'

311

The lawyer shook his head. 'Oh dear, I haven't made myself clear enough, have I?' he mocked.

Lydia frowned, still holding his gaze.

'I want you, dear Lydia. I want you to be my wife.'

At these words, she suddenly felt nausea rise in her stomach. 'Your wife?' she mouthed. The words stuck in her gullet, like barbs. His insensitivity amazed her. 'Sir, you are too hasty,' she cried, suddenly finding her voice again.

Exasperated, Lavington clenched his fists. 'How much longer do you have to play the grieving widow, Lydia? Do not tell me you need time. Time is what they said was needed to heal these wounds,' he barked, pointing to his disfigurement. 'But time did not heal the scars. They were left for all to see. Time is vastly overrated.'

He was walking toward her now, his eyes on fire. She cowered away from him, afraid that he would lash out.

'Do not tell me you need time. You were the one who was whoring with that colonist when your husband was rotting in jail.'

At these words, Lydia brought her hands up to her head to cover her ears. 'No. No. It wasn't like that. It was...'

'Love? Is that the word you have for it, you poor deluded slut?'

'Stop it, I beg of you,' she pleaded, but still he lumbered toward her, his eyes fixed on her. From somewhere deep within her she summoned up the courage to straighten herself and face her accuser.

'Get out,' she cried. 'Leave my house and never come back here again.' Her outburst left her panting for breath as she watched for Lavington's reaction. Yet instead of retreating, his back stiffened and his jaw set firm in a gesture of defiance. His head then began to shake slowly from side to side in a way that both puzzled and infuriated Lydia.

Finally, after what seemed like an age of holding her gaze, he said: 'You cannot ask me to leave what is rightfully mine.'

Lydia was confused. 'I do not understand you,' she said in a half whisper.

The lawyer's lip curled in a half smile. It was the same infuriating look that her husband had often given her to make her feel small and insignificant and worthless.

'You are standing on my property,' he told her plainly.

Lydia's eyes narrowed. 'What?'

'Boughton Hall, or at least most of it, belongs to me.'

Lydia dropped like a stone onto the sofa, closing her eyes as she did so. When her opened eyes scanned the room once more, they settled upon the card table in the corner and she began to make sense of Lavington's words.

'He lost the estate?' she asked incredulously.

Lavington smiled, twisting the disfigured side of his face. 'No, no. Nothing as obvious as that,' he said cruelly. 'But I do have in my possession debtors' notes worth ten thousand guineas, and unless I am very much mistaken, you would be unable to honor that debt without selling off your beautiful home.'

Lydia felt a great swell of anger surge through her body and suddenly leapt up from the sofa. 'I

313

will never sell Boughton,' she screamed, her fists clenched in unbridled anger.

Lavington threw his head back and snorted. 'My dear Lydia, whoever suggested that?' he sneered. 'I could no more make you homeless than turn poor demented Lady Crick out on the streets.'

Lydia thought of her sad, confused mother. It would be the death of her if ever she were to leave her beloved Boughton.

'Speak plainly, sir, if you please,' she urged.

Lavington limped forward. 'Your mother shall stay here and so shall you' – he said softly, taking her hand in his – 'as my wife.'

Lydia wrenched herself away from his grasp. 'So, this is what you planned all along,' she said softly, pulling away. 'But Michael trusted you.'

Lavington drew near once more. 'He had every right to. I was a good friend, but an even better card player.' He shrugged. 'Come, come, Lydia,' he began, reaching for her hand once more. 'Michael would have won it all back from me eventually. It is just that now, poor fellow, he will never have the chance.'

Lydia pulled away once more, shaking her head. 'You drove him to the rope,' she screamed. 'It suited you that he took his own life.'

The sneer disappeared from Lavington's contorted face. He looked offended. 'How can you say that?' he whimpered. 'Your husband was a brother to me. I would never have said nor done anything that would encourage him to do harm to himself,' he protested vehemently. He took a deep breath, as if trying to restore calm to his troubled soul. 'Believe me, it is out of loyalty to Michael

314

that I could not bear to see you sell your family home,' he said softly. 'As your husband I can protect Boughton and...' he looked at her knowingly, 'your tarnished reputation.'

Lydia sank once more, as if weighed down by the gravity of what Lavington had just disclosed. Her guard was down and she did not resist when the lawyer took her hand. 'I am sure we can come to some sort of mutually acceptable and beneficial arrangement,' he said softly and with these words, he lowered his face and let his scarred lips brush lightly against the back of her milk-white hand. 'You have until tomorrow to decide.'

Chapter 48

Thomas read the letter once more. The unforgettable smell of Lydia's scent wafted in the air at the touch of the paper. He had lost count of the number of times he had scanned each line, each sentence, and then searched it again for innuendo and double entendre. He looked for clues in each letter, each dotting of the i's and crossing of t's and from it, he deduced the message was clear. Lydia was in grave danger.

Dear Dr. Silkstone,

Please forgive me for not having thanked you in person for carrying out your duties in regard to my late husband so diligently. I deeply regret not having seen you before your departure from Oxford, but my state of mind was such that I could not receive anyone. As a man of medicine, I am sure you will understand.

I also write to inform you that Mr. James Lavington has asked for my hand in marriage and I have consented. We are to marry within the next few days.

Please do not think ill of me in these matters. I realize that the haste may appear unseemly, but I have my reasons.

Yours truly,
Lydia Farrell.

A terrible, sickly feeling gripped hold of Thomas's stomach. He looked at the letter once more, this time with unseeing eyes. Something was wrong – very wrong. Although Lydia had written only a few terse words, to Thomas they spoke volumes. They told him of betrayal and of duplicity and of malice and coercion. Lydia had been a good wife. She may have admonished her husband on a number of occasions, but these chastisements were deserved. She had been trapped in a loveless marriage and yet she endured her lot with fortitude. Thomas knew her to be constant and dutiful and she would never be so disrespectful to his memory so soon after his passing. She 'had her reasons,' she said. Could those reasons be that Lavington was threatening her in some way, wondered Thomas. There was wrongdoing afoot, he knew it, and he determined to find out in person. On the morrow he would take the coach to Oxford and find out for himself the real meaning behind Lydia's cautiously sparse words.

First he would approach Sir Theodisius and

show him the letter. Surely he would have to act now and allow him to perform a postmortem on Captain Farrell's body? Surely now Lavington had shown his true colors and provided enough evidence for any court to investigate the captain's death? Lavington must have Farrell's blood on his hands, thought Thomas, and it was up to him to prove it. Hastily he began to pack his medical bag with all the instruments he would require to perform an autopsy. Just as he was securing the last specimen jar there came a knock at his door.

'Yes,' he shouted, buckling a leather strap. When he glanced toward the door, he saw Francis Crick. 'Crick,' he exclaimed. 'What brings you here, my friend?'

The student looked grave.

'I do, sir,' came the unseen voice of a woman from outside and, as soon as its owner came into view, Thomas's face turned deathly white.

'Hannah!' he cried, rushing forward to greet her. 'But I thought you were…'

The maidservant looked gaunt and troubled. 'Dead, sir,' she obligingly finished the sentence. 'I should be, should I not?'

Thomas suddenly remembered that she had not been told of the outcome of his experiments and, as far as she knew, she still believed herself responsible for the death of her young master.

'No. No,' interjected the young physician. 'Thank God you have been spared, Hannah. I have much to tell you, and you me, I am sure.'

The maid looked at Thomas warily, but sat as he bade her. She looked exhausted and drained.

First Thomas felt it his duty to inform Hannah

317

of the outcome of his tests on the *Digitalis purpurea.* 'Then 'twas not me who...' Her voice trailed off incredulously.

'No,' replied Thomas. 'You did not kill Lord Crick.'

Hannah looked up, her face drawn and mottled. There was not a trace of the relief that the young doctor had anticipated, only mistrust. 'Did Mr. Lavington know this?' she asked cautiously.

Thomas nodded. 'I informed him as soon as I found out.'

'And what of Captain Farrell?' Her question cut Thomas to the quick. She did not know. How could she? Crick and Thomas exchanged anxious glances and the maid knew something was amiss.

'What is it? Have they found him guilty?'

Thomas paused for a moment, thinking how best to frame the shocking news. 'Hannah, I am afraid that Captain Farrell was found hanged in his cell.'

At these words Hannah leapt up from her seat. 'No. No,' she said, wringing her hands. Her state became so agitated that she began to pace the room from wall to wall, her hands clutching at her head. 'Lord, no!' she screamed.

Thomas stepped forward and took hold of her by the shoulders. 'Hannah, please. Calm yourself,' he urged her, holding a cup of water to her lips, but she merely dashed it out of his hand and sent it flying across the room.

''Tis all my doing,' she sobbed.

Francis intervened. 'You must not blame yourself, Mistress Lovelock,' he said, trying to ease her into her seat once more.

'''Twas him. He made me...' Her voice once more trailed off in an avalanche of sobs.

'Who?' urged Thomas. 'Hannah, please explain yourself.'

'Mr. Lavington, sir. He told me not to say...'

'Have you any idea how important it is that you tell us all you know?' insisted Thomas, grabbing the maid by the shoulders so that she faced him.

'He said he'd turn them out, Jacob and the children. I ... I thought it best to take the money and go. He told me never to come back again.

'I told him, Dr. Silkstone, that I could not see an innocent hang,' she wailed. 'But he says to me: "The captain is a guilty man. Make no mistake of that." And he came up to me and stood by me with that stick of his, as if he was about to beat me, so I took the money and I ran, sir. I left that place as fast as I could and I ran.'

Thomas had suspected as much, but now he had a witness. Hannah's testimony was not proof, but her words would carry weight with Sir Theodisius.

'We must leave for Oxford at first light,' he told Hannah. The maidservant nodded, but Thomas could see she was afraid. He put a comforting hand on her shoulder. 'You do the right thing, Hannah, and the law will look on you with mercy for it.'

Chapter 49

The Oxford coroner endeavored to rise out of his chair as he saw Thomas enter the room, but his weight pulled him down again so that his efforts to stand were futile. Instead, he proffered his plump hand to the young doctor.

'And what brings you here, Dr. Silkstone?' he enquired in a friendly manner. A half-empty glass of claret stood on his desk and Thomas deduced the strong wine had put him in a relaxed mood. 'I thought we had closed the sad and sorry Crick saga.'

'Would that we had,' replied Thomas.

The coroner motioned him to sit, but before he did so, Thomas retrieved Lydia's letter from his pocket and handed it over the desk to Sir Theodisius.

'Please, sir, read this.'

The coroner looked at him warily, then, taking the piece of paper, unfurled it and scanned the letter. His expression grew graver with each line until he looked up at the end of it with an angry scowl.

'But this is preposterous,' he boomed. 'Farrell is barely cold in his grave and Lavington creeps into his bed.'

Thomas tried to blot out the image of the lawyer lying with Lydia, but he was heartened by the coroner's reaction. Indeed, such was Sir Theodisius's ire that he tried, and this time succeeded, in easing himself out of his chair.

'There is more to implicate Lavington. Much more,' Thomas revealed. 'He threatened Hannah–'

'The maidservant?' interrupted the coroner. 'She is alive?'

'Indeed, sir, and she has much to relate, but that is not all.'

Thomas produced the silken cord from his coat pocket and dangled it in front of Sir Theodisius. 'I have good reason, scientific reason, to believe that this rope did not kill Captain Farrell,' he said. 'It came from Mr. Lavington's Merton Street rooms.'

The coroner could not disguise his alarm.

'Now will you consider a postmortem?' urged Thomas.

By now Sir Theodisius had made his laborious way over to the window and looked out on the street below. It had been raining steadily for the past forty-eight hours. Already it was growing dark and the lamplighters were about their business.

'So, Lavington killed the Irishman,' he said. His words were framed as a statement, not a question, and Thomas did not reply. 'And young Crick, too?'

The doctor shifted uneasily. Obviously the thought had occurred to him, but he could think of no motive.

'I cannot say, sir,' he replied hesitantly.

The coroner turned to face him. 'Then I shall give you the means to find out,' he said and, returning to his desk and easing himself down into his chair, he took up his quill, dipped the nib into

321

his inkpot, and signed the necessary papers.

Lydia Farrell lay on her bed in a white cotton nightgown and wished it were her shroud. She closed her eyes and pictured herself next to her dead husband on top of the hill. Her heart was so filled with remorse that she thought it would overflow and spill out into her very blood, but then she remembered that Michael had left her through his own choice and her sorrow turned to anger. How dare he take his own life and leave her to face the world alone? Had he done it out of self-pity or out of kindness to her? If he had believed it to be the latter, then he was mistaken. Perhaps in some perverse way he had planned that Lavington should be there to pick up the pieces of his broken life and rebuild them again with her? Had he not asked him to take care of her in the event anything should happen to him? Or was there some truth in what Dr. Silkstone had to say that afternoon in Oxford when he had been the bearer of such fateful news? What was it he had told her? 'I do not think your husband took his own life. I have reason to believe he was murdered.' She recalled his face; his handsome features, his kindness to her. She had mentioned his words to no one, but hid them in her heart. If Dr. Silkstone's suspicions were well-founded, Sir Theodisius would have ordered an enquiry. As it was, he had not and the true circumstances surrounding her husband's death would probably remain a mystery until she joined him in death.

Lydia had thought about ending her own life many times, too, since Michael had gone, but it was always the same thought that prevented her: What would become of her mother? The old woman was incapable of looking out for herself for much of the time and was often in a perplexed state, not knowing what day it was nor even her own name. At other times, however, she could be quite lucid, able to make judgments and eloquent statements of fact. Lydia had no notion of what ailed her. All she knew was that she, and she alone, was the reason she had consented to Lavington's ludicrous and untimely proposal.

She cared not what the people of Brandwick, or even farther afield, would say. The goings-on at Boughton Hall had fueled the fires of the gossips and tittle-tattlers for months now. Her hasty marriage would only add more kindling to the noxious flames. Lavington had bribed some poor curate with the promise of a living on the estate if he but perform the marriage service without first having read the banns, and it had not been difficult to find a man of the cloth to comply, such was the income of a country parson.

While she had reluctantly consented to marry Lavington, she had laid down a condition to which he had agreed. She had asked him not to come to the marriage bed until such times as she was ready to receive him. The thought of his scarred hands wandering over her naked breasts and thighs, the notion of his gnarled fingers probing her secret place, filled her with such utter revulsion that she thought she might retch. She would be his wife in name, but not in body, nor mind.

As she lay in the cold, still room she became

aware of a noise at the window. Was it heavy rain or hail? Or was it the sound of pebbles being thrown at the pane? Her heart began to race and she leapt out of bed and rushed toward the window. There it was again. She could see nothing in the darkness outside, but lifted the sash as gently as she could.

'Thomas? Thomas, is that you?' she whispered hoarsely.

Suddenly a tall, thin figure stepped out of the shadows below.

'Thomas?' she called faintly, as the man began to climb up the wisteria that draped itself over the facade of the house and up around Lydia's casement. She was alarmed at first, but then she realized, as the figure came nearer, there was no need to be afraid.

'Francis,' she mouthed, as the young student drew level with the window and eased himself through the frame.

'Dear Lydia,' he greeted her, putting his arms around her.

She hugged him tightly. 'Oh my dear Francis, it is so good to see you,' she whispered.

Still holding her by the shoulders, Francis studied his cousin's face. 'My poor dear Lydia,' he whispered.

'Did Dr. Silkstone tell you?'

Francis nodded.

'Is he here? Is he with you?' she asked eagerly, glancing over Francis's shoulder.

Her cousin shook his head. 'No, my dear.'

'But you have word from him?' she urged, tugging Francis's sleeves.

'Trust me and all will be well,' he told her, pulling her head toward his shoulder once more and stroking her chestnut curls. 'You are in safe hands.'

Hannah Lovelock picked her way along the rain-sodden lanes, hiding behind hedgerows as the need arose. Her shoes and the hem of her calico skirt were caked in mud and slowed her progress, but she pressed on. The carriage had dropped her perhaps half a mile away from Boughton Hall and she was to make her way to her home and alert her husband to the plans.

Through the window she saw him, mending the fire, with William and Rachel at the table, eating rye bread and sipping milk from their bowls. This was a scene she thought she would never again see and a great surge of love overwhelmed her as she rushed in through the door.

'Ma! Ma!' shouted the children, rushing toward her as soon as they clapped eyes on her. Jacob instantly dropped his poker and, open-mouthed, held out his arms to embrace her.

'Hannah. Oh my dearest,' he cried, tears rolling down his pockmarked cheeks.

Hannah, too, could not hold back her tears, but pressed a muddy finger to her lips, calling for quiet. 'Hush yourselves. No one is to know I am here,' she told them, urging them to be silent.

'By what miracle are you free?' asked her incredulous husband.

'I will tell all in time,' replied Hannah, 'but right now, I am needing your help. Down the road a carriage waits. It carries the coroner. Dr. Silkstone has gone ahead. He is going to cut the captain open.' She turned to Jacob. 'You and Amos must be the bury men and dig up the coffin.'

Jacob looked at her questioningly.

'Dr. Silkstone thinks that the captain may not have taken himself to the rope,' said Hannah.

Her husband frowned. 'Then who...?' His voice trailed off thinly.

When Hannah spoke the name, her husband nodded. 'I knew as much,' he muttered.

'What do you say?' urged Hannah.

He looked earnestly at his wife. 'We have no time to lose,' he told her. 'Lavington is to marry Lady Lydia in the chapel this morn.'

Hannah's hands rose to her face to signify her shock. 'Today? In the chapel?'

'The service will take place at ten o'clock. Amos and I will go and fetch picks and shovels and meet the gentlemen at the grave at that hour, so that we are not seen,' said Jacob.

Hannah nodded. 'May God save her ladyship,' she muttered under her breath.

'May God save us all,' corrected her husband.

Chapter 50

A man's grave, though silent, can speak volumes in death. As Thomas stood by the newly dug pit on top of the hill by the pavilion at Boughton, he paused in silent reflection by the simple wooden cross. Even if the place had been marked with an elaborate mausoleum or a mortsafe, there was no escaping what had happened. Men may consider the earthly trappings of death to be of the highest importance and yet, in reality, they are only of interest to those left behind, thought Thomas.

The rain had begun to fall steadily and it stung his eyes and gouged small rivulets in the bare mound of earth. From his vantage point behind the pavilion, Thomas could see the chapel clearly. Lovelock had broken the news to him of the wedding and he had received it with horrified indignation. His first thought was governed by passion. He would burst into Boughton and rescue Lydia from Lavington's clutches. But then a physician's logic took over and he realized that, in order to prove that Lavington was, indeed, responsible for Farrell's death, he needed to conduct a post-mortem. He knew it would be hard seeing Lydia enter the chapel, but her fate now lay in his hands.

At precisely a quarter to ten James Lavington arrived, accompanied by the curate and Rafferty. Thomas felt tense. Looking through a spyglass, he could see the lawyer clearly as he dismounted from the curricle and limped into the chapel.

A few minutes later Lydia arrived, escorted by Eliza and Mistress Claddingbowl. No ribbons or flowers bedecked the phaeton and, as he looked through the spyglass he could see Lydia was in no mood to celebrate. Her face was pale and her demeanor nervous. She was looking about her as she alighted from the carriage. Was she looking for him?

'Not long now,' Thomas told her under his breath.

Waiting until the chapel door was shut, he walked a little farther down the slope and gave the signal for Kidd, Sir Theodisius, and Hannah to set off in the dogcart up the slippery hill. Less than five minutes later they had reached the brow.

The soil was so damp that it was easily worked. Lovelock and Kidd dug quickly, so that in a few minutes they had brought the simple pine coffin to the surface. Thomas gave the order to prize off the lid and the men took crowbars and opened it up.

The jailer had done his work well, thought Thomas. The captain's face, although beginning to discolor, was better preserved than if nature's decaying processes had been allowed to work unimpeded.

The corpse was dressed in a white silk shirt and satin breeches, as if about to go to a wedding. The tragic irony of the sight struck Thomas and the thought of Lydia going to her own wedding still in widow's weeds spurred him on. Unlike the postmortem he carried out on the young earl, where he worked literally and metaphorically in the dark, this time he knew exactly what he was hoping to find.

As Sir Theodisius held a kerchief to his face and Lovelock and Amos kept guard, with Hannah looking out over the chapel, Thomas reached into the coffin and unfastened the collar around Captain Farrell's neck. As he did so two flies flew out from the dead man's nose. The marks of the cord were still visible, but more importantly, so was the deeper wound at the front of the neck. It was this that interested Thomas. It was this, he surmised, that held the key to the Irishman's death.

At the base of the epiglottis appeared to be a puncture wound, about the size of a farthing. Some instrument had clearly been applied to the captain's throat and pressed down with great force, blocking off air into the lungs and piercing the flesh as it did so. The wound could not possibly have been self-inflicted. Wiping his hands on a cloth, Thomas called Sir Theodisius over.

'You wanted proof, sir, that Captain Farrell did not hang himself? Well, here it is,' he said, pointing to the neck wound.

With his kerchief clamped to his mouth and nose, the coroner peered gingerly into the coffin. He saw for himself the circular patch on the neck.

'And what, pray, would have caused this?' he asked.

'Something small, but to which great pressure could be applied,' replied Thomas reflectively.

'A thumb, perhaps,' suggested the coroner.

Thomas shook his head. 'That would not have pierced the skin.' His gaze had dropped to the ground, where the men's shovels and pickaxes lay. Seeing the shafts of the tools, he was suddenly reminded.

'A walking stick!' he said deliberately, as if a light had suddenly illuminated his thinking. 'I'll wager my life it was Lavington's walking stick that did this.'

Wide-eyed, Sir Theodisius nodded. ''Tis proof enough.'

Just then, a cry went up from Hannah, who had been keeping watch over the chapel. 'They're coming out,' she called hoarsely.

Knowing there was no time to lose, Lovelock

and Kidd quickly replaced the coffin lid. 'Take Sir Theodisius to the chapel in the cart,' Thomas directed.

'But what of you, sir?' asked Amos. Thomas did not reply. He was already scrambling down the muddy bank, heading for the chapel. Halfway down, he slipped on the wet grass and tumbled a few feet, but he soon righted himself and continued charging down the steep incline.

In the distance he could see Lydia and Lavington, now man and wife, walking slowly toward the wedding carriage. He could not yet make out Lydia's face, but he knew there would be no smiles of joy on her lips. He saw her climbing up dolefully onto the carriage, followed by Lavington, who pulled the wretched side of his body up awkwardly to sit on the driver's seat.

All Thomas could hear now was the blood pounding through his ears as he ran the last few yards toward the wedding party. 'Stop,' he called out. 'Stop!'

All eyes turned to see his mud-spattered figure racing toward them.

'Thomas,' cried Lydia, rising in her seat, but she was firmly pushed back by her new husband.

'Another guest for our wedding breakfast,' called Lavington as the doctor drew level with the carriage.

'There will be no wedding breakfast, Lavington,' panted Thomas. 'You are under arrest.'

The lawyer snorted. 'On whose authority?'

'On mine,' called Sir Theodisius as the dogcart pulled up.

Lavington looked contemptuous. 'This has to

be a sick jest,' he said disdainfully.

'No joke, sir,' warned Sir Theodisius. 'I would ask you to accompany me to Oxford.'

'On what charge?' chided Lavington.

'On that of the murder of Captain Michael Farrell.'

Lydia, still seated on the phaeton, let out an involuntary cry.

Lavington suddenly changed his tone. 'And you have proof of this?'

'A postmortem has just been conducted on Captain Farrell's body,' replied Sir Theodisius.

Lavington paused for a moment, mulling over the implications. 'No doubt that was performed by our man of medicine here,' he said, sneering at Thomas.

Lydia turned to Lavington once more, her eyes wide in horror. 'You killed Michael?'

At first he looked shocked that she could even contemplate such a thing, but then his expression of dismay gave way to an almost demonic smile. 'Just as he killed me on the day he did this to me,' he said, touching his disfigured face.

Lydia frowned. 'What do you mean?'

Lavington's tone suddenly became agitated. 'He did this to me,' he reiterated, pointing to his cheek and then his limp arm. Suddenly he stood up, as if addressing some imaginary rally or a meeting.

'Come down, sir,' urged Sir Theodisius.

But Lavington ignored him and instead began to call out to his stunned audience. ''Twas in India. It was Farrell's watch, but he took too much liquor that night. Almost senseless, he was. I knew if the senior officers found him, he would

331

be court-martialed, so I tried to get him to his quarters. We were walking back under cover of darkness when he suddenly stopped by the ammunition shed. I saw him take out a cheroot and strike a match, then toss it over his shoulder. I shouted and pushed him out of the way before the first explosion. I took the full force of the blast from a barrel of gunpowder. Farrell was injured, but only slightly. He must suddenly have come to his senses, for he pulled me out of the burning rubble, my skin hanging off my bones. They awarded him a medal for his paltry efforts and me, well, I was rewarded with this.' He lifted up his limp hand and turned to Lydia. 'So, you see, my dearest, your beloved husband owed me. He felt obliged to me. That is why I came to live on the estate, his poor crippled friend to whom he gave charity, in return for silence.'

Lydia looked at him askance.

'He owed me and now I have collected my debt,' he said calmly.

'So, you would treat his widow as a repayment?' cried Thomas, incensed by Lavington's revelations. The doctor lurched forward, tugging at Lavington's sound leg, but with the full force of his body he kicked Thomas to the ground. Lydia screamed and Lavington turned, pushing her off the phaeton with a single blow, so that she, too, landed on the sodden earth, causing the horse to rear up.

As Lovelock ran to Lydia's aid, Thomas grabbed hold of the rail of the phaeton and pulled himself up onto the back just as the horse set off at full gallop.

'In God's name, stop,' shouted Thomas, trying to grab hold of the reins. But, like a man possessed, Lavington kept lashing the whip so that the horse was in a frenzy and went careering along the track, throwing up mud and stones in the phaeton's wake.

'You'll get us both killed,' pleaded Thomas, wrestling with Lavington, but he was just pushed back each time with greater force. He knew he would have to take drastic action and was just about to deliver a heavy punch to the madman's jaw when the phaeton suddenly veered sharply to the left. Both men looked ahead to see the wooden bridge over the lake ahead.

The heavy rains had swelled the waters so that they lapped over the planks. Seeing this, the horse suddenly took even more fright. It pulled up short and then reared, sending both Thomas and Lavington falling.

Thomas landed with a thud on the bank, but when he recovered his composure, Lavington was nowhere to be seen. Suddenly he heard a sharp cry and ran to the edge of the lake. Lavington was in the water, fighting for breath, his sound arm waving in the air.

Grabbing a fallen branch, Thomas edged out onto the bridge and, lying on his belly, proffered the stick to Lavington. 'Take hold,' he shouted above the sound of the torrent. Flailing in the black waters, Lavington managed to reach the branch and grasp it as Thomas pulled it closer to the bank. He hauled an exhausted Lavington up through the reeds, coughing and spluttering. Putting an arm around him, Thomas sat him upright, supporting him, so that he could breathe more easily.

'Take deep breaths, now,' he told him, suddenly adopting the role of rescuer and carer. But instead of submitting, Lavington, once he had regained his composure, punched Thomas in the face with such force that he was sent flying backward. He then started to run off toward the woods.

Thomas leapt up and followed. He knew with his crippled leg Lavington could not go far. He caught up with him seconds later by the bridge, grabbed him by the shoulder, pulled him 'round, and delivered a blow to his face, knocking him backward. Bending over him, Thomas felt in no mood to be charitable.

'So, you killed Farrell. Did you kill Crick, too?' he cried, pitting his voice against the nearby waterfall.

Lavington looked at him with scorn. 'Well, did you?' screamed Thomas angrily, bringing his foot down hard on Lavington's hand. He cried out in pain.

'No. No, I did not kill him.'

Thomas found himself believing him and, taking a deep breath, offered his own hand to help Lavington up. But instead of accepting the offer, the lawyer took hold of Thomas's hand and jerked it, pulling him forward and wrong-footing him, so that he fell to the ground near the bank once more. This time Lavington fell on top of him like a mad dog, pounding him with the fist of his sound hand. Thomas managed to prize him off and Lavington rolled over, perilously close to the lakeside.

'Give yourself up, Lavington,' shouted Thomas. 'This is hopeless.'

'Not to one who has already lost all hope, it isn't,' he replied almost gleefully. He heaved himself up and began running again, this time toward the bridge, the weight of his soaked clothes dragging him down. The rain was heavier now, too, slicing through the air like needles, whipping the waters into an even greater frenzy.

'Come back,' called Thomas, as he watched Lavington drag himself out over the bridge as the waters lapped over it. 'Come back, you fool.'

But his words fell on deaf ears and Lavington struggled on until suddenly he heard a terrible creaking sound. Thomas heard it, too. 'The bridge!' he cried. Lavington turned to see the planks suddenly give way under the weight of the floodwater. Frantically he tried to grab hold of the rail, but he lost his grip. His arm shot out, trying to regain his balance, but he could not and he fell, his body disappearing into the murky depths. Thomas rushed to the bridge, but the waters had gathered apace and had now covered most of it, so that only a few posts remained visible like jagged teeth.

A few seconds later, as Thomas watched helplessly on the bank, he saw Lavington's black cloak float to the surface not far from where the bridge had collapsed. Racing toward it, he lay down on the bank and, using a long branch, hooked the material toward him. It came easily, without its owner. Puzzled, Thomas looked up just in time to see Lavington struggling out of the lake on the opposite shore.

'For God's sake!' he cried, scrambling to his feet and giving chase.

The fugitive was only a few yards ahead, but in front of him lay the thick beech woods. A few seconds later and he had disappeared into them, vanishing from sight.

Thomas arrived at the edge of the woods only a minute or two later, but Lavington was nowhere to be seen. He stopped in his tracks and listened. The dry crack of calling crows overhead was the only sound that could be heard. Lavington must be hiding somewhere, thought Thomas. He picked up a large stick and proceeded slowly onward, edging from tree to tree, stopping at every pheasant call and every rustle of the undergrowth. The wetness of the ground muffled his footsteps and the rasping of his breath rose and filled his own ears, blocking out all other sounds.

In this strange, eerie half silence he walked on toward the clearing until his foot caught something in his path and he stumbled over it, sending his stick falling from his hand. Shaken, Thomas looked backward, expecting to see Lavington behind him. But there was no one there. He had tripped over a log, half hidden by sodden leaves. It was only when he allowed himself the luxury of propping his weary body up against the lichen-covered trunk of a beech tree by the clearing to catch his breath that he caught sight of his quarry.

Lavington, too, was propped up against a nearby tree. Thomas looked at him and he seemed to return the gaze, but remained motionless. Reaching for another large stick for protection, Thomas approached him warily.

'For God's sake, man. Stop playing games,' he said, edging forward. But there was no movement. No reply. Thomas moved closer, his heart beating faster with every step. Only when he came to within three or four yards of him did the awful truth dawn.

'Lavington,' he called to him again. 'Lavington!' But the eyes remained fixed in a stare and the mouth remained half open and from it appeared a thin trickle of blood. 'Lavington!' Thomas cried, this time reaching out to him.

With this touch, he knocked him on the shoulder and sent him off balance, so that he fell, facedown, onto the sodden ground.

It was then that the full horror of what had happened was revealed. The back of the lawyer's skull had been smashed to a bloody pulp.

Chapter 51

Jacob Lovelock and Amos Kidd arrived at the scene a few moments later to find Thomas crouching over Lavington, the large stick still in his hand. As they drew closer they saw, too, the smears of blood on the doctor's shirt.

Thomas looked up at the men, dazed and unsure. They returned his gaze, but the difference was they were certain of what they saw.

'Dr. Silkstone!' exclaimed Kidd.

Still stunned, Thomas looked at the men, then at the thick branch he held in his hand. He let it drop to the ground. 'Oh no,' he said, shaking his head. 'No, I did not... He was like this. I found him like this.'

Lovelock and Amos remained silent for a moment, stunned by what they saw.

'Did you see anyone?' pleaded Thomas. 'Search the woods.' But the men remained rooted to the spot. 'The murderer must be nearby!' he shouted.

'Yes, he must,' replied Kidd, fixing a stare on the doctor.

'"Twas self-defense,' chimed in Lovelock. 'We know that, sir.'

Thomas shook his head. 'No. No. I found him like this. Look at his skull. Someone hit him. Someone hit him with...'

'With this?' said Kidd, holding up the heavy stick that Thomas had just dropped.

'There was a fight, sir,' intervened Lovelock, trying to ease the tension.

Thomas looked at him incredulously. 'There was no fight with me. He was murdered, I tell you. Someone hit him from behind.'

'But where did the murderer go, sir?' asked Lovelock. He pointed ahead to the high stone wall that ran around the perimeter of the estate. 'He could not have scaled the wall and he didn't come our way.'

Thomas swallowed hard. 'You think I did this?' The reality of his situation dawned on him for the first time.

'You better come with us, sir,' said Kidd, stepping forward and taking Thomas by the arm, but he fended them off in a gesture of defiance.

'I can give a good account of myself, gentlemen,' he told them. 'I do not need restraining.'

Back at Boughton Hall Lydia and Sir Theodisius waited for news in the drawing room. By this time Francis Crick had also arrived and was helping to comfort his cousin when Kidd and Lovelock arrived with Thomas.

Seeing Thomas's shirt ripped and muddy, with blood on his face and shoulder, Lydia began to rush forward, but Francis prevented her, taking her by the arm.

'No, Lydia,' he said firmly.

'But Thomas, what is happening?' she cried. 'Where is he? Where is Lavington?'

'He is dead, my lady,' said Thomas slowly.

'Dead?' echoed Sir Theodisius.

'Murdered,' said Kidd.

Lydia gasped. All eyes turned on Thomas. 'But who...?' she cried.

'I found him. His skull had been struck from behind,' Thomas told her.

Kidd and Lovelock both looked at him accusingly.

'So who is responsible for this crime?' intervened Sir Theodisius.

'I have no idea, sir,' retorted Thomas. 'I saw no one.'

Aware that his version of events lacked credibility, Thomas stumbled to find an explanation. 'He can only have been dead two or three minutes before I found him, sir.'

'And yet you neither heard nor saw anyone else in the wood? Nor did these men?' ventured Sir Theodisius.

Thomas closed his eyes momentarily, hoping to awake from this nightmare when he reopened them. Instead he saw Kidd hand the heavy stick that he had found in the woods to Sir Theodisius.

'Dr. Silkstone was holding this when we saw him. Hunched over the body, he were,' he said.

'Is that true?' asked the coroner, perplexed.

'Yes, sir, but...'

It was Francis who came to the doctor's rescue. 'Perhaps we should carry on this investigation in the study,' he suggested. Thomas looked at him. He had not seen him for a few days and his whole demeanor seemed changed. He appeared more confident in the way he conducted himself, as if the events of the past weeks had made him grow in wisdom and character.

Thomas watched him usher Lydia into the study, followed by the coroner.

'Please, sir,' he said, showing Sir Theodisius to a seat. The young student then proceeded to sit next to his cousin on the chaise longue and took her hand in his in a gesture of comfort.

'Pray tell me what is happening,' pleaded a distressed Lydia.

Sir Theodisius looked grave. 'This is a serious situation, Doctor,' he said. 'You give me little choice.'

'I do not understand,' replied Thomas.

'Dr. Silkstone, by the power invested in me by His Majesty King George III, I am arresting you for the murder of James Lavington.'

''Tis not true!' shouted Thomas. Kidd came forward to restrain him once more, but Sir Theodisius called him off.

340

'Who else could have killed him, Dr. Silkstone?' quizzed the coroner. 'We all saw you fighting with him before. You had the wherewithal and,' he said, pointedly looking at Lydia, 'it seems, the motive.'

'Motive?' questioned Thomas.

Sir Theodisius shook his head. 'I am not blind, Dr. Silkstone. Your hatred of Lavington was obvious.'

The young doctor darted a look at Lydia, then hung his head in exasperation, but just as he lowered his gaze to the floor, he noticed Francis Crick's shoes. They were spattered with mud. What especially caught Thomas's eye, however, were some other gray deposits that clung to the student's stockings.

'Perhaps you should ask Mr. Crick what he was doing while I was going after Mr. Lavington in the woods,' ventured Thomas, his voice suddenly more assured.

All eyes now moved to Francis, who shifted awkwardly.

'Well, Mr. Crick,' urged the coroner.

'I came up from London this morning, sir. I arrived just as Lady Lydia returned from the chapel.' His voice was slightly indignant.

'So, why are your shoes and stockings so dirty, may I ask?' pressed Thomas.

Francis looked uneasy. 'It was raining, sir, and I had to walk from the carriage to the door,' he replied.

'My cousin arrived not more than ten minutes after I came back,' interjected Lydia.

Sir Theodisius nodded. 'That seems to me to be a perfectly reasonable explanation,' he concluded.

Thomas nodded. 'Indeed it is, sir, until you ask him how he came to have that grayish powder on his stockings.'

Sir Theodisius peered down at Francis's legs and clearly saw the strange substance to which Thomas referred. 'What is the meaning of this?' he quizzed.

The young doctor stood up and walked over to Sir Theodisius. Holding up a flap of his torn shirt in front of the coroner, he said: 'You see this?' Sir Theodisius scrutinized the piece of linen. 'That gray powder resembles the powder on Mr. Crick's stockings, does it not?'

The coroner nodded. 'It appears so.'

'It is beech lichen. Otherwise known as *enterographa elaborata*.'

Sir Theodisius sniffed. 'What of it?'

'It grows on the trunks of ancient beech trees,' explained Thomas. 'I picked it up in the wood just now.'

Sir Theodisius was becoming impatient. 'Very well, Dr. Silkstone, but where is all this leading?'

Thomas looked at Francis Crick, whose cheeks had suddenly lost their entire color. 'It is exactly the same beech lichen that is on Mr. Crick's stockings.'

Lydia turned and stared at her cousin, a look of mistrust etched on her face.

'You were in the woods, Francis,' said Thomas softly. 'And you killed James Lavington.'

At this accusation Francis darted up from the chaise longue. 'How dare you, sir?' he cried.

Sir Theodisius interjected. 'What can you say in your defense, Mr. Crick? If you were not in the

342

woods, how do you explain the lichen?'

Francis grew increasingly agitated. 'What motive would I have to kill Lavington?' he blurted defensively.

'Money. Power. Love. I could go on,' taunted Thomas.

'Explain yourself, Dr. Silkstone,' barked Sir Theodisius.

It had been Dr. Carruthers who had first drawn his attention to it. 'What did you say that young earl's name was?' he had asked one evening after dinner a few weeks ago. When Thomas replied, somewhat puzzled, that it was Crick, his mentor had clapped his hands gleefully.

'I thought so,' he replied.

When Thomas enquired why that particular fact should be of significance, the old anatomist leaned forward in his chair. 'I remember now,' he whispered enigmatically.

'Remember what?' urged Thomas.

'I remember two or three years ago, when I could read the newspaper for myself, there was an engagement announced between a Crick and another Crick in the court pages of *The Universal Daily Register*. I remember it particularly because the father of the boy was a patient of mine, until he drank himself to death.'

Using this snippet of information, Thomas had visited the offices of the newspaper and asked to look at their back issues. Sure enough the engagement of Lady Lydia Sarah Crick to Mr. Francis Henry Crick had been announced on May 30, 1775.

'You were betrothed,' said Thomas.

Francis suddenly began to tremble. 'Yes.'

Lydia lowered her head in embarrassment. 'We were young and foolish,' she mumbled.

'Foolish?' repeated Francis. 'Foolish?' He looked at her incredulously. 'Is that what you call it now? We had everything planned. We had your parents' blessing. How can you say our union would have been foolish?' Thomas watched the young student grow more tense. 'If anyone was foolish it was you, leaving me for that Irish wastrel.'

Lydia's elopement with Farrell had been exposed in court, but what only a few people knew or remembered was the fact that she and Francis had been childhood sweethearts.

'Your mother always wanted us to be together, you know that.' Francis was staring at Lydia reproachfully now. 'I was the one you were meant to marry. I was the one who was meant to take on all this.' He waved his hand in a grand gesture that suddenly took on a poignant impotence.

'You did not need to kill for it, Francis,' cried Lydia.

He clenched his fists and brought them up to his chest in a gesture of frustration. 'I could not let Lavington have you, after all we had been through,' he sobbed.

'So, you confess to his murder?' interrupted Sir Theodisius.

Francis took a deep breath and drew himself upright, as if he were proud of the confession. 'That I do sir, just as I would have killed Silkstone if he had taken her away from me.'

'Then, Francis Crick, I arrest you for the murder of James Lavington.' At these words Lovelock and

344

Kidd marched forward and took hold of Crick. He made no attempt to resist, but simply looked forlornly at Lydia. 'I will always love you,' he whispered before they marched him out.

'I owe you an apology, Dr. Silkstone,' admitted Sir Theodisius graciously as he was about to leave.

'No need,' replied Thomas, proffering his hand. 'No doubt we will see each other again in court,' he said.

As soon as the coroner left to return to Oxford, Thomas walked over to where Lydia was sitting, a glazed expression on her face. Sitting beside her he took her hand in his. She flinched and turned away momentarily.

'Oh my dear Lydia,' Thomas began. 'Look at me, please.'

She turned to face him slowly. 'Mama wanted us to marry so badly. She could see no future for Edward, but Francis was always her favorite.'

Thomas stroked her cheek. 'And because Francis was family it did not matter he had no other inheritance.'

Lydia jolted upright. 'You knew?'

Thomas nodded. 'I could tell that Francis was not called to medicine by some greater good, but by necessity. Then I found out his father was a drunkard and a gambler and had squandered his only son's inheritance. Francis had to work for his living, until he saw a way of marrying the woman he loved and inheriting her fortune. He may not have killed the captain himself, but his execution would have suited his purpose.'

Lydia now stared ahead of her, as if she could see the scenario played out before her.

'So, it was Francis who sent you that threat and who had you attacked?'

'Yes,' said Thomas. 'But he had not bargained on Lavington's designs on you.'

Lydia thought for a moment. 'Is it possible that he killed Edward, too?' she asked, almost childlike.

'No doubt he will be questioned,' replied Thomas.

At that moment Lady Crick flounced into the room, wearing a bright straw bonnet and a woolen shawl.

'Where is Francis?' she asked. 'I thought I heard Francis. He promised to take me out.'

Thomas and Lydia eyed each other awkwardly. 'He was called away on urgent business,' said Thomas quickly.

The old dowager looked deeply disappointed, her countenance visibly drooping at the news. 'What a pity,' she bleated. 'I do so enjoy our walks in the woods.' And with that she trailed forlornly out of the room.

'Poor soul,' whispered Lydia as she watched her crestfallen mother leave. 'She didn't even know about my marriage to Lavington.'

Chapter 52

Francis Crick was spared the degradation of the barber-surgeons' scalpels after his execution. The judge had ruled that, while he showed no remorse for his crime, he had at least confessed to it.

The trial had been held at the same Oxford court where Captain Michael Farrell had been tried not three months before. Thomas and Lydia had attended, but as Francis had confessed, it was a summary affair, without any of the intricacies and legal arguments that had been aired at the Irishman's trial.

Lydia had visited her cousin in his condemned cell afterward and given him what little comfort she could in his last hours. But there was something she needed to ask him before the noose was tightened around his neck and she knew her question might prove almost as painful.

'Do you know who killed Edward?' she said, forcing the words from her mouth.

Francis looked at her, his eyes red from crying, and shook his head.

'You cannot ask me that,' he said and turned away, but Lydia grabbed his hand.

'Surely you cannot take the answer with you to the gallows?' she asked incredulously.

He looked at her earnestly once more. 'I love you, Lydia. I have loved you for years and you should have been mine.' His words wounded her like arrows because she knew them to be true. 'If it wasn't for Farrell, we would have been together, wouldn't we, Lydia?' There was an urgency in his voice that suddenly frightened her. 'Wouldn't we?' he cried, taking her by the shoulders and shaking her.

'Stop it, Francis,' she called. 'You're hurting me.' She pulled herself away from his grasp and he relented, taking two or three steps back and composing himself once more.

'Do not take your secret with you to the grave, Francis,' pleaded Lydia.

The young man looked at her intently once more. There was still a family likeness between them, he thought to himself. The same blood ran through their veins. He could never be robbed of that. 'I can and I must,' he replied. 'For all our sakes.'

And so it was that on the morning of August 15, 1781, Francis Henry Crick was hanged by the neck until he died, taking with him to his grave the secret that still haunted Boughton Hall.

For the next few days Lydia shut herself away in her room. 'The mistress does not wish to see anyone,' Eliza told Thomas when he called.

'Tell her ladyship I can give her a draught to soothe her,' pleaded Thomas.

The maid went away and returned shortly afterward, shaking her head.

'My mistress thanks you, but says she would rather be left alone,' reported Eliza.

Forlorn, Thomas returned to London to his dissecting rooms. He tried to immerse himself in his work, but the passion of Vesalius had deserted him. He no longer felt compelled to probe the intricacies of the human body, to tease out tubules, to dissect tissue. Its mysteries no longer held out a promise of redemption, but of damnation. Each organ became a Medusa's head that would turn him blind, just like Dr. Carruthers, should he set his inquisitive eyes upon it.

Furthermore, he received word from his father in Philadelphia that Charleston had fallen to the British and that much of South Carolina was being coerced to return to British allegiance.

Nothing made sense to him anymore. Into his ordered, structured existence chaos had come and brought with it destruction and death. Not only that, with it had come love, too – an emotion he had never felt before, and now that had also been taken away from him. He felt confused and bereft. Lydia had given his work a purpose. He had been on a mission for her. Now that she chose to exclude him, he felt deprived of any reason to go on.

It was therefore hardly surprising that on the ninth day after his return, having received word that Lydia wished to see him, he was on the coach that left from London to Oxford within the hour.

She greeted him in the drawing room, holding out her delicate hand for Thomas to kiss.

'I have been so worried about you,' he told her, continuing to hold her hand. She made no attempt to withdraw it.

'Let us sit,' she said softly, guiding him to the sofa. Thomas studied her face. She looked gaunt. It was obvious to him she had lost a great deal of weight.

'You should have let me stay with you,' he chided gently.

She looked at him, slowly shaking her head. 'You have done more than your duty asks of you.'

Thomas felt wounded by this remark. 'I would do anything for you,' he replied. 'I thought you knew that.'

'I know it,' she acknowledged, 'and yet I wish it were not so.'

Thomas frowned. 'What do you mean?'

She rose deliberately and walked to the window, gazing out at the gardens beyond. 'Three men I once loved, my brother, my husband, and my cousin, not to mention James Lavington, are now dead because of me.'

Thomas could not believe what he heard. 'No, Lydia,' he said, rising and walking toward her.

'Lavington almost killed you, too,' she continued.

'You cannot blame yourself for any of this, Lydia,' he assured her, but he detected his words were of little comfort. So often he had witnessed the cruel aftermath of bereavement that left loneliness, depression, and guilt in its wake. He wanted to share her pain and he suddenly found himself acknowledging his own guilt. He sighed deeply. 'You asked me to find your brother's killer, but I failed. If I had been successful early on, then your husband and Francis, and Lavington, might still be alive. We can all blame ourselves if we look back,' he told her.

Lydia smiled meekly. 'You have done more than any man,' she assured him, pressing her hand onto his in a gesture of intimacy.

Just then, Lady Crick came into view, passing the drawing room window carrying a pannier and wearing a moth-eaten bonnet adorned with pheasant feathers.

'Dear Mama,' sighed Lydia, watching the old woman shuffle toward the garden gate. An air of fragile melancholy seemed to surround her. 'I cannot understand what ails her. One day she is in some far-off land of her own and another, she seems perfectly well.'

Together they watched the old dowager walk out of the walled garden and down the path.

'Where is she going?' asked Thomas.

'For her walk in the woods. She and Francis would often go and she misses him.'

'Does she know?'

Lydia shook her head. 'If she does, she has not spoken of it, but she is sad, that much I do know. It will be a year tomorrow since Edward died. She mentioned the date only yesterday. I wasn't even sure that she had grasped he was dead. I only wish I knew what went on inside her head.'

'Would you like me to speak with her?' Thomas ventured.

Lydia swung 'round. 'Would you?' she said.

The day was bright, but the air was chill as Thomas followed Lady Crick as she ventured into the beech wood. He kept his distance so that he could observe her and watched curiously as she weaved in and out of trees, entering deeper and deeper into the forest.

Once or twice he had snapped a twig underfoot and the old woman had stopped in her tracks. Perhaps sensing she was being followed, she had turned and looked about her, then shrugged and carried on, going ever deeper under the forest canopy. Was she nervous about being detected? She seemed to be on a mission. Her steps were purposeful and confident, as if she were going to meet with someone.

Presently the track became narrower. The sun no longer reached into the dark places and the smell of rotting vegetation assailed the nostrils. There was no birdsong now and Thomas was growing increasingly uneasy. If he revealed himself to her, he would frighten her out of her skin and risk causing heart failure. He would have to bide his time and be silent.

A few seconds later, however, the old woman stopped for the first time in her foray and began looking at the ground. Thomas strained his eyes to see what she was doing. It appeared as though she was looking for something. Suddenly she bent down, plucked something from the ground, and put it in her pannier, then again and again.

Thomas, too, shifted his gaze, trying to see what the dowager could be collecting. The answer was quick to reveal itself to him. On the trunks of fallen trees, nestling in dead leaves, in little clearings, Thomas could see them everywhere. Flat purple ones, rounded scarlet ones, ochre helmets, brown mushrooms: the fungi were everywhere in various stages of growth or decay. The old woman was doing nothing more sinister, or strange, than collecting mushrooms. He smiled to himself, more out of relief than anything else. After all the intrigue and mystery he had encountered over the past few months, his mind had become suspicious. He upbraided himself for being so mistrustful and allowing himself to doubt the innocent intentions of an elderly gentlewoman. He was just about to turn and go back to the hall quietly, without attracting attention, when he noticed Lady Crick do something rather unexpected. He saw her eat what he assumed was a raw mushroom. Chewing it slowly and deliberately as a cow chews cud, she pulled another from her basket, then ate it before straightening herself and turning to leave the forest the same way she had entered it.

Thomas ducked behind a tree, not wishing to be seen, and watched the dowager pass, carrying her pannier full of mushrooms. He remained at a discreet distance behind her for the next few minutes. He estimated the old woman had traveled almost a mile into the woods and it would take her almost half an hour to reach the garden gate moving at her steady but slow pace.

It was not until she came to the edge of the forest that Thomas noticed something else. The sun was dappling the ground now and the path was only a few feet away when Lady Crick appeared to stagger slightly. She put her hand out against the trunk of a tree to steady herself, took a deep breath, then carried on.

Not wishing to alarm her, but being near enough to the garden to pretend he had come from that direction, Thomas decided to approach the old woman from the side.

'Are you well, my lady?' he asked her gently.

She stopped and looked at him quizzically. 'Francis? Is that you, Francis?' she asked.

'No. I am Dr. Thomas Silkstone, a friend of Lady Lydia. May I help you?'

Lady Crick cocked her head at an odd angle as if trying to orientate herself.

'Where am I?' she asked weakly.

'In the grounds of Boughton Hall, your ladyship,' replied a puzzled Thomas.

She looked at him with the dull eyes of a fish and then seemed to have difficulty focusing. The young doctor was just about to take her by the arm and guide her inside when she suddenly let out a shriek and started pointing at his head.

'There's a monkey. Look,' she screamed. Her breathing became harsh and labored.

Unsettled by this sudden outburst, Thomas once again began to take her by the arm, but she refused. 'No. No. Get the monkey away,' she yelled, flailing her arms and dropping her basket so that its contents scattered on the ground below.

Alerted by the old lady's cries, Lovelock, who had been working the garden nearby, approached to see if he could help.

'Come, my lady,' he told her soothingly. ''Twill be all right,' he told her, taking her gently by the hand. She smiled at the burly servant. 'Francis,' she said calmly. 'I am tired,' and she surrendered herself into his arms as he picked her up with ease and began walking back to the hall. Thomas followed swiftly behind. Lady Crick was humming gently now, like a contented babe, and by Lovelock's demeanor Thomas surmised this was not the first time she had behaved in such an odd manner. 'Pretty penny,' she mumbled. 'Pretty penny and white roses.'

'Yes, my lady,' soothed the servant. 'All will be well.'

With the help of Eliza they managed to put the old woman to bed. She struggled a little before lapsing into a strange state, neither awake nor asleep. Thomas took her pulse. It raced like a hunted fox's. 'Has she been like this before?' asked Thomas of Lydia as she sat by her mother's bedside.

'Yes. Maybe half a dozen times.'

'How long does the madness last?'

'Three or four hours, sometimes more.' Lydia looked at the dowager as she lay staring at the ceiling, as if watching something up above, an unseen drama playing out only for her eyes. 'What is it? What ails her?' She folded her mother's cold hands under the linen sheets.

Thomas looked at her and saw the same forlorn expression and the brown doelike eyes that had first appealed to him all those months ago. 'I cannot say,' he answered.

What he did not admit to Lydia, however, was that he had a very good idea.

Chapter 53

The library at Boughton Hall was not a large room, yet judicious planning meant that as many volumes could be packed into its four walls as in many another grander library. Lined from floor to ceiling with shelves that were filled with scores of musty tomes covered in the dust of neglect, the library was probably the least visited room in the house. Nevertheless Lydia's father, the fifth earl, had by all accounts been a man of some erudition and had collected many volumes fitting for a man of his position.

Scanning the long-untouched shelves Thomas observed the volumes that seemed to be the staple diet of every English gentleman's library. There were the complete works of all the ancient philosophers, from Homer to Herodotus, together with the more contemporary volumes from those as diverse as Sir Thomas More and Thomas Hobbes. Moreover there were treatises from John Locke, the physician and philosopher oft quoted by his fellow countrymen in their struggle for independence.

The young doctor was even pleasantly surprised to find such fine works as Dr. Lorenz Heister's *A General System of Surgery*, together with William Hunter's acclaimed *The Anatomy of the Gravid Uterus*. They gave him hope that he might find just what he was looking for. Sure enough, after twenty minutes or so, a book by the great Robert Hooke, whose work he greatly admired, leapt out from the shelves of obscure periodicals and journals on forestry and the preservation of game. In its yellowing leaves, Thomas discovered all he needed to know.

Later that day Thomas sat behind the large desk at one end of the library as a bewildered Mistress Claddingbowl approached. On the desk sat a pannier, the sort used by Lydia and her mother to collect fruit and flowers from the kitchen garden. By the pannier was a large book, opened at a page of illustrations of various types of fungi.

The cook curtsied nervously. 'Good day, Mistress Claddingbowl,' greeted Thomas.

'Good day, sir,' she replied, twisting her apron as if it were the dough she had left behind to prove in the kitchen.

'Take a seat,' instructed the doctor, gesturing to a chair on the other side of the desk. She did so, at the same time eyeing the basket.

'Are you familiar with these fungi, Mistress Claddingbowl?' asked Thomas. Before he came into the library, he had revisited the spot where Lady Crick had begun to hallucinate and had dropped the pannier. Carefully he had retrieved all the spilled mushrooms and fungi that had fallen. They now sat in the basket, a motley assortment of musty-smelling specimens. 'These, here,' said Thomas, pointing to the four or five plump, sandy-colored mushrooms in the basket.

The cook shook her head. 'No, sir. I ain't never seen them before,' she replied confidently. 'Never.'

She seemed so sure that Thomas felt there was no point in pressing her further. 'Do you want me to cook them, sir?' she asked innocently. 'I could fry them in a nice bit of butter and–'

Thomas smiled. 'Thank you. No, Mistress Claddingbowl. These are the very mushrooms that I fear have led to Lady Crick's condition.'

A horrified look darted across the cook's flaccid face. 'Oh no, sir. I ain't never seen those sort before, but...' She trailed off.

'Yes?' urged Thomas.

'But I did see that,' she said, pointing to a fungus with greenish yellow gills.

Thomas looked at her uneasily. 'You are sure?'

Bending over the basket, she sniffed it, just as a dog would, then pulling herself upright she declared: 'Withered roses. I'd know that smell anywhere, sir. Lady Crick asked me to cook some for his lordship's breakfast one morning.'

'Can you recall when that was?' Thomas pressed her.

The cook sat back in her seat. 'A week or so before he died, sir. I remember it because later that day he was taken real bad with the sickness and I wondered if it was the mushrooms what ailed him.'

As soon as the fat cook had waddled out of the library, obviously feeling pleased about her revelations, Thomas began to turn the pages of the large book. Soon he came to a page headed 'fungi found in woodlands.' The intricate illustration showed a pale cap with black streaks radiating outward. The caption confirmed his suspicions. It read: 'Yellowish green cap. Found in beech woods in the autumn months.' Thomas looked in the pannier once more. There was no doubt about it. This fungus was an *amanita phalloides*, commonly called the death cap – the most poisonous fungus known to man.

Chapter 54

'What have you gleaned?' asked Lydia over dinner that evening. She noticed that Thomas seemed preoccupied, playing with the food on his plate and unwilling to engage in conversation. It was not until the servants had cleared away that he felt free to unburden himself.

As they sat by the fire in the drawing room Thomas made known his innermost thoughts. 'I believe I know how your brother died,' he said slowly.

Lydia was silent for a moment, shocked by this sudden revelation. 'You have discovered the murderer?'

He shook his head. 'Edward was not murdered,' he told her plainly.

Lydia frowned. 'What do you mean?'

Thomas looked at her directly. 'His death was an accident,' he said.

'An accident?' repeated Lydia incredulously. 'How so?'

All evening Thomas had been wondering how to couch his revelation in a way that did not apportion blame. It would not be easy. 'I believe your brother ate some deadly mushrooms, given him in error.'

Lydia looked at him in stunned silence. Thomas could almost see her mind at work, then, in her shock, she mouthed the word: 'Mama.'

Thomas nodded. 'I am afraid she mistook a death cap for an edible mushroom and Edward breakfasted on it.'

Lydia thought for a moment. ''Tis true. He was very nauseous and pale and suffered cruelly with the cramps, but that was a full fortnight before he died.'

Thomas nodded. What he had ascertained that afternoon in the library was that the poison of the death cap took effect up to two days after ingestion, causing vomiting and diarrhea, a terrible thirst, and a haggard appearance in its victims.

'Afterward, a recovery seems to take place and the victim grows in strength,' he explained.

'Yes,' agreed Lydia. 'Edward seemed fully restored.'

'But the death cap is a great deceiver and although your brother may have felt well, his liver and other organs would have been damaged beyond repair.

'It can be another ten days before the victim is suddenly struck down again to die in unspeakable agony,' said Thomas with a convincing finality.

Lydia was silent for a while. 'My mother must know nothing of this,' she said emphatically.

Thomas nodded, but he also knew he must now reveal Lady Crick's mystery ailment. 'I have also discovered the reason for her strange behavior,' he said. Delving into his pocket he brought out a small mushroom and held it up to the light. 'I believe this is the cause of her hallucinations. I saw her pick them in the woods.'

Lydia's jaw dropped in astonishment. Thomas saw that the simple truth was as difficult for her to grasp as it had been for him to discover.

'I cannot find words,' she said, shaking her head in disbelief.

'You do not have to,' said Thomas comfortingly. He held out his hand and she took it, but said nothing. Both of them knew that silence was the price they had to pay.

Thomas went to Lydia's room not as a physician but as a lover that night. Not a word was spoken as Lydia pulled back the sheets and he slid into bed beside her. At first they simply held each other, luxuriating in each other's arms; then, unable to hold back any longer, Thomas began to kiss her chestnut hair before he found her willing lips.

'I have waited so long for this moment,' he whispered. This time he could see no sadness in her eyes, as he had so often before. 'I want to make you happy.'

'We shall be happy, my love,' she replied, cupping his face in her small hands. Her gesture was one of such sweet tenderness that he felt his heart would break with joy. He kissed her lips once more and again and again and with each kiss their mutual desire became more urgent.

A knock at the door broke the moment. 'My lady. My lady,' came an anxious voice. It was Eliza. 'Lady Crick is unwell,' she called.

Lydia covered herself instinctively and rose from the bed. 'I shall come,' she said.

Eliza had been charged with keeping watch over the old woman during the night. It was now just past midnight.

Thomas rose, too, and pulled Lydia toward him for one more kiss before the facade was put firmly in place once more in front of the servants.

'I shall come shortly,' he told her.

Moments later he arrived to find the old woman retching into a bowl.

'How long has this been going on?' he asked Eliza.

'About twenty minutes, sir,' came the reply. 'This be the second bowl.'

Thomas glanced down at a pail beside the bed. It was half full of cream-colored vomit that reeked of acid. Now the dowager was retching up green bile, voiding her stomach of all its contents.

Eliza stood by the dowager, dabbing her clammy forehead with a damp cloth, while Lydia simply looked on in dismay. She had tried to hold her mother's hand, but the old woman was so agitated and confused that she had repulsed her.

'Mama, 'tis Lydia,' she cried wanly. But there was no recognition in the agonized look that was returned.

'Are the mushrooms the cause of this?' asked Lydia.

''Tis difficult to say,' replied Thomas, taking the dowager's pulse. 'If they are, their effects should wear off in a few hours and she should be restored by tomorrow.' He gave Lydia a reassuring smile.

But Lady Crick's agonies continued into the night. She became doubled with the cramps and her bowels emptied themselves in a continuous stream, so that Eliza had to bring towels to cover the mattress. The stench became almost unbearable and all the casements had to be opened wide.

When Thomas examined the dowager's abdomen he found it completely rigid. *Défense musculaire,* he believed the French called it. He could have bounced a farthing off it. The slightest pressure from his hand caused the old woman to let out a cry, raising her skeletal hand in a forlorn effort to ward him off.

As the night wore on, Thomas grew increasingly concerned about her condition until, just before three o'clock, there was a sudden change in the old woman's demeanor. Color began to return to her ashen cheeks and her fever seemed to subside. Her labored breathing became softer, easier, and the eyelids that had been clenched tight in agony now opened, fluttered gently, and then closed in a sublime rest.

Lydia, who had been sitting anxiously outside at Thomas's request, entered the room when she heard the noise had died down. She feared the worst, but Thomas reassured her.

'The pain seems to have eased. We must let her sleep now,' he urged.

'I will stay here with her.'

'But you need to rest.'

'I cannot,' she replied. 'I will call you if she wakes.'

Knowing it was useless to try and persuade Lydia to take to her bed, Thomas nodded and smiled. He found himself utterly exhausted and was grateful for the promise of rest.

Chapter 55

As the young doctor had predicted, Lady Crick was indeed over the worst. In fact, later on the following day, she was sitting up in bed taking broth and on the third day she ventured to walk around the room, albeit on Lydia's arm.

'Your mother makes excellent progress,' noted Thomas as he and Lydia watched the old lady walk around her bed unaided two days later.

Lydia smiled. 'Yes. She talks of going out into the garden tomorrow.'

'That is good news,' said Thomas, but Lydia could tell there was a certain distance in his voice.

'What is it, Thomas?' she asked.

She was aware from his pained expression that

he had bad news to impart. 'Your mother's recovery means I have no reason to stay here at Boughton Hall,' he told her. 'I'm afraid I must return to London.'

Lydia looked at him with large, sad eyes. 'I dread that day,' she said softly.

'You know I do, too, but there is no other way,' countered Thomas. 'You have your mother and I have my work. For the time being we cannot be together. But perhaps later...' His voice trailed off.

'I pray God it will be so,' replied Lydia.

For the remaining few nights Thomas shared Lydia's bed, creeping into her room at night, then leaving with the first rays. For the first time in his life he felt truly happy, but they both knew it was a happiness that needed to be interrupted, for a short while at least.

On the morning of October 11, 1781, Thomas made ready to leave Boughton Hall for what he envisaged would be the next few months, or at least until the spring had thawed out treacherous roads and banished icy puddles.

He hated protracted farewells, so he had decided to leave early so as not to prolong the sadness of his departure. He kissed Lydia on her forehead as she slept and it was only young Will who was on hand to see him leave Boughton Hall for what he assumed was a very long time.

'We shall miss you, sir,' said the youngster, helping Thomas into the saddle of a chestnut mare.

'And I you, Will,' replied the doctor, 'but I shall return as soon as I am able.' And with that he pulled on the reins and began the journey to

Oxford to catch a coach.

As he rode down the drive on that chill autumn morning, Thomas felt a great sense of sadness and of loss. The thought of not seeing Lydia for another four or five months was difficult to bear. They would write, but cold parchment was no substitute for the touch of her hand or the warmth of her smile.

He had just rounded the great sweeping drive, lined by the golden-leaved chestnuts and deep green laurels, when something made him glance up toward the pavilion where Captain Michael Farrell lay buried. Perhaps an inner voice was telling him to bid the captain a final farewell, but as he looked up toward the brow of the hill, to his surprise, he saw a figure standing, looking out at the vista.

As he drew nearer he could make out that it was a woman. Straining his eyes, he suddenly realized it was Lady Crick. Urging his horse to canter up the steep incline, he soon arrived at the pavilion. A ghostly blanket of early morning mist shrouded the valley below.

Hearing the sound of hooves behind her, the old woman, dressed in a crimson shawl and a lace cap, turned and smiled calmly when she saw the young doctor.

'You are leaving us, Dr. Silkstone,' she said. It seemed to be an observation rather than a question.

'Regrettably I must,' said Thomas. 'But it is good to see you so restored before I go.'

The dowager let out a strange laugh. 'Do not be fooled, Dr. Silkstone,' she replied enigmatically.

Thomas frowned, uncertain as to what she meant by these cryptic words. 'I am afraid I do not follow.'

Lady Crick turned to look at him. Her face seemed oddly contorted and Thomas noted her skin had a strange yellowish hue. 'It was a year ago last week that my son died,' she said.

Thomas nodded. 'Yes, Lady Lydia told me.'

'And by this time next week I will have joined him,' she added.

Thomas was uncertain as to how he should respond to this curious statement. 'How so, my lady?' he asked, thinking that perhaps the full effects of the hallucinogenic mushrooms had not worn off.

Now, as she looked at him directly, the American noted the old woman's pupils were fully dilated and her countenance strangely altered. 'I picked two death caps the day you followed me into the woods, Dr. Silkstone,' she smiled.

Thomas gazed at the aged widow in silent amazement, trying to comprehend the enormity of her statement. She studied his face as he computed her words and watched as the horror spread across his features.

'Yes, Dr. Silkstone. I will die within the next few days.'

'But why?'

'Because I have failed.'

'In what way?' Thomas needed to make sense of the momentous news he had just received.

The dowager raised her head to take in the vista of the rolling hills that stretched before them in a patchwork of earthy colors.

'Edward was not fit to have all this,' she began. 'You saw the sort of women who kept him company. His dear father would have turned in his grave to see how his only son behaved.'

'So, you killed him to let Captain Farrell inherit the estate?' asked Thomas. But the dowager simply smiled and shrugged her narrow shoulders.

'Good God, no. The Irishman was a wastrel, too. Not much better than Edward. He stole my Lydia's heart and repaid her with his gambling and womanizing.'

Thomas thought for a moment, trying to make sense of what he had just heard. It suddenly dawned on him what the old dowager had planned from the beginning. He stared at her in disbelief, unable to find any words to express his utter shock. The woman who stood before him mockingly had played the part of a senile old widow to a fault, gaining sympathy from all who encountered her. Yet all the time she was watching and waiting, manipulating events in the cruelest and most vile ways. She had planned her own son's death with all the cunning and guile of the devil himself.

'Francis!' he blurted. 'You wanted Francis to marry Lydia and inherit all this,' he cried, gesturing to the lush farmland below.

'Francis. Dear Francis,' she repeated. 'He taught me so much on our walks.'

Thomas shook his head in disbelief. 'You wanted the captain to be found guilty so that Lydia would be free to marry Francis.'

'But what I had not bargained for was James Lavington,' interrupted Lady Crick.

The doctor nodded. 'If only Francis's jealousy had not got the better of him. Lavington would have hanged for Farrell's murder and he could still have inherited Boughton.' Everything suddenly fitted into its undeniably awful place.

Thomas stood in stunned silence, contemplating what he had just heard. Lady Crick remained looking out at the view. 'Of course,' she said after a few moments, 'this could all be yours, if you wanted it.'

Thomas looked at her disbelievingly.

'You love Lydia. She loves you. You may be of lowly birth and a colonist, but I believe you are a good man.'

It was as if the scales had suddenly fallen from Thomas's eyes and he could see, for the first time, the dark inner core of this outwardly harmless old woman. As she stood on the crest of the hill, surveying the countryside for miles around, it was as if she was some grotesque puppeteer, pulling the strings of her helpless puppets below.

'You would hand me a poisoned chalice?' he said incredulously.

Lady Crick smiled. 'Poisoned,' she laughed. 'How very apt. No, not poisoned. A little tainted perhaps.'

Thomas felt the anger rise up in him, like a great wave that threatened to engulf him if he did not take control. 'I want your daughter as my wife, 'tis true,' he began, keeping his rage in check, 'and I believe she would consent, but if we do marry, Lady Crick, 'twill be on our terms and not because you wish it so.'

A sneer curled the dowager's thin lips. 'So be

it,' she said, her voice tinged with scorn.

Thomas's heart beat like a drum in his chest but he tried to compose himself. What he had just heard had turned his world upside down, and if Lydia were to discover what he now knew, it would destroy hers. There was no time to lose.

Galloping back to Boughton, Thomas dismounted hurriedly.

'I have changed my plans,' he told the startled Will. 'Please say nothing of this to her ladyship.'

So it was that Thomas slipped back into the daily routine of Boughton Hall as if he had never intended to leave that morning, trying to act as if nothing untoward had happened. He ate breakfast with Lydia in the dining room and tried to make pleasantries over plates of bacon and eggs, yet all the time he was waiting, waiting for the first stab of pain, the first spasm to grip, the first sharp intake of breath from Lady Crick.

The old dowager had not joined them for breakfast, but had chosen instead to go for a walk in the woods. Only Thomas guessed her purpose.

'I cannot believe how restored Mama seems,' smiled Lydia as they sat at the table.

Thomas felt a pang of guilt but simply said: 'Yes. She seems well enough.'

'And you can rest assured she will never touch, those mushrooms again,' laughed Lydia innocently. Thomas merely smiled.

Shortly after luncheon that day Lady Crick took to her bed, complaining of feeling tired. Although Lydia expressed concern, her mother assured her that she should not worry.

'I will see that she is comfortable,' Thomas told

Lydia and he followed the dowager a few minutes later.

The bedroom was dark and still. 'My time has come,' said the old woman from her bed. Thomas saw that beads of sweat now dotted her brow. 'Water. I need water.'

An insatiable thirst was one of the symptoms of the poisoning and Thomas poured her a glass. 'Are you in pain?' he asked.

'Does it please you that I am?' she answered.

Thomas felt insulted. 'I have pledged to alleviate suffering.'

The old woman let out a contemptuous laugh. 'Remember, I heard my son in his death throes. I heard him scream and gurgle enough to chill the blood. Do you think I am prepared to go through that agony?'

Thomas looked at her bewildered before recalling that she had been into the woods for the last time that morning.

'You have eaten more mushrooms?'

'They will soon work their magic,' she smiled, 'and I will float blissfully into oblivion.'

It seemed almost too painless a fate for one so evil, thought Thomas, but he held his tongue and began his reluctant vigil. How long it would last, he could not tell, but he hoped it would be swift for everyone's sake.

As he sat in silence, watching the poison take hold, he imagined the old woman's liver, crouched like some sleeping cat deep in the abdomen, being assailed by the deadly poison. It would be smothered rather than beaten to death, anesthetized by the toxins in the mushrooms. It may well feel some pain before it failed completely, but just how much and when that would be, Thomas could not say. All he knew was that it was his duty to prepare Lydia for the dowager's imminent demise. To her it would be wholly unexpected and therefore a terrible blow, but he knew it was a task he had to fulfill.

'I am afraid your mother is slipping into unconsciousness,' he told Lydia gently, taking her by the hand.

She withdrew from his grasp immediately in disbelief. 'How so? She was better. What has happened?'

'She suffered a relapse. 'Tis only a matter of time now.' As Thomas watched the grim realization of her mother's impending death creep across Lydia's face he felt guilty, for the first time in his life, of a sense of terrible betrayal. Lies and deceit did not sit easily in his soul, but stay there they must to protect Lydia from a truth that would be too awful for her to bear.

The young woman walked to the window and looked out onto the manicured lawns. 'Thank you, Thomas,' she sighed. 'You have done all you could.'

The pastor was called, but it was too late. There was no deathbed confession, no repentance, no atonement, simply the sound of labored breathing.

It was another forty-eight hours before death descended on Boughton Hall for the fourth time in a year. It had made its presence felt on a few occasions before it finally carried off its prize. Once or twice Lady Crick had let out a muffled cry. Once or twice she had drawn her legs up to her belly and whimpered and once she had even lashed out with her arm, as if fending off the devil himself. Other than those few moments of obvious discomfort, death's visit was uneventful and relatively silent, just how the dowager had planned it. Not for her the gross agonies and indignities that she had inflicted on her son, thought Thomas. Her body would be allowed to rest in peace and the black soul that surely lurked within it would never be exposed by a surgeon's knife.

They buried Lady Crick in the crypt next to her husband and son. Thomas remained at Boughton until the interment, hoping that his presence might give some comfort to Lydia, but the time soon came, as he knew it would, for his return to London.

'What shall I do without you, my love?' asked Lydia, looking up at Thomas on the morning of his departure. 'You have been my strength through all of this.'

'You know I am always here for you,' he said, taking both her hands in his and kissing them tenderly. Her eyes were full of tears and it was all he could do to stem his own. He could not let the moment pass. 'If you would be my wife, then we need not be apart again. Will you marry me, my dearest love?'

Lydia gazed at him and smiled. 'Yes. Yes, I will,' she whispered, nestling her head on his shoulder and holding his body tight against hers. It was a moment he knew would warm him through the long winter months of separation that now faced him.

Time, they say, is the great physician. Time would heal the wounds inflicted by so many deaths, so many personal tragedies, Thomas was sure of that. For the moment, however, those wounds must remain bandaged, allowed to heal naturally. Sometimes, he mused, the knife of a surgeon can do harm as well as good. Sometimes natural processes must be allowed to do their work away from the intervention of the scalpel and the trocar. Sometimes silent prayer and meditation is what is needed without a show of priestly pomp.

And so it was, in quiet contemplation, that Thomas said his farewells and rode down the drive of Boughton Hall for what he knew would be the last time for many months. It was just as he was passing the churchyard where young Rebecca lay, her grave still decked with fresh flowers, when he heard shouts. He craned his neck to look 'round and saw Will Lovelock, his carrot-colored hair flapping as he ran, calling after him down the drive.

'Dr. Silkstone! Dr. Silkstone,' he cried.

Thomas ordered his horse to halt. 'What is it, Will?' he asked as the boy ran alongside him. He was out of breath and gulped down air as fast as he could to relate his message.

'I am to give you this, sir,' he panted, holding out the silver locket that Lydia had once dropped in the stable yard.

Thomas frowned as he took it. 'But I told you to return this to her ladyship,' he chided.

'I did, sir,' replied the boy. 'Just as you said. But

Lady Lydia told me to give it to you, as a keepsake.'

Thomas smiled, thanked the boy, and closed his fingers 'round the pendant before putting it in his breast pocket and riding on. No doctor had ever devised a remedy to ease lovesickness, but during the cold and unforgiving season that lay ahead without his beloved, the token, he told himself, would help warm his aching heart.

Glossary

Chapter 1

rabid dog: Serious outbreaks of rabies in England from 1759 onward meant that rewards were paid for each dog killed. Rabies broke out in Boston and other North American towns in 1768.

sack: a style of sherry.

Chapter 2

lymphatics: Dr. William Hunter and his brother John discovered that the lymphatic flow runs toward the heart. Up until the mid-1700s the opposite was the received wisdom.

decaying flesh: Spring and autumn were considered the most favorable seasons for operations. A medical guide for surgeons (1712) read: 'In the Spring, the blood is revived with greater heat whilst in the Autumn blood is calm. In the Winter the cold locks up the paws, hinders transpiration and the blood has not the vivacity required to animate our bodies.'

miasma: It was commonly held that diseases such as cholera or the Black Plague were caused by a miasma, a noxious form of 'bad air.'

Corporation of Surgeons: From 1752 the body of any criminal executed in London and Middlesex counties could, if the judge decreed it, be dissected for the purposes of anatomical research at Surgeons' Hall.

Mr. Garrick: David Garrick was the most famous actor of the age and managed the Theatre Royal in London's Drury Lane until 1779.

phthisis: By the early eighteenth century tuberculosis was recognized as a contagious condition and hospitals started to exclude infected patients.

albino rat: The first recorded instance of an albino mutant rat being used for laboratory study was in 1828.

black rat: Black rats are notorious for carrying the fleas widely thought to have been responsible for bringing bubonic plague to Britain. However, more recent researches show that a waterborne intestinal disease may have been responsible.

The Daily Advertiser: Launched in 1773 in London, with a dependence on advertisements, this is sometimes regarded as the first modern newspaper.

gout: The eighteenth-century physician George

Cheyne singled out the disease for well-fed and hearty types.

goiter: A condition that used to be common in many areas deficient in iodine in the soil.

laudanum: From the eighteenth century and well into the nineteenth, laudanum was recommended as the drug for practically every ailment.

The Royal Academy of Arts: This was founded in 1768 through a personal act of King George III, who wished to promote the arts.

Chapter 3

The Pantheon: This once stood in Oxford Street and was a place of public entertainment that opened in 1772.

Pump Room: The social heart of Bath, where spa waters are drunk in a neoclassical salon.

foul-smelling liquid: The putrefaction process of a human body normally begins on the second or third day after death. The body becomes bloated and the skin discolored, but it is the smell that is most distinctive, being produced by the intestinal bacteria

doxy: The modern sense of 'a sexually promiscuous woman' dates to at least 1450.

French pox: Venereal disease, the former name of syphilis.

Chapter 4

Their days in India: By 1765, Britain's influence in India was in the ascendancy and Bengal was ceded to Clive of India.

ivory: Artificial noses were usually carved of ivory or made of plated metal and were made to replace original noses, which may have been congenitally absent or deformed, lost through accident or combat, or through a degenerative disease, such as syphilis.

Chapter 5

St. Bartholomew's Hospital: Almost always known as Bart's, this hospital was founded in 1123.

stillborn child: Infant mortality at this time in both the UK and the U.S. was about 500/1,000 compared with under 7/1,000 in 2000–05.

Chapter 6

cutpurse: A violent mugger.

muckworm: One who scrapes together a living by mean labor.

Hanoverians: The line of kings that began in 1714 with George I and ended in 1837 with William IV. The major opposition to the Hanoverians came from the Jacobites, who supported the restoration of the Stuarts to the throne.

The Sheldonian Theatre: Built in 1667, it was the first major commission for an aspiring young architect named Christopher Wren.

inglenook: A medieval-style fireplace, with a large recessed opening.

Christ Church Anatomy School: Erected in the School Quadrangle in 1766–67 by Henry Keene on the site of the organist's house, it became the Christ Church science laboratory.

Chapter 8

iodine: When dissolved in alcohol it was commonly used as an antiseptic in the past.

caries: The formation of cavities in the teeth by the action of bacteria; tooth decay.

Chapter 10

Great Tom: The name of the bell from Tom Tower, whose hundred and one peals traditionally signal the closing of the college gates.

fag: In English public schools, a fag was a young pupil who was tasked with being an older pupil's servant.

Chapter 12

potager: A vegetable garden.

jalap: A medicinal herb.

bunter: A destitute prostitute.

Chapter 13

hatchments: A hatchment is a funeral demonstration of honors displayed on a black frame that used to be suspended against the wall of a deceased person's house. Hatchments have now largely fallen into disuse, but many remain in parish churches throughout England.

chancre: The primary stage of syphilis is usually marked by the appearance of a single sore (called a chancre).

Chapter 14

the dome: This was designed by Sir Christopher Wren.

farthing: A low-value coin.

laurel water: A distillate of cherry laurel leaves containing hydrocyanic acid that smells like bitter almonds.

retort: A vessel in which substances are subjected to distillation or decomposition by heat.

Chapter 15

loofah: Made from a plant called the *Luffa cylindrica* of the gourd family. The fruit is picked when the skin turns a dark orange color and the seeds are removed to leave a spongelike pod, which, when soaked, is ideal for rubbing the skin when bathing.

salve: A soothing herbal cream.

febrifuge: A medication that reduces fever.

Chapter 16

attar: An alcohol-free perfume.

'the smell of bitter almonds': Cyanide is found in small amounts in the nuts.

Chapter 17

litmus: Litmus paper was brought into general use first in the 1600s by Robert Boyle (1627–91). Paper chromatography was, in reality, first developed in Russia by Mikhail Semenovich Tswett in 1903.

Chapter 19

palliasse: A straw-filled mattress.

Chapter 20

Vesalius: Andreas Vesalius's anatomical text *Fabrica,* published in 1543, was a foundation stone upon which all surgical practice was based.

anosmia: A lack of functioning olfaction, or in other words, an inability to perceive odors. Some people may be anosmic for one particular odor. This is called 'specific anosmia' and may be genetically based.

carboys: Large glass jars that were symbols of pharmacy from the 1600s onward.

Chapter 21

Dr. Samuel Johnson (1709–1784) was an English author, poet, essayist, moralist, novelist, literary critic, biographer, editor, and lexicographer.

Bedford Coffee House: A haunt of intellectuals in Covent Garden.

Radcliffe Camera: The word 'camera' means simply 'room' and was built 1737–49 with £40,000 bequeathed by Dr. John Radcliffe, the royal physician.

John Friend: A physician to Queen Caroline, he bequeathed money for the foundation of an anatomy school at Oxford on his death.

Nathan Alcock: An Oxford physician who died in 1779.

A brace of shiners: Two coins.

At least four pounds: The price of a corpse was measured in feet and inches.

Chapter 23

Hogarth: William Hogarth (1697–1764) was a famous satirist and artist.

paphians and doxies: Women of ill repute.

Chapter 25

hierophant: An interpreter of sacred mysteries.

Chapter 26

cinder sifters: These men made their living off the discarded rubbish of the capital.

costermongers: Street sellers of fruit and vegetables.

whisket: A basket.

unguent: Ointment, salves, or balm for soothing.

didicoy: A person who lives like a Gypsy but is not a true Romany.

'biting their thumbs at him': a huge insult in the seventeenth century.

Chapter 28

Robert Hooke's Micrographia: Published in 1665 and famous for its stunning illustrations of microscopic bodies.

Philosophical Transactions of the Royal Society: First published in 1665.

Chapter 31

feverfew: A herb believed to ease headaches.

Crown Inn: A five-hundred-year-old hostelry that

still exists.

Amersham: One of the main towns along the London-to-Oxford coaching route in the Chiltern Hills.

Chapter 33

nosegay: A posy of medicinal plants and herbs used to disguise bad odors.

Chapter 34

Britain was still in the grip of 'the Little Ice Age' – a series of particularly harsh winters in which the River Thames regularly froze over.

wherries: A wherry was a type of boat traditionally used for carrying cargo or passengers on rivers and canals in England, and is particularly associated with the River Thames.

sack-'em-up men: Grave robbers who sold corpses to anatomists.

Chapter 35

gallimaufry: A motley assortment of things.

gallipots: A gallipot was a small, glazed earthenware jar used by druggists for medicaments.

Chapter 36

Balliol: An Oxford college.

Gray's Inn: A London Inn of Court.

Chapter 37

peascods: The pod of the pea.

nostrum mongers: Quacks who peddled false remedies for ailments.

furbelows: A gathered or pleated piece of material, especially as an ornament on a woman's garment.

guglet: A bottle.

Digitalis purpurea: Staffordshire doctor William Withering is credited with discovering the powers of the purple foxglove, *Digitalis purpurea*. In 1775, one of his patients who was suffering from a heart complaint consulted a local Gypsy, took a secret herbal remedy, and promptly got much better. The active ingredient was *Digitalis purpurea* and Withering subsequently wrote a paper on it.

Chapter 38

crossroads burial: In England until 1823, a suicide's

body was buried at a crossroads with a stake through the heart.

Chapter 42

Cherwell: A tributary of the Thames that runs through Oxford.

bargees: People employed on or in charge of a barge.

guineas: A guinea was worth one pound and one shilling.

Magdelene: An Oxford college on the Cherwell; pronounced 'mord-lin.'

Chapter 44

tricorn: A three-cornered hat fashionable at the time.

Chapter 46

Bedford Lane: In Covent Garden, an area which by the 1760s had acquired such a dubious reputation that a magistrate dubbed it 'the Great Square of Venus.'

St. George's Hospital: Founded in 1733.

vinegar: Used as an antiseptic.

Chapter 50

mortsafe: An elaborate tomb to foil any attempts by grave robbers.

phaeton: A carriage drawn by a single horse or a pair, typically with four large wheels.

Chapter 51

lichen: A composite organism that grows on the shaded bases and trunks of mature trees, usually beech, in ancient woodland.

Chapter 53

Anatomy of the Human Gravid Uterus: A masterwork by the anatomist and obstetrician Dr. William Hunter, published in 1774.

Robert Hooke's *Micrographia* contained detailed drawings of fungi.